My Name Is
Russell Fink

Clever, memorable, unpredictable. I want to write like Mike Snyder when I grow up. He makes it look easy. And he doesn't settle for easy answers, which is good, since there are none.

BRAD WHITTINGTON,
author of *The Fred Books*
and *The Cooper Books*

* * *

My Name is Russell Fink is laugh-out-loud storytelling — inventive, surprising, and chock-full of quirky authenticity. It will grab you by the heart, tickle your funny bone, and highlight the intrinsic, fragile beauty of humanity in a way you didn't expect. An exceptional first book by a refreshing voice.

MARY E. DEMUTH,
author of *Watching the Tree Limbs*,
Wishing on Dandelions,
and *Daisy Chain*

* * *

A laugh-out-loud, wild romp of a mystery.

BRANDILYN COLLINS,
bestselling author
of *Crimson Eve*

* * *

Russell Fink is hapless and hilarious in this insightful and highly entertaining look at redemption. Michael Snyder is a great new voice in Christian fiction, and we can't wait to see what he comes up with next!

ANNE DAYTON AND MAY VANDERBILT,
authors of *The Book of Jane*

My Name Is Russell Fink

A Novel by
Michael Snyder

ZONDERVAN®

ZONDERVAN.com/
AUTHORTRACKER
follow your favorite authors

We want to hear from you. Please send your comments about this
book to us in care of zreview@zondervan.com. Thank you.

My Name Is Russell Fink
Copyright © 2008 by Michael Snyder

Requests for information should be addressed to:

Zondervan, *Grand Rapids, Michigan* 49530

Library of Congress Cataloging-in-Publication Data

Snyder, Michael, 1965–
    My name is Russell Fink : a novel / by Michael Snyder.
      p.   cm.
    ISBN-13: 978-0-310-27727-9
    ISBN-10: 0-310-27727-2
    1. Young men — Fiction. I. Title.
  PS3619.N938M9 2007
  813'.6 — dc22   2007032249

Internet addresses (websites, blogs, etc.) and telephone numbers printed in this book
are offered as a resource to you. These are not intended in any way to be or imply an
endorsement on the part of Zondervan, nor do we vouch for the content of these sites
and numbers for the life of this book.

This is a work of fiction. Any people, places, or things mentioned between the dog on the
front and the bar code on the back are made up by the author. Any likeness or similarity
to real people, places, or things is either (a) purely accidental, (b) a momentary lapse of
subliminal borrowing, or (c) a nifty coincidence. If you are a person, place, or thing and
think that you have somehow made a cameo in this purely fictional dramatization of a boy
and his dog/a boy and various girlfriends/a boy and his frigid and multilingual friend, Dan,
… um, I think I'd be way too embarrassed to admit it. But either way, it was a total accident
and I'm really, really sorry about it.

Interior design by Beth Shagene
Animation illustrations by Erwin Haya

Printed in the United States of America

08 09 10 11 12 13 14 • 23 22 21 20 19 18 17 16 15 14 13 12 11 10 9 8 7 6 5 4 3 2 1

This book is for Alicia,

my wife, my lover, my very best friend.
You already know I couldn't do this
without your unending support.
Now everyone else does too.
I love you.

Acknowledgments

Everyone thanks their editors and says nice stuff about them ... I actually mean it! Andy Meisenheimer's enthusiasm for the World of Russell never wavered from day one, eventually spilling over into these very pages. Becky Shingledecker became infected along the way and made our hero (not to mention our author!) respectable. Not only did they push me to make this a better book, they're just really great people. And I cannot thank them enough. So far I haven't found one person at Zondervan that's not great at their job. But I'm still looking!

When I first met Steve Laube, he was the "big, scary editor-guy." Although he doesn't remember that day, he was the first industry insider to say something nice about my writing ... well, sort of. Now he's my agent and a darn good one too. Thanks, Steve, for everything. You are the best.

Gayle Roper was the first real author to take an interest in my writing. I think she believed in "The Cow Guy" before I did. She hasn't stopped teaching or encouraging me yet. Thank you, Gayle.

Don Hoesel and Mark Mynheir are my two oldest writing pals. Thanks guys.

Conventional wisdom dictates that one never writes in a vacuum. I think that would be really weird and uncomfortable (and dusty!) so I write in a chair. That said, I have the greatest groups of iron sharpeners a guy could ask for: The *Hammer & Anvil* is comprised of Chris Fisher, Jeanne Damoff, and J. Mark Bertrand. And the *Misfits* include Angie Poole, Chris Mikesell, Heather Goodman, Jennifer Cary, Jennifer Tiszai, and Michelle Pendergrass. Great writers, one and all, who had to deal with Russell while still in his training pants. What a blessing to call each of you a friend.

A special thank you to my dear friends at *The Master's Artist* — B. J., Deb, Dee, Donna, Jeanne, Jen, Lisa, Madison, Mark, Mary, Melanie, Simon, and Steve. Please visit us at www.aratus.typepad.com/tma.

Also, many heartfelt thanks to *Relief: A Quarterly Christian Expression* (www.reliefjournal.com), The American Christian Fiction Writers (www.americanchristianfictionwriters.com), *Faith in Fiction* (www.faithinfiction.blogspot.com), *Infuze* (www.infuzemag.com).

To Aubrey, Jesse, Luke, and Isaac ... Daddy loves you guys the most.

Finally, I would like to thank Shai. You are an inspiration to me and my family every hour of every day. We love you, girl.

Part One

Thursday

My conscience must be out of order.

Otherwise I'd feel at least a tinge of guilt as I consider making this call. Only two reasons exist for dialing this number: first, to inform Max Hengle III that I'm about to land a big sale, and to say this is rare would be an understatement. It's happened exactly twice. And neither transaction was the result of any Herculean effort on my part, more like fortuitous timing or dumb luck. But this did not prevent me from taking full credit. Sales is a tough business.

The second reason for dialing this number — the egregiously more common reason — is to call in sick. One could argue hypochondria, but I prefer preventive maintenance. Still, I contend that over the life of my career, these measures will have made me a happier and more productive employee. And who wouldn't want a whole stable full of happy and productive employees?

I hear a click, followed by a habitual throat clearing, then the voice.

"Max Hengle speaking."

"Good morning, sir." I pause to adjust the timbre of my voice to a spot between grogginess and pain, careful not to overdo it. "It's Russell here, and I'm afraid I won't be able to make it in this morning."

"Uh-huh," he says, fingers clacking on a keyboard in the background. Mr. Hengle prides himself on his ability to multitask, but the reality is, he's terrible at it. For all he knows, I just told him I saw his daughter on *Springer*. When his brain catches up, he says, "Pardon?"

"That's right, feeling pretty lousy, sir." And this is not entirely untrue. Fact is, the more I talk, the worse I feel. The causes range from indigestion to pre-cancerous moles. I cough twice and add, "Pretty lousy."

"Doesn't this make your third absence this month?"

"March has never been my month, you know, healthwise."

"Nor saleswise. My patience is wearing thin, son."

"As well it should, sir."

Mr. Hengle sighs long and loud, purging himself of all things Russell.

I've always dreamed of making history, but I pray this isn't it. In the sixty-year history of Hengle's Supply, no one's ever been fired. Although firing me would make Mr. Hengle's life much easier, he's convinced that doing so would create some bad mojo or throw his karma out of whack, mainly because he owes my dad a pretty big favor. Still, I feel bad. So I silently and solemnly swear to resign as soon as I can claw my way out of debt, come up with the security deposit and first-and-last month's rent on my own apartment, and move out of my parents' house.

"There's going to be some changes around here, Russell. I just don't see how we can continue on like this, do you?"

Since I'm hardwired to respond to rhetorical questions with sarcasm, I remain mute, save for the sound of my stubble scraping against the phone's mouthpiece. It sounds like static.

"Tell you what, Russell." His weary, patronizing whine is nothing

12

new, though the trace of sincerity is. "Why don't you take tomorrow off as well? Then you'll have the whole weekend to recuperate."

"That's very generous, sir."

"I was aiming for sarcastic and condescending."

"Oh, well, thanks anyway, I guess." I should just hang up and stop the bleeding, but pangs of self-preservation urge my vocal cords into action. "Did I mention to you that Tyler, Billingham & Sneed is right on the cusp of issuing a huge purchase order?"

"About a week ago, as I recall. The *last* time you called in sick. I fully expect to see you at Monday morning's staff meeting where, by the way, you'll get to meet our new office manager." He makes "office manager" sound ominous, as if Charles Manson will be handling payroll and implementing office policy. "Are we understood?"

Over the dial tone, I say, "Hardly ever, sir. Hardly ever."

* * *

On the way to Dr. Kozinski's office I decide to stop in to Tyler, Billingham & Sneed and see Geri — typically my first call of the week. It's a routine boon for my flagging confidence, but this is more of an emergency visit. If I'm going to hide behind my potentially career-defining order, I guess it makes some sense to check on its status. As usual, I bring along two giant vanilla lattes from the Bean Bag.

Geri's on the phone when I get there so I set her coffee down in front of her and scan the pastry tray. I select a bloated éclair, take a bite, and wait. The reception area is done up in blocks of mahogany, with haughty magazines and rental plants. I suspect the pretension is piped in with the Muzak.

Geri's voice has barely trailed off when I hear a loud slurping sound. I turn around and grin in expectation of a hearty "thank you."

"Ack. I can taste the caffeine."

"Is that a problem?"

"I'm temporarily off caffeine. Except for an occasional dark choco-late of course." She pops the plastic lid off, uses her finger to spoon out a dollop of whipped cream, and sticks it into her mouth. I watch her freckles dance as she talks, trying not to be too obvious. "So, what're you doing here on your day off?"

"How did you know I was off today?"

"For starters, you're in jeans." Geri absently straightens a small framed photograph on her desk—a formal-wear shot of her and some guy, presumably her former fiancé. But he's been scratched out. "Plus I called your office looking for you earlier, and they told me you were out sick."

"What if I said I came by here to check on the status of that big order?"

"What if I said that's why I called your office this morning?" She motions me forward and glances around as if we're being watched. "One of those new salesgirls from Office Something-Or-Other called on us last week. And she really got Mr. Billingham's attention."

"That's no great feat." Billingham is an ogler *par excellence*.

"I think the partners might be seriously considering her offer."

My salesman's smile remains intact while panic leaches into my bloodstream. Geri's law firm plans to replace over a hundred-thousand-dollars worth of copiers, scanners, and swanky office furniture, and until this morning I had no competition. The commission check's al-ready been earmarked for a down payment on a new apartment and my two loudest creditors.

"Must be your imagination, Geri. What could one of those big-box conglomerates possibly have to offer that I don't?"

"The salesgirl looks like a supermodel."

"There's always that."

"And *she* brought the pastries this morning."

14

So much for the éclair tasting better than normal. "I thought you said she came by last week."

Geri uses the photograph as a shield. "She did. She dropped in and introduced herself last Friday. Then she came back yesterday, then again this morning. Now she's in there meeting the other partners."

I stare at Baxter Billingham's office door, mushed éclair coating my tongue.

"Sorry to have to be the one to tell you. But I thought you at least ought to be aware. So you can plan your strategy."

Even if I were capable of devising a strategy, I couldn't compete with the image of a swimsuit model galvanizing a trio of salivating attorneys with a sultry PowerPoint presentation behind Billingham's door. This is not an account that I prepare for. Rather, I perform routine maintenance, stroke egos, and make small talk with the partners — the Braves and bad TV sitcoms with Tyler, UT football and sailboats with Billingham, the stock market with Sneed.

This account is mine. Or at least it always has been.

I take another spiteful bite of the éclair, and a cool glop of Bavarian cream squirts out onto my chin. Geri laughs and hands me a Kleenex.

Then the supermodel emerges and makes some comment about the quarterback for the White Sox. The partners all guffaw and slap each other on the back. Suddenly, I feel like I'm on a bad sitcom, where she's the starlet and I'm the hapless, beer-swilling cousin who lives over the garage.

Geri rolls her eyes, and for a few brief moments we're bound together by mutual disgust. She has no patience for vacuous stick-women, even less for the men who do. My issues are less noble — plain old-fashioned fear and greed.

* * *

The waiting room at Nashville City Medical Clinic is much less pretentious, but the magazines are several months out of date, with pages bent and crusted with all manner of bacteria. So I ignore them and steal glances at the other patients, making sketches of them on a legal pad. It's an old habit, inventing imaginary ailments for complete strangers, then rendering their symptoms with flurried pen strokes. Normally, I show my work to Alyssa and see if she can accurately diagnose the afflictions. I draw the burly guy in coveralls with a puckered and humiliated look on his face, with cartoonish motion lines implying constant shifting as if he can't quite get comfortable in his chair, and tiny flaming tendrils rising from his nether regions. When I can't think of a way to portray itching, I move on to the young girl in the opposite corner.

She is staring up at the TV bolted to the wall, but it's obvious her mind is viewing her own private soap opera. She's pretty but mousy, and keeps telling herself she has the flu, but her brain is an adding machine counting the days since her last period. I'm darkening the wrinkles on her forehead when my phone erupts.

The patients all glance up at me, the observer observed. It rings again and I study the number.

Alyssa.

My greeting is polite but terse, a funeral whisper meant to convey urgent business. A tone that Alyssa completely misses. Or chooses to ignore.

"Hey babe." Her voice is too loud, too happy. "Good day so far?"

"Not bad." I get up, walk toward the door that opens into the hallway, and narrowly dodge a zombielike toddler with two streams of green goo on his upper lip. "I'm kind of in the middle of something here."

"Well ex-*cuse* me. I guess you're in some big meeting — selling what? Packing peanuts? Desk blotters?" My fiancée has reduced my livelihood to hawking trivial gadgets that fuel the corporate monoliths responsible for starving Third World kids, botching the environment, and exploiting generations of Asian laborers.

In the hallway now, I pitch my voice just above a whisper. "Do you need something? Or did you call just to make fun of my job?"

"Touchy, touchy."

Someone's calling my name through the closed door; it sounds like Cassandra, my favorite nurse. But the voice is garbled, like Charlie Brown's teacher.

"Seriously," I say. "What do you need?"

"Ooh, you sound so sexy when you're mad."

"Listen, Alyssa. I really do need to go. They're waiting." The implied subject of *they* is on the darker side of honesty.

The nurse calls my name again, louder and more clearly this time, definitely Cassandra. I silently count to ten before I push back through the door into the waiting room.

"Alright, I can tell when I'm not wanted. But you need to knock off a little early tomorrow. I need some assistance setting things up for Saturday."

It irks me the way she assumes that I'll just blow off work whenever she asks. As if her whims automatically trump my responsibilities. Never mind that I am, in fact, blowing off work; one could argue that I've trained her to think that way. I guess I just resent her attitude about it.

"I'll see what I can do. But I'll have to call you later and let you know if I can break away." Another half-truth, which I camouflage by changing the subject. "Are we still on for dinner ... sometime?"

A spooky presence just over my left shoulder interrupts Alyssa's answer. I turn to find Cassandra, six inches from my face and smiling.

"Oh, there you are," she says. "Dr. Kozinski will see you now."

I hear an angry intake of air in my left ear. Busted.

"What was that?" Alyssa yells. "Are you at the doctor again, you lying—"

I scrape stubble across the mouthpiece in a lame and desperate attempt to simulate static.

"Sorry, must be bad reception." I snap the phone shut.

After a moment's deliberation, I power it all the way off and follow the squeaky-shoed Cassandra into the bowels of modern medicine.

* * *

My bare feet stick to the cold tile floor as I strip down to my skivvies. The room (a glorified closet, really) reeks of antiseptic and is chilly enough to infringe upon my civil rights. Medical implements stand at attention: swabs, syringes, secret potions, and all manner of probes and invasive thingies meant to invoke fear and vulnerability in the paying customer—an insidious ploy unique to horror movies, amusement parks, and doctors' offices. Sure, there's the illusion of sovereignty when the nurse guides you to your lofty throne atop the padded, overly high examination table. But then it dawns on you that your feet are dangling like a toddler on the toilet. You're in your underwear. And you had to use a stool to get up there in the first place. All this after they stick you with needles and make you pee in a plastic shot glass. No, you'll do as instructed, as if you're working for the doctor instead of the other way around.

I climb up on the stool, perch myself on the crinkly deli paper, and absentmindedly swing my feet. Cassandra was all business this morning when she escorted me to the examination room. Despite the enormous diamond on her finger, I think she has a crush on me, so I practice clenching my stomach muscles in case she pops in. The trick is to avoid looking intentional or vain about it: overdo it and you look hollowed out, creepy; not enough and a six-pack of abs can look like a jumbo pack of hairy dinner rolls. By the time she barges in ten minutes later to tell me that the doctor will be right with me, I've abandoned my posing to inspect various moles on my shoulders and back. At the sound of the opening door, I flex everything at once and try to smile nonchalantly. The effect is likely a cross between a deranged Chippendale and a serial killer with a toothache, but it happens so quick that I doubt she even got a decent look, thank God.

When Dr. Kozinski strides in moments later reviewing my chart, I hear the demoralizing sound of laughing nurses through the open door.

"Well, well. What's it been, Russell? A whole week since your last visit?"

"A lot can happen in a week."

Instructions are no longer necessary to get through this part of our routine. It's been choreographed to the point where simple nudges or gestures are all that's needed to have me blow deeper, look this way or that, lie back, sit up, turn my head and cough. In the old days he would even breathe warm air on the business end of his stethoscope before he slapped it on my chest. Now he seems to take pleasure — a little too much pleasure, if you ask me — from inflicting small discomforts. Like holding the tongue depressor down until I gag. Or giving the blood pressure pump a few extra squeezes. He flips the light switch off and jams his fancy pupil-dilating flashlight at my left eye.

"You using the high beams there, Doc?" I say this every time. He never laughs.

He turns the lights back on. "So, what brings us here today? Another mole, I presume?"

"Right here," I say, turning my left shoulder toward him and pointing it out with my right hand. "I'm pretty sure it's turning colors."

"We'll get to that in a moment." Dr. K refuses to break routine. I'm not sure if it's habit, or if his conscience won't allow him to charge

19

me for a full examination unless he performs his entire complement of invasions. He makes small talk while probing my ears, nose, and throat, then asks about my parents' welfare while feeling for lumps or hernias. It tickles like mad and he knows it.

Finally, he leans in and shines his light on the mole in question. "Oh yeah, you're right. It is changing colors, like a mood ring. Or maybe a disco ball."

"Seriously. I think it looks different."

"That's because you're stretching the skin." He places both his thumbs on my forearm and applies outward pressure. "See, your skin turns white."

"Ouch." He's pulling the hair on my arms, probably on purpose.

"Now back to pink," he says, ignoring my outburst. "And if I keep doing this long enough, it will eventually turn an angry red."

"So I guess I'm not dying then."

"Don't put words in my mouth." He grins at the temporary panic in my eyes. "My professional opinion is that you've only got five or six decades left. Seven tops."

"Your bedside manner could use some work."

"You still selling copiers?"

"In theory. You need a new one?"

"No, Russell. I was just working on my bedside manner."

"Because we're running a killer special on HP models for—"

He turns me so I'm facing the wall while he runs his hands across my shoulders and spine.

"Have you given any thought to our last conversation? About looking for another line of work? Something you don't hate?"

"There's nothing else I really want to do. Nothing that pays benefits. And whether you admit it or not, you'd miss me."

"I'm surprised Hengle doesn't just fire you. As much as you hate that job, you couldn't possibly be any good at it."

"It's a long story."

His fingers return to a spot in the middle of my back. "Humor me."

I should know better than to delve into all this, especially with him. But before I can change the subject, I feel my body heave a pro-tracted sigh followed by the sound of my own voice. "My old man healed his kid several years ago."

"Bernie?"

"Nah, he's beyond help. His other kid, the war hero."

"Ray," Dr. K says, clearly distracted. He mumbles something and scribbles in my chart. "Nice kid."

And it's true, at least as far as I can tell. Ray Hengle returned from the Persian Gulf with a leg full of shrapnel and migraines that seemed to last for weeks at a time. Too many metal fragments to operate, the doctors had said.

Finally, Max brought Ray to my father, who had agreed to pray for the boy.

My father extended his hands toward Ray's head, tentative at first, as if warming them over a fire. His prayers were whispered, calm and lilting, devoid of his usual histrionics. But it was intense, like a lover's quarrel in a library. He worked his fingers into the man's scalp, then began kneading the injured leg. When Ray roused and started moan-ing, I had to get out of there.

I thought the story would be bigger. The newspaper devoted a few hundred words to the local hero's improved health, but no men-tion of Gary Fink. The CBS affiliate ran a feel-good piece, complete with before-and-after X-rays of the restored shrapnel-less leg. They even used the word *miracle*. But I'm not sure anyone believed it as much as Max Hengle III.

"Something wrong?"

"No, just making some notes. You were saying? About your job?"

"Yeah, Dad healed his kid about ten years ago, and Hengle's been bugging him ever since to repay the favor. I guess tolerating me is like his penance or something."

"You don't really believe that your father actually *heals* people."

"Technically, I think God gets credit for the actual healing."

His amused look falters a bit. "Does God even *want* the credit? Just last week one of those *60 Minutes* or *Primetime* shows did an exposé on Christian miracle workers and the gullible followers they supposedly 'heal.' "

"It was *48 Hours*, actually." I know this because the show spent the better part of ten minutes rehashing the decade-old shenanigans of Reverend Gary Fink — my father. In the weeks following his arrest, "Reverend Fink" became a punch line. Then a prison nickname.

"It's obviously the power of suggestion. Either that or they're scam artists bent on …" Then he remembers who he's talking to.

"Trust me, Doc. I don't want to believe it either. Dad and his cronies deserve all the bad press they get." I pause, barely able to believe the words coming out of my mouth. I stopped defending my father in grade school. "But he's actually healed people too. I've seen it."

"Thought you said God did the actual healing." If it's possible to infuse a wink with sarcasm, the good doctor pulls it off.

"You know what I mean."

I feel his fingers plying the now vulnerable skin in the middle of my back. He makes a small laughing sound through his nose and says, "You know, you could save us both some trouble."

"How's that?"

"You could quit your job and find something you love to do. That should solve most of your problems …" He allows this last line to trail off, a setup for the punch line he's been waiting for. "Then maybe your father can work his hocus pocus on the rest of your phantom maladies."

"Won't work."

"Please," he says. "Do tell."

"Because I don't think I believe anymore."

"You just said you saw it with your own eyes. Now you say you don't believe it? Which is it?"

"It's complicated."

He shakes his head and hands me the form he's been scribbling on.

"What's this?" I say.

"Looks like you finally got your wish."

"How's that?" I scan the tiny form in my hand. One word leaps out from the page — *biopsy*. The translation in my head: *cancer.*

"I'm sure it's nothing," he says, "but we're going to need to remove that mole there in the small of your back. Quick procedure. You'll be in and out in an hour or so."

Then he leaves me in my underwear, alone with my darkest thoughts.

* * *

My first trip on an airplane was to New York City. The plan was to visit the NYU campus, complete all the registration hoopla, then hang around long enough to watch the big New Year's ball drop in Times Square. I loved looking down on the clouds, wondering if my sister Katie ever got her wish — to wake up every morning on a fluffy pink bed of cotton candy. I wasn't crazy about the turbulence or the salted peanuts or the way the air inside the cabin smelled like the bottom of a stranger's closet. The pilot's voice crackled over the PA system and told us all to stay in our seats, that we would begin our initial descent into JFK as soon as we were cleared for landing. After circling the airport twice, the tipsy know-it-all in the seat behind me began floating unsolicited theories about iced-over runways, terrorist threats, and running out of fuel before smashing into the Hudson River. Finally the grizzled businessman in the seat next to me turned around and told him to shut up. I peered through the tiny window as several other jets emerged and disappeared in the gray mist. For some reason, I really wanted to see the look on the other pilots' faces.

We kept circling the city. No one slept. Our captain chimed in periodically to reassure us. But the know-it-all had predicted we'd be out of fuel in forty-five minutes. That was nearly an hour ago. Conversations dried up, except for an occasional nervous whisper. I closed my eyes and tried to remember how to pray.

But my thoughts drifted. It dawned on me that since Katie's funeral, my whole life had been just like this, a holding pattern. I'd spent the last decade and a half going in circles, hovering, marking time, waiting for tragedy to strike. All the while, life happened on the other side of the clouds. I jolted awake when the plane's tires thumped onto the tarmac. Somehow I'd managed to stave off my date with destiny by nodding off.

So I wasn't shocked when Dr. K told me about the mole. Nor was I surprised that he didn't mention cancer. I knew this was coming. I've been expecting it.

But I'm going to need to talk to Sonny about it.

* * *

After making me sign a stack of insurance documents and scanning my credit card for the thirty-dollar co-pay, Dr. K's office manager hands me a folded note. "Someone called and left you a message. Sounds like she has anger management issues."

The handwriting is foreign to me, but the tone is pure Alyssa: "Our relationship is like a geometry proof. *If* you ever want to see this engagement ring again, *then* you better show up in the parking lot of *As a Jaybird.* Saturday morning. 9:00 sharp."

I tell myself that this is it, that I will not succumb to another of her ridiculous demands. But of course, my resolve will disintegrate and I'll show up. I always have. It's what I do.

Friday

I awake Friday morning and grin at the silent alarm clock. For a brief moment I flirt with the idea of "calling in well," or maybe just showing up at the office. But Mr. Hengle hardly ever works Fridays, so the only people there to impress would be his obnoxious kid, Bernie, and the other salesgirls. Besides, who am I to trample the joy out of my boss's charity? No, he gave me the day off and I need to make good use of it.

I nestle deeper into my pillow and listen for any signs of movement. At some point I must have nodded off because I could have sworn I heard Katie tapping out one of her secret messages on the wall that separates our bedrooms. But it's just Sonny's clumsy tail.

When my brain starts manufacturing regret and dumping it into my veins, I sit up and rub the sleep from my eyes. I notice a sketch I was working on the night before, and visions of filling canvases and drinking too much coffee dance in my groggy head. Maybe today will be the day I can coax my muse out of hiding and get some painting done.

Then I remember *why* Hengle gave me the day off. All my good cheer gathers at the base of my neck, metastasizes, then burns a trail toward the offending spot on my lower back. It itches but I'm afraid to touch it. Somewhere along the way, I got it in my head that if a mole is indeed malignant, then one wrong touch could dump millions of cancer cells into my bloodstream and spread to all my extremities. So I do what I do best—ignore it. Or try to. Sonny greets me in the kitchen, performing his geriatric doggy dance. If I'm not mistaken, his need to make water seems to have tripled in recent months. He's a walking urine factory. I open the back door and watch him waddle through.

"Make sure you do your business in your own yard."

As I watch, temptation seizes me like an ice cream headache. I have the house to myself for at least a few hours. And maybe it's my imagination, but Sonny does look thirsty. The combination of my parents' gun safe—which doubles as Mom's liquor cabinet—scrolls across my brain like a stock ticker ... *Right – 4 ... Left – 10 ... Right – 21 ... Left – 8 ... Right – 12 ...*

"Grow up," I say to the empty kitchen.

After chasing a second bowl of cereal with a third mug of gourmet coffee, I don my painting pants—a baggy pair of plaid boxers, flecked with stiff paint blotches—and get to work. I begin with a few exercises: the mousy girl from the waiting room, hemorrhoid man, a preliminary sketch of a piece I call *Fault Lines* (which, like my unfinished portrait of Katie, seems too personal, too heavy for this early in the morning). After an hour or so I realize that I don't feel so much warmed up as worn down.

So I decide to check on Sonny and retrieve yesterday's mail.

He's howling at the back door, so I let him in and spend a few minutes massaging his neck until he starts nodding off in my lap. I fill his bowls with smelly pellets and water, then head out to the mailbox.

I squint at the sun and inhale the musk of dogwoods, blooming dangerously early this year. The muggy morning air warms my skin, making it tingle, reminding me of Tuesday's surgery — and the dismal reality of having to call in sick yet again. At least I'll have a valid excuse.

My thoughts are breached by a clicking-and-shuffling sound to my left. I look up to see my parents' neighbor, Ernest Simmons, hobbling up his aggregate driveway, a cane in one hand and something metallic in the other. A small shovel? A pair of clippers? A handgun? Whatever it is, he's trying to hide it in the skirt of his bathrobe.

If the rumors are true, Simmons made a fortune during the dot-com boom of the nineties, when a debilitating computer virus coupled with the disappearance of his wife distracted the young entrepreneur just long enough to see his burgeoning empire crumble. He chose to litigate instead of revamp, wasting years in the courtroom suing his competitors for theft of intellectual property. No one knows how old Simmons really is, only that his mixed bag of allergies and illnesses makes him appear decades older. He's called the cops on Sonny no less than a dozen times, claiming disturbance of the peace. He even tried to sue us once for destruction of private property, but my father's lawyer was able to prove that Sonny's urine actually nourished our surly neighbor's rosebushes. He's convinced that Sonny impregnated his precious Betsy, a hairless terrier. Who could really blame him, what with the way she flits around her immaculate yard in her argyle sweaters and cutesy hair bows? But whether Simmons chooses to believe it or not, Sonny's been fixed for ages.

My strategy has always been to kill my neighbor with kindness. I shout an obnoxiously friendly greeting in his direction, which he pretends not to hear, but his quickening pace gives him away. The *click-shuffle-shuffle, click-shuffle-shuffle* pattern has a light waltz feel to it. I shake my head, thankful that I'm not that miserable. At least not yet.

When I get to the mailbox, I hear the muffled sound of Sonny's bark. His old and grizzled snout is at the living room window. Simmons slams his door. The mailbox shrieks on its hinges. I raise my right hand in a satirical wave, hoping he appears at the window, and reach inside for the mail. My first thought is, *Who filled our mailbox with mashed potatoes? And why are they still warm?* Then the synapse that connects my brain to my nostrils fires, and I realize that my hand is covered in dog crap.

I swivel my head toward Simmons' house in time to see his drapes fall back into place in the living room window.

When I shake the excess off the soiled letters, a handwritten note tumbles groundward and wedges between the spindles of our Bermuda grass. I hold the edge down with a toe and read:

Keep your idiot canine and his DNA sculptures out of my yard.

I also notice a letter from State Farm addressed to me. Since the last two letters I received from my agent were past-due notices, I assume the same here and pitch the smelly envelope in the trash.

* * *

After two-and-a-half showers, I decide to call the police.

"Afternoon, this is Officer Peebles at your service. What can I do for you?" His voice conjures an aging professor moonlighting as a pump jockey from Mayberry. I can't help picturing a thin bow tie on a police uniform and an oily rag dangling from his holster.

"I'd like to report my neighbor."

"Report how? Is he dead or drunk or peeking in your windows?"

"No, nothing like that." Something about the way he says the word *drunk* brings me up short. "It's more like desecration of, you know, someone else's possessions."

"You mean destruction of private property?"

"That's it."

"What kind of property we talking about here?"

"Well, he loaded my mailbox full of dog poop."

Friday

I'd swear he's trying to suppress laughter. "That's it?"

"What? That's not enough?"

"Sure, yeah, it's a crime alright. But you got yourself a couple of problems as far as I can tell. First off, you need to talk to a postal inspector, not the police. Second, did you actually see this neighbor of yours messing with your mailbox?"

"Not exactly. But I still want to go on record or file a public complaint or whatever you call it."

At this point he types all my personal information into his computer. I've already resigned myself to hear a standard issue reply, something about sending an officer over to investigate and not getting my hopes up. Then I remember the one blight on my record.

A DUI.

The third time Alyssa broke up with me was three days before my twenty-second birthday. That was only the second — and last — time I ever abused alcohol (at least on myself). The newspaper played up the son-of-a-preacher angle, much to my parents' chagrin.

The memory makes me paranoid, twisting each of the officer's droning questions into an indictment, and in turn, every word spilling from my dry mouth sounds increasingly guiltier. Finally, I blurt out, "You know what? I changed my mind. Simmons is not such a bad guy. Maybe it wasn't even dog poop after all. Let's just forget the whole thing."

"Sir?" The exasperation packed into that one word frightens me. "Have you been drinking?"

I try the stubble trick again.

When the phone rings moments later, I check the caller ID. It says *NASHVILLE P.D.*

I don't pick up.

I try a couple of breathing exercises to calm down, but it does no good. My mind just conjures one ridiculous scheme after another. But no answers to the question: *How do you exact revenge on an ailing, crotchety neighbor without risking either jail time or a rather severe dent in your self-esteem?*

Sonny waddles into my bedroom, looking older and more pathetic than normal. Even by basset hound standards, he seems thoroughly humbled. I massage his scruff until I find the magic spot that reduces him to a quivering mass of flesh and fur.

"Don't worry, buddy. It's not your fault."

He moans a soft apology.

"And you have my permission to bite him whenever you want. Or pee on his bedroom slippers."

"Well, well." My mother appears and leans against the doorframe, arms folded. She must have come in while I was in the shower. "I can hardly wait to hear this one. Please tell me you're not referring to your father."

"Ernest Simmons."

I fill her in, avoiding the more gory details. "The cops said that I had to actually witness him shoveling Sonny's DNA into our mailbox."

"Let it go, Russell. He's sickly and practically out of his mind. Are you alright?"

"I'm fine. The question is, how are *you* doing?"

The effects of her lunchtime cocktails show up in her red, glassy eyes and splotchy complexion. But her words are as sharp and fluid as ever.

"I'm okay," she says. "But I'm not the one who called in sick yesterday."

"You talked to Alyssa."

My mother simply nods. I suspect that although she still doesn't like Alyssa very much, she's coming to terms with the fact that we're her best shot at ever having grandbabies to spoil. "She says you're being morbid again. I don't know why you do that to yourself."

She's referring to the fact that I gave my twin sister cancer when we were nine years old.

It was the last Saturday before school started. The leaves were browning and the air reeked of exhaust and burnt rubber from a nearby tire factory. I was Peter Pan and she was Tinker Bell, dueling imaginary pirates when I executed a graceless pirouette and knocked Katie out of our tree fort.

She landed with a thud.

I peered over the side. She didn't move. I knew she was dead. But in typical Katie style, she waved with her good hand and attempted a weak smile.

The ambulance carted her off with a broken collarbone. She came home three weeks later with leukemia.

After that we spent every waking hour together. I tried to make her laugh and she tried to make me stop crying. Katie called me a silly boy for blaming myself, said that we were lucky that the broken collarbone helped them find the cancer so that God and Daddy could get her all healed up. That's what she'd say, *all healed up*, with a pink-and-green inflection that made you believe it. I loved her even more for that.

Katie died eighteen months later, on our birthday.

We buried her on a sweltering Tuesday morning, along with the best of what was left of our family.

My mother pretended that nothing happened. My father quit meeting my eyes. My brain told me I killed my twin sister. We shared the same womb. She got the looks and brains. I got the attitude and all the healthy cells.

Until recently. My mole starts to tingle.

Mom snaps her fingers. "Russell. I don't have the energy to deal with you moping around in a funk all weekend. I've got a little job for you."

I suddenly want to tell her about my mole, to turn back the clock and climb into her lap and have her tell me not to worry, that everything will be okay. But I can't bring myself to even insinuate that she could lose another child to cancer.

"Your father finally managed to get his meeting with Geoffrey Sinclair."

Sinclair owns and operates the second largest Christian broadcasting company in the world. And my father's been campaigning for months to get a job interview. I guess having dinner together is like reconnaissance. Sinclair gets to pull back the curtain and see just how nutty our family is before making the job offer official.

"It's Monday evening and you need to be there."

"I don't see why."

"Because we're a family and we need to show a unified front. Your father needs this job. And Lord knows he's not qualified to do anything else."

He's not really qualified for ministry either, but I keep that to myself. Mom fails to mention the real reason my father needs to land this job. Ever since his fall from grace, both of my parents have been working for my Aunt Wanda's insurance firm to make ends meet. Not only does Wanda overpay them, she allows my father time off for ministry trips and overlooks my mother's alleged sick days when she needs to indulge her habit. But Wanda never misses an opportunity to remind us all of her generosity. Of course their only other alternative would be to work for my brother as painfully unhip baristas.

"Is Peter coming?" Sonny is snoring at my feet now, but I keep rubbing him anyway.

"As a matter of fact, you need to find him for me and make sure that he does. And bring him to church on Sunday too. Your father has said and done all the right things, so the church is renewing his membership with a ceremony of some sort."

The symmetry is not lost on me. This is the same church that threw him a small going away party when they publicly revoked his membership. No one actually mentioned the word *excommunication*. But I could taste the disgrace in the back of my throat for months.

"Why me?"

"Because your father is not here. Because Peter listens to you. Because I need to spend the next three-and-a-half days relearning how to smile without looking like a recently paroled used car salesman."

"Okay, Mom. Don't sweat it. I'll find Peter."

"I know you don't respect your father. I get that. But you still live in his house and eat his food. So the least you can do is show up and smile and offer a little support."

"Okay, we'll be there. As long as Dad's not preaching." I decide not to tell her about the mole until after the surgery. And maybe not even then. Sonny whimpers in his sleep. "Does he look thinner to you?"

Mom looks at Sonny, her mouth opening and closing soundlessly, then back at me.

"Because I think he's losing weight."

"No, Russell. I'm sure he's just fine."

* * *

My big brother owns and operates the Bean Bag, a moderately successful coffee bar in the Vanderbilt area. Peter claims he won the shop in a poker game, and although I've never believed his story, I cannot fathom any legitimate means by which he could have acquired it. He doesn't have any rich friends that I know of, his credit is as shaky as my self-esteem, and our father ran out of money years ago. Peter's real talent is writing, not business. But instead of applying himself to his boyhood dream of becoming a novelist, he's obsessed with winning a Pulitzer with the Fink family memoirs. He's chronicled our dysfunction and my father's fall from grace in excruciating detail, keeping it

33

all in notebooks, convinced that someone will hack into his computer and steal all his good ideas.

For once, Peter's not hard to find. He's in his office, looking paranoid and listening to his messages.

"Still screening your calls?" I say. "That can't be too good for business."

"Oh, hey Russell." He points to a rickety guest chair directly across from his giant desk. "Take a load off."

"Nah, this place makes me claustrophobic. Why don't we grab a seat out front?"

"Let me show you something first." He motions me over and points to a grainy screen that stutters and blinks from one frame to the next. "Security cameras. Pretty cool, eh?"

We watch two silhouetted forms enter through the shop's front door. A moment later the scene flickers, revealing an upended paper cup rotating in lazy arcs on the pavement by the dumpster.

"Fascinating," I say. "How much did it cost?"

"Safety first, little brother." He slaps me on the back, then retreats into a shadowboxing stance, a silent invitation to pretend we're carefree teenagers again. I decline. He follows me into the dining room, still feigning, weaving, and punching the air. He stops long enough to bark orders at his staff of three high schoolers.

The décor in the café is garage sale chic with plenty of room for rich college kids to spread out and play on the Internet while sixties jazz spills from hidden speakers. The menu consists of sandwiches, exotic desserts, retro T-shirts, and used compact discs. And of course, all manner and variety of overpriced coffees and teas.

We select a couple of decrepit-yet-artsy wingbacks near the back of the shop and I tell him about my run-in with Simmons. My every syllable and gesture is calculated to garner sympathy, but his smirk telegraphs his primary concern—whether or not my story is memoir-worthy.

The barista brings us steaming mugs of exotic mocha-somethings and turns to leave, but not before Peter tells her to straighten the newspaper rack and run out back and pick up parking lot trash. He's a much better overseer than businessman.

"Where's your uniform?" Peter is referring to my customary khakis, starched button-down, and necktie. "Don't tell me Hengle's embraced the twenty-first century and allows casual Friday."

"Gave me the day off."

"So what's up? You didn't come all the way down here to tell me about Simmons turning our mailbox into a Play-Doh factory."

"Mom sent me."

He sighs and turns toward the hissing espresso machine.

"She needs you in church on Sunday, then Monday night at the house for dinner. They're entertaining Geoffrey Sinclair."

"That's big time. Are you going to be there?"

"Unless Dad starts preaching."

Peter flicks his eyes at mine, then changes the subject. "So I guess we're supposed to smile a lot and pretend we're a happy, close-knit family?"

I sip the chocolaty concoction. It burns my tongue and makes my eyes water. But it's delicious and I tell Peter so.

"My own recipe," he says and nods a greeting to a guy in his early fifties who looks like Santa's first cousin—only less jolly and more physically fit. He's emptying a small packet of sweetener into his coffee and stirring. "Is Sinclair really considering Dad for a TV gig?"

"Apparently." I wait until he meets my gaze. "Can I tell Mom you're coming?"

Peter stares at his coffee mug, running his index finger around the rim. "I don't know why I should. But I can tell by the look in your eyes that you're not leaving until I say yes."

I slouch further into my chair and cross my arms, as if I could sit there all day if necessary.

"Alright, but I'm bringing my notebook, just in case."

"Thanks, Peter."

The Santa man slurps his drink, then unleashes a series of violent, sputtering coughs. The other patrons turn to see his face redden, deepening his resemblance to St. Nick.

"You okay?" Peter asks with enough panic in his voice to make me wonder if his insurance premiums are paid up.

"Fine, thanks." The man's jowls fill with color as he dabs his stiff shirt and beard with crumpled napkins.

Peter is staring at the bottom of his mug again. I know that look, a look that tells me I should jump up and flee the premises before it's too late.

"Russell, I hate to ask you this."

"It's never stopped you before."

"This is the last time, I swear. The very last time."

"That's what you said the last *three* times."

"Don't make me grovel. I just need a couple grand to tide me over."

"You know I don't have a couple grand."

Everyone knows I don't have a couple grand. When I was four and Peter eight, my grandfather set up a savings account for each of us before going off to prison. He left strict instructions that it only be used for college expenses for my brother and me. Peter eventually used his to buy a Jaguar — just to spite Gramps — and for some reason has had the self-control to gamble away everything he owns but that car. I took out a loan against it to finance Alyssa's engagement ring, and I'm still paying for it. My freshman roommate must have discovered

36

my PIN (scribbled on a movie stub and crammed into the toe of my Gumby bedroom slippers), because at the same time all my money disappeared, he moved to Europe with the wife of his professor. While I moved back home with my parents.

I shake my head, angry now. "And even if I did have it, I wouldn't give it to you. I'd check you into whatever the gambling equivalent of the Betty Ford Clinic is. You're sick and you need help, not more money."

"You're right. I know. But it's the other way around this time. I need the money so that I *can* get help. I might be in some real trouble this time."

I stare at him, daring him to lie to me.

"I'm being followed, Russell."

His expression is resolved and I have to look away when his bottom lip starts to tremble. That's when I see the Santa man leaning forward, one ear craned in our direction, staring at nothing in particular.

"I'm serious. This has never happened before and it's got me a little freaked out."

"Look, I can probably scrape together another five hundred or so. But that's it."

"Thanks, man. Seriously, I owe you big time."

Then, as if he flipped a switch, Peter's demeanor changes back to the fun-loving youthful entrepreneur. "Hey, is Alyssa coming to dinner?"

"I seriously doubt it. Why?"

"I was wondering if she'd be interested in doing a television commercial for me."

What he's really wondering is if she'll ever dump me so he can ask her out. He thinks I'm oblivious to his subtle flirting. Actually, it bores me. I'm midway through rolling my eyes when St. Nick's cousin approaches our table, hands folded in front of him.

"Pardon me, fellas. The name's Claude Beaman and I promise I didn't mean to eavesdrop. But I couldn't help hearing one of you mention that you were, um, being followed? I was a private investigator in Austin for fifteen years. I just moved to Nashville and wanted to see if maybe we couldn't help each other out."

Peter grins and says, "You carry a gun?"

"Nah." He smoothes his beard slowly, then again, before resting his hand over his breast pocket. A white crease runs the length of his jeans, and his shirt is so brittle from over-starching that I fear one wrong move will shatter it. "I'm more of a laptop and telephoto lens guy."

"We appreciate the offer," I say. "But I'm afraid we can't really afford—"

"I'm sure we can work something out, maybe cut a deal in exchange for some good word-of-mouth marketing."

I can see Peter is enamored with the idea of retaining a real live PI so I try to head things off before they begin. "Tell you what, leave us a card and we'll call you if something comes up."

The man looks embarrassed again, but rallies quickly by snatching a napkin from the table and clicking his ballpoint pen.

"I haven't gotten around to getting my cards updated, so I'll just scribble down my number and you boys can give me a call if you need me. Or if you have any friends who could use some professional snooping ..." He slides the napkin in front of me and I can't help noticing his blocky handwriting, how it seems to lean forward; how he piles his eights, more like snowmen than racetracks. He then offers a faint salute. "Sorry to bother you. And I do appreciate your time."

The plan is to cram the napkin into the bottom of my coffee mug, dousing it in watery dregs, but Peter snatches it up first. He drains his own mug and begins bussing our table so he won't have to look me in the eye.

"So anyway, about the money ..."

I write my big brother a check for a thousand dollars. Before handing it over, I make sure I have his undivided attention. "You cannot cash this check until Tuesday — literally. It will bounce. And if you give one penny of this to your new investigator friend, so help me, I will find the guy who's following you and help him break both of your legs. Got it? Tuesday."

"Got it. Thanks again. And hey, don't worry about the coffee. It's on the house."

Funny, had I known I was drinking a thousand-dollar cup of coffee, I would've savored it more.

* * *

I manage to kill one hour in the art supply store and another in a used record shop before heading back home to my parents' house for a nap. Mom is snoring softly on the sofa with cheesy religious broadcasting blaring in the background. A half-gallon container of spiked lemonade sits on the coffee table — empty of course. I tiptoe toward my bedroom for a fitful nap, littered with dreams of routine mole-removing surgeries gone horribly wrong. I get up and try to paint, wondering when Alyssa will call to yell at me some more. But it's no use; my muse is still napping.

Alyssa finally calls at a little after ten with a list of cryptic instructions that I'm too groggy to comprehend.

Whatever she's up to, I'm sure it has to do with her recent bout with philanthropy; she's spent countless hours in recent weeks organizing a rally to protest the grand opening of a new topless bar near a neighborhood full of widows. Although I applaud her effort, suspicion slithers around my insides. I can't help thinking that this is yet another publicity stunt.

Alyssa and I started dating in high school, but I didn't realize until much later that I had no choice in the matter. It was fun at first, tagging along with the most popular girl in school. I was in awe of her looks, her audacity, her ability to command a room. We all were. My role was less romantic. I was a safe bet for Alyssa, a sure thing, a buffer against the advances of jocks, nerds, and even a few grimy teachers. If the ghastliness of high school could be reduced to a game of tag, I was Alyssa's home base.

Over time I concluded that her lust for attention was hereditary. Her father had developed a Messiah complex and her mother was a jealous disciple, systematically intercepting and hoarding any affection directed from father to daughter. It's no wonder Alyssa joked she was more like an orphan than an only child. She played the role well — Dickensian, almost. I was her sidekick, more of an accomplice than a lover.

Her transition from high school to college reminded me of Nashville — the quaint, southern façade remains intact, but the inner workings bustle with progressive energy, a cosmopolitan discontent for something bigger and brighter and more significant. Alyssa was the glittery skyline. I kept the streets safe and litter-free, carrying her makeup bag to auditions all over town. One gig led to another, and I found myself lounging in recording studios, television sets, and photo shoots sketching ideas in my portfolio and basking in the afterglow of my girlfriend's rising star. She's most famous for a series of low-budget, highly effervescent commercials for a local hot tub company. Playing off the name of her ditzy character, perfect strangers (mostly post-pubescent boys shouting from car windows) often refer to me as *Mister* Bubbles.

Alyssa claims she wants to leave her mark on the world. I think she just wants to matter. I'm not sure how that squares with whatever she's dreamed up for tomorrow, or if I really want to find out.

I should just blow it off completely, pretend I overslept or something. But I won't. My impending surgery has me more than a little freaked out. And if nine years of tumultuous dating, an engagement ring worth half my annual salary, and an entire weekend of picking out china patterns doesn't entitle me to a little sympathy, then nothing will. As pathetic as it sounds — even in my own mind — I want someone to feel sorry for me. Someone besides me.

Saturday

Entering the parking lot of a so-called gentlemen's club — even for a good cause and in broad daylight — gives me the heebie-jeebies. It doesn't help that it's filled with placard-wielding senior citizens in expensive running shoes, a handful of serious-looking clergymen, and a half-dozen homeless men in various degrees of dishevelment squinting at the sun and fighting over a box of donuts. Not a bad turnout for a Saturday morning.

Giant neon tubes spell out the name of the risqué nightclub in loopy cursive.

As a Jaybird.

The structure itself is a two-story cinderblock cube with blackened windows. It's painted pink and purple and adorned with life-sized versions of those silhouetted mud flap girls.

I park just below a Nashville landmark — the city's oldest living oak tree. According to the gilded sign, it's a Swamp Chestnut Oak with a circumference of 152 inches, stands 132 feet, and has a crown spread of 86 feet. It's supposedly three hundred years old. The most impressive feature to me is the dilapidated tree fort, complete with makeshift rungs nailed to its trunk.

The sound of voices swells like Little League infield chatter as I approach Alyssa's makeshift command center, which consists of one large folding table, two chairs, and three giant coffee urns. Soiled petition forms are taped in place between rows of empty donut boxes. Her clamoring cries for attention go mostly unheeded. Moving through the crowd, I am able to make out snippets of conversation about Medicare benefits, the separation of church and state, and the fact there is no cream for the lukewarm coffee. Finally, Alyssa reaches into a gym bag and removes an electric bullhorn. She presses the trigger, and the air ignites with static and piercing feedback.

Alyssa's typically creamy complexion is flushed. Her hair is starting to frizz and several buoyant curls are now pasted to her forehead. She checks her wristwatch and then looks toward the entrance to the parking lot. Her face darkens. She thanks everyone for coming and starts doling out instructions. The plan is to reenact the battle of Jericho sans trumpets. I sit on the edge of the table and watch as she lines up a group of volunteers, wheelchairs and walkers in the rear. She gives the signal, and the demonstration lurches forward.

Things start badly when a grim octogenarian lifts her aluminum walker and sets it down on the tasseled loafer of the skeletal man in front of her. For one frightening moment, it looks like they may topple the whole group like geriatric dominoes.

Alyssa leaps into action, scooping up his shoe and trying to slip it back on his foot like a toddler. The man, red-faced from exertion or embarrassment or an overtaxed artery, slaps her hands and scolds her. She gives him a dirty look, brushes by him, and approaches the petition table, leading with a scowl.

"Hey babe," I say. "How's it going so far?"

"I'm not speaking to you."

"Ah, but you just did."

"Oh, shut up."

A pimply teenager steps between us. He has the air of a young man looking for his first friend — a real bundle of nerves, licking his chapped lips, blinking like a strobe light, and shifting the weight of his slight frame from one foot to the other. He's obviously another one of Alyssa's adoring fans. Since he doesn't call her Bubbles, I'm guessing this guy's a fan of Alyssa's other claim to fame — a barroom floozy in a Toby Keith video.

"Would you sign my forehead?" the kid asks, wielding a Sharpie. He leans forward and Alyssa mindlessly scribbles her name. The kid turns to me, grinning. "How does it look?"

"Brilliant," I say, and the kid pumps his fist once and dashes off to join the rally. Alyssa falls into one of the folding chairs, leans one elbow on the table, and begins tallying the signatures.

"You're obviously upset about something," I say to the top of her head.

"For starters, you skipped work so you could go to the doctor." She looks up. "Again. Then you lied about it. *Again.*"

"Did it ever occur to you that I might be working? They do use office supplies at doctor's *offices.*"

She looks up from her tabulation and says, "Did it ever occur to you that maybe I called your office and they told me you called in sick?"

"Did you?"

"Next time I will."

"What do you care if I call in sick every now and then?"

She holds up her hand, and for one frightening instant, I think she's going to flip me off in front of all these nice old ladies. But then she uses her thumb to wiggle her engagement ring, a gesture that seems to imply she's not looking forward to making babies with an unemployed hypochondriac.

"I'm pretty sure I have cancer."

"Spare me."

"Seriously, I think even Dr. Kozinski is worried this time."

"You really need to get a place of your own. Living with your parents makes you morbid."

So much for garnering sympathy.

"Look Russell, I don't have time for this now. The homeless guys are mad because we're out of donuts, and the preachers would rather debate theology than actually protest anything."

"I tried to warn you about all this. I think it was Confucius who said you should never mix philanthropy and cheap publicity."

"Please, Russell. Just try and make yourself useful."

"Useful how?"

"For starters, you could call the local networks and find out why their news crews haven't arrived yet."

I shouldn't be surprised when she hands me a yellow sticky note with the local numbers for the ABC, CBS, Fox, and NBC affiliates. I shove it into my back pocket and concentrate on not rolling my eyes.

She points past a cluster of shouting clergymen toward an arriving Sunrise Retirement Community van, snaps her fingers and says, "There's something else you can do. Some of the senior citizens want me to come up with something they can shout while they march around the building. You know, like a song or a chant or something."

"And?"

"You're creative. Make something up and go teach it to them."

"You're kidding."

"Make sure it rhymes. Old people like rhymes."

"I think I'd rather make a run to the donut store."

Just then a *News 4* van careens into the parking lot and dumps off a skinny cameraman with a bushy beard, followed by a blonde woman with a microphone and an expensive suit. She's the kind of wholesome, lightweight celebrity you recognize at once but have no chance of re-calling her name or why you recognize her.

"And one more thing, while I'm coordinating protestors, why don't you see if you can coordinate that camera with my face? You even have my permission to flirt with the news babe if necessary."

Then the reporter lady saunters toward us, her lowly cameraman in tow, and shoves a microphone in my face.

"Excuse me, sir, could you please give us your take on the gentle-men's club controversy?"

I feign deep thought, then say, "A monumentally bad idea."

"Would you care to elaborate?"

I point to a handpainted sign by the door that advertises an all-you-can-eat buffet. "I just don't think food and nudity belong in the same room."

She rolls her eyes and lowers the microphone. Alyssa steps in and introduces herself as the protest organizer. She is in her element. I can't bear to watch so I decide to take Alyssa's challenge. I greet the newcom-ers with a handshake and a smile, then invite them to crowd around me. I teach them their new battle cry, complete with hand motions I remember from Sunday school.

"It's imperative that you teach this chant to your fellow protes-tors. The entire city of Nashville — and her children — are counting on you."

That done, I decide to check on the hubbub surrounding Alys-sa's interview. She's trying to focus on the reporter's questions, but she comes off looking perturbed and frazzled at the turmoil swirling around her. Behind her, a preacher in a cheap suit, the pimply teenager, and a homeless man with a head like a football have broken ranks with the other marchers and are vying for their own fifteen minutes of fame. The preacher is calling down plagues and brimstone for all those who deign to worship on any day but Saturday. The autographed

47

teenager keeps jumping in front of the camera and making silly faces. And Football Head is demanding hot coffee, Krispy Kremes, and some strippers or he's going to report Alyssa to the Better Business Bureau. She counters with a few witty sound bites, but I can see the worry snake across her forehead like fissures. This is not the publicity she was looking for. And a tiny sliver of my heart hurts for her.

The wholesome reporter mutters a creative string of profanity and motions her sidekick to wrap things up.

I sidle up to Alyssa as the front line of the marchers appears around the far corner of the building, chanting with muddled vigor. I can hardly wait to hear my creation.

"At least they're having a good time." I motion toward the line of chanting senior citizens.

Here's our church ...

Here's our steeple ...

We don't want your naked people ...

The pride swelling inside me is stifled when Alyssa punches me in the chest.

"This is all a big joke to you, isn't it? Like everything else in your world."

"No. What? What are you talking about?"

"All I ask for is a little support from the man who's supposed to love me. And the best you can come up with is that ridiculous nursery rhyme."

"What more do you want? I did exactly what you asked." I try my best disarming grin. "Even included hand motions."

"Maybe you could act like you care about something other than yourself."

"Me? You're the one who staged this whole charade just to get your face on television. *Again.*" She recoils at my mocking tone.

"You don't care about anything or anybody but your stupid painting and your fascination with dying."

"That's ... that's just not fair."

"Oh, don't go all pitiful on me. Maybe it's not fair. But it's true and you know it. Face it, Russell. You suck at your job. You suck as a boyfriend. And until you get over it, you're wasting *my* time and *your* life."

I'm too stunned to speak. This is familiar terrain for us, using words like knives. But Alyssa just hit bone.

"Well?" she says.

"I'm having surgery on Tuesday."

"What? Is that supposed to be funny too?"

I shake my head. "Dr. Kozinski found a mole."

A small gasp escapes her. And for one blissful moment, I'm convinced that she'll actually step outside of herself and indulge me the one pathetic thing I came here looking for—sympathy. But she's looking past me, over my shoulder toward the giant oak tree.

I follow her gaze to a mewling kitten, stranded on a fat branch fifteen feet above us.

"Don't just stand there, Russell. Get up there and get that kitty down."

Staring up through the limbs makes my head tingle and my stomach hurt. I lick my lips and lean against the tree's massive trunk for support, vaguely aware of Alyssa saying, "Oh, brother!" as she shoves past me. It's all I can do to keep from spilling into the street like a crumpled beer can.

She's a fast climber. In mere seconds, Alyssa navigates the network of limbs and is seated on the floor of the tree house, cradling the kitten to her chest.

I'm vaguely aware of murmuring behind me. Then all I hear is the whir of the camera and the clipped and sturdy voice of a news professional.

"We are reporting live from the site of a protest rally at a gentlemen's lounge set to open its doors tonight. It appears the rally's organizer has taken her protest to another level — literally. Having scaled the city's oldest living oak tree, she appears to be staging some sort of prayer vigil ..."

Alyssa blinks once, then again. She closes her eyes, folds her hands under her chin, and mumbles her way through the Lord's Prayer.

Sunday

My church attendance is in advanced stages of atrophy. But I can't think about it without feeling guilty, so I don't. Even though superstition doesn't exactly square with my religion — or what's left of it — I figure an eleventh-hour visit to the house of God couldn't hurt, given my upcoming surgery and all.

The auditorium at Nashville Community Church is enormous, and on this Sunday morning, it is filled to capacity. Familiar hymnlike melodies eddy and swirl above me, mixing with the crisp air that reeks of coffee breath, cologne, and Juicy Fruit.

I find my mother and sit down in one of the empty seats next to her. Minimalist architecture and folding chairs have replaced the gaudy floral furnishings and hardback pews that I remember from my youth; the padding on these humble foldouts is thicker than our best sofa.

My eye picks up on a familiar name under the heading of "Guest Speaker."

Pastor Gary Fink.

I can't believe it. She lied to me. My own mother. And about church even.

It's been over a decade since I sat through one of my father's sermons. And my lucky streak will not end today. I say a quick prayer of thanksgiving for having driven my own car, then a second one of forgiveness for what I'm about to say.

I lean toward my mother, careful not to meet her eyes, and whisper out of the corner of my mouth, "I'm going to the restroom. Maybe see if I can find Peter and tell him where we're sitting."

The white of my lie must be showing, but I can see that she's not ready to get into it. Without her bottle of courage, she's no match for the angst I've accumulated since Katie's death. The look on her face tugs at the pant leg of my heart. But then I remind myself that she fudged first.

As I make my way through the crowded vestibule, I realize I'm fantasizing about my mother's liquor cabinet and Sonny's special gift. That's when I hear a familiar voice.

"Russell? Is that you?"

It takes a second to match the voice with the face. "Geri. Nice dress. Let me guess, Romania?"

Geri examines the bright yellow and white of her own outfit, as if seeing it for the first time. Her latest pastime is that of amateur seamstress, transforming government-issued parachutes, tarps, flags, and tents into surprisingly fashionable outerwear. Baggier than I'd prefer, but tasteful. "Nope. It's the Vatican flag."

"That's very, um, I don't know ... *religious* of you."

"Yeah," she turns and points at the large symbol on her back. "These are supposed to be the crossed keys of Saint Peter."

"Cool, two keys. I always assumed there would be a back gate." I pause for comedic effect. Satisfied, I add, "Like at the zoo."

Nostalgia blooms in Geri's grin. She was my assigned lab partner in sophomore biology at Belmont University. Thus our friendship predates our current copier salesman/law firm secretary relationship.

Of course, I liked her at once. She dressed funny, smelled delicious, and hated music with synthesizers. The bridge of her nose crinkled when she smiled, which never failed to weaken my knees. She had opinions about everything but had to be coaxed into sharing them. I saw her as a seamless mix of irony, pathos, and humor. And she was so darn subtle about it all, able to self-deprecate without invoking pity. The only time her subtlety faltered was when we played board games. Geri was a fierce competitor when it came to Monopoly, Yahtzee, Battleship, or Operation.

At first we just studied together. Then we began eating together, often two or three times a day. I suppose I should have felt some degree of guilt. But Alyssa was the one who convinced me to move back home and then went away to college herself. *She* decided when it was convenient for us to break up or get back together. By the time Geri and I started doing laundry together, it finally dawned on me that we might be more than just friends. One night in particular — during a noisy rinse cycle — I felt myself leaning in to kiss her. I didn't plan it, it just happened. Eyes closed, lips parted, I moved in. Then I felt something stiff and cool on my tongue — Geri had popped a stick of Teaberry gum in my mouth. When I opened my eyes again, she was balling socks together on the dryer. Still, my heart beats a bit faster whenever I smell fabric softener.

We routinely snuck into the Nashville Zoo through a back gate. She loved feeding the lambs, and I loved the naughty feeling of getting away with something. That, and nurturing a crush I knew I couldn't act on.

I'm surprised to find her in church. Our running joke in college was that if cynicism were a religion, we'd be shoe-ins for ordination. Making fun of TV preachers — my father included — became the recreational equivalent of intramural sports or Xbox addiction.

"Heaven's back gate, huh? Never thought of that." She seems

distracted, glancing over my left shoulder. It's hard to tell if she's trying to find this someone, or avoid them. "Wonder if they're any less pearly?"

"What are you doing here anyway?"

She shrugs, causing the shiny material of her homemade pantsuit to swish together. "I think they call it 'going to church'."

"Last I remember, you were experimenting with atheism."

"Guess it failed. The question is, what are you doing rushing out of here before the service even starts?"

"I'm abstaining." I point out my father's name on the church bulletin. "For religious reasons."

Geri nods, distracted, knowing all about my family's dysfunction. But then she's scanning the horizon behind me again. It dawns on me that her former fiancé was a bit of a religious nut — surely they haven't gotten back together.

The door to the auditorium opens and we hear the music giving way to an opening prayer. A sour-faced usher offers a benevolent dirty look, which I take as my cue to head out.

"Well, it was great seeing you. I'm sure I'll stop by your office tomorrow so you can help me figure out how to keep the supermodel from stealing my order."

I get a kick out of watching disgust flash in her face as she remembers the ditzy salesgirl. "Sounds good to me."

Once outside, I pause long enough to pretend to tie my shoelaces — and to sneak a look back through the smoky glass doors. A tall, gangly man approaches Geri and extends his arm in an overly chivalrous way. I feel a pinprick inside, then the slow gaseous leak of some foreign solution. The sensation amplifies until there's no mistaking it — *jealousy*. She not only takes his arm, but leans her head on his shoulder as they disappear inside.

I was always attracted to Geri but never admitted it until the night we played Life in the student center. I was enamored with the sound of the spinner, the obscene wads of cash I was accumulating, and simply hanging out with Geri when I should have been studying. But her mood was souring with every turn. She started with a pitifully low salary, and then the little blue husband figurine kept falling out of her car. When I suggested she swap her defective orange car in for another color, she snapped at me. "I'm always orange, okay? Now shut up and spin."

Meanwhile, my little blue man won lotteries, bore children, wrote books, and amassed a small fortune. But I couldn't enjoy it. By the time Geri was nearing the finish line, she was childless, mostly broke, and her little blue husband was forced to recline in his seat like an invalid. Before her final spin, Geri's nose did that adorable scrunchy thing. But instead of a snarky remark, she broke down and began sobbing. I shoved the game aside and held her. She cried harder, in part, I suspected because she hated to cry in public. So I held her tighter, frightened at the realization that I might be in love with the wrong girl, and wishing we could talk about it. We never did. Three days later, Geri announced she was engaged.

Looking back, I'm sure she knew I was crazy about her all along. And I think it must have scared her as much as it did me because she always found subtle but convenient ways to remind me of our mutual status of engaged-to-someone-else.

Thankfully I don't see Peter until I'm safely behind the wheel of my Ford Taurus. But he doesn't notice me. And as much as I'd like to see his face when he realizes that he's been duped, another plan is materializing in my brain, against my will. Entertaining this notion is the emotional equivalent of a pinhole in the Hoover Dam.

Technically, I'm not sneaking into my own house, since it is my official residence and all. But that's how it feels, like I'm an imposter trying to get away with something. Which, as it turns out, is exactly what I'm doing, and I can't shake the mental image of God shaking His head and tsking as He slides beads across a gilded abacus ...

Skipping church + Lying to mother +
Liquoring up a defenseless dog = Deadly cancerous mole

The air inside the house feels thick and ominous, like in those dorky movies about teenagers and serial killers. So I get to work before I lose my nerve.

After a cursory examination of the pantry, I find the first of my supplies — a half-empty bag of gourmet dog treats. I make my way to the catchall drawer for Mom's industrial-sized turkey baster. Next, I pad up to my parents' bedroom closet and whiz through the combination on their massive gun safe. Despite Mom's covert alcoholism, my parents are still naïve enough to think Peter and I have never found her stash. I uncap a bottle of premium vodka, use the baster to suction out about a half cup, then head downstairs in search of Sonny.

I find him asleep on his mat in the laundry room. He wakes up when I come in and shivers through a series of yawns, looking every one of his seventy-two dog years. I stroke his head, back, and belly and he rewards me with a wet kiss on the mouth. He sniffs the dog biscuit in my closed fist and begins pacing in place and twitching uncontrollably.

I sit on the tile, resting my back against a kitchen cabinet, and I try to stave off the guilt for what I'm about to do. I remind myself that Sonny enjoys this routine, and that he should be able to indulge a few guilty pleasures with what little time he has left. Unlike me, he's a happy drunk.

* * *

I discovered Sonny's gift the first time Alyssa broke up with me. It was Super Bowl Sunday and we were supposed to attend a church-sponsored party to watch our beloved Tennessee Titans in the big game. We'd signed up to bring the salsa—a gallon each of the mild and hot. But when she came to pick me up, she sat me down on my parents' corduroy sectional for one of her serious talks. We were both about to turn eighteen and were only months away from graduation, then off to our respective universities—me in New York City and Alyssa in Tennessee. I'd just made my first payment on her engagement ring. The plan was to pop the question on the eve of our leaving for college.

"The truth is," she'd said, as if reciting lines from a script, "I just don't think I can trust myself at college. You know, what with all those new faces and athletes and musicians and whatnot."

She tried to make it all sound noble. And I was too stunned to mount a credible protest.

"Look, I know this hurts, Russell. But there's no point prolonging the inevitable. I'm really sorry—being Super Bowl Sunday and all—but I just didn't want to have to think about it during the game. I'm sure it'll save us both a lot of heartache in the end."

No amount of tear-filled stuttering could dissuade her. She collected the jars of salsa and went to the party without me. With my parents and Peter on a mission trip to South America, I immediately broke into the gun safe and commenced drowning my sorrows. Sonny watched my deterioration in silence. And the more I drank, the sadder he looked. So I decided to share.

On a whim, I soaked one of his doggie biscuits in a small glass of vodka. It only took one whiskey biscuit to get him hooked. Now I had a drinking buddy.

Sonny had always been a good listener, but for the first time ever, he was *responding*. My rhetorical questions about the football game were directed at the TV screen, but the answers were coming from Sonny—correct answers—about things that hadn't even happened yet. His accuracy improved with each marinated doggie treat; he was able to forecast third-down conversions with stunning accuracy, eventually predicting field goal attempts, touchdowns, and whether the Titans would run or pass. Sonny had become my Magic 8-Ball.

Of course he was limited to yes or no questions. And it took the entire first quarter to decipher his shorthand. Two short, spastic barks indicated "yes." Incessant blinking and a failure to meet my eyes meant "no." By the end of the third quarter, our inebriation took on an inverse relationship. His increased clairvoyance sobered me up. But he just kept munching spiked doggie biscuits, predicting plays, and getting more and more wasted.

By the final play of the game I asked Sonny if the Titans would score. His eyelids fluttered and he pretended to look nonchalantly around the room. The Titans would lose. Sonny said so. Right before he passed out.

The next day I checked on Sonny to make sure that I hadn't dreamed the entire ordeal. But sure enough, the air around his sleeping mat was staler than normal. And he was snoring. When he did wake an hour later, he stumbled and staggered around until he peed on the linoleum.

I never could figure out how to make money off Sonny's talent. He worked strictly in the moment, which meant no off-track betting or big lottery paydays. He had no affinity for game shows. And besides, I had a terrible time transposing *Jeopardy* questions into a yes-or-no format before the smart people on the show blurted the answers. But he was able to duplicate his prophetic gift during telecasts of the US Open and the NBA playoffs. I couldn't go public, as I'm sure there's some law against contributing to the delinquency of an aging canine.

Eventually Sonny advised me to accept a scholarship offer from New York University to pursue my dream of becoming an artist. I figured the distance would make it easier to forget Alyssa. But I was wrong. The following summer I ignored Sonny's advice, returned to

Nashville, and enrolled at Belmont University to major in business, all because Alyssa had decided she missed me and begged me to move back home.

* * *

The phone rings; I'm guessing it's Mom, anxious to unload another ripe batch of guilt on me about skipping out on church. So I stare at the phone until it stops.

Sonny meanders toward me, nuzzling the turkey baster. I can't help but be amused by the fading twinkle in his eye — my sweet alcoholic dog. Even as I empty the treats into his bowl I promise myself that this is it. This is the last time I will stoop to this level of wretched inadequacy. Of course I've broken this same promise no less than a dozen times. It seems I'm as addicted to his gift as he is to the sweet nectar of ninety proof.

I've become an enabler.

He sniffs the dry wafers and eyes me impatiently, like a junkie trying to keep it together while the deal goes down. I coat the biscuits with my mother's vodka. He attacks the bowl, panting and slurping with ferocious abandon while I check all the windows and doors again for potential witnesses. I even inspect the garage door. Mom's been after my father for months to have the automatic opener repaired. She claims it's a security risk, but I suspect she's just tired of having to raise and lower it the old-fashioned way.

I return to see him lapping up the rest of the whiskey biscuits, which have disintegrated into a disgusting chunky broth. He tilts his head at me, panting. It seems like he's thirsty all the time now. By the time Sonny licks his bowl dry, I decide he's sufficiently tipsy to begin.

The process seems to work better if I start with easier questions. And I've learned that dummy questions don't work either. Sonny can detect the insincerity a mile away.

I clear my throat, look him in the eye, and say, "Sonny, should I quit my job at Hengle's or hold out until I can afford my own place?"

He tilts his head, unblinking.

"Sorry, I forgot."

I lick my lips, wishing I had one last baster full of elixir for me.

"Okay. Is old man Hengle going to fire me?"

Sonny blinks and looks at his paws, as if checking an invisible wristwatch.

So far, so good. I can make next month's car payment. I massage Sonny's neck and slip him another biscuit. A dry one.

"Ready boy?" Our eyes meet again and I say, "Is my mole cancerous?"

What Sonny does next scares me to death. He holds my gaze, lies flat on the floor, and sticks his nose against my leg. What could that possibly mean? I rephrase the question several times, but he doesn't move. Panic threatens to derail me, so I change the subject.

"Okay, I've got one for you." Sonny rises into a sitting position. "Should I break up with Alyssa?"

He barks twice, then stands and spins around. Then he unleashes a barrage of double-barks, as if to say, "Yes, yes, you idiot. What are you waiting for? Break up with her now, this instant, before she ruins your life forever."

Relief washes over me like a hot shower on a frosty morning. I begin to laugh, a hysterical sputtering cough that borders on insanity. And I would swear that Sonny is laughing too as we spin around the room, barking and giggling at one another in frenzied celebration. The joy is as sweet as any I've known.

Until I hear Peter's voice.

He's standing in the door frame that separates the living room and kitchen, grinning like a lobotomized monkey and wielding his dreaded notebook.

* * *

Peter's laughter echoes in my head as I steer my Taurus through the streets of suburban Nashville in an embarrassed rage. I can just picture him scribbling in his notebook, thanking God Almighty for his good fortune.

This random drive feels just like my life.

And it's all Alyssa's fault. She's the one who drove Sonny to drinking in the first place.

Several miles later, my breathing has returned to normal and I'm finally able to string a few rational thoughts together. Unfortunately, they all have to do with Alyssa and the fact that our relationship can be reduced to a jumble of mixed metaphors. We've plumbed the depths of our dysfunction. We've added a lower rung to the ladder of codependency. Our relationship is less than the sum of its parts, where one plus one still equals one, or maybe even less. We've covered our wounds in a patchwork quilt of Band-Aids.

Then it dawns on me — why not do it now? With only six months or so to live, why spend another day in a mortally wounded relationship?

Sonny has given me the impetus I need. And since I'm a big chicken when it comes to confrontation, why not channel this emotion into action and get it over with? Just rip the Band-Aid quilt right off and brace myself for the sight of blood.

It takes a full minute for me to get my bearings. It appears that I've been driving through the neighborhood of my youth, to the house on Ravenwood where I killed my sister.

* * *

The parking lot of the nightclub is empty, but I park illegally on the street anyway. As I approach the giant oak tree, I hear the sound of muffled voices. After a few seconds of squinting and craning, I'm able to make out two distinct shapes in the branches.

"Alyssa? Is that you?"

"She's over there." The voice sounds oddly familiar. "I think she's meditating again. Or maybe taking a nap. She does that a lot."

It's the pimply kid from the protest, the one with the autographed forehead. He's using a curator's voice, whispered and arrogant, as if he's the foremost expert on the sleeping habits of neurotic publicity hounds. I move around the trunk until I can make out the dilapidated tree house.

"Russell?" Alyssa says, sounding groggy. The top of her head appears, her hair hanging like cheap curtains around her face. "What are you doing here?"

"We need to talk," I say.

"Ooh, sounds serious," Alyssa says. "Harold, you think you could hop down and make a coffee run? I think my fiancé wants to yell at me."

"Wait a second," the kid says, angry now. "You mean I sit up here with you for two days, bringing you magazines and makeup and Taco Bell and listening to your life story, and now you want to dismiss me like a child?" A lowrider drives past, bass thumping. "Unbelievable." The kid's sneakers scrape against bark and leaves rustle as he makes his way down. "This blows."

He pauses, regarding me as he would a crusty bedpan, then trudges away mumbling to himself.

"So ..." Alyssa peers at me over the side of her wooden roost.

"So ..." Since I've never asked anyone out before, much less broken up with anyone, I have no clue where to begin. I think back to movies I've seen to come up with an icebreaker or the perfect segue. But the best I can come up with is, " ... you're still up there."

Instead of a pithy remark, she laughs and says, "Yeah, hard to believe, but I'm still up here. And you know what's funny? I was just sitting up here feeling sorry for myself when that reporter lady said something about me staging a prayer vigil. I thought it was funny at the time. But when everybody left, I did start praying for real. And not on purpose, mind you. It was like an accident. But then I couldn't seem to stop. Weird, huh?"

It *is* weird. And a little scary as well. Alyssa and I were thrown together when our fathers joined forces to plant a church in east Nashville. The church flourished for a few years, despite the fact that it was strong on personality but practically devoid of leadership or direction. My father was itching to get back into the healing racket and Alyssa's father began experimenting with New Age ideas. He now runs a commune in Mexico where nudity and smoking hallucinogenic toad venom are viewed as legitimate paths to enlightenment. Maybe that's what this protest is really all about. From the dreamy sound of Alyssa's voice, I fear that the sins of her father may have finally found her.

"Russell?"

"Yeah, yeah, I'm here." My mouth is suddenly dry, my resolve as sturdy as a soggy cracker. So I'm as shocked as Alyssa when the syllables forming at the back of my throat burn a path across my lips. "And well, um, I think we should break up."

She stares hard at me over the floor of her tree fort, no doubt trying to gauge how serious I am. "No you don't. Not really. You're just upset because of all those awful things I said. And because I didn't react well when you told me about your surgery. I'm sorry I didn't believe you, Russell."

I stare up at her.

"You know how I get when I'm stressed, just fly off and say whatever pops into my head."

She isn't making this easy. "So what makes you believe me now?"

"I called your doctor's office. Told them I was your ride home and needed to verify the time."

"I still want to break up."

"Look, Russell. I said I was sorry. Just postpone your surgery until I win this battle." She makes a sweeping gesture toward the dormant building. "Then I'll come down and go with you and we can sort this all out."

"What battle? You're the only one here. This whole thing is a publicity stunt and not a very effective one, I might add."

"It's not just a stunt. It's a matter of principle." I hear her shuffling above me. And for a moment I think she's coming down for a confrontation. But I guess she's just trying to get comfortable. "Besides praying, I've been thinking a lot about what Confucius said."

"Who?"

"You know who. You're the one who told me what he said about mixing philanthropy and publicity. See, that's my problem. I've been going about it all wrong. I realize now that there's nothing wrong with a little self-promotion, but it's got to have some heart."

"Confucius never said that. I just made it up."

"Don't flatter yourself, hon. Maybe you should spend some time up here with me. It's done wonders for my state of mind."

"Don't change the subject. We're breaking up. And I'm going to need that ring back."

"We're not breaking up. Not like this."

"Look, if I want to break up, then we're breaking up. You don't get to dictate the terms."

"Okay, fine. But you could at least come up here and do it like a man, so I can see the look in your eye."

"You know I'm afraid of heights."

"Suit yourself then. But I'm keeping the ring until you break up with me properly."

And with that she pulls her head back into the tree fort, like a turtle going in for the night.

Fueled with my newfound audacity, I grab the lowest, fattest branch and hoist myself upward. It's been awhile and my tree-climbing muscles have withered. If I don't fall and kill myself, I'll surely be sore tomorrow. After much groaning on my part, I finally make it to a sitting position in the nest of big branches and try to catch my breath.

Then I remember why I'm afraid of heights.

Instead of catching my breath, it's coming in short, suffocating gasps.

I feel something whiz by my left ear, something which shatters on the pavement below, and I snap my head in that direction — too quickly, and it makes me dizzy. Through the branches I see a red pool on the pavement and I'm convinced that it's blood. I have to blink away a horrifying image of Katie, sprawled on the pavement below me. Then I see a plastic white cap and realize it's fingernail polish.

I'm climbing again, and Alyssa is now pelting me with one strange object after another — a tube of toothpaste, tiny bottles of makeup, an apple, her cell phone, a Hall & Oates CD, a handful of romance novels, a leftover burrito, and at least one shoe.

I raise my right hand for protection against the barrage of flying shrapnel. Then something that feels like a small sewing machine smashes into my left hand and I'm tumbling toward the earth. Thankfully, I land on my butt in the grass instead of breaking bones on the pavement. Alyssa's portable generator lies in pieces all around me.

She takes a few calming breaths, then whispers, "Father, forgive him for what he's trying to do."

Then I hear her scream the word *creep* as a picture frame explodes at my feet. The photo was taken by a stranger, just moments after I asked Alyssa to marry me.

The last sound I hear before slamming my car door is Alyssa shouting, "We are not broken up until I say so!"

Monday

My morning commute is fraught with all manner of dread as one neurotic thought caroms off the next, like spastic carbon bubbles exploding in the fizzy head of a soda. What if I just skip my surgery? Will it hurt when they cut the mole off? Did I really break up with Alyssa? Am I doomed to live with my parents forever? How much longer do I have left to live anyway? Shouldn't I make a list of important things to do before I die? How come my throat hurts every time I swallow? Is that what it feels like when you start to grow a double chin? And if it hurts so bad, why do I keep swallowing in the first place?

Then all the questions funnel into a single one: *Why won't the incompetent driver in front of me exercise his God-given right to make a right turn on red?* He's halfway through the intersection already when he starts backing up. The rear end of his station wagon looms larger in my windshield until I'm able to read the fine print on his bumper stickers.

I'm blowing the horn and thinking about how much I hate bumper stickers, when the station wagon shoots backward and slams into my front bumper. Hot coffee cascades from my spill-proof travel mug down the front of my shirt, making puddles in the pleats of my khakis. The dread comes bubbling back as I paw through my glove compartment looking for my registration and insurance card. I really hate conflict; of course the upside is that I'll have a bona fide excuse for being late for work.

But then the station wagon lurches forward, makes the right turn on red and speeds off.

I get out to inspect the damage to the front end of my Taurus only to find the bumper splayed on the pavement like a giant grin. I remember the past-due notice from State Farm caked with dog poo, and I try to convince myself that I still have time to write the check, but I'm not in a very convincing mood this morning. A horn honks, somehow ceding permission for everyone else to honk their horns as well.

The bumper is surprisingly light, its surface pebbled with a thousand caramelized insect carcasses. I toss it in the back seat, flash a peace sign at the logjam of angry horn-honkers, then point my car toward the office and go. The inside of my car now smells rubbery, like tar, like the tire factory the day I knocked Katie out of the tree fort.

* * *

When it comes to sales meetings, I define success by staying awake until the end, then ducking out without having to answer to anyone in authority. As it turns out, I make it to the office in plenty of time. The conference room is alive with chatter, like a forest full of crickets. Since I'm wearing my last cup, I pour myself a fresh mug of strong coffee and decide to drink it black for a change to match my mood. I assume my customary spot in the back of the room and act like I'm searching for something important in my briefcase so I won't have to make small talk with anyone.

If you choose to believe the gilded string of letters on my premium embossed business card, I'm an Office Machines Specialist for Hengle's Supply. Yet here I sit, waiting for our staff meeting to begin and rifling through my stash of unused cards — just to be sure. I'm indulging a rather pathetic Bradbury-esque fantasy where I discover a misprint, then magically morph into the occupation on the card — maybe I should have some printed with *Artiste* just to see if it'll trigger some kind of self-fulfilling prophecy.

Max Hengle III approaches the lectern to deliver his Monday morning state-of-the-business address. He has a little extra juice in his step this morning, which scares me. These sales meetings last exactly one hour, and the format is as predictable as the evening news: Hengle waxes nostalgic for the first thirty minutes, then spends another thirty yelling at us for not selling enough paper clips, ink cartridges, and bulletproof filing cabinets. "It's the small stuff, people," he cries. "That's why you'll never see an elephant hunter driving a Rolls Royce."

Hengle's Supply, Inc. was born in 1954, making it the same vintage as Oprah, Travolta, Seinfeld, and *Sports Illustrated*. Max Senior began peddling his wares amid rumors of McCarthyism, hydrogen bomb testing in the Pacific, and Elvis crooning through the first transistor radio. It took less than three years to establish Hengle's as the leading supplier of office supplies in middle Tennessee. Max Junior, God rest his lazy soul, presided over the family business through the eras of disco, punk, and new wave, and faring about as well. He died prematurely in a bizarre plumbing accident. The family kept things quiet, probably a mistake, since the rumors grew to involve all manner of bathroom humor. Max the Third took the helm in 1989, when drum machines, hair metal, and a guy named Garth tried to strangle the last bit of art out of the airwaves. And despite the proliferation of the big box stores, deep discounts, and teenagers who don't know the difference between a three-drawer full-suspension vertical file cabinet and a three-hole punch, he's managed to recapture and maintain the lion's share of Nashville's office supply businesses.

He dispenses with the history lesson in record time this morning so he can introduce our new office manager. Her name is Nancy — no last name, like Cher or Madonna, only frumpier, bookish, mid-thirties. Her profile reveals a prodigious nose that must have been broken at least once. Nancy stands, nods tersely, then smoothes her gray linen skirt before reseating herself. In the nanosecond our eyes meet I can tell she's already sized me up — and she's not impressed.

Mr. Hengle is almost giddy as he announces a sales contest. This news causes exactly one half of the Hengle's sales force to perk up, all but Bernie Hengle and me. Bernie, because he's so smug, his sense of entitlement so great, that he's already won the contest in his mind. Besides, he probably helped his father come up with the idea. I slouch in my chair and remember *Glengarry Glen Ross* where the richest of the Baldwin brothers berates a roomful of Oscar winners, then announces a vicious contest in which the top salesman wins a Cadillac and the loser receives a set of steak knives and a pink slip. I could use the steak knives, but only if I can keep this job long enough to dig my way out of debt and make the deposit on my own apartment. Alyssa's right, living with my parents is sucking the marrow from my soul.

Fortunately, today's stakes are much less severe. First place earns a weekend getaway to a golf resort (Bernie), second and third place winners, their choice of a deluxe filing cabinet or a leather office chair (Mandy and Robin respectively). Fourth place merits the distinction of being the only salesperson not to win either first, second, or third (me).

The meeting adjourns and we pack up our notes, sample cases, and dreg-filled coffee mugs. Mandy and Robin actually quiver with anticipation, each vowing to bring the other along if they happen to edge Bernie out of the first-place trip. Bernie directs his arrogant eyes down the length of his nose at me.

"So, Fink," he says, "how's your golf game these days?"

"Starving," I say. "From lack of attention."

"That's too bad," he says, much louder than necessary. "I had you pegged as the frontrunner in the contest."

Mandy and Robin exchange giggles. It's no secret that my languishing sales numbers are a blip or two away from flatlining.

"Seriously," he says, then winks over my shoulder, no doubt trying to catch Mandy's eye. The fact that she's married only seems to fan Bernie's juvenile advances. He's a hormone factory. "I'd be willing to bet my next commission check on your chances."

As much as I'd like to get into it with Bernie, what I really need to do is get out of here before getting cornered by Hengle or his new henchwoman. They're engaged in a whispered conversation in the front of the room. So I give Bernie a disinterested wave and continue packing up my briefcase.

"You never know, Fink," he says, playing to the girls. "Maybe your luck is changing."

A more mature man would walk away. Instead I say, "Speaking of lucky breaks, have you ever cashed a check your daddy didn't sign?"

It's a low blow, lower if you happen to know that Bernie Hengle spends twenty-three hours a day consumed with trying to prove something to somebody. Although no one's exactly sure what or to whom.

"Let me tell you something, Fink." He's in my face now, jabbing his finger into my chest. "The numbers don't lie. I earn every penny I make. In fact, I practically carry the whole lot of you."

When Bernie gets mad, a wormlike vein pulses in the middle of his forehead, his neck turns purple, and spit flies from the corners of his mouth. His arm stops mid-gesture as he realizes that his flaming indictment has lumped poor Mandy and Robin in with me. I almost feel bad, but not quite. Robin and Mandy giggle louder now and head for the door. Bernie sneers at me like a B-movie villain, then trails after the ladies, sputtering feeble apologies.

Hengle and Nancy break from their powwow and are headed my way.

I try to make myself invisible by putting my head down and hunching my shoulders, like a toddler who thinks you can't see him when his eyes are shut. I'm less than five feet from the front door when I feel a tap on my shoulder.

"Mr. Fink, might we have a word?" It's Mr. Hengle.

"In private," Nancy says.

* * *

Nancy's office smells like coffee, cardboard, and permanent markers. Except for the colorful bouquet on her credenza, the room looks like a page from Hengle's quarterly flyer — tidy, efficient, antiseptic. Nancy sits, then motions for Mr. Hengle and me to do the same. All is quiet, save for the hum of her computer and the whispered beat of a lite-rock station.

Mr. Hengle clears his throat, picks an invisible piece of lint off his pant leg, and says, "Russell, the rest of the staff got the chance to meet Nancy in a less formal session Friday. Since you were out sick ..." His voice trails off. "How are you feeling today?"

"Much better, thanks. Dr. Kozinski sends his regards. And he asked about Ray."

Hengle's grin falters, then rallies back strong. "Glad to hear it. Russell, we've hired Nancy here to handle most of the day-to-day functions. Chief among her duties will be managing the sales force and finding creative ways to maximize potential. I think you'll find her to be an invaluable resource."

"I'm sure I will." I smile at Nancy but she's unmoved. I turn back toward Mr. Hengle and say, "So, I guess that means you'll be spending more quality time with your nine iron, eh?"

Mr. Hengle chuckles. Nancy doesn't.

Hengle continues, "Now Russell, you and I have discussed your sales performance numerous times in the past — and I don't want you to see this as any kind of threat, mind you — but obviously there's a great deal of room for improvement. So I want you to view Nancy as a mentor of sorts."

"You mean like that bald guy on *Kung Fu*?" Hengle labors to conceal the smile tugging at the corners of his mouth.

"Something like that."

"Does that mean I finally get a company car when I snatch the pebble from her hand?"

Hengle is laughing in earnest now so I turn to Nancy, "Just promise me you won't call me Grasshopper."

She smiles then. A high school principal smile. An undertaker's smile.

"Mr. Hengle, could Mr. Fink and I have a few minutes in private? To get acquainted."

"That's a good idea." He unfolds himself and stands in the doorway, looking relieved and a little worried. "Remember, Russell, you report to Nancy now."

Then he's gone.

Nancy gets up and closes her office door behind him. It dawns on me that she's not frumpy at all, more like frugal and plodding. Nothing is wasted, no extraneous gestures, tics, or arm swings. Everything is calculated, from her gray linen blouse to her streamlined approach to jewelry and makeup — Hester Prynne meets Elizabeth Arden.

She sits and swivels, facing her computer monitor. A few keystrokes later and I can see the grid of an Excel spreadsheet reflecting in her rimless glasses. She studies the screen for a moment, then turns to me, places her folded hands on her desk blotter, and says, "Well, Mr. Fink."

"Nancy."

"Tell me something. Do you like your job?"

"Sure, yeah. Probably the best job I've ever had."

"Interesting." She examines an unmanicured fingernail for no apparent reason. "Why don't you tell me a little bit about yourself? What else do you like to do? Hobbies? Girlfriend?"

"I have a fiancée — an ex-fiancée. She claims that my art is my mistress. You know, because I'm a painter."

"Interesting."

"You said that already."

"Excuse me?"

"You've said 'interesting' twice." Something tells me to tread lightly, but I ignore it. My only chance with authority figures is to amuse or disarm them. "But see, you didn't really look interested either time you said it. So I'm wondering if you're really interested in my personal life at all, or if we're leading up to something."

She inspects the fingernail again, then tilts her head so she can regard me over her glasses. "Okay, Mr. Fink. I'll play along. You tell me, what exactly do you think we were leading up to?"

"My guess is that you wanted a small list of things that I'm passionate about, or at least *interested* in. Then you were going to ask a few probing questions about how much time and attention I pay to those things so you could make some point about how often I call in sick. You know, 'How can you say you love your job when you're always calling in sick?' Something like that?"

"Very good, Mr. Fink. Then I'm sure you're aware that your personnel record has more gaps than a hockey player's grin."

"That's pretty funny."

"I'm not certain what kind of leverage you have over Mr. Hengle. And frankly, it's none of my concern. But I, for one, will not treat you like a mascot. There will be certain expectations and standards of conduct that will apply to everyone in my charge. Failure to comply will result in extermination, regardless of bloodlines, prior loyalties, or who can tell the best jokes."

"Did you say extermination?"

"You know what I meant."

"Because I think poisoning underachievers in the workplace is generally frowned upon."

Not even a hint of a smile.

"Mr. Fink, do you know why Mr. Hengle hired me? Profitability. I was hired to make money for this company. Not to sell staplers or answer the phone or make new friends. And I've been given full authority to accomplish that goal. *Full* authority, Mr. Fink."

I want to ask her why she needs authority to *not* make friends, but we've already established that she's impervious to my sense of humor.

She says, "Now don't get me wrong, I'm a reasonable person. I'm even willing to …" She makes talonlike quotation marks with her fingers … "'start over.' And I think a good first step is actually showing up for work. What do you say, Mr. Fink?"

"Well, I hate to bring this up, but I do have surgery tomorrow."

"Surgery?"

"It's an outpatient thing. I'm having a mole removed." Part of me wants to insinuate that a team of world-renowned surgeons has already reviewed my case and that the prognosis is dismal. If I can't amuse her, maybe I can make her feel sorry for me. But I just can't bring myself to utter the *C* word. "My doctor said it would only take an hour or so. So, you know, I could probably make it to work in the afternoon."

"Not to impugn your character or anything, but I suppose you'll be able to produce proof of this operation."

"I'll see if they'll let me videotape it if you want."

"Don't be a smart aleck."

"Sorry. I'll bring a doctor's note."

75

"That would be fine. Now for the sake of clarity, are there any other surgeries or weddings or prospective flat tires that I need to know about?"

"Nothing that I know of."

"I'll make it simple for you then. You have exhausted all of your sick days, personal days, and vacation days for this calendar year. In other words, if you're breathing, I expect to see you at work — on time. Otherwise I'll have no choice but to terminate your employment with Hengle's Supply."

"You know that's never been done before."

"I'm somewhat of a pioneer in these matters." So was Attila the Hun, I'm thinking. "Now, are we understood?"

"Yes ma'am."

"My name is Nancy, not ma'am."

"Oh, I'm sorry. I guess I didn't catch your last name."

She eyes that fingernail again, this time like she wants to bite it. "Now if you'll excuse me, I have to prepare for a meeting with Mr. Hengle. And you have some selling to do."

* * *

The fastest way to prove Nancy wrong — and for that matter, the Hengles, Mandy and Robin, my parents, my brother, my fiancée-in-limbo, and the freaky teenager in the SUV behind me — is to pin down the humongous copier order at Tyler, Billingham & Sneed. And the fastest way to do *that* is to enlist the help of Geri. My hunch is that she wields more power than her administrative assistant title would indicate, and it's gloriously obvious she doesn't like that supermodel salesgirl from the big chain store. Geri had regarded her like a fresh wad of bubblegum on the bottom of her favorite sneakers.

When I enter the law office waiting room, Geri is standing in front of the law firm's main copier, alternating between pounding the meaty part of her fist on the green *copy* button and kicking the side of the machine with the toe of her fashion-conscious work boots. When she flails around like that, her shirt pulls taut around her middle. She's gained weight since college. But she wears it well.

"Is there a problem?" I say, feeling like an intruder.

She turns, freckles shimmering, her cheeks flushed with perspiration. "Did you sell us this giant piece of crap?"

"No, not really. I mean, somebody from Hengle's sold it to you guys. But that was before my time."

The machine beeps and spits out another legal-sized copy of a *Far Side* cartoon. Geri pivots on her left foot and kicks the copier again with her right. I don't have the heart to point out that she's merely denting the cabinet base that supports the actual machinery.

"Well, unless you can help me figure out how to get this motion to dismiss copied and delivered to the courthouse in the next thirty-five minutes, I'm holding you and your company personally responsible."

"Okay, calm down. I'm sure we can figure something out." I drop my briefcase and begin troubleshooting. I must admit, I like the sensation of taking charge, of assuming the role of calm expert. What I like even better is the close proximity to Geri's body, the heat of our shoulders touching. "But, if I help you get this done, you need to help me figure out a way to close the deal on the new copiers."

"Fine. Whatever."

After five more minutes of careful study, I admit that the problem exceeds my level of expertise and that her next best option is the neighborhood Kinko's.

"It's raining," she says with more than a trace of desperation.

The logical question would be, *Well, couldn't you just drive?* But Geri's life runs in cycles. For instance, she's always lamented the fact that her weight can fluctuate as much as twenty-five pounds, depending on the season. She also has an acute fear of driving that seems to come and go without provocation.

"I'll give you a lift. But you're gonna owe me."

We share an umbrella out to my Taurus, and I'm struck by how great she smells. Some delicious combination of mint, cucumber, and fresh rainwater that makes me wish I'd parked farther away. Shockingly cool raindrops trickle down my neck as I gather up fast food bags, dog-eared sales literature, and CD jewel cases to toss into the backseat. She gets in, still clutching her bundle of legal documents to her chest.

"What's that smell?" she says.

"Oh, that." I jerk my thumb toward the backseat, suddenly embarrassed. "Someone slammed into my car and knocked the bumper off."

She looks dubious. "That's one smelly bumper."

Then she lapses into an uncharacteristic silence, punctuated only by the clatter of raindrops. I glance her way and watch her use her fingers to trace water droplets shimmying up the passenger window.

"Are you okay?" I hear myself ask.

"I'm great, just looking for rainbows."

"Let me know if you find one. I'll drive you to the end of it and we can go halfsies on the pot of gold."

She doesn't respond, just keeps tracing and staring until I park the car. Kinko's is a nonevent, and we make it to the courthouse with a healthy five minutes to spare. The rain has settled into a comfortable drizzle, and Geri pauses on the courthouse steps. She scans the horizon, no doubt rainbow hunting.

"How about you let me buy you some lunch? You know, to make amends."

"Amends?" She tilts her head and looks at me. "For what?"

"For the broken copier, for the near-miss on filing your brief, for dragging you out in the rain."

"Okay." She doesn't realize that none of those things are my fault — her mind is somewhere else.

Geri claims to have no preference where we eat. But then she systematically whittles my list of suggestions down to Waffle House and a couple of fifties-themed diners. When it finally dawns on her that she's in the mood for fried bologna, she directs me to a quaint diner in the Vanderbilt area.

We take a red and white leatherette booth in the back, under autographed headshots of Gene Autry, Hank Williams, and Goober. The scarred Formica tabletop teeters when we rest our elbows on it. I retrieve a couple of tattered menus and review our options aloud while Geri cranks the silver knob on an old-fashioned tabletop jukebox.

"Too bad this thing's not hooked up. I'm starting to think that all the good songs were written before I was born."

"I don't think it was your fault."

Our waitress arrives without a sound, a pad in one hand and skeletal fingers gripping a wooden pencil in the other. Her wispy bouffant, gloppy red lipstick, and permanently bowed posture make me wonder if she served the diner's inaugural BLT.

"What'll you have?"

Geri orders her fried bologna sandwich, french fries, and extra pickles. As an afterthought she adds a giant malted milkshake.

"I'll have what she's having."

I'm surprised to see our waitress transcribe our order, pausing often to touch the pencil point to her tongue. Then she lumbers off, collecting dirties and wiping tables as she goes. I resist an overwhelming urge to get up and lend her a hand.

We spend the next fifteen minutes reminiscing over our college glory days and making small talk about life since. Geri spends her nights and weekends journaling, concocting homemade perfume mixtures, making her own clothes, heckling reality TV shows, and occasionally picking her trumpet back up. She was a phenomenal jazz trumpeter in college, even toured with a Miles Davis tribute band for one summer. But she gave it up when she got engaged. Thomas, it turns out, was not looking for a soul mate so much as a clone of his mother.

Finally, Geri points to my left hand and says, "What happened to your thumb? That looks nasty."

"Domestic dispute involving a tree fort and a flying generator."

"Guess it could have been worse." She's never met Alyssa, but she's heard the stories.

"So ..." I'm attempting to sound casual, if not slightly ironic. "What about your love life? Don't tell me it ended with Tom."

"I've retired."

"Right."

"I'm serious, Russell."

"You mean like the Rolling Stones, working on their fourteenth farewell tour?" She unwraps a straw and rolls the paper between her fingers. Gauging by the black look on her face, I can only guess I've said something stupid. So I quickly add, "I don't mean to say 'I told you so' but, come on, *Tom and Geri*?"

Her face darkens, but she recovers in an instant and flicks the balled-up wrapper at me. "So anyway, I guess I owe you an apology, huh? I can be a real drama queen sometimes, especially when my hormones kick in."

"Are you kidding? That's nothing. Alyssa still says that *God* wants her to be an actress."

Geri makes her if-you-can't-say-anything-nice face. Then she says it anyway. "I can't believe that you put up with — I mean, that you guys are still together."

"We're not. I broke up with her yesterday. She didn't accept."

Her grin packs enough wattage to power a small island. "I owe you twenty bucks then."

"What?"

"Think about it. It'll come to you. But if you can't remember, I'm not paying."

I'm not sure how to respond so I watch our waitress shuffle toward us under the burden of steaming plates and giant milkshakes. Based on her progress, I'm guessing our fries and shakes will be the same temperature when they finally reach our table.

I point to Geri's homemade olive-colored outfit. "What happened to the grunge look?"

"It was grunge-lite, actually. And I burned it all when Kurt Cobain died. Then I woke up the next day and realized that I had no clothes and no money. That's when I started making my own stuff. Like this jumpsuit."

She holds up her arm for me to inspect it.

"Completely waterproof. Go ahead, feel it."

I do, all too aware of the flesh and blood vibrating beneath the thin layer of space-age material.

"I had no idea. That's really cool."

"No, Russell. It's not cool. It's weird, like the fear of driving thing."

We finish our meal with small talk and long patches of silence. At some point I look up and notice that Geri's attention is captivated by a bloated fly hovering over the remnants of her bologna sandwich. I raise my arm to shoo it away, but she tells me to leave him alone. She leans forward cautiously and peers at the disgusting little thing with something akin to awe.

"When's the last time you looked at a fly?" she says. "I mean really looked?"

It's not a real question, I realize, but rather an invitation for me to see with new eyes. I drag a few fries through a puddle of ketchup and try to think of something clever. But her fascination is contagious, and before I know it, I'm hunkered down eyeballing the tiny disease bag.

"Look at that detail," Geri says, "so intricate, and so … tiny. And all those eyes …"

"Wait, I only see two. Big red bulging ones."

"And all those shades of purple. Forget the fact that it can actually take flight. You've got to believe God was having fun the day He came up with this idea."

"A lot of people consider those things flying garbage cans."

"Yeah." She thinks I'm actually agreeing with her. "Probably the same people that can't find the beauty in spider webs and tornadoes and old people. Look, he's rubbing his little hands together."

"I'll bet he's devising a sinister plan to fly away with one of your pickles."

"Actually, he's washing up. Did you know flies groom themselves? Anyway, I like to think he's praying."

And then he's gone, off to prayerfully groom himself in a bowl of potato salad.

"Well, I probably need to get you back to work, young lady. But if you remember, you did kind of promise to help me out."

"I did?"

"I agreed to help you with the busted copier, and in return, you agreed to help me salvage the order for the new copiers."

"Sorry, I don't think so. The copier's still busted." She pauses for a moment, her expression distant and unreadable. Just when I think she's looking for rainbow patterns in the wall behind me and deciding to protest, she flashes that crooked grin again and says, "I'm messing with you."

"Do you have any ideas?"

"Absolutely. But it's going to cost you."

We meet our waitress at the cash register. Geri fishes her wallet out of her purse, but I make her put it away, insisting that she let me pay for lunch. The waitress winks at me as if we're in on the same secret, that if Geri lets me treat her to lunch, then I get to pretend it's a date. Am I really that obvious? I hand over my check card, but the waitress points to a handwritten sign: CASH OR CHECK ONLY.

"Oh," I say, followed by a "huh."

Geri stops fiddling with the toothpick dispenser and takes in my dilemma with a glance. I thumb through my money clip, as if rubbing my thumb across the few singles there will magically make them multiply.

"I got it, Russell." Geri produces a twenty for the meal and five for the tip.

"I'm sorry. I'll hit a cash machine on the way home and pay you back."

"Don't sweat it. Like I said, it's going to cost you."

* * *

I head back to the office to piddle around with email and move papers around my cubicle before heading home to obsess about my lack of selling ability, the peculiar state of my relationships, and tomorrow's surgery. On the way home, I almost stop by Alyssa's tree. The plan is to start an argument for no other reason than to blow off some steam and make myself feel better by comparison, but I don't have the requisite energy. So I drive home, hook Sonny to his leash, and walk him around the neighborhood until dinner. For some reason, despite the lousy week I'm having, I keep wondering what Geri's up to. It'd be great if she were coming to dinner tonight. Her special brand of sarcasm would make the evening almost bearable.

Sonny's gait is a bit wobbly. Either it's my imagination or his hangovers seem to defy dog years. He seems more lethargic than ever. He sniffs along the curb, raises his leg, and fires.

"That's ten times in ten minutes, boy." He swivels his big head up at me, panting and trying to look thirsty. "Keep this up and I'm taking you to the vet."

We loop around the block until the driveway starts filling up with cars — Mom's, Dad's, and Peter's. I catch Simmons watching us from his window, and I'm half-tempted to break down his door and have Sonny exact retribution in person, right on his no-doubt pristine carpet. But the unmistakable sound of Alyssa's perforated muffler prevents me from compounding my misery. I whip my head around, more than a little surprised to see her.

She nearly kills Sonny as she swings into the driveway, parks, and lugs out two cartons of ice cream.

"You okay Russell? You look like you just saw your mother in a tube top."

She bends down and attempts to trade kisses with Sonny. But he'll have none of it.

"No offense, but what are you doing here?"

"Peter invited me. And besides, how many opportunities do you get to break bread with a broadcasting tycoon?"

Her eccentric get-up makes sense now — plaid skirt, pale cashmere sweater, sensible shoes, and a simple cross on a chain, like a librarian en route to a prayer meeting. Alyssa is not only here for dinner, but for an audition.

"So you gave up on the vigil, huh?"

"Heavens no. Harold came back and now he's sitting in for me."

"The angry kid from the protest?"

"You should see him in a wig. It's adorable."

"Good, he saved me the trouble of having to climb the tree to get my ring back."

"I got your point, Russell. Let it go already."

"I'm not making a point. I want my ring back."

"Technically, it's my ring."

"Then maybe you should take over the payments."

"No, you gave it to me." She pretends to search her finger for it. "And wouldn't you know it? I accidentally left it on my dresser when I got out of the shower."

I'm about to protest, but she claims the ice cream is melting and she hurries up the sidewalk. When I can't think of a good reason not to, Sonny and I follow suit.

Despite my funk, the house smells as warm and golden as a Thanksgiving casserole. Peter is hunched over his notebook when we come in. When he notices Alyssa, he leaps up and wraps her in a lingering embrace. His eyes laugh at me over her shoulder. He's always had a thing for her.

Sonny growls at them. My hero.

While my theoretical fiancée and actual brother lapse into playful banter about her career, I escort Sonny to his giant pillow in the laundry room. I stop mid-stride when I hear Peter mention something about a private investigator. I gape at him, which he answers with a conniving wink. I decide right there to stop payment on the check — if it's not too late — then spend a few quiet moments with Sonny, whispering lame apologies and rubbing his belly. He's asleep in no time, and I find myself wishing I could just skip dinner and snuggle up next to him and try to sleep off my life.

The doorbell rings, followed by animated voices and forced laughter. Our guest has arrived. I kiss Sonny between the eyes and head to the living room, practicing fake smiles along the way.

Geoffrey Sinclair looks much older in person, despite wrinkle-free skin and a hairline staunchly defended by thousands of little salt-and-pepper sentries. He sits at one end of the table with my father at the other, like ecclesiastical bookends (except for the infamous Fink double chin on my father).

It's funny; I realize that I haven't seen my father in almost a month. After putting in long hours at his sister's insurance mill, he works nights and weekends trying to resurrect his ministry. He travels the country teaching seminars on building healthier father/son relationships. Makes me wonder if he can even spell *irony*.

Memories of us as a happy, close-knit family blanket my thoughts. But they're in black-and-white, which makes me wonder if they're real or if I've somehow superimposed *Leave It to Beaver* or *Father Knows Best* reruns onto my otherwise ordinary childhood. My parents never fought, nor did they embarrass us with flamboyant movie kisses in the kitchen. They just were.

They did all the usual parental things, yelling when necessary and paying the mortgage on time. The workaholic father arrived home each evening to a pristine house and a warm dinner. In those rare moments of spare time, he alternated between perfecting Peter's batting stance and doting on Katie, his princess. I mostly stood around and waited my turn.

I got along fine with my father and in turn, he got along fine with me. But that was about it. I remember feeling we were nothing more than roommates, until Katie died, and then we became cell mates. I'm sure we blamed each other for Katie's death. Or maybe we were more alike than I cared to admit. Maybe he blamed himself.

I guess I always assumed his healing spectacles were a sham. And it wasn't like I didn't try. Many nights I lay awake, begging God to make me believe in my father. But then breakfast would come and our eyes would meet while passing the pepper or a bottle of Aunt Jemima. His rueful expression would confirm the obvious — my prayers failed yet again. When his ministry began to crumble, I stopped begging God.

The day the warrant was signed for his arrest on charges of tax evasion, he holed himself up in his office and refused to speak to Mom, his colleagues, or even his lawyer. He kept dialing our home number until I got home from school and picked up. For some reason he wanted to tell me first. "Because, Russell." His voice faltered when he said my name. "I can trust you."

I would have preferred a hug.

Mom hands me a basket of warm bread, asks me to pass it down, then takes her seat at the immaculately set table. This used to be her element, the gracious hostess regaling guests in culinary splendor. Now she looks like Martha Stewart — the prison version — sour and cagey, like maybe her teeth hurt or she needs a drink. And I'm struck with a sudden urge to try and protect her.

Peter waits for Alyssa to sit down, then grabs the seat directly across from her. His eyes radiate an eagerness that borders on pornographic. He is genuinely fascinated with my girlfriend's celebrity, and she feeds off it. They chat each other up and ignore me, once again reducing me to an accessory. We haven't spoken since he caught me abusing Sonny the other day. And every time he opens his mouth, dread courses through me with funny bone zeal. If Sonny's extended hangover doesn't somehow give me away, it'll be Peter's word against mine.

The plan for the evening is to swim below the surface, to fade into the background, to become the proverbial fly on the wall. But the wall in question feels like it's in the factory where they make swatters.

I'm thinking that maybe Peter and Alyssa would make a good couple after all — that maybe they deserve each other — when the room settles into an awkward silence. It's time to say grace.

My insides clench, and I'm suddenly fascinated by the frayed hem of my zipper flap. The act of praying aloud has always filled me with severe trepidation; it started in Sunday school when I mangled the Lord's Prayer with "Halloween be thy name," then got so frazzled at the whispered giggles that I ended with "lead us not into Tarnation."

It never fails, my mouth dries up and my eyelids flutter like mad as I scrutinize every word, every syllable, every stepping-stone of silence between the words, as if failure to wax eloquent enough will result in holy demerits. That and my praying voice sounds like it's being played back through some cheap tape recorder.

Finally, I hear my father beseeching the heavens and my heart throttles back to idle. There's a foreign quality to his voice. He says "Amen" and the room crackles again with polite conversation and the medley of serving spoons scraping bowls and ice tinkling in glasses. It dawns on me that he looks different somehow.

"You okay, little brother?" Peter says, not even trying to hide his smirk.

"Actually, I'm not feeling —"

"Oh, he's fine," Alyssa says. "Just dreaming of his next trip to see Dr. Kozinski. I'm starting to think he has the hots for one of the nurses."

Everyone gets a good chuckle — everyone but Sinclair. He regards me with a pinched, sympathetic expression, as if he really wants to know what's bothering me. I look away in time to catch Peter winking at Alyssa.

The moment passes, along with the bucket brigade of serving dishes brimming with fried chicken and gravy, corn and mashed potatoes. After a few grunts of approval and compliments to the chef, the conversation begins in earnest. I keep waiting for my father to work in bits of his résumé, but instead he defers to our esteemed guest, goading him to talk about his new ministry. Sinclair seems reluctant, choosing instead to probe the rest of us with questions about our work and our hobbies. He seems to have a knack for wading through pretense and pleasantries to get to the heart of the person in front of him, though he makes a tactical error by asking Alyssa about her acting, an open invitation for her to hijack the spotlight.

She does.

And I feel myself slipping back down into my stupor, vaguely aware of the voices swirling around me. My brain registers a few choice phrases. But most of it seems distant to me, like a stereo blaring through a dorm room wall. I have a sudden urge to go check on Sonny. Instead, I push vegetables around my plate with a fork.

"Russell." It's Sinclair, and now all eyes are on me. "Your father tells me you're quite the artist. Says you have an amazing gift for blending the simple and the surreal, and all without sacrificing the spiritual."

I feel my jaw unhinge like a puppet. I cannot remember a time when my father spoke of my art with anything other than derision or boredom.

Sinclair continues, "I'd really love to see some of your work."

"Sure," I say. "Yeah, that'd be great."

He smiles, almost embarrassed, and says, "I've been known to dabble in some charcoal and watercolors, but I'm afraid that I'm basically a hack." He has the longest fingers I've ever seen. They seem to go on forever, like one of those old-fashioned, foldout wooden rulers.

I can't think of a single thing to say, which Alyssa takes as her cue to shower my artistic abilities with hyperactive praise.

"Oh, Russell's art has this, this, what do you call it? You know ..." Alyssa stammers, eyes pleading for help. "Like, you know, not necessarily artsy. But it has this like a real, um, *artistic* quality about it." What she lacks in appreciation for nuance, she makes up for with enthusiasm. I'm vaguely aware of my father nodding, my mother biting back a wry smile, and my brother laboring to not roll his eyes. Yet even through the thickening cloud of idiocy, Sinclair never takes his eyes off me.

When the phone rings, I scrape my chair across the hardwood floor and am halfway up when my mother bolts from the table.

"Keep your seats everybody," she says and scoops up a handful of dirty dishes. The phone rings again. "I'll see who that is and put the coffee on."

While Peter panders to Alyssa's hyper-receptive ego, my father tries to steer the conversation back to Sinclair's new ministry. He's less desperate than Alyssa, yet equally persistent. But now Sinclair is bent on learning about Peter's coffee shop.

Mom returns with a snide comment about telemarketers. She takes her place at the table again and we regard each other amid the crossfire of dialogue that neither of us cares anything about. That's when I notice the color in her cheeks. And that she seems a bit more relaxed than before. Her grin is taut, conspiratorial, as we again feign interest in the conversation.

We smell Sonny before we see him.

Until that moment, I'd forgotten that the flatulent effects of alcohol on his digestive system can sometimes last for days. He's a walking outhouse, waddling around the table, sniffing for scraps.

When he finds none, he decides to groin our guest.

I hear, "Russell!" in four-part harmony, as if I'm the one with my nose in Sinclair's lap.

Geoffrey Sinclair is the picture of grace under pressure. "It's okay, really." He uses both hands to massage Sonny's neck and steer his long wet nose toward safer terrain. I refuse to look at Peter, but I can tell by his constant squirming that he's dying to relay the source of Sonny's behavior.

"Well," my father says, almost pleased with the distraction. "Why don't you share your vision with the rest of the family, Geoffrey?"

Sinclair spares few details about *Second Chances*, a ministry that helps former religious leaders and athletes and businessmen reassemble the broken pieces of their lives. Apparently he wants my father to host a weekly talk show that will feature live interviews with a variety of famous prodigals.

I'm vaguely aware of Peter removing his notebook from his lap and placing it on the table. Anyone named Fink takes this as a bad omen. "So that's your angle, eh?"

My father blanches. Mother smiles into her lap, her shoulders quaking imperceptibly. Alyssa and I stare dumbly at Sinclair. If discretion is the better part of valor, my brother is a quivering sissy. Peter is convinced he can bully people into confessing their most salacious faults, thus providing fodder for his memoir-in-progress. If history holds, however, he's about to be embarrassed or get himself popped in the nose. Maybe both.

"Excuse me?" Sinclair's voice is calm, genuine, as if he really didn't hear.

"That's how you're gonna do it? Bring in famous adulterers and druggies to grub for money? Pretty ingenious."

"Peter — " My father chuckles, but not like he means it.

But Peter continues, unabashed. "I suppose they get a hefty cut, right? Or will they come on just to get some cheap publicity?"

"That's enough." My father sounds genuinely angry, and old.

Sinclair waves him off. "No, no. I insist. Let's hear Peter out."

"Well, tell me I'm wrong."

"I'll admit, mine is a rather unique calling. And quite frankly, a dangerous one. Most of our guests will have been addicted to something. And as such, run the risk of lapsing back into destructive and embarrassing behavior. So trust me, I'd much rather air Billy Graham reruns or another benign Bible study show. But I believe this is what God wants me to do."

"Fair enough," Peter says. "But how does that translate to the bottom line? If it's a ministry, someone's gotta beg, right?"

"For the sake of argument, I'll concede your point, being not-for-

91

profit. But let me assure you that the one thing I will not tolerate is tweaking people's emotions, or as you call it, 'grubbing' for money."

It could just be my imagination, but I'd swear Sinclair cut his eyes at my father.

"I'll believe it when I see it."

Sonny disappears under the table. I can feel his hot breath on my ankles, coming in short blasts, as if he's sniffing for familiar territory.

"Anyway," my father says. "We plan to feature my own, um, indiscretions on one of the earlier shows." All heads but Sonny's swivel toward my father. "I'd like each of you to think about participating — on camera — with the segment on our family."

"Really?" Alyssa says. "That'd be fantastic."

"Well," my father says. "I guess we could find a spot for you."

The awkward silence is filled by the unmistakable sound of wetness — specifically, a concentrated stream making contact with fabric.

"Oh … my …" Sinclair leans back, tipping his chair up on two legs. "What have we here?"

I look over in time to see Sonny, leg raised, whizzing on Sinclair's pant leg and loafers.

Peter leaps back from the table, trying to avoid the splatter and sending his silverware, his notebook, and a crystal butter dish toward the floor.

"Oh, man," I say, running to Sinclair's aid, but it's too late. Sonny has all four legs on the ground and is sniffing for crumbs under the table. "I am so sorry."

Peter and my father begin shoving napkins at Sinclair. Alyssa keeps repeating, "Eww." And my mother disappears into the kitchen to actually find something useful to clean up our guest. I'm too mortified to do anything but stand there and say, "I'm sorry. Really, I can't believe this."

Sinclair has his hand on my shoulder. "Not to worry, it's not my first christening."

I grab Sonny by his collar — tugging way harder than necessary — and drag him back toward the laundry room, still apologizing over my shoulder and offering to bring a wet washcloth. I manage to tuck Sonny back into his bed without kicking him or calling him names. Only then do I notice Peter's notebook in Sonny's mouth, riddled with teeth marks, slick with butter and dog slobber.

I leave to the sweet, sweet sound of gnashing teeth and shredding pages.

* * *

Sleep eludes me like a watermelon seed on freshly waxed tile.

After several hours of staring at the ceiling and obsessing over the dreadful dinner, I manage to focus all my anxiety on my impending surgery. It gets so bad I find myself praying for nightmares, figuring that fitful sleep is better than none at all. When that doesn't work, I get out of bed, pad out to the living room, fire up the computer, and google every possible combination of "moles" and "surgery" and "cancer" to try to convince myself that one tiny slip of the scalpel won't multiply malignancies faster that the US National Debt Counter.

At some point, Sonny toddles out with dried scraps of notebook paper stuck to his whiskers. "I'm still mad at you," I say, not meaning it. Truth be told, I'm pleased to have the company. The one consolation of his vulgar antics was watching Peter search in vain for his precious notebook. Of course, when my brother realizes what's happened, I may have to enlist Sonny in the canine version of the Witness Protection Program.

I check my email — nothing but discount Viagra and refinancing offers.

"You know this is all your fault, don't you?" Sonny yawns at me, then nudges my hand with his snout. Before I know it I'm petting him against my will. "My job was to supply the whiskey biscuits. Yours was to tell me not to worry about the mole, that everything would be fine, to quit acting like such a baby."

Tuesday

Here I am again, staring at people I don't know in Dr. Kozinski's waiting room, too uptight to sketch their ailments. If I did, they'd all be spotted like Dalmatians with giant cancerous moles. I'm mulling the irony of calling in sick for a doctor's appointment when Cassandra calls my name — and my nerves are too frazzled this morning to even pretend that she harbors romantic fantasies about me.

I round the waiting room partition and am surprised by her appearance. She looks rough, her eyes rimmed red, her skin puffy in all the wrong places. Her smile looks genuine but sad, as if she knows I won't survive the procedure. Without a word, she escorts me back to the same examination room I was in last week — or maybe its evil twin.

"Go ahead and peel off your shirt and hop up on the table. I'll go round up Dr. Kozinski and we'll get started."

"Are you okay, Cassandra? You look down."

She brightens a bit and smiles again, this time pinning her bottom lip under her teeth. "Yeah, I think I'll be just fine. Thanks for asking. You're too sweet."

She turns to leave and my insides freeze. "Cassandra? You're com-ing back, right? For the surgery?"

"You'll be fine." She pats me on the arm, giving my bicep a light squeeze, allowing her hand to loiter there. It feels nice, warm, and a bit naughty. "This procedure is nothing. I'll be right here."

"Promise you won't tell anyone if I break down and start blubber-ing like a baby?"

She cocks her jaw to one side, as if debating. "Yeah, I promise." Then she offers a half-wave before she disappears. That's when I see the white loop around her finger where the engagement ring used to be. Now it looks like scar tissue. Guess that explains the sad face.

I try to imagine asking Cassandra out and realize that I don't feel free *or* single. If anything, the whole breakup ordeal feels as hollow and pointless as renouncing my spleen. I can tell it to shut down or get lost, but it's still in there, churning away, doing whatever it is spleens do. No matter what I say, it's still a pretty crucial part of me.

After a quick rap, the door swings open and Dr. Kozinski stalks in with Cassandra and another nurse in tow. They're all busi-ness — washing hands, ripping open sterile packages, filling syringes, and exchanging somber doctor-speak. Cassandra instructs me to roll over and lie facedown on the deli paper. Then she slides a flimsy ex-cuse for a pillow under my head and drapes what feels like a giant papery tablecloth over my back.

Finally, Dr. Kozinski asks me if I'm ready to proceed.

"Can a person survive without a spleen?" I ask.

He laughs like he means it. "Not to worry, Russell. We're going in the other way."

"Sure, but could you live without it?"

"Splenectomies are fairly common and rarely fatal. The real dif-ficulty comes in dealing with the changes after the fact. The body is more susceptible to disease and whatnot. Immunization is the key."

"Huh," I say.

Everyone assumes their positions. Dr. K hovers over my left shoulder, and it smells like his mouthwash has gone sour. From what I can tell, the extent of Cassandra's job is to hold a book open where Dr. K can see it. She rests the spine of the book on my right shoulder.

I begin to speak but have to stop and clear my throat. "Please tell me you've done this before, Doc. That you're not reading the instructions as you go."

"Actually, I'm using this paint-by-numbers kit that came with my mail-order medical license."

Then I feel the hands on my back — warm and rubbery — prodding, stretching, swabbing. The room now reeks of alcohol and I feel the cool, wet drizzle where the warm hands were.

"You may feel a little pinch here."

Actually, I feel at least three. My body aches in all the places I'm clenching. And I realize that I've stopped breathing.

"If you can hold your breath for the whole operation, your chances of bleeding to death go way down."

The unnamed nurse laughs along with Dr. K. But Cassandra remains silent. She squeezes my shoulder again under the book and rests her hand there. I try to look at her, but my face is smashed into the stiff little airplane pillow. Is my behavior so pathetic that I need constant reassuring? Or could she really have a crush on me?

Then Dr. Kozinski says, "Oops!"

Someone is screeching, and it sounds an awful lot like the pubescent version of Russell Fink. My body goes taut and several realizations hit me at once. The corner of Cassandra's book is cutting into my skin. There are tears pooling in my right nostril. Worst of all, I now have about sixty seconds until my entire bloodstream is riddled with disease.

"What do you mean 'oops'?" My voice cracks but I don't care.

Dr. K and the mystery nurse exchange nervous chuckles.

"It's nothing, really. Your skin separated a little. Just going to re-quire another stitch or two."

"You said 'oops.'"

"I didn't mean to alarm you." But the sound of his quelled laughter indicates otherwise. "I promise, the worst that can happen here is you might actually have a scar."

"Or have cancer spread all over my body."

"What are you talking about?"

"Nothing," I say under my breath. For some reason I'm thinking of Sonny and his evasive answers to my questions about the mole. Maybe I'll have to ask him again.

Then it's over.

* * *

They hoist me into a sitting position and it takes a moment for the vertigo to subside. Dr. Kozinski gives me my post-op instructions about bathing and pain medication while the ladies tidy up.

"Any questions?" he says.

"Yeah, when do we find out if I have cancer?"

"The lab results should be back from pathology in a week or so. But really, Russell, in all likelihood, you've got nothing to worry about. I can assure you that this is preventative, all very routine. Think about it this way. If the mole was a problem, it's gone now."

"So you're telling me that I definitely don't have cancer?"

He waves me off. "Listen, I've got some good news for you. It turns out we do need a new copier after all."

"You're just saying that because you botched my surgery."

"Just talk to Cindy on the way out. You'll recognize her as the one who gleefully takes your money when you leave."

When Dr. K and the mystery nurse leave, Cassandra helps me into my shirt and says, "You okay, Russell?"

"Except for the crater in my back?"

She turns and begins rifling through a small drawer. Then she turns and begins scribbling on a prescription pad.

"I thought only doctors were allowed to do that."

"Let's just call it a precaution, you know, in case you have any questions." Her cheeks fill with color. "Or if you need anything this weekend, well, you know ..."

How can a woman so far out of my league possibly be nervous about flirting with me?

"That's my home number." She absently rubs the white ring around her finger. "You know, just in case."

My eyebrows arch in direct proportion to the descent of my jaw.

I emerge feeling like I swallowed a pinball machine. The glitz of flashing lights and frantic sound effects are a direct result of Cassandra offering me her phone number, yet the lead ball of fatalism pounds my insides, reminding me how little time I have left to live. It's all very distracting, so much so that Cindy has to resort to fake throat-clearing and waving her arms to get my attention.

"Ah, the dreaded co-pay," I say.

She nods once, takes my debit card, and slides it through her machine. Moments later she frowns at the little screen and swipes it again. The warmth in my cheeks turns to heat when the scanner rejects it again. I suspect Cassandra will walk out any second and realize the folly of dating such a poor man.

"Tell you what," Cindy says. "Since you're such a good customer, I'm going to make an executive decision and waive the co-pay just this once."

I resist the urge to hug her. "Thanks, I owe you one."

"How about you make it up to me with a great deal on a new copier?"

I do some quick math in my head. Since my paycheck is direct-deposited, the only possible explanation for insufficient funds is if Peter cashed my check first thing Monday morning.

The Bible says if Man A covets Man B's wife, it's no different than committing real live adultery. So I guess it's safe to assume, as I stand here picturing my brother cashing a thousand-dollar check, that I'm already guilty of administering a rather vicious beating.

* * *

It seems like I should be limping or something, but amazingly nothing hurts, not yet. And the fact that I survived my surgery has somehow made the air thinner and crisper. My shoes feel lighter, the pavement springier, my lungs more pliable and vigorous.

It takes a while to find my car in the parking lot of Dr. Kozinski's office. I'm still not used to seeing it without the front bumper. The Ford Taurus has never been considered a jolly kind of car, but mine seems to be grinning all the time now. I smile back, until I remember that I need to call my insurance lady and see if I'm still covered. A quick scan of my checkbook register last night netted exactly nothing. I only record deposits. It's less depressing.

The drive home is uneventful, save for me trying to keep my back from touching the seat. The injected painkillers haven't worn off yet, but it weirds me out to think about pressing my fresh wound against anything. Of course if I do something stupid and break open my stitches, then I'll have an excuse to call Cassandra. Her note is burning a hole in my breast pocket. Not because I anticipate some long, drawn-out romance. It just feels nice to be pursued for once, by someone who's not crazy.

Mentally, I brace myself for an onslaught of self-doubt, but it doesn't come. Not this time. Instead, a foreign sensation has wormed its way into my mind, something more subliminal than cerebral, something déjà vu-esque. It's confidence. And why not? I just survived surgery without a single whimper. What started as a mere trickle is now gushing through my veins. I'm the star of my own Gatorade commercial.

Of course I can call Cassandra. And of course she'll say yes. These are no mere speculations or fantasies, only foregone conclusions. I'm going to call Alyssa and demand she return the ring, and while the receiver is still warm in my hand, I'll call Cassandra and ask her — no, *tell* her — when and where to meet me for dinner. I'll call Hengle and inform him that I will not be bullied by his new henchwoman, I'll march down to Tyler, Billingham & Sneed and demand that they buy their copiers from me, I'll cash the enormous commission check and move into my own place.

I turn onto my parents' street and swing my wounded Taurus into their driveway. When I enter the house, I find it empty, which is more than a little depressing. Is it too much to ask for a note or some flowers? Even Sonny is sleeping under the kitchen table, the ingrate. I put on a pair of sweats and a loose T-shirt before making my way to the kitchen to brew some gourmet coffee and pop a couple of pain killers. I secretly hope they'll make me loopy; I've always wanted to paint under the influence — like Jimi Hendrix with a paintbrush. But I'm too chicken to try it.

Since I did promise to make a showing at work this afternoon, all I have time for is a cup of coffee, some bad TV, and a quick nap before heading to the office. Given the prolific output of Sonny's bladder lately, I decide to take him out so he won't interrupt my nap.

As I approach, I notice that on top of the kitchen table, my mother's pristine stacks of bills have toppled into each other. The junk mail and bills and personal correspondence have formed one cascading pile, like a half-shuffled deck of cards. There's a chewed-up envelope next to Sonny on the ground, addressed in blocky ballpoint script, and it looks like it has been colored with an orange crayon, or maybe a highlighter pen. I begin resorting Mom's stacks when Sonny makes a wet, guttural noise, followed by a hushed rattle. I crouch to get a better look, then spring backward, nearly toppling the kitchen table in the process.

A mixture of reddish brown fluids is pooled around Sonny's long snout.

Sonny is dead. Someone killed my dog.

* * *

I slump to the floor and scroll through a mental Rolodex of potential suspects — I've yet to accumulate a decent list of enemies or ex-girl-friends, which now has me pondering the woefully short list of real friends I've accumulated so far. If it takes night to make day, pain to know pleasure, black to make white, then doesn't it stand to reason that the depth of our friendships could be measured by the quality of our enemies? The only two people I can think of willing to take a bullet for me are both dead, Katie and Jesus. And I imagine they're up there somewhere shaking their heads and tsking at me right now.

I dial the Nashville Police Department from memory, wondering what the odds are that Officer Peebles will answer the line. I don't have to wait long to find out.

"Afternoon, this is Officer Jacobson." My mouth is open and I'm ready to launch when he continues, "Can you please hold?" He doesn't wait for my reply. Instead of silence or on-hold music, I hear a dull thunk, followed by the sounds of serious voices and the busy hum of activity — intercoms, machinery, splintered conversations. After a metallic scrape and a loud intake of air, a familiar voice comes on the line.

"This is Officer Wally Peebles."

I can almost picture the two-fingered salute as I blurt, "Someone killed my dog."

"Wait, I know you. Fink, right? The DUI guy who hangs up on people."

"Someone broke into my house and killed my dog, now what are you going to do about it?"

"Let me guess, the next-door neighbor." I hear keys clicking in the background. "Ernest Simmons of 2504 Halo Drive ... Let's see here, dispute with a neighbor over a pet basset hound ... these computers are marvelous, what with the way they keep up with everything ... oh, and I made a note here that you were intoxicated when you called."

"I was not intoxicated."

"Let me get this straight. First, he loads feces into your mailbox. Now you say he's killed your dog?"

"Yes, that's right. That's exactly what I'm saying."

"You don't sound all that confident. You see him do it?"

"No."

"How do you even know it was murder then? Any weapons or blood or anything?"

"There's some blood, among other things."

An amplified female voice blares something in the background.

"What other things we talking about?"

I give him the entire disgusting list of body fluids. Then I tell him exactly how I found Sonny.

"So you're saying your neighbor broke into your house and made your dog throw up and die?"

"He wouldn't have to break in. He has a key. You know, like to check on our house when we're out of town and whatnot."

"His own key?" More stilted typing, then, "This just keeps getting better."

It's dawning on me just how ridiculous all this sounds. But I've come this far.

"He was chewing on a letter, and it had some kind of weird orange stuff on it too. Probably drugs or poison or something."

"These are pretty serious charges you're slinging around. It sounds to me like Rover just got into some rat poison."

"We don't have any rat poison."

"Any chance he has access to your liquor cabinet?"

"I don't *have* a liquor cabinet."

"It wouldn't be the first time a dog died from alcohol poisoning."

My anger and grief have now been eclipsed by fear. Maybe I did accidentally poison Sonny with whiskey biscuits. Do they do doggie autopsies in these cases? Could I possibly be responsible for killing my own dog?

"Fink? You still with me?"

"Never mind."

"What do you *mean* never mind? You can't just call up here and report a murder, then try to take it back with *never mind*."

"I'm sorry I bothered you. Sonny was old and I'm upset and I guess I just wanted to take it out on someone." I pause and try to catch my breath, wishing I could just hang up and forget the whole thing. But before I know it, my mouth is moving again. "Hey, I don't suppose there's any way to track a beat-up station wagon with fake wood on the side and a bunch of bumper stickers?"

"You need help, Fink."

Then he hangs up on me. Which is okay, because the next thing I was going to say may have gotten me arrested.

I dial work and Hengle answers on the third ring. My throat is bloated with uncried tears, making my words slur and warble.

"Russell, is that you?"

"Yes sir, and I'm afraid I've got some bad news. I'm not going to—"

"No you don't. Please hold for Nancy."

I hear a click followed by a tinny version of Elton John entreating the sun not to go down on him. Too late for me I suppose.

"Mr. Fink?" Hengle must have warned her. "I trust your surgery was a success."

"I won't be able to make it in this afternoon after all."

I imagine her inspecting her nails again, sifting her words, and the wan smile as she mulls her options like a menu.

"I thought I made myself clear — either you show up here this afternoon or I'll have no choice but to — "

"Sonny is dead."

"Excuse me?"

"He's dead. As in murdered. As in not breathing." Even as I say this, Officer Peebles's suggestion that I poisoned Sonny is ringing in my head.

"I can tell you're upset, Mr. Fink, but I'm afraid you're not making any sense."

"Someone killed my dog."

We listen to each other breathe.

"Mr. Fink, I can appreciate your — "

"It's *Russell*. And I'm not coming back to work until I bury my dog."

* * *

I root around in the attic for the better part of forty-five minutes, pausing occasionally to wipe my eyes and nose on my T-shirt, before I find what I'm looking for. It's right behind Katie's cedar hope chest, which as far as I know, has not been opened since the months following her funeral.

The inside of my grandfather's footlocker smells like a cross between a new baseball bat and an old photo album. My high school letter jacket is folded neatly at the bottom, the maroon fabric natty and worn like thrift store carpet. Cracks and creases spider out in the white faux-leather sleeves like a road map. When Sonny was a puppy he slept at the foot of my bed, nestled into the gold lining of my prized jacket. I plunge my face into the fabric and breathe deeply, but any traces of Sonny have been masked by dry cleaning solution. That's about to change. I also find his favorite puppy squeaky chew toy—a gnarled, faceless, one-armed replica of Fred Flintstone. I press his middle. He still squeaks.

I return to the kitchen and thumb through the Yellow Pages. It's a useless endeavor, partly because the ads all blur together, but mostly because I seemed to have forgotten the alphabet.

Then it dawns on me to call Geri. She has a cousin who works for a pet cemetery. His name is Dan, but I can't remember the name of the place where he works.

Geri answers on the third ring, breathless. "Oh hey, Russell. You just barely caught me. I was on my way to lunch."

"I'm sorry to bother you, but, um ..."

"What's wrong, Russell? You sound terrible."

"It's Sonny. He's, um ... well, he's dead."

It's quiet for a while, but not uncomfortable.

"What's the name of the cemetery your cousin Dan works for?"

"It's called Heavenly Pastures. Dan just works there part-time so he may not be in. You want me to call him for you?"

"No thanks." I lick my finger and turn the page. "Here it is. Thanks, Geri. I really appreciate it."

"I'm so sorry about Sonny. If there's anything I can do ..."

I thank her and promise to call her later. Then I dial the number and study the Yellow Pages ad while it rings. The ad boasts features such as same-day service, widest selection of comfort fit caskets in the southeast, eulogies for all occasions, walk-ins welcome (appointments preferred), and grief counseling.

"Heavenly Pastures, Cecil here." The man sounds like an asthmatic mafia don. "What can we do for you?"

"My friend gave me your number. She's a friend of Dan's and well —"

"Say no more, I understand. It's a very painful thing, having to bury a pet. So tell me this, what kind of time frame we looking at here?"

I glance at the lifeless form of Sonny and shudder. "Ad says same-day service."

There's a rustling sound, then the telltale thump of a phone bouncing off a tabletop. "Oh geez, sorry about that. Today's good. What time were you thinking?"

"As soon as I can get there, I guess."

"Good, good. Just a couple more questions."

Cecil probes delicately until I've relayed most of the particulars about Sonny. When he launches into the features and benefits of premium caskets and the laundry list of ancillary services provided, I cut him off.

"Just make it nice," I say. "And not too terribly expensive."

After a series of wet coughs, he sniffles once and says, "Wouldn't dream of it. Don't you worry about nothing. I'll take care of everything. You get here, you talk to Dan."

"Great, thanks."

"Oh yeah, one last thing. Can you tell me how big a pup we talking about here?"

"Basset hound," I say, nearly choking on the lump in my throat. Why such a harmless answer uncorks so much grief is a mystery. I swallow hard, blink back more tears, and carry my dead dog out to the Taurus. Sonny is heavier than I expected, yet somehow lighter than he should be. I lay him on the passenger seat and get in beside him, resting my hand on his neck.

As soon as I'm out of the driveway, the hiccups start. I hate hiccups like cats hate baths, like vampires hate garlic, and Frosty hates sunshine. That's what I get for holding back my tears. It's not like I don't want to cry. I just can't.

The radio dial is plagued with sad songs, screaming talk radio, and more sad songs. I click the radio off and the windshield becomes a movie screen playing translucent video snippets, like a sappy Kodak commercial — Sonny as a pup tripping on his own ears and sliding on the kitchen tile, Sonny greeting me at the door so excited that he pees himself, Sonny's blank stare as I throw him a Frisbee, Sonny whimpering in my arms after getting clipped by a slow-moving Volkswagen, and on and on it goes. By the time I reach the gravel driveway of Heavenly Pastures, I'm a hiccupping, non-crying mess.

It's not quite as heavenly as I'd anticipated.

If you weren't looking for it, you'd never notice the quaint, hand-painted sign in the yard with happy caricatures of winged pets. The lawn is a combination of brown spots and dandelion patches with tiny white afros. I park my car and watch a skinny little man with thick glasses and a greasy comb-over hurry out and climb into a shiny Lincoln Town Car. His open-collared shirt is pasted to his skin and reveals a gaudy cross-on-a-chain. If that's Cecil, he's not at all what I expected. He looks more like a malnourished shoe salesman than a gangster. He keeps his gaze straight ahead as he swings his car onto the road.

I turn the ignition off, pocket the keys, then sit and listen to the engine tick. Every tick is a reminder not only of time lost, but of my own morbidity, as if I needed further reminders today. What's the etiquette here? Do I scoop Sonny into my arms and lug him in the front door like a toaster that needs repair? Do I go in alone and leave my poor dead dog in the hot car? Before I can decide, another man exits. Must be Dan. So I get out and prepare to greet him.

He skips the introduction and hugs me. I offer him a few awkward pats on the back, then extract myself. We stand there a while, me hiccupping and Dan smiling sadly. He's tall, about six-five or better. His hair is a cross between Mark Twain and Don King, his facial hair random and scraggly. A white priest's collar peeks out from the overlapping collars of a flannel shirt and what appears to be a silky church choir robe. I can't help thinking he looks familiar.

"I'm Dan," he says, extending his hand in greeting. It's like shaking hands with a Popsicle.

His smile reveals perfect teeth, save for a gap where an incisor used to be. I'm not sure but I think this is the guy I saw with Geri at church. "Geri called and said not to wait for her, but that she'll get here if she can. Do you mind?" he says, stooping to pick up Sonny. He cradles him like a newborn, all delicate and full of awe, making me feel like a bystander intruding on a private moment. He seems oblivious to the sour bouquet of body fluids. I follow him into a living room-turned-showroom and watch Dan place Sonny on a giant plastic shroud lying atop a lush bed of satin. It takes a moment for my brain to register this as a coffin, Sonny's final resting place.

The smell of fresh flowers goes from pleasing to cloying in mere minutes. Now I have a headache to go with my lingering hiccups.

Dan's mournful gaze lingers over Sonny's still body until my grief gives way to a new and familiar sensation — jealousy. I am actually bothered by the fact that this total stranger appears to be a better griever than me. I feel like a petri dish, shallow, filled with something mysterious and rancid.

I lean on a glass display case, studying the personalized key chains, ceramic sculptures, and glitzy urns. The wall behind the cash register boasts black-and-white photos of famous dogs — or rather the dogs of famous people. It seems Heavenly Pastures has the deceased pet market cornered on country music stars and local TV personalities. Alyssa would definitely approve.

Finally, Dan turns to me and says, "Is this the model you discussed with Cecil?"

"I guess so, I don't know."

Dan bites his lip and stares at the floor with an expression that wavers between suspicion and anger. His trance is interrupted by a ringing telephone. He excuses himself and answers. After another intense bout of silence, he delivers a string of syllables, baffling yet beautiful. The sound is Middle-Eastern, and fluent.

"I'm sorry about that. Thought it might be Geri. I'll let the machine pick up if anyone else calls."

"No problem."

Dan sifts through a pile of papers in front of him, absently scratching his scalp. When I'm sure he's forgotten about me, I clear my throat, which sets off another annoying round of hiccups.

"Did you want any additional services?"

"Services?"

"Yeah, you know. I can perform a standard eulogy in English. Or you can choose from a variety of languages or orthodoxies. We can have music or just a few moments of silence. Pretty much whatever you want, we can do."

Dan's words sound as if they've been dipped in caramel. He's in no particular hurry. But his hands fly around in tiny half-gestures that suggest a degree of urgency, as if he's used to being misunderstood.

"Why don't we stick with English?"

Dan nods, obviously disappointed.

" ... and Sonny always liked music." This is a complete fabrication. But Dan looks like he could use a concession about now.

"Give me a few minutes to clean him up and we'll get started." He eases the lid down with great ceremony, releases a concealed foot brake, and pushes the coffin down a long corridor. Down the hall, there's a chapel, a grooming room, a drying room, and a kennel, which strikes me as the animal equivalent of death row. I collapse into a leather sofa — all black and billowy suede — and wait for the tears to come, for the dam to burst and wash me away. But all I can think about is standing in front of Katie's casket and the feel of my father beside me, his warm, trembling hand squeezing my shoulder, the mixed scent of his failing deodorant and a million carnations, the edge of his belt digging into my cheekbone as I try to hide my face in the pleats of his dress pants. I cried myself dry that day.

Some time later, the squeaky caster announces Dan's return and I follow him outside. The backyard is as lush and green as the front is crusty and dead. There's an American flag flapping at half-mast, statuettes of kittens and puppies, hanging planters, and a babbling swanlike birdbath. If not for the Mexican restaurant and tanning salon that back up to it, the cemetery's view would seem enchanted.

The eulogy is somber and beautiful, even poignant at times, although I can only understand about half of it. Dan loses himself in the process, slipping between exotic languages and breaking into croaky a cappella dirges at will. He's a passable singer, but his gap-toothed whistle accompaniment more than makes up for it. About the time I think I've had enough, Dan's voice settles into a simple refrain. I recognize the melody but not the language, yet his sincerity runs so deep that I find myself humming along. At some point, I realize he's weeping. And my hiccups are back.

"Would you like to say something?" he asks me.

I approach the casket, kiss Sonny on his cold dry nose, and whisper, "I love you, buddy."

"Could you speak up a little?"

"What?" I turn to see a small microphone in my face.

He taps the lapel microphone and says, "I'm recording the entire service. Later you can provide me a list of some of Sonny's favorite music, or if you and your family want to record some additional

111

messages or greetings, I can pipe it in on an endless loop." Sure enough, I notice tiny speakers tucked into the lid of the casket. "Don't worry though. I can program it with plenty of quiet time as well."

"How much is this going to cost me?" I feel like such a weenie for asking.

"I'm throwing it in for free. I'm the inventor, so I can do that. Plus you're a friend of Geri's." He looks so proud as he adjusts the micro-phone. "I'll leave you alone so you can say your good-byes. Just take your time and I'll help you finalize everything inside. Remember to speak clearly if you can manage it."

There's not much to say really. I stroke the fur under Sonny's neck and try to remember the last thing I ever said to him. I hope it was nice. The feeling of grief is so strong I can almost hear Taps being played over my left shoulder. Then I *do* hear Taps being played over my left shoulder. I don't even have to turn around; I know it's Geri. As usual, her dulcet tone is as sweet and lilting as it is bold. It's the sound of angels, smiling through tears. When the last note fades, I hear her footsteps softly fade away.

* * *

Back inside, Dan is gnawing on an eraser and squinting at an invoice. He blows air into his cupped hands and says, "I forgot to ask, what was the cause of death?"

A toilet flushes somewhere in the house, followed by the sound of water rushing through pipes.

"Well, actually, I'm afraid he might have been poisoned."

Dan looks up. The eraser falls from his lips and takes a couple of crazy bounces before shooting out of sight behind the counter.

Geri appears and says, "What's this about poison?"

"I could run a couple of tests for you." Dan looks almost giddy at the prospect. "Not a complete necropsy or anything like that. But I might be able to find traces of something."

"I'd love to know what happened if I could."

"That's dreadful," Geri says. "Who would want to hurt poor Sonny?"

Dan's distracted now, and anxious, as if he can't wait to snap on the rubber gloves and get to work. But he turns his attention back to the pile of papers in front of him. Finally, he scratches through two more lines and turns the papers around for my inspection. "You can make your check out to Heavenly Past—"

"No," I say, eyes bulging at the total and feeling the blood drain from my extremities. "I can't."

"What's wrong? Didn't you discuss costs with Cecil?"

I shake my head. "I believe my words were 'make it nice, but not too expensive'."

Dan mumbles a few multilingual curses under his breath, "No wonder he bolted out of here in such a hurry."

Geri is by my side now, close enough to whisper. "Look, Russell. Let me help out. You can pay me back whenever."

I can only shake my head in response, grateful and ashamed.

Dan studies the invoice for few moments, then scratches through a few more lines. I can hear his molars grinding from across the desk. He raises his eyebrows and shows me the changes.

"I really appreciate it, but ..."

"We do take credit cards."

"Not these," I say tapping my hip pocket. "Don't suppose you have a layaway plan?"

Geri is at the counter now, thrusting her credit card in Dan's face.

"Come on, Geri. I haven't even paid you back for lunch yet."

She ignores me and wags her credit card at Dan. I warn him not to take it. But he's not listening. Something flashes in his eyes, and he snaps his fingers.

"Say, you wouldn't be interested in house sitting for me, would you?"

Geri's face lights up, and she pulls her card back. "That's a brilliant idea."

"How's that going to help?" I say.

With a gleam in his eye, Dan pinches one corner of the invoice. A grin splits his chapped lips as he begins to rip.

"Hold it," I say, louder and more panicky than intended. "You think I could hang on to that?"

His face sags. But he hands me the now voided invoice anyway.

"Thanks. I really don't know what to say."

"Yeah," Geri says. "Thanks Danno. You're the best."

His cheeks fill with red. And for once, he doesn't look like he's freezing.

"And you," Geri says, giving my shoulder a playful shove. "You just saved me from having to trek back and forth between my place and Dan's. See how brilliant this is?"

"Where do you live exactly?"

Dan points to a spot over my shoulder.

"Across the street?" An admittedly stupid question.

Dan nods, still grinning. I can see the pink of his tongue through the gap in his teeth.

"No funny business going on, right? No drugs or porn or anything?"

His face cracks like a cartoon egg hatching. Then he practically detonates with full-bodied guffaws. He rocks and trembles and slaps his palm on the desk as spit flies from the corner of his mouth. And the sound—a raucous, chortling baritone—rattles the picture frames and nearly alters the rhythm of my heart.

It is infectious, though, and I find myself laughing along.

Finally he says, "Nope, nothing illicit. Just heading to Cape Canaveral to see my girlfriend blast off into space."

I expect another round of hilarity. But he appears to be dead serious.

* * *

His name is Russell Fink too. His friends called him Sonny. But I've always called him Gramps. The guards at Middle Tennessee Detention and Correction Facility call him prisoner #TN68702. On my sixteenth birthday, against my parents' most stringent objections, he bought me a puppy. It didn't seem right not to tell him in person.

We're seated across from one another at table #19, an industrial strength version of a school cafeteria table with its legs imbedded in concrete. The air is tinged with secondhand smoke, cheap disinfectant, and body odor, but it reeks of desperation. To my left is a giant of a man, blubbering over a small pink bundle in his arms. A man's first encounter with his newborn daughter ought not be a spectator sport.

My grandfather's orange jumpsuit has faded to match the rosacea in constant bloom in his cheeks. The sight of his denture-less grin crawls all over me like a clown in a scary movie.

"What happened to your teeth?" I say.

"Traded them."

"You traded your teeth?"

He nods, amused. His mouth is in constant motion, as if tying an imaginary cherry stem with his tongue. What he's really doing is sucking on a Checkers piece, a red one today. His reputation as a master Checkers player has graduated to legendary status since coming to prison. The wet, smacking sounds don't even register in his ears anymore, a by-product of too many years locked away with the old, hopeless, and criminally insane. Social graces and self-esteem have been eroded by boredom, despair, regret, and little blue pills. Sucking on plastic game pieces as if they were Lifesavers now seems normal to him.

"Who could possibly want your dentures?"

"Harry Delaney."

"I'll bite. Why?"

"Thinks his last few meals will taste better with teeth." I feel my face arrange itself into a question mark. Gramps shrugs and says, "Harry'll be dead soon and don't have any of his own."

"What did you get out of the deal?"

"Three cartons of cigarettes."

"Was that smart?"

This tickles him. He'd asked me the same question hundreds of times in our weekly phone calls. It was his idea of gentle persuasion. A signpost on the path to grandfatherly wisdom. Ironic coming from a double-murderer.

"I'll get 'em back. I redid Harry's will. So when he kicks off in a month or two, I'll get my teeth back, along with a '65 Mustang and a '68 Les Paul."

"Okay, so it's a good deal for you. But last time I checked, you don't smoke, drive, or play the guitar."

"Thinking about taking up all three. I want to look sexy for the ladies when I tunnel out of this joint."

Gramps is a country lawyer-turned-convicted felon-turned-jailhouse preacher, and has always had a thing for the ladies. According to my parents, his constant philandering is what caused Grandma to pretend she was having an affair in the first place. Her accomplice was the local tennis pro Freddy Westmoreland. It drove Gramps nuts. He tried everything to win back her affections—which, as it turned out, he'd never really lost in the first place. He gave up the girlfriends and the drinking. Yet Grandma milked her imaginary fling for all it was worth, basking in the rekindled affections of her first and only love.

But she took it too far. And never one to be outdone, Gramps took it one step further.

His first line of defense was to steal the unsuspecting tennis pro's money. But Westmoreland was either so fiscally apathetic or insanely wealthy that he didn't seem to notice. Then Gramps began stalking his wife and her supposed lover to restaurants and dance halls and afternoon tennis lessons. Eventually Grandma realized that things were getting out of hand and decided to come clean. According to her journals, she planned her final make-believe tryst as if it were a surprise party. But her grand visions of a tearful reconciliation ended in bloodshed.

From the humid front seat of his car, Gramps watched his wife enter the tennis pro's apartment, then barged in twenty minutes later, inebriated, waving a handgun and making threats.

Someone in the shadows shot first. Surprised, my grandfather returned fire. His first bullet caught my grandmother in the chest. When he realized what he'd done, Gramps locked his gaze on the stricken tennis pro. Two shots fired at once. Gramps was merely winged. He crumpled in a heap atop my grandmother. Westmoreland died on the way to the hospital.

It turned out Westmoreland's roommate fired the warning shot. He took his own life months later, before he could testify.

"Ten more minutes," a security guard barks in our direction.

Gramps clears his throat and says, "What's eating you? I know you didn't drive all the way out here to talk about my dentures. You need money or something?"

"Nah," I say, ignoring the guilt that usually accompanies this conversation. "I'm good."

"Liar."

"What difference does it make? I thought you ran out years ago."

"I get by okay." Gramps flexes his left arm as if hefting an imaginary dumbbell.

"Sonny's dead."

His expression doesn't change but his breath catches, then his eyes begin to glisten.

"I'm sorry, Russell. I know you loved that pup."

I nod. "Someone murdered him."

His mouth stops moving and he rests his elbows on the table. He folds, unfolds, and refolds his hands. The dry skin sounds raspy in the relative stillness. The thing I love most about Gramps is that he never doubts me. His faith in me has always been devout.

And unwarranted.

The red plastic game piece flashes in his cheek when he talks. "Now who would murder a tired old hound dog?"

"I have some ideas," I say. Actually I haven't a clue what really happened. I just feel like being petulant. "And I plan to find out."

He shakes his head. For a moment, I think he's encouraging my thirst for vengeance.

"Let it go, son."

"What? You'd never let something like that go."

"Yeah, but you ain't me." He pauses to make sure I'm looking at him. "You're better than me. There's power in forgiveness."

"I've never shared my family's hang-ups about power."

"Fair enough. You just remember that the good Lord's got the market cornered on vengeance."

* * *

The tedium of the hour-long drive from the Podunk, Tennessee, prison town is almost enough to make me consider calling Alyssa, but I can't risk undoing what took me months to work up the courage to do, just for a few minutes of sympathy. Thankfully I'm so deep in the boonies that my cell phone has no reception, so I'm left alone with my thoughts, able to ponder the very real possibility that I did indeed kill Sonny. I mean, he was almost eleven years old. Maybe his body couldn't process the whiskey biscuits any longer. Maybe it built up in his system until it reached toxic levels, then unleashed its poisonous wrath on his central nervous system. Like everything else, maybe Sonny's death is my fault, just like my mother's drinking, Peter's gambling, and Katie's cancer. My father is the only exception; his grab bag of dysfunction predates my first birthday.

My phone rings in the seat beside me. Without thinking, I answer it.

Alyssa says, "Hey babe, where are you?"

"Been to see Gramps."

"Oh." The idea of me inheriting the genes of a convicted murderer has always frightened Alyssa. "Well, anyway. I finally replaced my phone so, you know, you can find me if you need me."

"If I need you, I could just drive by your tree."

"Nope, not anymore. My protest worked. The owner never even got the place open. Which is why I'm calling. I wanted to take you to dinner, you know, to celebrate. And so I can apologize."

"Maybe not. It's been kind of a rough day."

"Well then, I can cheer you up." I'm about to mount a protest of my own, but she keeps talking. "I've got reservations at The Boundary for eight o'clock. I can't wait to see you and I'm going to hang up now before you can say no. Seeyoutonightloveyoubye."

And she does.

Out of habit, I'm deciding what I'll wear, when I'll need to leave the house to make it to Alyssa's on time, imagining the look on her face when I tell her about Sonny and —

Wait, isn't this exactly how I ended up in this anemic relationship in the first place? She leads and I follow. And it's always been that way. It was her decision for us to become *more than friends* — which I eagerly agreed to. She initiated the first date, the first kiss, and the first three breakups. She's the director and the leading lady. My role as supporting actor is to grovel until we get back together again.

I realize I'm still holding my phone open. Alyssa will not bully me back into this relationship. Not today, anyway. What I need is to make a clean break, emotionally speaking. To *immunize*, as it were. And who better to help than Cassandra? I pause, waiting for the guilt to catch up. How can I sit here and ponder my love life when I should be thinking of Sonny? But the only sensation I recognize is light-headedness and a tinge of hunger.

I'm pondering the strange dichotomy of my mind when my phone emits another abbreviated ring. I assume it's Alyssa and thank God for the scattered cell phone reception. Half-formed thoughts ricochet between Alyssa, Cassandra, and trying to figure out who killed my dog. It doesn't dawn on me that I'm mostly wondering what Geri would have to say about it all until I turn into the parking lot of Hengle's Supply.

* * *

The parking lot is mostly empty at this hour. I park between Bernie's BMW and Nancy's Volvo, wondering if I've missed another of Hengle's impromptu after-hours sales meetings. I imagine them huddled together and brainstorming ways to replace me without actually having to fire me. I fish a necktie out of the glove box for good measure.

I slip into my cubicle and begin sifting through voice mails and emails. Not bad, only three angry customers to deal with tomorrow. I'm about to pat myself on the back for getting *any* amount of work done on the day of Sonny's funeral, when my intercom crackles to life.

Nancy wants to see me in her office. Before leaving mine, I grab the proof of my surgery and Sonny's murder. It's supposed to bolster my confidence, which now feels as flimsy as the carbon paper invoice from Dr. K's office. She's squinting at her computer terminal when I enter, clicking her nails on the keyboard. The sight of her scrambles my thoughts, derailing both of my imagined strategies. Should I go for suave and cocky, like a TV lawyer? Or brash and menacing? Now, with the war drums pounding in my veins, I can't decide between the two.

"Mr. Fink," she says without looking up from her work. "I must admit, I'm surprised to see you this evening."

I open my mouth, but nothing happens. My pent-up audacity is draining like tepid bathwater. I can feel the panic gathering in the form of a small knot in my throat. So before I lose my nerve altogether, I step toward Nancy's desk, arm raised, prepared to slam the documents on her desk. But I realize too late that I've juxtaposed my strategies. The signals collide in my brain — suave, brash, sarcastic, threatening. The result of my first bold step is a slippery maneuver, part pit bull and part duck waddle.

My right foot catches on the leg of her guest chair, and I feel my upper body tipping forward. I overcompensate and try to plant my left foot for balance. But my left knee smashes into the corner of her desk. On my way to the carpet, my chin clips the edge of her desk. That's when I see my precious documents fluttering like giant confetti — the invoice from Dr. Kozinski's office, gruesome before-and-after Polaroids of my surgery, the torn invoice from Heavenly Pastures, and of course the picture of Sonny in his casket.

With stars in my eyes and something warm and wet oozing down my neck, I'm aware of footsteps in the doorway. At first I think I'm seeing double. But then I realize that I'm staring at Max Hengle III and his obnoxious son, Bernie. The elder Hengle looks horrified, the younger delighted.

In the restroom, it takes a full ten minutes to get my chin to stop bleeding. A wad of gauze is suspended by a half-dozen bandages. My shirt and tie are a disaster.

After I make my way from the men's room to my desk, Nancy appears in the doorway and motions me into her office. "How's your chin, Mr. Fink?" She has collected my documents and stacked them in a neat little pile on the corner of her desk. A speck of blood is drying on the edge of the doctor's bill. It looks like a cancer cell from my Google search the other night.

"Same as my shirt." I use the end of my tie to point to the evidence. "And of course, my pride."

"I just want you to know that I spent my entire morning drafting the requisite paperwork to process your termination from Hengle's Supply. Although I can sympathize with your situation, I believe I made myself perfectly clear earlier today. But it appears that Mr. Hengle has come to your defense yet again."

"I'll be sure and thank him."

"Just so you know, I put Mr. Hengle on notice as well. He can either respect my authority and let me do what he hired me to do, or he can find someone else to play the flunky. Unless something drastic happens, one of us won't be around much longer."

In the span of time it takes her last syllable to close the distance between us, I realize that I'm listening with new ears. Nancy's special brand of smug condescension has found the light switch in my soul and flipped it. Screenwriters call it an epiphany, I think. Whatever it is, there's a mystical, almost tangible quality to it. My entire body quakes with that battery-on-the-tongue sizzle. She's thrown down an invisible gauntlet, and I fully intend to pick it up and slap her with it —

Figuratively, of course. I don't hit girls.

* * *

The plan is to drive to my parents' house and pack an overnight bag for Dan's. The house looks desolate from here; I'm guessing that Dad's off teaching one of his seminars and Mom's curled up in bed with either a bottle or a book. Or both.

As I make my way up the sidewalk, I don't know whether to worry about the mess I've left behind or the fact that I probably killed Sonny. Through the door I hear the muffled sound of a vacuum cleaner. Once inside, I'm more than a little surprised to see my father pushing the vacuum. Patches of sweat darken his white undershirt. His face is creased with anger.

My first impulse is to sneak past him and do what I came here for — to grab some toiletries and clothes for my house-sitting gig. But there's a stronger urge, a sudden desire to engage my father, to sit down over a cup of coffee, to meet each other's eyes and have some semblance of a real conversation. I realize I'm remembering Sinclair's words, that my father not only noticed my paintings, but actually liked them. I want to ask him about it. Then I want to ask him what he remembers most about Katie, how he copes with Mother's "problem," and what he really thinks of me. I don't even realize I'm staring until my father looks up, notices me, and scowls.

"Nice timing," he says, then bends to wrap the cord.

That's when I remember Sonny's mess. "Oh, I forgot to warn you about that."

He doesn't hear me, or pretends not to. This is not the first time he's made me feel like somebody else's kid, like if he ignores me long enough, I'll just go away.

"I've spent the last hour cleaning up dog vomit while you've been off playing with your girlfriend or painting pictures or whatever it is you do in all your spare time."

"But that's just it. Sonny was — "

He backhands the air in front of him. "Save it."

Then he disappears into the kitchen. When I hear the water running, I head down the hallway toward my bedroom to collect my things. I notice some mail on my bed, bills mostly. I grab some clothes, double-check my shaving kit, and toss it all into an oversized gym bag. I break down my easel and load a handful of my favorite sable brushes, some paints, and fresh canvases into a large portfolio. On a whim, I check my chest of drawers. The sight fills me with unspeakable joy. Underwear, freshly laundered and folded with love. I add them to my stash and lie across my old bed and try to think. The house creaks with familiarity, like the ghost of an old friend saying hello.

The phone rings. Then again. And again. The machine clicks on and I hear the muted recording of my father's voice through the wall, followed by another voice — angry and threatening and somehow familiar. After a soft pounding noise, the machine stops. A few moments later a door slams, followed by the sound of my father's footfalls going down the wooden steps into the garage.

I decide it's a good time to head out, but not before snooping around the kitchen to search for that orange-stained, half-chewed letter. But it's gone. Everything has been cleaned up. I check a couple of drawers and inside the bread box until I notice my father is back, hands on his hips, glowering.

When I can't think of anything else, I say, "Where's Mom?"

"She's not well."

In our home, *not well* is code for sleeping off another drunk.

"Do you realize that he's yet to return my calls since your performance last night?"

"Who?"

"Sinclair," he says, as if it's the most obvious thing in the world.

"Hey, I didn't pee on anybody." Despite my indignation, I'm unable to meet his gaze. "And I said I was sorry."

"You say that a lot."

I ignore the wet, stinging sensation in my eyes, focusing instead on my fingernails digging into the flesh of my balled fists.

"Your mother was right." He jerks his thumb toward the kitchen. "We should have put him to sleep a long time ago."

He's just being mean now. I stand there, chewing my lip like a child. I try to count to ten but keep getting stuck on three.

"Not that you care, but I was supposed to have an interview here tonight."

I look up, more than a little horrified.

"That's right," he continues. "Sinclair had recommended me for an associate pastor position in town. But instead of a hot meal, Pastor Randolph and his chief elder were treated to the stench of dog vomit and the sight of your mother asleep on the sofa."

The phone rings again. My father glances at it warily, his face twitching. It rings again, deepening the look on his face. Then he turns back to me, as if surprised to see me still standing there.

"My surgery went fine, by the way. Thanks for asking." He blinks recognition, but says nothing and looks off toward the bedroom as if waiting for the phone to ring again. "Then I came home and—"

"Look, Russell. This isn't working out."

"What's not?"

"This whole arrangement. You don't pay rent. You call in sick half the time. And you can't seem to control your stupid dog."

"Are you kicking me out?"

"I'm saying you need to grow up, and I'm not sure you can do that here."

I watch my father disappear into the hallway.

* * *

From the street, Dan's house looks like any other. Brick with black shutters. A sprawling ranch with a descending driveway. Since I'm officially homeless now, I take this as good news. Unless he's a complete nutcase, I may be able to parlay this house-sitting jaunt into something more permanent.

The doorbell plays "Smells Like Teen Spirit," complete with distorted guitar and the first drum fill. No answer. Followed by no footsteps and no *I'll be right there*'s. I try to remember what Dan looks like. I can see the outline of his long face and a few contours, but no significant details. The harder I try, the murkier it gets, like trying to recall the name of a game show host or the scent of a dead relative.

I ring the bell again and am treated to a medley of four-second snippets of every song from *Abbey Road*, but still no signs of life.

The welcome mat looks diseased, with large patches of faux grass missing. A rusty mailbox hangs at a forty-five degree slant. At my prompting, the doorbell works its way through the Partridge Family theme song, "Foxy Lady," the "Hallelujah Chorus," and "The Monster Mash." I've forgotten all about Dan when he finally answers the door.

Strands of wet hair dangle from beneath his toboggan hat like baby snakes, some sticking to his face and forehead. He grins with what appears to be real joy.

"Follow me," he says. He's wearing jeans, at least two shirts, and a wool sweater. "I'll give you the nickel tour while I finish getting ready."

The living room is huge and could easily serve as the Smithsonian exhibit of early 1980s Americana. I trail him down a hardwood hallway, noticing the weather stripping on the bedroom doors. One even has an inspection window. He stops at the last door on the left and opens it with a flourish.

"This'll be your room."

I'm not sure what I was expecting but am a bit disappointed by how ordinary it all looks. A queen-sized bed, chest of drawers, reading lamp — all very pedestrian and predictable.

"Feel free to snoop around the house," Dan says. He seems to relish dispensing mystery in small doses. "But if you're not sure what a particular button or dial does, I wouldn't touch it. The fridge and the pantry are loaded. Towels and toiletries are in the hall closet. I've stocked a variety of toilet papers to suit your preferences. You like aloe?"

"Sure, I'm a big fan." My friendly sarcasm has no visible effect on him. "How long will you be gone, exactly?"

"No more than a week." He checks his watch, getting antsy. "Anything else you can think of?"

"You look familiar. Have we met somewhere before?"

Pride seeps through the crack in his embarrassed grin. "I get that a lot. I guess you could say that I'm a bit of a celebrity. There's my inventions, and of course you may have seen me on *America's Most Wanted*."

I don't even try to camouflage my surprise. I'm about to house-sit for a mass murderer. The mysterious rooms make sense now. They're probably filled with body parts.

"It's not what you think. I *caught* a guy, one of the FBI's ten most wanted, in fact."

I shake my head. "I don't think that's it."

"Well," he shrugs defensively, "there *was* the whole incident with the Wal-Mart greeter."

A horn honks outside. Dan peeks out the curtain, scribbles his cell phone number on a notepad, and slings his duffel bag over his shoulder. Then I watch him slip into the backseat of an idling limo.

The first thing I do is order a pizza. Then I explore the premises, following my ears and nose into the various rooms. Overall, the place is cluttered but habitable, staking out the comfortable middle ground between frat house squalor and serial killer fastidiousness. Occasionally, some beep or hiss or mechanical whirring sound causes my hackles to stand at attention. Remote controls, unlabeled and homemade, litter almost every surface. The first one I pick up makes the walls resound with lush music, although I can't seem to locate any speakers. Another controls the color and intensity of various light fixtures. Still another dispenses small puffs of air freshener. The bright red remote makes a toilet flush somewhere in the house. The last one I pick up elicits a mechanical female voice that keeps repeating "Abort, abort, abort" until I stab the right series of buttons to make her stop.

When the pizza arrives, I settle into the living room sofa, scarf down a slice of pineapple-ham-and-double-cheese, then decide to see what's on TV. I find eleven more remote controls. But not a single television set.

At some point I must have nodded off because I awake hours later with a limp, half-eaten pizza slice soaking into my T-shirt. I brush my teeth and climb into the most comfortable bed in the world. The alarm clock looks normal except for a bundle of wires protruding from its backside and disappearing under the bed. This time the bedside remote has temperature markings with what appears to be a humidity control. I dial in 71 degrees and 29 percent relative humidity, then pull freshly laundered sheets up to my chin and close my eyes.

* * *

"Are you wearing cologne?" I ask Sonny.

"Yep. Got a date later." He's sitting on a folding chair, one row in front of me. His paws are crossed at the ankles; he shakes one nervously, making his claws click on the cement floor. And he has thumbs; how else would he be able to hold the pen?

"A date?"

He shrugs. "Things are different here."

I let my eyes wander. The seats seem to go on forever in every direction. We are all facing the same way, but there's nothing to see but white. And there's a breeze that smells like cinnamon toast and tangerines. It reminds me of Geri's homemade fragrances.

"Where is 'here,' exactly? Surely this isn't heaven."

"Not hardly." Sonny points to a trio of yapping dogs with ribbons in their kinky hair. Poodles!

"I see."

"That, and the cats here have claws." Sonny flips a page in what appears to be Peter's notebook. It still has teeth marks.

"What are you working on?" It feels like a perfectly natural question. Of course, the fact that I perceive it as normal only heightens its peculiarity.

"The Twelve Steps."

"*The* Twelve Steps? As in AA?"

"I'm on number nine, the one where I have to make amends to all the people I've harmed."

Before I can fully digest his words, an elevator car falls from above and lands right in front of us with a cartoon shimmy. The doors fly open to reveal a jail cell with stark furnishings. I could swear I smell fabric softener. A man lifts himself off a thin mattress and rubs the sleep from his eyes with meaty palms. A two-day stubble litters his jowls. That's when I recognize the familiar figure before me—Otis, Mayberry's town drunk. And he's in black-and-white. He squints at us from behind the bars, clears his throat and says, "Any questions?"

My hand goes up, but without any help from me.

"Yes, you there. Russell Fink, is it?" A murmur ripples through the crowd that wasn't there a moment ago. Then Otis makes a sour face and stamps his foot. "I'm sorry. I know better than that. No last names. Anyway, your question?"

"Did I kill my dog?"

Before Otis can answer, the scene changes and Sonny is standing on all fours in the witness stand. When he speaks, his lips don't match the words, like one of those Japanese dub films.

"You want me to tell you that it's not your fault. But I honestly don't have any idea. It's not like the movies, you know. I wasn't hovering above, dodging the ceiling fan blades, staring down at my lifeless body. But even if I did know, I'm not sure I'd tell you."

"Why not?"

"Because no matter what I say, you're going to blame yourself. It's what you do."

This time the scene doesn't change, but somehow we're in my bedroom in my parents' house.

"Look, Russell, if it's not too much trouble ..." He pauses to scrape dirt from under his thumbnail. "I could really use your help."

"Yeah? How so?"

"Like I said, if I'm going to check the box next to step number nine, then I need to make amends. And since I'm dead, I'll need you to do it for me."

"Do what?"

"Make amends. Tell people I'm sorry. Replace the stuff I've chewed. Sprinkle deodorizer all over Simmons' lawn. That kind of stuff."

"Simmons? I knew it!"

A buzzer goes off, like the wrong answer on a game show. Then Sonny's gone before I can say good-bye.

Part Two

Friday

Over the past few days, Nancy's words have morphed into an annoying jingle on endless repeat. *One of us won't be around much longer.* The version in my head is a low-budget eighties dance number, complete with an overly happy studio choir. I'm more determined now than ever, if for no other reason than to obliterate this sappy musical mantra from my subconscious.

I made ten cold calls this week on neighboring offices. Only one administrative assistant treated me as if I were a radioactive street preacher. Four of the calls turned into decent leads: three construction companies and a travel agency that specializes in extreme vacations. My last call of the day on Friday resulted in a purchase order totaling more than my previous two weeks' sales combined.

Amazing what a little desperation — mixed with grief and a dash of spite — can do to a man's motivation.

And that's not all I'm going to do. As crazy as it sounds, I'm going to keep my dreamy promise to Sonny. Just the idea fills my throat with battery acid, but I'm determined to make amends for Sonny. It's the least I can do.

First things first, however; I dream up excuses to go see Geri at work.

"Hey," she says before my loafered foot lands on the plush carpet of Tyler, Billingham & Sneed. "I was just about to call you. Yikes! What happened to your chin?"

"Oh that." I finger the bandage absently. "New disciplinary policy at work."

She frowns at me and says, "How are you holding up?"

I can tell by her tone that she's referring to Sonny, not my injury. "I'm fine, I guess."

"I'm so sorry about all this. "

She has that look in her eye like she's going to hug me. I wish she would. Instead, she says, "But hey, I do have some good news."

"Good, I could use some. And I hope it has to do with a giant copier order from your boss."

"Nothing definite yet." She grins at me. "But a deal's a deal and I need a ride."

She forwards her phone to one of the paralegals and follows me out to my car.

Instead of telling me where we're going, she yells out directions intermittently while she talks. Apparently, the supermodel salesgirl made a couple of errors on her initial proposal. Nothing crucial, but enough for Geri to sit the partners down and explain why the lowest bidder is not always the best deal.

"Barbie will probably get the paper clips and desk blotters. But if you play your cards right, you'll get the big stuff."

Barbie? "Man, you really don't like her, do you?"

"She pities me. I can see it in her eyes. I'm the dumpy sorority sister with no sense of style. Turn right."

"Come on, that's ridiculous."

"No it's not. But I'm used to it. To girls like her, she's the skinny blonde singer and I'm Mama Cass. She's Marcia and I'm Jan, or maybe even Alice. Keep going straight. She's Mary Ann *and* Ginger; I'm a cross between the Skipper and Mrs. Howell."

"I think you're overreacting. And as much as I'd like to spend twenty minutes convincing you just how wrong you are, I really need your help."

"Yeah, well, you're going to need it. You're scheduled to give a —right at the light—a formal presentation to all the partners on Friday."

I ask her again where we're going.

"I told you that it's private. If you ask me again, I may have to reconsider my offer to help you."

We stop at a red light and I have the peculiar sensation that we're being watched.

"Hey, isn't that your girlfriend?" Geri points diagonally across the intersection to Alyssa's baby blue Beemer. "Man, she's pretty."

Alyssa sees us, and she looks less than pleased. When the light turns green, I gun the engine and keep an eye on the rearview. Sure enough, Alyssa's left blinker flashes twice before she nearly causes a three-car pileup with a U-turn. Against Geri's orders, I make a series of unauthorized turns until I'm sure I've lost her.

"Sorry about that," I say. "I kind of stood her up last night."

"How do you *kind of* stand someone up? Turn in here."

I do as instructed. Geri gets out and makes me promise to stay put, warning me that if I follow her or try to figure out what she's up to, not only will she sabotage my chances at landing the sale, she'll also have Dan kick me out of his house, and she'll find a way to get me fired. So I watch her disappear into an office building. The sign out front boasts a construction company, a radio station, an adoption agency, a law firm, a dental surgeon, and an oncologist. Her cryptic behavior has more than piqued my interest. I bounce around the radio dial, wondering if her mission is personal or professional. I decide she's probably going for a job interview and doesn't want to jinx her chances by talking about it. After distracting myself with the box scores from *The Tennessean*, I'm surprised to see an official announcement that my father has indeed secured the *Second Chances* gig. So much so, that I almost miss the article about the proprietor of *As a Jaybird*. Seems he was convicted for tax evasion, fraud, and weapons charges.

A car backfires behind me, jolting me from my musings. Then a shadow passes over my window. I look up, hoping to see a hot air balloon, or maybe even a blimp. But it's the angry silhouette of my former fiancée. The urge to hit the power locks and drive away is primal and all-consuming, but I'll have to face her sometime. May as well get it over with now. She inches backward, just enough for me to get the door open and stand.

"Listen, about the other night. I tried to call but —"

"Oh, shut up. I don't know what's gotten into you lately, but I've had just about enough of whatever it is. I've indulged your little breakup whim long enough. Now I want an apology and —"

"Apology for what?"

"For acting like a jerk. For standing me up last night — do you have any idea how embarrassing that was?"

"I didn't stand you up. You called me out of the blue, told me where and when to show up, then hung up on me. And as far as acting like a jerk, I'd say I have a pretty good excuse for once."

"Please. What is it this time? Another mole? Brain tumor? Terminal case of Tourette's?"

"When I got home from my mole *surgery*, I found Sonny murdered, my father kicked me out of the house, and my new boss threatened to fire me."

She blinks at me, mouth open.

"See what you miss when you spend a few nights in a tree? And by the way, I heard the owner of the naked joint was arrested for trafficking dope. *That's* why he never opened for business."

I can't help noticing how good this feels until I see that I've genuinely hurt her feelings. She rummages through her purse with a crazed expression. I hope she's looking for mace and not a gun. Finally, she brings out a pair of needle-nose pliers.

"I was wrong," she says. "You're not sexy when you're mad. You're mean."

She raises her left hand to eye level. The sun glints off the diamond on her finger, the one I'm still paying for. She squeezes the stone between the ridged teeth of the pliers, then starts to wiggle them back and forth.

"What are you doing?"

"You want the ring back so bad?"

"Please stop."

The diamond comes free with a faint popping sound.

"Here you go. Here's your ring back." She tosses it to me. "I'll just hold onto this stone for you until you come to your senses and are ready to have a reasonable conversation."

My thumb plays over the mangled prongs while I try to think of something to say.

"You know where to find me when you're ready to apologize."

"Apologize?" It's Geri. The thought of her overhearing our conversation embarrasses me to my core. But then she does the unthinkable — she loops her arm into mine and puts her head on my shoulder. "Apologize for what, dear?"

Alyssa says, "And who are you supposed to be?"

"I'm supposed to be the Queen of Sheba. But since that's not working for me, I thought I'd settle for being Russell's girlfriend."

I'm breathless as one lung fills with exhilaration, the other dread. It's all I can do to keep from grinning.

"Russell already has a girlfriend; in fact, we're engaged. So I'd appreciate you taking your pudgy hands off him."

I flinch, tempted to break my own rule about hitting girls. Geri senses this and squeezes my arm.

"I don't know," Geri says, plucking the mangled gold band from my palm and slipping it on. "I don't see any ring on *your* finger."

Then she raises her own hand ceremoniously, a dainty imitation of Alyssa's gesture from moments ago. Amazingly, the sun glints off the spot on the ring where the diamond used to be.

* * *

"Thank you," I manage to whisper when we're alone in the car headed back to Geri's.

"That," she says with a grin, "will *really* cost you."

Saturday

I'm sitting outside my parents' house, feeling remarkably better than I have in weeks and watching their next-door neighbor's windows for any sign of activity. A few short moments later, I notice curtains falling back into place in Simmons's window. An even shorter moment later, I march up his front steps and pound the meaty part of my fist on his door.

"What do you want?" he shouts from inside.

"I need to talk to you for a minute."

I listen to the syncopation of locks and latches and chains, wondering how I'll broach the subject without sounding like a mental patient. Then his door swings open to reveal the legendary curmudgeon himself. My breath catches as all the gory details from the neighborhood ghost stories come flooding back. I've never stood this close to the man. Even on those rare occasions he dropped by to deliver our mail after a vacation or to accost my father about his bratty kid and his defecating basset hound, I always kept my distance.

My first thought is that he looks brittle, a quivering stick man in a tattered bathrobe and stained undershirt. According to my mother, the man is not yet forty, but from

139

this distance he looks twice that. His eyes are milky and set so far back in their dark sockets that I feel like I'm staring down the double barrel of a shotgun. His hand shakes as he runs his forefinger along the side of his nose, a maneuver that seems to accomplish nothing more than burning off nervous energy.

"It's a little early for chitchatting," he says. "Speak your piece or I'm calling the cops."

"It's about Sonny."

"Who?"

"My dog."

"What about him?" Despite the nauseous look on his face, his voice is surprisingly clear and strong.

"Would you mind telling me exactly where you were Tuesday?"

"Same place I am every Tuesday." He points with his whole head toward the inside of his house. Simmons starts blinking, and his face twitches as if someone's tugging on an invisible fishhook lodged in his cheek. "Reading the paper, popping pills, and watching TV. What's it to you?"

"Do you have any witnesses? Anybody who can verify that?"

"As a matter of fact I do."

This brings me up short. I'm trying to think back to all the detective reruns from my youth for a follow-up question, a real Jim Rockford zinger.

"Well then … could you … I mean … do you have like an alibi or something?" This isn't going well. "Or, I don't know, some names I can check out?"

"It's kind of a long list." A flicker of a grin cracks his chapped lips. "Let's see, there's Sheriff Taylor and his boy, Opie. That Montel fella. Oprah. Gilligan. Who else? Clint Eastwood made an appearance too. As much as I'd love to stand here and watch you play Dick Tracy, I really have to pee. So either tell me what's on your mind or you may end up having to change my diaper for me."

"Someone poisoned Sonny."

His face does that twitching thing again. "Makes sense why you'd think it was me. I hated that dog. But you can be sure I didn't poison him."

"Yeah? How so?"

"Cause I would have shot him, not poisoned him. Now if you'll excuse me."

He tries to shut the door in my face, but I plant my foot and forearm across the threshold. "I have something else I need to say to you. Or, at least, Sonny does."

He tilts his head to one side and releases his grip on the doorknob. "This I gotta hear."

"I'm supposed to tell you that Sonny says he's sorry. About the rose bushes, about pooping in your yard, about digging the holes and eating your newspapers. Pretty much everything. Sonny wanted me to make amends."

"Nice try, kid. I may be frail, but I'm not quite crazy yet."

He grabs the door again as if he means to slam it. Then it dawns on me that he thinks I'm making fun of him. That he sees this as just another prank from another clueless kid. I've never thought of Simmons as anything but a cranky neighbor to be ridiculed. Standing here, seeing the helpless and wounded expression, makes me wonder which came first — his ornery nature, or our conclusions about him.

"I know you're not crazy. I'd appreciate it if you'd at least consider my apology."

He does consider it, so long in fact, I'd swear he's fallen asleep on his feet.

Finally, he says, "You want some tea?"

"Well, I'm supposed to be headed to work."

His pained expression telegraphs that he knows it's Saturday. "Never mind. Of course you are."

"Wait, no. Do you have Orange pekoe?"

Simmons moves back and I step inside. "Here, put these on." He hands me a ball of wadded up items and disappears into the kitchen. I place the allergy mask over my face, slip the hairnet on, and end up shoving the paper booties and gloves into my pocket. The air in the room seems clean, yet laden with the monotony of solitude. The first thing I notice is an enormous multiscreened entertainment center replete with one giant TV screen and several smaller ones tuned to twenty-four-hour news programming, stock tickers, and an open browser to the World Wide Web. It takes a second to realize why everything seems so shiny. The house has been vinylized — clear plastic floor runners, lamp shades, and couch covers. The walls and most flat surfaces are covered in picture frames. There's an eerie quality to them until I realize that there's no more than a half-dozen poses of the same woman.

"That's my wife, Sherry." Simmons shuffles back toward the living room with two steaming mugs of thick brown liquid. "And for the record, she didn't disappear. She left me. I know it's creepy, but those photos are all I've got left. And I like having them around."

"No, it's not creepy at all." Sometimes lying is justified.

"Heard your old man was going to be on TV again."

"Yeah? How'd you hear about that?" My face is hot under the mask. And when my lips move, the paper makes my nose itch.

He sets the mugs down and, like a magician, flips the television on. The screen comes alive in tacky furniture, expensive dental work, and an acre of over-coiffed hair. The set is tuned to Sinclair's station. A trio in matching denim outfits belts out some old-time gospel in perfect harmony while we sip our drinks. The constant raising and lowering of my mask keeps me from having to make small talk. Besides, my longtime neighbor seems more than a little content to have a visitor. And I don't want to ruin the moment for him.

After several minutes, he sets his cup down with trembling hands and says, "You say it was Tuesday morning? The day your dog died?"

I turn too quickly, causing hot liquid to spill over the rim and into my lap.

"I might have seen something that could help you out. But I'm not sure."

"Really? I'll take any help I can get."

"Now I don't want you to get the impression that I'm always watching your house or anything. But my prostate is shot, so I'm back and forth to the john much more than I'd care to admit." He points a trembling finger at the window behind him. "I got a pretty clear and natural view of your place from here."

"So what did you see?"

"A whole parade of cars. First, your mother leaves — for work, I'm guessing. Then you drive off in your smashed-up Ford. Your brother's car shows up fifteen minutes later. He lets himself in through your busted garage door — you guys really ought to get that fixed — and rummages around a bit. Twenty minutes later he comes out with his typical paranoid look, then speeds off. But I figure, he's family, so I didn't think much about it."

Simmons drains his cup with a loud slurp. Then he stares at the bottom of the cup for a long, thoughtful moment before speaking again. "At some point another car pulled into your driveway. Just sat there idling a while, then backed out and pulled up alongside your mailbox." Simmons glances at me, then looks away again. "Anyway, um, I'm really sorry about that."

It takes me a second to catch up.

"Shoveling dog mess into your mailbox. I get a little worked up sometimes."

143

"It's okay, really. What else can you tell me about that car? It wasn't a beat-up station wagon was it? With a bunch of bumper stickers?"

"Nah, it was a compact, one of them foreign jobs — Nissan or Toyota or something."

"Did you get a look at the driver?"

"Nope, sorry. Had his dry cleaning hanging in the passenger window. Probably a big fella though, judging by the size of his forearm."

We're both quiet for a while. Then Simmons starts coughing. It's a violent retching sound that seems to go on forever. Just sitting there feels helpless and awkward, so I fetch him a glass of tap water and resist the urge to pound on his back. He downs the glass in one long swallow and continues.

"Not much happened until your mother got home and let herself in through the garage. I'm sure you already knew that though because you showed up about an hour later. And that's the last I saw or heard."

Simmons drums a fingernail on his mug while I try to process this new information. Not only did a complete stranger drop by the house, but it appears my mother was there the whole time too, most likely passed out on her bed.

"Don't know if that helps at all ..."

"I'm not sure how, but I think it does."

I jot down my cell number and tell him to please call me if he thinks of anything else that might help. He looks a little insulted, so I quickly add that he can call me if he just wants to get together for tea again sometime too.

* * *

As my Nikes make the transition from Simmons's pristine, spongy lawn onto the crusty, thinning hairline of my parents' yard, I can see the derailed state of the closed garage door. One corner is flush with the driveway. The other is cockeyed, revealing a triangle of shadowy blackness underneath. My knee pops as I kneel and grasp the rotting weather strip. It feels like sandpaper and takes surprisingly little effort to get the door gliding upward. Then I hear a series of shrieks — the first is the metallic friction of screeching metals, the next two are the girlie screams of two grown men, both named Fink.

To our mutual surprise, Peter and I are standing nose to nose on the threshold of my parents' garage. For one split second, I'm assaulted with a snapshot of good versus evil — me backlit by a March sun and Peter shrouded in darkness with a pinched and squinty expression.

He recovers quickly and says, "Hey little brother. What are you doing here?"

"Checking something out. What are *you* doing?"

"Oh, um, looking for my notebook." Peter is holding a plastic yellow funnel by the throat. He spins it in his hand, staring at it for inspiration. "I know I had it here the other night." Peter hammers the funnel into his opposing palm as he talks. He stops when a splatter of green goo soils his golf shirt. "Listen, I guess I owe you an apology."

"Just one?"

"Seriously. I did you wrong, man. And I'm really sorry."

It's always taken real effort to stay mad at Peter. "It's alright. I'm sure I'll recover. But it's a good thing I haven't seen you around in a while. I might have saved those gambling goons some dirty work."

Peter laughs nervously, his eyes pinballing and unable to settle on anything. "So, we're okay now? You're not going to strangle me or anything?"

"Not this week. Besides, it was only money."

"Oh, well. I never thought about it like that." He licks his lips in a way that suggests more than sheer ignorance. He tosses the funnel behind a pile of boxes.

"Speaking of apologies, I kind of promised Sonny I'd make amends for him too."

"Well that's a bit weird."

"Yeah, I know. And I'll save you the whole list." But I can see it in my head—love letters, two leather wallets, his high school diploma, a Mickey Mantle rookie baseball card, and supposedly a winning lottery ticket worth two million dollars. "Suffice to say that he's sorry for everything of yours he ever ate or pooped on."

"What if I don't accept?"

"That's between you and Sonny. And one other thing—I'm asking everybody I know where they were the day Sonny died."

"Died?" His eyes bulge and his voice cracks on the last word. Now his Adam's apple telegraphs a series of gulps.

"I figured Mom told you."

"Man, that's rough. I'm, um, really sorry about that."

"Thanks." We're both quiet for a while, too quiet. "Haven't seen much of you lately. Where've you been hiding?"

"I've been forced underground."

"Look, if you're convinced you're being followed, why not go to the cops? The *real* cops, not that wannabe Magnum PI."

"These are not the kind of folks who back down easy," Peter says, affecting a know-it-all voice of experience. But he still sounds scared. "Siccing the cops on them would be like using a BB gun on a Bengal tiger. It won't stop them, just make 'em mad. Besides, Beaman works cheap. Hey, listen, I need a favor. I need you to run by my apartment and grab some paperwork for me."

"No."

"What do you mean no?"

"I'm out of the favor-doing business. If you remember, I wrote you a check with two simple stipulations—don't cash it until Tuesday and don't use it to hire your investigator friend. You did both. And now I'm even more broke than normal."

"Oh, I'm sorry. I had no idea."

"Didn't you just spend five minutes apologizing for that?"

Peter gnaws on his lower lip and looks longingly outside. "Um, yeah. I guess I did. Sorry, I don't know what's wrong with me. Will you do this for me? I swear this is the last time."

"Nope. Find somebody else."

"I can't, Russell. You're my last resort."

"Flattery won't help."

"You know what I mean. I'm begging you."

"Why can't you get Inspector Beaman to do it? You know, since he's getting paid?"

"I ... I just can't. That's all."

If I didn't know better, I'd swear he's on the verge of tears. He tries to say something else and stops.

"I can't believe I'm about to say this, but here goes. What do you need?"

Peter's detailed instructions sound more like a scavenger hunt than a simple errand. I'm supposed to let myself into his apartment and partially disassemble his computer tower. There I'll find a small key taped inside that unlocks a strongbox buried in a huge bag of dog food in his bedroom closet. When I point out that he doesn't have a dog, he rolls his eyes at me and forges ahead. The strongbox requires a combination as well as a key. He repeats it twice and looks over my shoulder to make sure I write it down properly. Then he makes me promise to swallow my note when I'm done with it. After a surprisingly heated and rather childish debate, we agree that I'll flush the note in a public restroom somewhere. The strongbox contains a little black book that I am to retrieve and hold onto until further notice.

147

Once he's satisfied that I have things under control, he thanks me profusely, then adds, "Look, about Sonny ... I really am sorry."

"You never actually said where you were the morning Sonny died."

"Don't be stupid, Russell."

Peter lowers the garage door, and I stand mute in the darkness, unsure of what just happened.

* * *

Since I'm here, I decide to nose around. Upstairs on my bed is a rubber-banded bundle of mail for me with a note from my mother. It starts with *I love you* and ends with an enumerated list of recent phone messages — four from Alyssa, all bossy and scatterbrained; and one from Geoffrey Sinclair asking me to return his call.

I lift my old cordless phone off its cradle and power it up. May as well get this over with. It's not like I have any real shot at getting the man on the phone. It is Saturday morning, after all. The receptionist says she'll put me right through, and seconds later, I hear the voice of Sinclair himself.

"This is Russell Fink calling. I hate to bother you, but — "

"Don't be ridiculous. No bother at all." He sounds like he means it too. "How's the painting coming along?"

"I haven't had a lot of extra time lately."

"That's too bad. You might like to know you really inspired me. That's why I called, by the way, to thank you. Seems I spend the bulk of my free time with a brush in my hand these days. I think Mrs. Sinclair is starting to suspect another woman."

"Maybe that's my problem. You stole my muse."

It takes him a second to realize I'm joking, probably due in large part to the lameness of the joke. In the quiet moment, I'd almost swear I heard someone walking across the kitchen floor. "Listen, I'm really pleased to hear from you, Russell. But I do need to run out of here in a few minutes for another dreadful meeting. So, tell me what I can do for you on this fine day."

I realize now I should have rehearsed my lines. "Well, it's about Sonny."

Sinclair chuckles. "How is Old Faithful?"

I'm not sure exactly how to phrase it. "Dead, actually."

I hear a metallic click, then a bit of static on the line. I check the handset to see if the batteries are running down.

"Russell, that's terrible. I'm so sorry."

"Thanks. I'm calling on Sonny's behalf. It's kind of a long story, but basically I'm making amends for Sonny. Trying to right a few of his wrongs for him."

"Okay." I can't tell if Sinclair is distracted or if he's checking his Rolodex for reliable shrinks.

"I just wanted to apologize again. From me and from Sonny."

"Like I said the other night, no real harm done. I wasn't crazy about those loafers anyway. Don't think another thing about it."

"Thanks. I guess that answers my other question."

"Which is?"

"It had to do with alibis. And somehow I think it's irrelevant now."

"Alibis, huh? You suspect foul play?"

"Something like that."

"Well, if it puts your mind at ease, I left the following morning for some emergency meetings in Southeast Asia. Didn't return home for about six days. Does that cover it?"

"Yes, sir. And you know, I didn't really suspect you or anything. Just trying to cover all the bases."

"Not to worry, Russell. Now is there anything else?"

"I'm glad that Sonny didn't ruin my dad's chances for getting that TV gig."

"Of course not. Unless your father's having second thoughts, we're good to go. We've been in preproduction for weeks. Tell me something, Russell. There's something between you and your father, something unsettled, am I right?"

"No, we're fine." A few weighty seconds pass in silence. How do you reduce years of a broken relationship into a sound bite? "Really."

"It's been my experience, Russell, that the first steps toward forgiveness are always the hardest. And waiting only makes the earth settle around your ankles until you're stuck in the sludge. I'm not privy to all the details in the Fink family history, but I pray that you folks will start taking those steps toward one another."

I'm about to say good-bye when he says, "In fact, we should pray about this." And without hesitation, he does. I miss most of it as my mind focuses on the word *we* — as in *we* need to pray. I hear words about reconciliation and forgiveness and healing and Sonny, but mostly I hear blood beating in my ears and malformed excuses about why I abhor praying out loud. I'm just about to scrape my stubble across the mouthpiece when he says, "Amen. Thanks for calling, Russell. I really do need to run."

I hear Sinclair disconnect. Then I see my red-faced father standing in the doorway, fists clenched at his sides.

"What are you trying to do to me, Russell?"

Ever since I was about twelve, no matter how our conversations start, they always devolve into an argument. This one is doomed from the start.

"Were you listening in on my conversation?"

He stares at me.

"Look, I made a list of every possible suspect and I'm systematically weeding them out. I can assure you I didn't accuse Sinclair of anything."

"So help me, son, if I lose this job, I'm holding you personally responsible."

We are at the point now where one of us says something we should regret. I doubt we ever do — regret it, that is.

"Well," he says. "What do you have to say for yourself?"

"Actually I wanted to tell you that Sonny is sorry. For all the times he chewed your stuff and barfed on the rug and got you in trouble with the neighbors."

"Are you high?"

"I don't expect you to understand, Dad. I just wanted you to know."

I can hear his teeth grinding from across the room. He looks older now, like Gramps working his jaw behind thin white lips. My father raises one hand, and for one insane second, I expect to see a gun. But he just waves me off, dismissing me with the back of his hand. Makes me wonder which hurts more.

Monday

Alyssa has called six more times since Friday, but I always let it go into voice mail. At first she cussed me out again for standing her up at The Boundary, but subsequent messages range from contrite to playfully aggressive. What bothers me most is the fact that she doesn't even mention Geri, my "new girlfriend," as if she knows I'm incapable of moving on.

I've not seen or heard anything from Dan since he left town. Although one night, after I discovered that every room in his house has been outfitted with ceiling-mounted TV lenses, all wired to a central satellite television receiver, I watched some CNN coverage of the upcoming space launch from Cape Canaveral and could have sworn I saw Dan in a crowd of NASA scientists. But I'm sure it was just my imagination, like the night I dreamed someone snuck into my room and covered me with a preheated blanket.

Somehow I managed to lose Cassandra's phone number while moving into Dan's house. So my numerous anonymous phone calls to Dr. Kozinski's office are of a duplicitous nature. On the one hand, I want to know if I have cancer—well, what I really want to know is that I *don't* have cancer, although I doubt Cassandra is authorized to deliver such news. On the other hand, I keep hoping she'll answer the phone, but she never does, and I panic and hang up before asking to speak to her. I realize now that I'm less excited about actually going out with her; rather, I just want to hear her *say* she wants to go out with me. The thought of an actual date with anyone other than Alyssa scares me to death.

Now it's Monday at noon and my confidence has hit a watershed moment. This morning I landed my biggest order to date. So I take the almost-direct approach by speed-dialing Dr. Kozinski's office and asking the receptionist if I can leave a message for Cassandra.

"Is this Russell Fink?"

"Yes it is. Um, who's this?"

"Cindy Tanner. The lady who bought a copier from you?" She seems hurt that I don't recognize her voice. But she sounds different when she's not swiping my debit card.

"Right. I hope it's working okay."

"Hang on. I'll go grab Cassandra."

"Wait. I mean, how did you know it was me?"

"For starters, I recognized your voice. We also have caller ID. So far you're averaging two-and-half hang-ups per day."

"Oh."

"Cassandra made me promise to keep you on the line the next time you called. So hang on, dear, and I'll go hunt her down."

The on-hold music is actually a super cheesy advertisement for Kozinski, Johnson, and Fluhart, M.D.'s. The narrator is midway through an enthusiastic pitch for routine colonoscopies when Cassandra picks up.

"Russell? Let me guess, you lost my number?"

"Guilty as charged."

"How are you healing up? Any complications that I need to know about?"

Her voice sounds all pink and flirty, giving my confidence a much-needed boost. But then I remember why I called, and it dawns on me again that I'm treading uncharted waters.

"So far, so good."

After several moments of dead air, she says, "Great."

My tongue is now a lethargic lump of flesh, dry and heavy and useless. I should have rehearsed this part. Finally I manage to say, "So ..."

"So ..."

"How would you like to ... hang on ... um ..."

"Yes, I'd love to."

"Great. Good. What day might you be able to ..." I pause, trying to swallow.

"How about tonight?"

I catch myself nodding at the phone.

"Russell? You still there?"

"Yes, absolutely, tonight sounds great."

"Pick me up at seven?"

"Seven. Yes, perfect. Seven."

I jot down her phone number again and directions to her apartment, then manage to tell her I'm looking forward to seeing her — without saying anything really stupid.

* * *

I turn onto Dan's street after work to find the driveway filled with cars. I park across the street in front of Heavenly Pastures and think about my next move now that Dan's home. We never discussed my exit strategy, and secretly I guess I was hoping he wouldn't return home for another month or so. Now that I'm homeless, I'm hoping he'll take some pity on me and let me stay a while longer. If not, I guess I'll be sleeping in the Taurus. Or maybe Peter's bachelor pad. It's not like he's using it, after all, or he wouldn't need me to run his errand for him. So, it appears the impromptu plan is to avoid the topic until Dan is forced to throw me out as well.

I pause at the door for a moment, listening to the muffled voices and pondering whether to ring the bell or use my key. Finally, I decide to split the difference with a light knock and a stealthy entrance. It almost works.

There are at least seven people seated on couches and folding chairs around Dan's living room. He's cross-legged on the floor with what appears to be a workbook open in his lap. His hair is blonder, his skin a bit more bronzed than a week ago. He's wearing thick corduroys, a thicker turtleneck, and even thicker bedroom slippers. A weepy thirtysomething pauses mid-sentence and looks up at me. This causes a chain reaction, and I find myself staring at eight pairs of questioning eyes.

"Russell," Dan says, sounding genuinely pleased to see me. He stays seated and motions me forward. "Everybody, this is Russell Fink. Russell, I'd like to introduce you to the local chapter of *Chagrinant.*"

Before I can ask what that actually means, Dan closes his eyes and moans something unintelligible through a series of elongated yoga breaths. This elicits more moaning and gasping from the two ladies closest to Dan. That's when I recognize his winglike pose and pretzel legs from the back of a workout tape.

When the wheezing subsides, I offer up a goofy wave and am greeted with a series of nods and polite hellos.

Dan says, "Why don't you grab a seat and join us?"

"Actually, I need to get cleaned up."

A severely freckled woman says, "I'll bet he's got a hot date."

"Well," I say, "I don't know how hot it is."

This information garners some harmless catcalls and feigned disappointment. I'm not sure what to say or where to look, so I turn toward the sound of footsteps in the hallway.

"Geri?"

We begin speaking at the same time. She looks as flustered and anxious as I feel, unsure what to do with her hands. She stutters a couple words about helping with Dan's group, like she needs to explain why she's there. Some of the ladies elbow each other and whisper behind their hands, obviously mistaking our awkward exchange as flirting.

"We work together," I say.

"A *lawyer* even." This from an auburn-bouffanted woman who apparently made an ill-advised raid on her teenage daughter's wardrobe.

Someone else yells, "You go, Geri."

"No, no. I'm not a lawyer." I have an irresistible urge to explain myself for some reason. "I'm, well ... Geri is — "

"Russell is my friend." Geri's voice carries a tone of finality. "So you girls knock it off and let the poor boy get ready for his date."

"It's not really a date anyway," I explain. "Just, you know, a friend of mine." It's obvious to everyone in the room that I'm lying. But I can't seem to stop myself. Finally I blurt out, "She's my nurse." As if that settles it.

Geri winks at me and takes a spot on the couch while I try not to take the "poor boy" comment personally. She has a peculiar look on her face. I'd like to believe it's jealousy.

"Well, it was nice meeting you all. But if you'll excuse me ..."

Dan snaps his fingers. "Oh, Russell. Got some preliminary results back on those tests." I'm sure I look confused, wondering if Dr. K finally mailed the pathology results and Dan took a peek at my mail. "The lab tests for Sonny?"

"Right." I'm surprised at his disregard for tact. But then, what is the etiquette for discussing the necropsy of a dead basset hound in a roomful of other people? Dan regards me with that earnest, moist-eyed expression, as affable as it is vacant. It's obvious now; tact is not an option for Dan. He's clueless.

"Russell's dog, Sonny, died last week." A smattering of sympathetic murmurs fills the room. A middle-aged woman with droopy blonde hair immediately begins dabbing her sparkling green eyes. "My preliminary tests showed signs of at least two kinds of poison. So I took the samples to NASA with me — hope you don't mind. I was able to confirm one of your initial suspicions."

I steady myself by placing both hands on the back of the La-Z-boy, but it reclines further, hinges shrieking, and I almost end up in the lap of the freckled woman. She's gripping the armrest with one hand and somehow not spilling the cup of tea in her other hand.

"You were right. The findings are consistent with alcohol poisoning."

The ladies gasp and shake their heads. My restless stomach churns at the silent indictment, my imagination having morphed their sympathetic stares into accusations.

"But that's not what killed Sonny."

"Oh, well, that's good I guess." My composure finds a little traction. "What did?"

The entire room seems to be tilting forward in anticipation. Dan, obviously relishing the proverbial spotlight, slows his delivery further.

"That's where things get complicated." He pauses for effect, fanning the flame of anticipation. "We found small traces of antifreeze. Not sure if it was enough to do him in, but his kidneys had begun to shut down. Dogs love the sweet taste. And as little as a teaspoon can cause kidney failure and be fatal."

"What does that mean, exactly?" I say.

"Nothing conclusive. Either of those could be the culprit, but those are just tests from external sources."

"Huh?"

Dan lowers his voice a tiny bit, a worthless concession to tact. "From the fluids around his body. I'll have the bloodwork results in about a week."

* * *

My stomach growls so loud I can hear it over the stiflingly hot shower. As I lather up, my mind metronomes between relief that I'm not solely responsible for Sonny's death and a bewildered rage as I try to figure out who is. But that eventually gives way to my more immediate dilemma — canceling on Cassandra at the last minute. Despite my rather bleak dating résumé, I do believe that this practice is generally frowned upon. I wipe the mist off the bathroom mirror and stare at the bleary reflection of a man with no home, a murdered pet, and one "hot date" he can't afford, financially or emotionally.

I lift the receiver, lose my nerve, and drop it.

I lift it again, feeling like I just swallowed a cinderblock. My hands are shaking, heart pounding with holy terror. I never imagined canceling a date was more nerve-wracking than asking for it in the first place. She picks up, but not before the answering machine kicks in. My mouth goes completely dry when I realize we're now being recorded.

"Russell, I wasn't expecting you to call." Cassandra's voice is flushed and buoyant. "I sure hope you're not planning on standing me up."

"I really, really hate to do this to you, but I'm afraid I'm coming down with something." And it's true. My stomach is still in revolt. When I can't handle the silence on the other end of the line, I jump back in. "Seriously, Cassandra, can we please reschedule? I'd love to get together tomorrow for dinner ... or even lunch or breakfast — "

"Alright, I'm convinced. You really don't sound so good."

"I hope you understand how much I hate this."

159

"Okay, okay. I believe you. But I'm afraid the rest of this week is spoken for."

"How about next weekend then?"

"I suppose I can give you a pass just this once. But remember, if you stand me up again, I can have Dr. Kozinski do all sorts of nasty things to you."

I drop the phone in the cradle and release the lungful of breath I'd been holding. The relief is short-lived, however. Canceling with Cassandra may have eliminated my frantic sense of worry, but it merely created a vacuum for its cousin, regret. I'm a fraud and a liar. I realize now that I really did want *a* date. Just not *this* date.

To distract myself, I pick up the bundle of mail I retrieved from my parents' house and sort through medical bills, requests for donations, and coupons for oil changes. Amidst the junk, I find a nondescript letter addressed to me. It looks like that computer-generated cursive advertisers use to add a personal touch to their mass mailings. Inside is a tri-folded sheet with similar script:

Russell,

Your brother has been kidnapped. The ransom is $500,000 cash. Your father and his new boss should have no problem coming up with it. You have one week.

I call Peter's cell phone. No answer. Same with his home phone.

* * *

I crane my ear toward the living room, trying to pick out Geri's voice.

It sounds like the odd gathering is breaking up so I get dressed and try to sneak into the kitchen for some leftover pizza. But Dan sees me and waves me over. He wastes no time sharing what's on his mind.

"We've got carpool issues and Geri needs a ride home."

"No, Dan. I'm fine, really. I take cabs all the time." I'd forgotten how cute she is when she's embarrassed.

160

"Nonsense," he says. "Russell would be happy to give you a lift."

"Leave him alone, Dan." Geri rolls her eyes. "He has a date tonight."

Dan waves her off. "He can drop you off. I'm sure it's on the way."

"Actually, the date's canceled. So I was going to run out and grab some dinner before coming back here to crash." This last comment is aimed at Dan, a trial balloon to see if he has a problem with me spending another night in his house. He's unfazed, so I appeal to Geri. "So, if it's okay with you?"

Dan claps us both on the back and rushes out the door with two of his devotees.

It turns out that the Bean Bag is on the way to Geri's. We stop in and I opt for a prepackaged Italian chicken sandwich and a slab of chocolate marble cake, and an extra hot version of Peter's decadent mocha drink. Geri goes for some frou-frou decaf drink with a double dollop of whipped cream. We grab a couple of overstuffed armchairs, separated by a scarred coffee table. Geri props her feet on the table, then squirms and grimaces her way into a comfortable position. She waits until I have a mouthful of food to ask, "What happened to your date?"

Her eyes are smiling behind the veil of steam emanating from her mug.

"Oh, that." For some reason I'm inclined to guard my words. I tell myself it's because I want to keep my private life private. But there's more to it than that. I'm just not exactly sure what. "Just didn't feel up to it."

"Yeah, poor Sonny."

"That ... and work." Since I'm not exactly sold on Peter's alleged kidnapping, I fudge a little and keep that part to myself.

"See, you shouldn't have canceled your date tonight. Might take your mind off things."

"As far as I'm concerned *this* is a date. I did pay for your coffee."

"For all you know I have a big burly boyfriend who could barge in here any minute and pound us both to smithereens."

"I thought I was your boyfriend." I mimic her performance with Alyssa, holding up my hand and flashing an imaginary diamond. "Maybe she'll finally take the hint."

Geri's face turns cloudy as she gets up. "Don't be mean, Russell." Then she turns and heads toward the restroom. She's right. There's no need to pile on when Alyssa's not around to defend herself. Geri returns minutes later wearing her cheery face again.

"Okay," I say, rubbing my hands together. "You have got to tell me what was up with that meeting. What did Dan call it? Chocolate something?"

"No, *Chagrinant.* It's a support group."

"What kind of support group? For terminally cold people? Brainiacs? Multilingual spouses of astronauts?"

Geri folds her napkin into the shape of a heart, then crumples it. "It's like grief counseling for owners of dead pets."

"Oh, I had no idea." Geri seems to be looking everywhere but at me. "But what were you doing there? As far as I know, you never even had a goldfish. So why do you need a support group for a problem you don't have?"

"They're pretty much all the same."

We sit quietly for a long time, each lost in our own thoughts. Then I hear a voice that sounds a lot like mine say, "I think I may be responsible for killing Sonny."

"Oh?"

I tell her everything, about finding Sonny in a pool of his own fluids, about the Super Bowl breakup and whiskey biscuits, about his clairvoyant tendencies. She knows very little about Katie, so I tell her that too, how it was all my fault. The words have a cleansing, almost redemptive effect, like I've always imagined a confessional. By the end of it, I'm staring into my coffee cup.

"You haven't changed a bit, have you?"

I look up. My feelings are hurt and I don't even know why.

"You're still carrying the weight of the world, still convinced that everything is your fault and that everyone is more worthy than you."

"Sorry," I say. "I didn't mean to go all pitiful on you."

"There you go again." At least she's smiling now. "It's really quite selfish when you think about it."

"You've got to be good at something. Maybe being pathetic is my special gift."

She shakes her head, then is temporarily distracted by something over my left shoulder. I resist the urge to turn around when she starts speaking again. "I'm not buying it. This whole pity party routine was a ploy for you to steer the conversation back to me helping you land your big sale. But I'm not helping until you answer a question for me."

"Uh-oh."

"If you hate your job so much — and don't pretend for a second that you don't — then why go to all this trouble? Why not quit and go find a job you don't hate?"

I wonder briefly if she's been talking to Dr. K. With no good answer ready, I default to obfuscation and humor. "If I told you, I'd have to kill you."

Geri's eyes keep flicking to a spot over my left shoulder, and I turn just in time to see a familiar face. It's Cassandra, radiating heat like a funeral pyre. When I open my mouth to speak, she leans toward me and grabs my mug of coffee as if she's going to gulp it down. But I know better.

In an instant, the mug is directly over my head and tipping forward. I bristle, arms down and head back, backpedaling in my seat. The stream of brown liquid barely misses my forehead, finding the target she'd intended from the start: my lap is now bathed in warm caffeinated brew.

She drops the mug. I manage to catch it before it causes more serious damage. Then she's gone.

"Let me guess," Geri says. "That was your date? The nurse?"

I grab two handfuls of napkins and try to mop the coffee out of my jeans. "You guessed it."

"Her bedside manner could use some work."

* * *

After dropping Geri off, I'm too wired to sleep. So I decide to swing by Peter's place to either: (a) wake him up to see what's going on with that bogus ransom note (if he's there) or (b) make good on my promise to retrieve his little black book (if he's not). I have to admit I enjoy the thought of burgling Peter's apartment. Or at least the illusion of breaking and entering. But when I swing the door open, it takes my mind a moment to rationalize the details coming from my eyes.

The place has been trashed. Thoroughly. And violently.

The floor is littered with papers, clothes, and shards of broken furniture and frames. It looks like someone used Peter's stereo to smash his portable TV, or vice versa. Even the drywall is pockmarked with gouges. Most shocking for some reason are the long gashes in the leather sofa. Like bloated roadkill, its bloodless innards spill out and make my stomach clench. At least his framed Hank Aaron rookie card survived unscathed.

I pick my way through the rubble and, per his instructions, find his computer tower. But by the time I dismantle it, I'm practically quaking with paranoia. Every creaking floorboard, muffled voice, and flushed toilet from neighboring apartments gives me the shivers, like crushed ice tumbling down the staircase of my spine.

The strongbox itself is right where Peter said it would be, covered in premium Purina dog chow. I blow the pungent dust off the locks and slip the key inside. Then I consult my note and align the six-digit combination. The lid pops open and I peer inside. The black book is on top, a thin volume with alphabetized index tabs down one side. A quick fan through the pages reveals little, just a bunch of names and numbers I don't recognize — like *$78K Slip* (sounds more like a landslide to me). The only variation is under the *M* tab — a section devoted to The Miracle Ward.

As I'm backing out, I notice the power light on Peter's coffee maker. I cross the room again, marveling that the coffee maker is still intact amid the broken dishes and battered microwave oven. I flip the lid on the coffee maker and look inside. The fill tank is beaded, like a sweaty forehead. The filtered grounds are still soggy. Apparently whoever trashed my brother's apartment paused for a coffee break. And it wasn't that long ago.

I switch the machine off, lock the front door, and run to my car. On the way out of the apartment complex I slam on the brakes. Peter's Jaguar is parked three buildings down from his own. How could I have missed that before? I slow as I pass, watching my supposedly kidnapped brother stare at his apartment through a pair of binoculars.

The urge to drag him out of his car and confront him passes. He doesn't see me, so why waste the energy? Guess that explains the alleged ransom note.

Tuesday

"I feel bad, Russell, making you miss work so you can drive me around." Geri's whole demeanor seems off today. She's uncharacteristically pensive, almost fearful.

"Who says I'm missing work? What do you think I do while you're gallivanting around to all these cryptic appointments?"

"I don't know." She offers a grin, albeit begrudgingly. I'll take it though. "I don't really care so long as you're not meddling in my business."

Following her directions, we enter an office park with four identical, two-story buildings. Tinted windows, framed in beige stucco, glower down at us. I find an empty spot between a shiny black Hummer and a dented Yugo.

"I mean it, Russell." Geri unbuckles herself and points at me. "No snooping."

"You realize of course that these are office buildings. I sell office supplies, so I can sell to any one of them anytime I want."

"Maybe so." She points for emphasis. "But if you know what's good for you, you'll stay away from that one today."

I agree to meet her back here in an hour. Then I watch

167

her walk away. Something about the way she walks makes me imagine Geri as an eight-year-old girl in a new town, entering her new school, putting on a brave front, but scared to death. It makes my heart hurt.

I ease the seat back and prepare to doze until Geri comes back. When I kill the engine and begin dialing in the one cool, independently owned radio station in Nashville, the flickering dashboard lights tweak something in the back of my brain. I calculate the distance from here to my parents' house and decide to investigate.

I ease into the driveway, one eye on Simmons' window to see just how blatant his spying really is. I'm a little disappointed when I don't see him. The garage door is still crookedly ajar and shrieks conspicuously on its hinges. I pause, waiting for my eyes to adjust, using the temporary blackness to recreate the image of Peter in the garage. *He spins the funnel in his hand, hammers it into his left palm, then tosses it behind a pile of boxes.* It's right where he left it.

I sniff the slick green spots, realizing only then that I have no earthly idea what antifreeze smells like. Another frantic moment of searching nets one mostly empty jar of Prestone. I uncap it, sniff once, then ignore the crazy urge to take a swig.

Peter was covering his tracks. He poisoned Sonny.

I stab his number into my cell phone, over and over until my anger turns numb. I make it back to the office complex with five minutes to spare. Geri emerges moments later looking even younger and less brave than before.

Thursday

The pizza arrives — our third one this week. Geri pours flat Coke into plastic cups and I hold my breath and write another check with a sizable tip. Apparently, my bank has a three-strikes-and-you're-out policy. I make a mental note to kick Peter in the shins — if I ever see him again.

This is our final strategy session. Geri has helped me tailor my PowerPoint presentation to each of the partners' personal tastes. We use a combination of statistics, movie clips, cartoons, and the obligatory graphics and sales info from Hengle's. If I don't nail this one, it will not be for a lack of effort. Win or lose, I owe Geri big time. I still can't help thinking there's more to her willingness to help than aiding an old college friend. I hope so anyway.

"Are you guys at it again?" Dan asks. He helps himself to a couple of slices. Part of me wants to protest, to instruct him to mind his manners. I mean, he could at least have the decency to ask. But maybe he's thinking the same thing about me. In the end, I decide that a few slices of pizza in exchange for rent-free lodging is a pretty good deal. Dan pours boiling water into a huge mug, drops a tea bag in, then places the hot tea and warm pizza into the microwave. "When you guys are done, I'll need a volunteer."

"Sure."

When I hear his laboratory door close behind him, I ask, "Do you believe all that nonsense about his astronaut girlfriend?"

"Why not? Astronauts have to date somebody." Her nose wrinkles when she takes another bite of pizza. A glop of cheese droops onto her chin, leaving a red mark. "Man, this is delicious."

"What? What happened to your — whatchamacallit — 'overly sophisticated sense of taste'?"

"Adventurous, not sophisticated."

"Whatever. All I remember is your chicken-pesto-oatmeal and peanut-butter-and-bologna sandwiches and popcorn-with-raisins and catfish au gratin. I used to wonder if you were experiencing some year-round pregnancy. I guess maybe your taste buds got tired and gave up on you."

"Yeah, something like that."

"Did I say something stupid?"

She brightens at this. "There you go again. I make a sad face and you automatically assume it was you."

"Well, was it?"

"No, Russell. Everything is great. I was just thinking. That's all."

"About what?"

"About what a nosy friend you've turned out to be. And about your big presentation. So, you ready for it or not?"

I close the lid on my laptop and announce, "Indeed I am. The harpoon is as sharp as it's gonna get. Now it's time to land that baby." I stand and thump my chest for emphasis. It makes me cough, which makes Geri laugh.

She says, "Barbie won't know what hit her."

"Man, you must really hate that girl."

"Who? Barbie?"

"You've pretty much admitted that you're helping me for spite. But I've never known you to be a name-caller before. I mean, just because she flaunts her supermodel looks ..."

Geri cracks up, gets herself together with a sip of Coke, then bursts into a fresh round of laughter. I shield my laptop in case she spews.

"What is so funny?"

"Her name *is* Barbie. Barbie Flannigan." The last few syllables are not so much spoken as ejected, forcibly, amid gale force laughter. I'd forgotten what a sweet sound it is, even when it's at my expense. She pulls herself together, but just for a second. Then, like a gasping hyena, she says, "Youthought?Youthought?Youthought I was ... ?"

Dan shows up again wearing thick goggles and a rubberized helmet. It's bright red and makes him look like a giant bloody finger. Geri falls off the sofa when she sees him.

"I need a volunteer." He's all business, oblivious to our hysterics. Geri's on all fours, pounding the floor with her fist.

She points at me and says, "His turn. I've got to pee."

"Again?" I say. "That's the hardest working bladder in show business."

Geri disappears and Dan removes his rubber hat. It makes a loud THWOP!

"Here put this on."

He tries to help, but I whine like a baby because it's pulling my hair. Geri's laughter echoes from down the hall. Once the headpiece is firmly ensconced on my head, Dan points a remote at me and says, "Now shut your eyes and think about lava!"

"About what?"

"Lava." His face is intense, bordering on rabid. "Or hot chocolate. Anything with heat."

I don't mean to but I think about Sonny's dog breath, coming out

171

in hot little clouds when he's winded. I used to call him Purina breath when he did that. I'm about to ask Dan what this is all about when I feel it—a warm sensation starting at the top of my scalp and oozing down my neck and face, then working its way down my shoulders like a deep massage. Dan is grinning his gap-toothed grin when I hear a pop. Then a hiss, like the initial blast of a tire gauge.

His expression sags, but the twinkle remains in his eyes. Whatever the heck that thing was, it worked. He tucks his helmet under his arm and wanders off, muttering calculations in some unknown tongue. I'm about to ask Geri if she fell in when I hear her cough. It sounds like it's coming from my room.

That's where I find her, studying my handiwork. A half-dozen recent paintings in various stages of completion are propped along the walls.

"These are good, Russell."

"You sound surprised."

"Don't be a doofus. You were always good, but I mean ... wow."

"Thanks."

"This piece is beautiful. And, well, so *normal*."

"It's for a friend," I say.

"Lucky friend," Geri says with real admiration. "She's pretty. And this one too; it's a bit creepy but I can't stop looking at it."

I stand behind her and try to see the painting through her eyes. It's a world within a world. The outer world is borderless, lush, and vibrant, Eden bordering on Pollyanna. But the action takes place in the inner world—an egg-shaped globe, drab and translucent. The man inside is shackled and straitjacketed, his face pressed against the inner wall.

"It's called *Fault Lines*. It scares me too, not because of the content, but because it feels important. I'm afraid that it's the best I'll ever be able to do. I'm afraid to finish it."

"The guy in the bubble is so real, frighteningly so. And he looks familiar."

I don't say anything, just stand there with restless hands, blushing.

"But as great as it is, I can tell you're not done with it. All the passion is inside the bubble. The stuff outside seems stilted, not as much fire or conviction. It's … too safe."

Although I'm self-conscious, it makes me feel important to let her stand there and stare at my work. The intimacy is unnerving, but sadly one-sided. It seems lost on Geri. Then the phone rings in the kitchen and ruins the moment. Geri and I walk down the hall, discussing the final details of my presentation.

Then Dan pops his head into view and says, "That was for you, Russell. Some girl."

"You didn't get her name?"

"Something-Uh."

Geri picks up another slice of pizza and gnaws it loudly.

"That's it?" I say.

"You know, like Melind-*uh* or Sandr-*uh* or Meliss-*uh*."

Well that narrows it right down. "What did she want?"

"The billion-dollar question." Dan is proud of his little joke. "What does any woman ever *really* want?"

At that, Geri tosses a slab of crust at Dan. It ricochets off his down vest and lands at his feet. Without ceremony, he picks it up, holds it to his cheek, and mouths the word *warm*.

Friday

I'm using overdue bills to construct a rickety tower on the kitchen table when Geri calls to remind me of some last minute details for this morning's big presentation for the bigwigs at TB&S. She sounds nervous, which makes me nervous — enough to consider going decaf this morning to quell the jitters. She wishes me luck then adds, "Oh, and if anyone asks you about the construction part of your bid, just roll with it."

"Construction?"

"Don't sweat it, Russell. I'm sure it won't even come up. Knock 'em dead and I'll talk to you this afternoon."

"This afternoon?"

"Yeah, afraid I need to take a personal day."

"Oh."

"Relax. You don't need me there. You're gonna do great."

I wish I could believe her. I hang up and pour myself a bowl of cereal. But the apprehension ballooning in my chest makes it hard to swallow.

Dan's slippers smack the hardwood as he pads out of his bedroom, all skinny white legs, pink sleeping scars, and bad breath. His bathrobe swishes as he straddles one of our mismatched kitchen chairs, stares at a spot behind my left ear, and sings a tune that I recognize but can't quite place. The lyrics could be the Lord's Prayer or maybe one of those oft-ignored flight attendant spiels, I don't know. But his choice of language confirms the obvious — today is Friday. (Dan assigns a different language to each day of the week — Japanese on Mondays, Latin on Tuesdays, and so on. Yesterday we nearly came to blows when I reminded him that British is an accent, not an official language.) As I shovel a spoonful of Cocoa Pebbles into my mouth, I'm vaguely aware of Dan scratching his inner thigh and his chalky eyes boring into the top of my head. When I finally slurp down the last soggy bite, he motions toward my empty bowl and says, "You mind?"

"You do realize that the cabinets are full of clean bowls?"

"I want that one."

"Whatever." I slide it toward him, upsetting my tower of bills. Small puddles of soiled milk slosh and glisten in the coved inner rim of the bowl. Dan fills it to overflowing then extends his opened palm toward me.

"Give me your spoon."

"No. No way, man. That's disgusting."

"Come on, give it to me."

"Get your own."

"But you already warmed it up."

Arguing with Dan is pointless so I seize the opportunity to deal. "I'll give you my spoon if you promise to stop microwaving your shoes."

"I've got poor circulation." As proof he places a big blue-veined foot on the table. "Go ahead, feel it. It's practically frozen."

Mulched chocolatey flakes percolate in my esophagus. Still, I have to admit that his foot does look cold. I double my resolve. "Forget it man, get your own—"

His hand springs forward and snatches the spoon like a toad plucking a fly from the air with his tongue. I'm about to unload a week's worth of pent up frustration — including my long-held suspicions that Dan has somehow calibrated his bowels to exploit the residual heat of my own trips to the throne — when the phone rings.

It's my mother. We haven't spoken since my father tossed me out. She sounds lonely so I suggest we have a late lunch.

Dan continues singing under his breath, pausing occasionally to release quiet burps and punch himself in the chest. After a particularly hard swallow, he says, "I've got some ideas about Sonny and what might have happened. If we're going to solve this little mystery we'll need to sit and brainstorm a bit."

"I know. You're right. But I've got to finish cramming for this presentation. How about later tonight?"

"Sure, works for me. Maybe Geri can come over and we can order another pizza."

I'm halfway down the hall when I recognize Dan's refrain — the Beatles' *Today Is Your Birthday*, sung in fluent Hebrew.

I silently retrace my steps and peer around the wall at Dan.

He looks up and winks at me.

* * *

Traffic is like a hearty broth this morning, thick and chunky. The rain has tapered off, making the air smell like earthworms. By the time I find a parking space and slog through a minefield of puddles, I'm eight minutes behind schedule and my pant legs are soggy. However, since my goal was to show up thirty minutes early, that leaves twenty-two minutes to get my act together. But when I factor in the reality that Geri's not here to help, it feels like I'm an hour late already.

The conference room is empty when I arrive. I take several deep, calming breaths and begin attaching cables to the corresponding ports in my laptop. Relief washes over me when I flip on the projector and the title page of my presentation flashes onto the screen. I click through a few panels to make sure the remote is working, then decide to reward myself with a trip to the urinal. For some reason, when I'm nervous, all the moisture leaves my mouth, gathers in my bladder, and expands.

I check the wall clock. I've got ten minutes to prepare my mind and body. There's a nagging feeling that I'm missing something. Something obvious and important. I chalk it up to nerves and rehearse my opening remarks as I make my way to and from the men's room. While washing up, the lights flicker and I hear the mechanical chirping of a dozen surge protectors.

I return with two minutes to spare, surprisingly confident. Until I look at the opening slide of my PowerPoint presentation glowing on the wall.

It's in Spanish.

I rush to my computer, ready to stab the required buttons to change it back to English. But of course I have no idea which buttons to push or how it got converted in the first place. I check the wall clock again; the partners are now three minutes late.

I tab through all the menus, looking for anything with the words "language" or "Spanish" or "English" in it. Nothing. I try all the function keys — twice, then again. Still nothing. My heart is pounding in my ears along with the second hand on the clock.

I hear footsteps but don't turn around. A shadow passes over my computer screen. I nearly cry out when I hear the voice behind me.

"Good morning, Mr. Fink." It's a female, one of several paralegals named Jenny. "Just wanted to let you know the partners are running a little late. Is there anything I can get for you?"

"No. Thank you. I mean, wait. Do you know how to work this thing?"

"Hmm, I'll bet the power surge got you." She looks over my shoulder, taps a few keys, then screws up her face. "Nope, sorry. But my hubby is an IT guy and says that almost any problem can be solved with a reboot."

"Thanks, I'll try that."

I power down, convinced now that this is somehow Barbie's fault. She sabotaged me. It takes forever for my computer to shut down, then another infinity or two for it to start up again. I decide that if this doesn't work, I'll just pack up my stuff and sneak out before the partners show up — if they ever decide to show up. Then I finally hear the digitized piano arpeggio that tells me my computer is finally ready.

Tyler, Billingham, and Sneed file into the conference room as I click to open PowerPoint. They mumble half-hearted greetings that make me think they can't remember my name. I don't realize that I've stopped breathing until my presentation pops up in glorious, red-white-and-blue American English. I can almost smell the apple pie.

"Good morning," I say in a gush of pent up air. "First, I want to thank you for taking the time to meet with me this morning. I know you're all busy and I —"

Tyler butts in. "Enough chitchat, son. Around here small talk and long-winded introductions are billable hours." As the comedian in the group, he pauses to gauge our reaction. "So let's go, chop-chop."

"Let's get started then." I dim the lights and feel better already. With all eyes forward and the room dark, my confidence climbs out of its hole and begins flexing its muscles.

The first two slides remind the lawyers of Hengle Supply's storied history and the long relationship between their company and mine. A half-dozen slides later, I find my groove. My voice is strong, my mind clear, and I'm able to deviate from my script with a few humorous asides. Even I'm impressed by the way I manage to humanize tired phrases like "value added," "multitasking," and "interdepartmental synergies." My tricolored pie chart is the hippest, mind-blowingest graphic in the history of corporate America. I'm considering a song-and-dance number finale when Sneed pipes up.

"Didn't we just see all this rot yesterday?"

Rot? My confidence just took a shot in the groin. "No sir. That wasn't me. That was Barbie."

"Ah yes, Baaarrrbbbiie," Billingham whispers. I'm sure it would sound harmless and dreamy with the lights on.

I click over to the next slide, trying to ignore the interruption. But it's no use; I'm rattled now. The voices — mine included — become a blur.

Sneed: "Seriously, Russell, if I have to listen to you read another one of these inane panels, I'm going to slip into a coma."

Tyler: "Not so fast, Sneed. Let's update your living will first. Russell here can be your witness. Billingham can have your boat. But I get to flip the switch!"

My finger slips and the next slide pops up. I begin reading.

Sneed: "Come on, man. We're lawyers. We can read for ourselves ..."

Tyler: "Speak for yourself."

Sneed: " ... Just tell us the difference between your proposal and, um, you know, what's her name's ..."

Billingham: "Baarrbbbie ..." He rolls the R this time. Sounds like he's been recently beaten with a love stick.

Me: "Well, let me skip ahead a few frames." I click forward fast enough to give us all vertigo.

Sneed: "No, no, no. Bottom-line it for us, son. I can't sit through another one of these."

Tyler: "Rhoids flaring up again?"

Sneed: "Shut up, Tyler. No one thinks you're funny but you."

Tyler: "I don't know. Barbie seemed to think so."

Billingham: "Barrr —"

I flip on the lights. They all look up at me, blinking as their pupils adjust. Sneed is standing now, looking more tired than perturbed. "Just spit it out already. Why do we need to buy from you, Russell? What do we get from your company that we don't get from *Barrrbbie*?"

His mocking tone cracks Tyler up. Even Billingham has to smile.

Desperate now, I clear my throat and say, "Well, sir, you get me."

Sneed: "*You*? What's that supposed to mean?"

"It means if you place your order with Hengle's Supply, I'll be here every Monday and Friday to check things out, to answer questions, even train new people if you need me to."

This garners a few grunts and thoughtful nods.

"If you think it'll help, I'll see if I can scrounge up a few pictures of Baaarrrbbbiie." At least Tyler thinks it's funny. Billingham actually looks hopeful. "I'll make sure that everyone in the building has my cell number. I'll be available 24/7."

The partners glance around at each other for a few tense moments. Then they're all talking at once. They pause once, Sneed asking if I'm sure my company can handle the remodeling portion of the project. I remember Geri's words, then nod enthusiastically. The conversation subsides and I see Billingham's shoulders slump, which I take as a very good omen.

Finally, Tyler looks at me and says, "Thanks for coming in, Russell. We'll let you know something by the end of the day."

* * *

It was Mom's idea to meet here for lunch, although I'm not a fan of curbside dining. It's a quaint café that specializes in gourmet chicken-and-dumplings and key lime pie so decadent it's worthy of an eleventh commandment. The typical clientele boasts lots of record producers and country singers I can never recognize. When I see my mother, I notice that her usual gray pallor has given way to a healthier, more ruddy complexion and I think she's added a few needed pounds. But I can tell she's been crying. Her silver flask, littered with ghostly finger-prints, sits in front of her like a small graven image. I scan the nearby tables to see who else might be staring at it. Next to the flask there's a small red bow lying on its head, glue side up. Makes me wonder where my birthday present is hiding.

The year Katie died, we skipped my birthday altogether. That was my idea. But it didn't keep the mailman from delivering colorful birthday cards. My father agreed to double Peter's allowance during those weeks as long as he intercepted the bright, oversized envelopes before they reached Mom. It took me three years to figure out Peter was replacing the crisp tens and twenties with crumpled one-dollar bills before they got to me.

There's no simple way to pay homage to the birth of one twin without dredging up the painful memories of the other. Since then we've made an event out of not celebrating the day I was born. The plan is to somehow pull off a birthday party without mentioning it aloud. I think it's silly, but have no choice but to play along. And why not? It usually ends with a sappy non-birthday card with a sizable check.

To further complicate matters, Katie and I don't actually share the same birthday. She was born at three minutes till midnight on March 31. I was born seven minutes later, in April, on the day reserved for fools.

My random non-birthday parties were a much bigger deal to every-one but me. I missed Katie every day like it was our birthday. Still do.

Mom picks up the flask and turns it over in her hand. Her dis-torted reflection shifts like a funhouse mirror. I want to say something, to do something. But it's nearly impossible to comfort the grieving when you're forbidden to mention the source.

"Maybe you should think about getting some help."

She sniffs proudly, if that's possible. "You mean like therapy?"

"There's no shame in it."

"This has provided all the therapy I need." She picks up the flask and shakes it. The contents make a thin, sloshing sound. "Or maybe it's all I deserve."

I lean my elbows on the table and hold both her hands in mine. She glances up, blinks a silent thank you, then stares at a faded stain on the tablecloth.

She squeezes my hand and says, "Going to see a shrink is just trading in one crutch for another. And I happen to be pretty fond of this one ... if it's all the same to the men in my life."

I've seen her like this before, but never so severe. There's more to it than birthday-induced heartache.

"What's wrong, Mom? You can't be this sad over Sonny."

"Well of course I'm sorry about Sonny. We're kindred spirits, after all." She winks, then mimes an imaginary toast in his honor while my blood turns to Freon. I drop my fork into my water glass and make a sound like I've been punched in the stomach. "Don't look so mortified, honey. So you slipped your dog a Mickey every now and then. Harmless, really. And I should know."

"I don't know, Mom. I had it checked out. There were traces of alcohol in Sonny's system."

"You did not kill Sonny, if that's what you're thinking." She bites her lip, then wipes her mouth with a napkin for no apparent reason. "Perish the thought, Russell. Just put it out of your mind, right here, right now. Do you hear me?"

I want to ask how she can be so sure, but that would just invite more sadness. And she should know — she was forced to drop out of veterinary school one semester prior to graduating back when she was newly married. Dad's ministry was taking off and he had serious reservations about the minister's wife being a career woman. When she got pregnant with Peter and quit school, Dad got what he wanted.

183

Sometime between Peter's birth and Katie's death, Mom began her surrogate vocation as a closet drunk.

"What's wrong, then?" I say.

She doesn't want to answer, probably so she won't have to lie. But her reprieve appears in the form of our waiter. We order the dumplings, garden salads, and sweet iced tea. Then she catches me up on all the latest gossip. My father's sister finished her screenplay last week, then her husband of eighteen years congratulated her by announcing he was going sailing — alone, and he wasn't coming back. My cousin, Michael, is flying home from Afghanistan this month after suffering a bullet wound to his left foot, possibly self-inflicted. And it appears that my mother's youngest cousin is still bent on dropping out of school to devote herself to becoming the next American Idol.

When she pauses to refold her napkin in her lap, I ask again.

"It's nothing new. It's been going on for years. The nature of your father's business."

"What's been going on for years?"

"Threats. Warnings. Prophecies of doom. So far they've just been by mail. But they're phone calls now too, and they just happen to be about *Second Chances*." She takes a moment to line up her fork and knife like little soldiers. "He's doing fine by the way."

"Meaning?"

"Meaning your father is overdosing on positive thinking books and tapes because he's confused and afraid but he'll never admit it."

"Confused? Afraid? Of what?"

"Everything." The waiter delivers our salads and drinks. Mother mashes a lemon wedge, then licks her fingers, somehow making it look classy. "This may be hard for you to believe, but despite all of your father's posturing and useless platitudes, he's a scared little boy. He second-guesses every decision he's ever made. He's convinced that

184

everything bad that ever happened is his fault. And he feels rotten about the way he left things with you."

"I wish I could say I felt sorry for him."

"He had no idea about Sonny. You're going to hate this, but you need to hear it. The reason you two butt heads all the time is because you're exactly alike."

"Ouch."

"It's not as bad as it sounds, Russell. I did marry the man, after all."

I want to make snide comments about my father's powers of persuasion. I mean, how many thousands of people has he duped into cashing in their savings to support one of his ministries? Or convinced that they've been healed of some phantom disease? To keep from saying anything mean or unnecessarily hurtful, I stuff my mouth with crisp salad.

Our silence is punctuated by the echoey double thud of a car driving over a manhole cover. After a while I feel like everyone around us can hear me chewing. When I catch Mom casting longing looks at the flask, I ask the first thing that comes to mind. "Why didn't you ever mention it before? The threats?"

"What good would it do? It would have given you nightmares as a kid, fueled your sick sense of humor as a teenager, and just make you worry as an adult. Besides, they're harmless. Nothing ever comes of it."

She stirs sugar into her tea and studies the soft eddy as if enchanted by the tiny waves. When she looks up, she's squinting at me. "So guess who dropped by the house to see me this morning?"

I shrug and push slimy bits of carrot and cabbage around my plate as a mutinous breeze tries to blow my napkin out of my lap.

"Alyssa." Mom pauses to gauge my reaction. "She came by for coffee. Wanted to enlist my help to talk some sense into you."

"Did she also tell you that she destroyed the engagement ring?"

"She said she was sorry." Mom nods and forks the last bit of lettuce, dressing, and bacon bits into her mouth. After a hard swallow she continues, "And that she was going to try and leave you alone, to get over you and move on with her life."

"She did?"

"Yeah, but I didn't buy it. Felt like a bad audition for a daytime soap. Want to know what I think?"

"Does it matter?"

"I think she'll hound you until things end on her terms. You want to know what else I think?" After a theatrical pause, she adds, "I think you're in love with someone else."

I find the hubcaps on a nearby parked car to be the most fascinating hubcaps I've ever seen. Mom says, "I knew it." A couple passing by on the sidewalk pause and stare. Mother looks right at them, points at me, and says to them, "I knew it."

I'm so happy with our waiter's timing that I could kiss his scuffed up Birkenstocks. He sets our entrees down and I engage him in all sorts of meaningless conversation about his favorite desserts, extra napkins, and if he can actually taste the difference between Dr. Pepper and Mr. Pibb. I stop short of asking him if we knew each other in college, despite our obvious age difference. He extricates himself with a lame excuse about other customers. Before my mother can steer the conversation back to my love life, I say, "So anyway, when's the last time you got one of those threatening phone calls?"

She swallows, then works her tongue to dislodge a scrap of chicken from her teeth. For the briefest moment, I think my subject-changing ploy might have worked.

"Alyssa's convinced that you're interested in one of Dr. Kozinski's nurses. But I don't think so."

" ... because I've been thinking. Maybe you should hire Peter's new friend, that obnoxious private investigator, to find out who's harassing you ..."

"So the only other girl I can think of is your friend from college. What was her name? Sherry? Terry?" I shovel food with renewed vigor and try like mad to keep my cheeks from filling with color. Then Mom snaps her fingers. "That's it. Geri, right?"

"Yes — I mean no. Yes, I did have a friend in college named Geri. In fact she works for one of my biggest customers. But I'm not — "

"I knew it," she says triumphantly.

"Would you cut it out? That's crazy. I mean, we've been spending some time together lately. But it's all work related."

"Right, sure, whatever. I remember now. I'd never seen you so smitten before. 'Geri did this. Geri said that. Geri helped me with my calculus. Geri hung the moon.' Nothing but Geri, Geri, Geri."

"Are you done?"

"Then she got engaged to someone else and you started moping around again, just like you did when Katie died."

I'm suddenly tired, jetlagged without the benefit of air travel. Mom can see it in my eyes.

"You don't have to say anything, Russell. But I'm happy for you. An answer to prayer, actually." She wipes both corners of her mouth with her napkin. "Also know that I'm going to need to meet this Geri face-to-face. This girl who has so enamored my son and turned his heart to goo. She still needs my stamp of approval, you know."

It's a freaky thing, having your mother point out something so earth-shatteringly obvious, so painfully simple, and yet so startling.

But it's true. I love Geri. I think maybe I always have.

It's not just because she's adorable. Or funny and talented and not afraid to speak her mind.

It's simply this. When I'm with Geri, the chatter in my head stops. Worry and regret meet in the middle of the ring and shake hands.

187

Then they bunk down with the lion and the lamb for an afternoon nap. And when Geri's not around, most of the mind-chatter in my head is all about her anyway.

Our waiter sloughs back into view and Mom orders coffee and two slices of key lime pie. Then she hands me a stack of envelopes rubber banded together. The first one is from her, a sweet birthday wish that makes her eyes water and gives me the hiccups. She did a lousy job forging my father's signature. I pretend not to notice. Instead I make my way around the table and give her a long hug.

I do a quick scan of the other envelopes. Two in particular are of note. One is from State Farm with ominous red letters; no need to even open it. The sight of another envelope makes my heart stutter, and one palpitation sparks the next until an angry cadence is pounding in my chest. It's an official-looking envelope from Dr. Kozinski's office. Inside, there's either a clean bill of health or an expiration date. I shuffle it to the bottom of the stack before my impending sense of doom manifests itself on my face.

I ask my mother about her work, sit back, and listen to her rant about her sister.

The dessert and coffee arrives. My first bite is ruined by the belching exhaust of a passing city bus. Mother raises her mug toward me and says, "Congratulations, son."

We clink our cups together. Hot coffee sloshes over the rim and scalds my thumb. "Thanks, Mom. It's just a birthday."

"I wasn't talking about that."

While I cram giant bites of pie into my mouth, my mother sits back and grins at my futile attempts to not grin back. I never knew love could be so embarrassing. I down the last sip of coffee and swipe the napkin across my face one final time. That's when I notice her expression falter. Whatever it is makes her look ten years older.

She stands too quickly, bumping her thighs on the table. The clattering dishes cause several heads to turn. She makes a clumsy attempt to reattach the red ribbon to the top of the flask, then slides it across the table to me. Her words are muddled, but I get the gist of it.

"Happy birthday, Russell."

I marvel at the receding image of my mother on the sidewalk. She just performed the two most courageous acts of her adult life and I didn't get a chance to thank her. Another breeze blows the bow off the flask, off the table, and down the sidewalk like the merriest of tumbleweeds. I stand and slip the flask into one hip pocket.

* * *

I don't claim to share any of Sonny's clairvoyant tendencies. But several blocks from Dan's house I have the sensation I'm being followed. My first clue is the incessant honking. Then my ears pick up on the sound of the BMW's congested muffler and my rearview is a blue streak of swerving metal. It's not clear from her reflection if Alyssa is overjoyed about something or homicidal.

I pull to the curb outside Dan's house, unbuckle my seatbelt, and kill the engine. The noisy Beemer careens around the block and rockets toward me. Something tells me to stay put — a wise move since Alyssa misses clipping my side view mirror by mere inches. She executes a sloppy three-point turn and parks twenty feet behind me, but makes no move to get out. Since she routinely inflates the importance of holidays and special occasions, I suspect she's here for my birthday. My mind conjures images of ripping the bow off a smashed iPod or a pair of shredded jeans. Or maybe she's whipped up a batch of Ex-Lax brownies.

I hear her engine whine. Her muffler sputters its way through a series of impotent backfires. I check the rearview in time to see the chassis buckle and hear the tires squeal. I grip the wheel and clench my eyes, waiting ...

The impact whips me around like a crash test dummy. My broken front bumper thumps off the seat behind me. Alyssa backs up. I watch her miniature version in my rearview. She's squinting through her windshield, no doubt inspecting her work. I hear the bucking Beemer whinny again. I scramble to get my seatbelt back on and brace myself for the next blow.

The impact is more vicious the second time. And it feels like our cars have locked horns. It takes Alyssa three tries to dislodge her bumper from the mess she's made of my rear end. I get out to inspect the damage as she speeds off, her hood bobbing up and down like a demented ventriloquist's dummy. The back bumper is splayed at a ninety-degree angle, hanging on by a threadbare layer of fiberglass. It jiggles in my hand like a giant loose tooth. I'm considering the creative use of duct tape when my cell phone chirps to life on my belt, signaling a new text message:

HAPPY BIRTHDAY, BUTTHEAD!

I hear a creaking sound, followed by a soft pop, and I feel the full weight of the rear bumper in my hands. I toss it in the back seat with the front bumper and wipe my hands on my pants.

Dan is doing yoga, emitting strange whimpers and groans, when I stalk through the living room. Part of me wants to report my ex-fiancée to the cops. But Officer Peebles would probably answer, find a way to take Alyssa's side, and then I'd end up spending the night in the drunk tank. I'm afraid I've become his white whale. Another part of me churns out rationalizations, that maybe this is Alyssa's deranged way of accepting the terms of our breakup. Since she insists on always having the last word, this must be her exclamation point. I try to tell myself that a smashed car is a small price to pay.

Maybe there's some miniscule chance I remembered to write the check to my insurance company.

I finally look up my State Farm agent's number. We endure each other's small talk for couple of minutes before I announce I'd like to file a claim. When I can't produce my policy number, she cheerily volunteers to look me up on the computer. Her first thoughtful pause alerts me to trouble. After much typing and troubled self-talk she says, "Russell, I hate to tell you this, but your policy's been canceled." When I don't respond, she says, "According to my computer, it looks like we sent a half-dozen past due notices."

"Any chance of finding some wiggle room? Maybe a loophole?"

"I'm sorry, Russell. Really. But if you want, we can renew your policy over the phone in a jiffy."

"Thanks. I'll get back to you."

One of two things happens when I'm angry. Either I seethe and break things until I slip into a miserable, self-loathing funk. Or my muse comes out of hibernation and takes my body and soul hostage. The ransom is typically a nasty headache and a finished painting or two.

At some point my imagination bypasses my limbs altogether, controlling the brush like a divining rod. I can see some strokes before they happen, but most are a series of small surprises. Occasionally my body and brain impose their will on my creative bubble, but my muse beats them back into submission.

An hour later I regain enough consciousness to realize that I've stripped down to an undershirt and my painting pants. I'm staring at the beginnings of a new version of *Fault Lines*. The man in the bubble looks a lot like me, his expression teetering between rage and rapture. Most shocking to me is the appearance of a new character, a child clinging fiercely to the man from behind, her face hidden from view. I can't be sure however if he's dragging her away from danger. Or into it.

Dan clears his throat. He's standing in the doorway, the look in his eyes eerily similar to the man in the painting.

"You okay?" he says.

"I think so."

"You were groaning."

He's right, I realize, and am instantly embarrassed. "So were you when I came in."

Dan points a half-eaten orange (the oven mitt confirms he's micro-waved it) at the canvas in front of me. "That's exquisite. Looks just like a manic version of you. Like the day you brought Sonny in to Heavenly Pastures."

I nod, not sure how to respond. Or if I even should.

"Guess you didn't hear the phone, but Geri called for you. She's on her way over."

I swivel my head toward Dan and blink.

"Dinner is at seven and she's buying."

"She said that?"

"Sounds like she's got a big celebration planned."

What's left of my slight humiliation dissolves in an instant. Geri knows my peculiar history with birthdays so I can't imagine she'd try a surprise party. So it must be the big copier order. I grin at Dan and he grins back. I have a sudden urge to hug him. But I fear my enthusiasm would create a heat wave and he wouldn't let go of me.

"Can I go?" Dan says while I search for my favorite blue T-shirt and the cargo pants Geri made for me.

"Sure," I say, eager to dismiss him. "I need to get changed anyway."

"No, I mean, can I go with you and Geri? You know, out to dinner with you guys?"

The pathetic look on his face is almost enough to make me recon-sider. But I'm more concerned with a sensation welling up inside me. It feels like a long-buried craving, something rooted in affection, watered with jealousy, and fortified with selfishness. I'm stunned by its power and simplicity. I want to be with Geri. And I don't want to share her with anyone.

"I don't think so, Dan." I climb into my clothes so I don't have to look at him. "Not this time. Geri and I have some business to discuss."

"That's okay. I'll bring a book or something to read so I won't be tempted to butt in much."

"You know how easily distracted she gets." The puzzled look on Dan's face reminds me that he knows Geri much better than I do. Eventually his confusion lapses into resignation and it's clear I've hurt his feelings.

"You kids have fun."

I'm about to reconsider when I hear a door slam outside. I peer through the window and see Geri bounding up the sidewalk and a yellow cab speeding off. I intercept her at the door before she gets any ideas about inviting Dan. I take her elbow and gently usher her toward my battered Taurus.

"Where's Dan?" she says. "On the phone he said he might join us."

"Oh, well, we talked about it. But I guess he made other plans." Now I feel like a complete heel. But before I can confess my deceit, Geri notices the front and back ends of my Taurus.

"Yikes! What happened to your car? A matching set."

"Ex-fiancée abuse."

"Guess she's still not crazy about the 'ex' part, huh?"

"Maybe a little too crazy," I say, opening the door for her.

Once inside, I turn the key and listen to the metallic wheezing of an engine that has no intention of turning over.

"Bummer," Geri says. "Guess we'll either have to cab it or take Dan's car."

"Dan has a car? I thought he traveled exclusively by limousine."

She turns and grins at me, "Oh yeah. Dan definitely has a car."

Ten minutes later, the three of us are lined up in the front seat of a brilliantly pink, 1991 Cadillac Seville. Evidently Dan keeps it locked away in a shed behind Heavenly Pastures. He's at the helm with Geri nestled between us, straddling the hump (the backseat is filled with dilapidated electronic gear and failed inventions). Like Pavlov's dog, I get excited whenever Dan engages the left blinker, anticipating the press of Geri's form against mine. En route to dinner, he regales with the story of how he tracked the ex-husband of Tennessee's top Mary Kay saleswoman with his handheld GPS system. He was running off to Europe with his favorite Hooters waitress, who happened to be the runaway daughter of a state senator. Dan tracked them to a nudist beach in Italy, whereupon the disgruntled Mary Kay lady delivered her divorce decree in person. The settlement made her day job unnecessary. She was so grateful to Dan that she gave him her car. He drove it until the heater gave out.

"You're in for a real treat, Dan." Geri's animated gestures coincide with a hard left turn and she practically falls into my lap. Her shampoo is fruity and wonderful. "Every time we end up in public, one of Russell's jilted lovers shows up and does something dreadful. Won't be long before he has his own reality TV show."

I want to remind her that, technically speaking, Alyssa is my *only* former girlfriend. And that I haven't spoken to Cassandra since she flooded my lap with latte. But explaining myself seems more pathetic than just keeping quiet.

"Here we are." Dan enters the parking lot of an exotic Asian steakhouse with a name I can't pronounce and a menu I can't afford.

Geri says, "Put your eyes back in your head, Russell. It's my treat tonight."

"You don't have to do that."

"It's your birthday."

She remembered. So much for thinking I've landed my career-saving order.

We skip appetizers and order enormous slabs of sizzling protein smothered in spicy vegetables. Before we eat, Dan bows his big head and ceremoniously makes praying hands. Geri asks me to pray and then closes her eyes as well, leaving me alone in my throat-clenching panic, my head filling with white noise and my tongue turning into a listless blob. I stutter through the beginning of a memorized rhyming prayer that Gramps used to say, but after one sentence, my mind splits down the middle. One side tries in vain to remember Gramps's prayerful punch line, while the other side cowers, certain that God and everybody else are listening in and trying not to laugh. Geri's hand grips mine, no doubt offering support. But I'm too far gone. The ensuing silence is worse than my crippled voice — almost. I open my mouth again, with the singular objective of setting my vocal cords into motion. But the sound comes from Dan's side of the table. He's singing the Doxology in either Greek or Hebrew. Or maybe Swahili. Whatever it is, it's the most beautifully disconcerting tune I've ever heard. Afterward, I chime in with a hearty amen and begin gulping ice water.

Dan says, "That was moving, Russell." My brain fires a sarcastic remark toward the tip of my tongue. But one look at Dan and it's obvious he's not joking. Somehow he mistook my choking silence for raw emotion. He pats me on the forearm. "Just beautiful."

The waiter arrives with our food and we all watch as Dan removes an aluminum contraption with foldout legs from his breast pocket. He points his PDA gizmo at it, which elicits a soft green light and a low hum.

"Dare I ask?" Geri says.

Dan opens his mouth, but I jump in. "Let me guess. Somehow that thing captures the heat coming off your platter and recycles it to keep your food hot longer?"

"Close," Dan says mid-chew. He wipes his mouth with his sleeve and says, "It's not about prolonging the highest possible temperature so much as maintaining a consistent internal food temperature of one-hundred and seventy-two degrees. That's my ideal temperature, you know."

"I had no idea," I say.

Geri squeezes a lemon directly into her mouth. "I thought it was one-sixty-nine."

"Can you believe it? My actual resting body temperature dropped another quarter degree. So I had to dial this baby up another notch or two."

Since Dan scarfs his food the quickest, he takes over the conversation. Geri and I struggle to finish our meals, and he tells us all about his recent trip to NASA. According to Dan, his girlfriend is the first alternate for the next space mission. His cheeks flush with color and he can't stop grinning as he talks about it.

"If just one of the primary crew members contracts the flu or breaks a bone or turns up pregnant, Trish will get to realize her dream of hurtling through the black and starry void." Dan swallows hard, wipes his mouth, and announces, "I'm thinking about popping the question."

"Wait a second," Geri says. "*The* question? The one that starts with 'Will you' and ends with 'Marry me'?"

Dan nods like a child, beaming. If giddiness were a drug, we'd be headed to the emergency room to have Dan's stomach pumped. He takes a greedy sip of hot tea that ends up dribbling down his chin.

"It's got to be special. Have you thought of a unique way to ask her?"

He does the childish, pink-faced nod again.

I give Geri a playful elbow in the ribs, which makes her wince and me feel bad. "Wow, I never pictured you as Cupid before."

"Oh, the things I could teach you about love."

I grin at Geri and she grins back. I have a sudden urge to lean over and kiss her. But I'm sure she'd just punch me.

"Well then," I say. "Whenever you're ready, *sensei*, tell me where to sign up. I could use some love lessons — obviously."

For the briefest moment, the air between us is charged. My nerve endings fire off conflicting signals, all spastic and haywire, like when you're tipping a chair back on two legs and almost fall.

"I don't know, Russell." She wiggles her fingers like a cartoon wizard. "These charms are not to be taken lightly. And I'm not sure I approve of your little nurse friend anyway. In fact, I'd say your problem is not the capacity to love well. You just need a better screening policy."

Before I can set her straight, a line of servers emerges from the kitchen with a candlelit cake and a chorus of creaky voices. They're singing a goofy version of "Happy Birthday" and looking at me. I close my eyes and make my wish.

I wish for Geri to wish what I'm wishing. I open my eyes to check, but she and Dan seem to be sharing some joke at my expense.

We eat our cake and drink our coffee. I tell them about my lunch with my mother, and about the threatening letters and phone calls.

"That sounds scary," Geri says.

"I don't know. She claims it's the nature of Dad's business." I point to Dan's heater gadget. "Don't suppose you have one of those for catching prank callers?"

Dan rubs his chin, lost in thought.

Just when I'm about to declare it the perfect evening, Geri removes a small wrapped package from her purse. It appears to be leftover Valentine's Day paper decorated with pictures of The Wiggles. I rip into it and remove a handwritten note. It says:

Congratulations, Russell Fink. The TB&S order is all yours. Happy Birthday!

(PS: Hope you didn't have any plans this weekend ...)

I'm too stunned to think. I jump up, yank Geri to her feet, and hug her like crazy. People look at us like we just got engaged. One couple even applauds. The hug is pure bliss until I feel Dan's cool, spindly arms wrapping around me. Geri and I separate just enough to allow him into our circle until we're a jumping, cheering little clump of humanity.

When the waiter runs off with Geri's credit card, Dan adds yet another layer of surprise. He too removes a small wrapped package and slides it toward me. His is wrapped in comic strips from the Sunday paper. I try to muster the same enthusiasm as I tear into Dan's gift, but it's tough after Geri's news. Inside are a few folded sheets of paper. I'm not sure exactly what I'm looking at when I get them all unfolded and spread out on the table. They appear to be unpaid invoices from various utility companies.

"I'm afraid I don't get it, Dan."

He claps me on the back and says, "Your share of the rent, Roomie."

Saturday

The number of cars in the parking garage on a Saturday morning surprises me. Makes me wonder whose work ethic is more out of whack—the single guy who resents the least infringement on his weekend (me) or the hard-charging type-A with two-point-four kids he'll never really get to know (any number of luxury SUV drivers with their name stenciled on their parking spot).

Geri is loading tools onto the freight elevator with a hand truck when Dan and I arrive. She's wearing a denim work shirt quilted together with remnants of South American flags. Beads of sweat bubble up along her hairline. To prove that chivalry is not quite dead yet, I trot over and wrench the two-wheeler from her hands. Sweaty or not, she still smells terrific, like warm cinnamon rolls on a bed of honeysuckle.

"Better save your energy, tough guy." Geri swipes her forearm across her brow, then points to piles of lumber and drywall strapped to pallets with metal bands. "I'm supervising. You and Dan will be doing most of the heavy lifting." She's referring to the part of the TB&S proposal she snuck in without asking me—the complete redesign of the firm's conference room, complete with all new furniture and an entire wall of audio/video equipment. Geri drew up the plans, picked out the colors, and hired herself as the general contractor. Barbie never had a chance.

"I know. Dan keeps reminding me between sips of his hot chocolate." As if on cue, he takes a loud slurp. I motion toward the half-full elevator and say, "Where'd all these power tools come from?"

"They're mine." Geri gets a kick out of the surprised look on my face.

The inside of the elevator smells like axle grease and old carpet. We take it up to the sixth floor where Geri unlocks the office while Dan and I take turns wheeling tools into the conference room. Afterward, she sends us back down to the garage for the really heavy stuff. Ten minutes on the job and Geri has established herself as foreman.

Although I'm indebted to Dan for his willingness to help, I have to admit I'm not exactly looking forward to lugging slabs of drywall and lumber with a gangly giant who suffers from insatiable hypothermia. I keep worrying that he'll drop his end of the load to blow warm air on his hands. But he's surprisingly strong. It takes an hour to stage all the tools and raw materials, and after our final load, Dan and I collapse onto the carpet and watch Geri attack a sheet of drywall. She measures twice, then plucks the pencil from between her teeth and marks her first cut. Satisfied, she wields a scary looking snaggletoothed dagger and voraciously saws through her fresh pencil markings. Her tongue pokes out from the side of her mouth while she works, but I have to look away when I notice Dan watching me with that goofy, gap-toothed grin on his face. I half expect him to break into *Russell and Geri sitting in a tree.*

Am I really that obvious?

Once Geri finishes her cuts, she stops long enough to uncap a bottle of water and take a long swig. "Okay, which one of you boys wants to break something?"

Dan and I look at each other as Geri hoists a sledgehammer and wiggles her eyebrows at us. She motions toward the south wall of the conference room and offers a theatrical bow. I jump up a little quicker than Dan and grab the giant bludgeon.

"Feels like a wrecking ball on a stick." A strange sensation courses through me, some illicit combination of power and naughtiness. "You really want me to smash that wall in?"

"Yes," Geri says. "And I'd prefer you do it soon. We have a lot of work to do today."

I glance at Dan, who looks positively giddy, then at Geri. Her face is flushed from exertion, but I can tell she's excited for me. It dawns on me that I'm entertaining the most juvenile of thoughts. Not only do I want to avoid embarrassing myself by missing the wall and smashing my own shins, but I realize I really want to impress Geri. I take aim and launch the sledge into the wall.

It feels good to switch roles, from artist to demolition man. But there's a level of guilt as well, for the guy who built this wall. As if on cue, my next blow hits a double stud, numbing both forearms at once. I pause, catch my breath, and wait for the tingles to subside. I look up, embarrassed. But Dan is building an insulated shoebox out of scraps while Geri studies the plans for the new glassed-in conference room. That's when it dawns on me that maybe destruction is not the opposite of creation. Rather, they're opposing points on the same cycle. All at once my wrecking ball feels like a giant chisel, a means of addition by subtraction. I regrip the sledgehammer and stare at a spot on the wall, a scarred and flimsy representation of all walls everywhere. I consider the wisdom of drawing up new plans before tearing down the old. And then I envision myself going from floor to floor, office to office, until the entire eighteen-story building has been reduced to a pile of smoky rubble.

Geri has her jaw cocked to one side, grinning. "You have a real passion for demolition work."

* * *

By the time we break for lunch, we're all shaky from hunger and exertion. I know we'll be sore tomorrow. Geri breaks open an insulated cooler filled with sandwiches, chips, fresh fruit, brownies, and gloriously delicious bottles of water. We eat in silence.

Finally, when my blood sugar returns to normal, I say, "Guess I should have asked you this before, but who's paying for all this stuff? The lumber and nails and whatever else is in those boxes?"

"That would be you, dear."

The brownie lodges in my throat.

"I mean your company is. But don't worry; I negotiated ninety-day terms with the hardware store. So Hengle's won't have to pay up until well after you guys cash the checks from TB&S. Your boss will think you're a hero. Didn't you even look at the purchase order?"

"Just the total. Once I started calculating the commission, my brain never really came back to the details."

"Wish I would have known that earlier. I would have padded my salary a bit more." She winks at Dan. "I could use a manicure. And I'm sure Dan could use a round-trip ticket to Cape Canaveral."

Dan stops chewing and starts talking. "Hey, did I tell you guys that one of Trish's crew members has pinkeye? She's one step closer."

I can't stand it any longer. "Come on, Dan. Do you really expect us to believe that you're dating an astronaut? That your girlfriend is about to attach herself to a rocket and orbit the earth?"

"Speak for yourself," Geri says. "I don't find it hard to believe at all."

Dan resumes his thoughtful chewing.

"Have you met this Trish?"

"Why do I have to meet her to believe she's an astronaut?"

Geri and I go on like this for a while until it becomes clear that Dan is lost in thought.

"Something wrong, Danno?" Geri asks. "Given half a chance, I've never known you to shy away from blabbing on and on about Trish."

"Yeah," I say. "Last time we talked about her, you were thinking of popping the question."

Dan kicks at a fresh roll of pink insulation. "I'm not sure she's ready."

"Maybe she has cold feet too," I say, giggling at the joke that no one seems to get but me.

Geri begins wrapping our leftovers and stowing them back in the cooler. "She's obviously got a lot on her mind. But like I've told you before, she needs to see you in hot pursuit, see that look in your eye that won't take 'no' for an answer. If you're not willing to follow her to the moon and back, she'll see it in your eyes."

"That's quite a locker room speech," I say. "You make it sound easy."

"No, not easy. But not nearly as complicated as men try to make it out to be. If it were rocket science, then Dan and Trish would have a marriage made in heaven."

Dan finds this hysterical.

Geri continues, obviously inspired. "Men typically spend countless hours trying to figure out how to impress women. Then they come up with all sorts of hair-brained ideas like lifting weights, sucking in their guts, and posing at stoplights — you know, gripping your steering wheels just so." Geri pauses to cock her arm on an imaginary steering wheel and fix her hair in a pretend rearview mirror. It's a ridiculously accurate dramatization. "You scheme and devise goofy theories about what you think women want. And when they don't work, you bellyache about the mysterious ways of the 'fairer sex.' Finally, when you can't think of anything else, you speed-dial the florist and stop off at Victoria's Secret for a gift certificate."

"Wait," Dan says. "Flowers are bad?"

"Flowers are wonderful, so long as they're not a cop out or an item on a checklist."

"I wonder if it's too late to cancel." He digs his clunky PDA out of his pants pocket and begins stabbing buttons.

"I've got to tell you, Geri. I find this all very fascinating. Especially coming from a girl who has sworn off men."

"Don't be a smart aleck, Russell." Geri seals the lid on the cooler, stretches her back, then motions for me to grab the end of a sheet of drywall.

"Who's being a smart aleck? This is information I can put to use. Like, right now." I try to amplify my not-so-subtle hint with a direct and fiery gaze. But she's frowning at the cutout she made for an electrical outlet. She motions for me to hold the drywall in place while she files off another quarter-inch, covering herself in a cloud of white dust.

"Oh brother," she says. "If you need advice, it can mean only one of two things. Either you made up with the actress or the nurse." My mind scrambles for something clever, but Geri waves me off. "Forget it. I don't want to know."

We grab our respective ends of the drywall, but Dan rushes over and shoos her out of the way. "Let me do that, Geri. You've got no business lifting that in your condition."

I look up in time to see Geri cut her eyes at Dan. "And what condition is that?"

"Never mind. Dan's being an idiot. He thinks that just because I threw my back out a while ago that I'm somehow an inferior specimen."

Dan and I hold the wall up while Geri fastens it in place with a drill. She motions for me to hand her the box of drywall screws. As soon as my back is turned, I hear a dull thud, followed immediately by a short, gasping groan. When I turn around, Geri is examining drywall and Dan is rubbing his stomach.

* * *

Dan is hunkered under a thick quilt and roasting marshmallows on a space heater in Geri's office. I'm shooting nails into a baseboard while Geri relaxes on the carpet, her fingers laced behind her head. She looks up suddenly and says, "Hey Dan, your boss ever say anything about not charging for Sonny's funeral?"

He keeps his eyes on the smoldering confection. "We're not exactly speaking right now." He pulls the gooey marshmallow from the unbent coat hanger and plops it in his mouth.

"You can't just say you're not speaking. We need details. Right, Russell?"

I nod, only a little disgusted at the sight and sound of Dan licking white sticky stuff from his fingers.

"I refused to eulogize a customer's dog."

"That's it?" I say.

"He was a German Shepherd named Hitler."

Geri and I stare at each other, dumbfounded.

He munches a few more marshmallows, then after a particularly loud swallow, he says, "Let's bug her phone."

"Bug who?" I say. "What are you talking about?"

"Your mother," Dan says. "You were saying before that someone's harassing her. It'd be simple enough to trace the calls. But why not bug them and make a recording? Would make for a much more dramatic courtroom scene."

I look at Geri and point at Dan as if to say, *Can you believe this guy?*

Geri shrugs. "Not a bad idea if you ask me."

"Are you guys serious? You want to break into my parents' house and tap the phones?"

Turns out they're plenty serious. Dan already has the equipment in the trunk of the Caddy. When I can't think of a good reason not to, we finish cleaning up Geri's office. It takes three trips in the freight elevator to stow all of her tools.

I dial my mother's cell number. We make small talk for a few minutes, then I inform her I'm stopping by the house to dig my tennis racket out of the attic.

"You sure I won't be disturbing Dad or anything?"

"He's driving home from Knoxville today. You should hang around a while. I'm sure he'd love to see you."

Somehow I doubt that.

* * *

Dan drives while I navigate through my old neighborhood, making him take a few extra left turns. When I direct Dan toward the driveway, he suggests we do a drive-by to get the lay of the land before going in. Then we argue about what to do with the car. I remind Dan and Geri that there's nothing suspicious about me parking in front of the house I lived in for years. But Dan wants to park in the garage.

"The garage door's busted," I say. "Besides, I thought you said we'd be in and out in ten minutes." I can't tell if he's paranoid or living out some *X-Files* fantasy, but he insists we keep the Caddy out of sight. The plan is for Geri to drop us off, then drive around for fifteen minutes until it's time to pick us up. But the awkward silence that follows reminds us all of her driving phobia.

"No," she says, making a real effort to muster confidence. "I can do this."

"I'm sorry," Dan says. "I didn't mean to put you on the spot. We'll think of something—"

"Don't be ridiculous," she says. "I'll drive to a convenience store and park, listen to the radio for ten minutes, then drive straight back here."

"I don't know, Geri," I say. "I don't like it."

"I appreciate your concern—both of you. But please hop out and get busy before someone calls the cops."

She's right. We're sitting in front of my parents' house in a pink behemoth. Then in one swift motion, she stabs the trunk release button on the key fob. The trunk creaks open and Dan and I hop out. I don't even think about trying to look casual until I notice Dan hunching his shoulders and jerking his head from side to side, like a gorilla making a prison break. He collects his box of gadgets and slams the trunk. Then Geri rockets off down the street.

"Try to look normal, would you?"

But Dan is too far into it, like a cartoon cat burglar. Forget the spectacle of a bright pink Cadillac. What could be more conspicuous than a hairy giant, hunched at the waist and tiptoeing across the lawn in a winter coat?

Once inside, he dons a giant headband that is part flashlight and part magnifying glass. In less than a minute, he's disassembled the handset and begins installing a small chip. I stand guard at the bay window, looking for any sign of my mother. Or the cops. Or Geri.

"Shouldn't you get that tennis racket?" Dan says. "You know, for the sake of plausibility? In case we get busted?"

He has a point. "Keep your ears open while I run up to the attic."

I root around for ten minutes, but there's no sign of my tennis racket. The hasp on my footlocker is undone, probably from the day I removed my letter jacket for Sonny. While I'm refastening it, I notice the same thing on Katie's hope chest. For the first time ever, curiosity gets the better of me and I lift the lid. Doing so feels sacred. As I kneel down for a closer look, Dan calls from the foot of the retractable ladder, "I'm done here, you about ready?"

"Yeah, give me a sec."

I trace my finger across the clumsy lettering scrawled on the cover of a spiral notebook.

Private Journal of Katherine A. Fink

Do Not Read

I can't bring myself to intrude on her private thoughts. Not today, anyway. There's a stack of faded Polaroids, most of which show Katie either dancing or laughing or both. My role was to egg her on. Peter's was to be annoyed by his obnoxious younger siblings.

"Hey Russell, hurry it up. We need to test this thing before we get out of here."

"Go ahead, I'll be right there."

"I need to call your parents' number, and I left my cell phone in the car."

Before I know it, I'm at the top of the stairs tossing my cell phone to Dan. He fumbles it twice before corralling it and cradling it to his chest.

"I'll be right down."

A moment later I hear the phone ring in the kitchen.

Then I'm lost again, digging through Katie's treasures — a dozen Breyer horses with chipped paint, a troll with lime green hair, a water-damaged sketchpad, dog-eared copies of Laura Ingalls books and *Charlotte's Web*, a knotted tangle of necklaces and bracelets, her favorite princess pajamas, and a dust-laden framed photograph of the Miracle Ward — a group of young cancer patients, some missing teeth, most missing hair. Katie is front and center with each arm draped across the shoulders of her pals. I'm suddenly wracked with regret for never taking the time to get to know her suffering friends. Back then, it seemed too much for a ten-year-old to take. But that seems hollow now, a pathetic excuse for my cowardice. I use my finger to clear the dust away from Katie's face. I don't realize that I'm hugging the frame, rocking back and forth, until I hear voices downstairs. I look at the photo once more and remember the page in Peter's little black book — namely, the Miracle Ward.

I put everything back like I found it, expecting to hear either Geri or Dan yelling for me to hurry it up. I'm about to close the lid when something else catches my eye. It's a colorful rendition of clouds and rainbows and spaceships and planets depicted behind glass.

Sand art.

I lift the jar and spin it in my hand, marveling at the attention to detail and wondering how on earth someone could fashion such an intricate scene out of colored sand. The kid sure had a thing for orange. Then I examine the fine print on the bottom of the jar — Tang, the astronaut drink.

"Russell? What are you doing up there?"

It's my mother. I cram everything back into the hope chest and scramble toward the landing.

"Oh, nothing. Just looking for my tennis racket."

"Who's that strange man on the lawn?"

"I'm guessing it's Dan, my roommate."

"Why is he wearing that funny hat? And a winter coat? It's seventy degrees out."

"It's hard to explain, actually." I make my way down the steps, then peek out the front window at Dan. He's hiding in the bushes. "He's, um, a little different."

My mother's face lights up. She pats me on the arm and says, "No need to be embarrassed, Russell. I think it's wonderful what you're doing."

I'm afraid to ask what she thinks I'm doing.

"All your old sports stuff is in the garage. I'll run get it for you while you check on your friend."

I sprint to the front door and hiss at Dan to get out of the bushes. He comes out, looking sheepish and out of sorts. "Where's Geri?" I ask, scanning the street for movement.

"Don't know, haven't seen her yet. And I'm starting to worry. Where's the tennis racket?"

"Couldn't find it."

Dan looks at me through his magnifying-flashlight headset like he's been had, and it's my fault.

Then my mother is there beside me, pressing the racket into my palm. She leans toward Dan, hands flat on her thighs and wearing her most docile, nonthreatening expression. When she speaks, her voice is too loud, her words too slow, like she's talking to a small child from another country.

"Hi, Dan. My name is Sharon. I'm Russell's mommy."

Dan nods, glancing at me for help.

"I really like your hat," she continues. "Very distinguished. Would you like to be a doctor someday?"

Before he can answer, the Mary Kay getaway car comes screaming down the street. Geri slams on the brakes, and the car wobbles on its chassis like a cartoon.

"Okay, we gotta run, Mom. Thanks for finding the racket for me."

Dan does his awkward stooped run to the idling car and piles into the driver's seat.

I'm about to follow when Mother grips my arm. "Look at that. He's even got his license."

"Mom, it's not what you think."

Back inside the car, a red-faced Dan asks, "Is your mother okay? Pardon me for saying so, but she seemed a little mental."

* * *

After a full day of manual labor and espionage, I can tell Dan wants to stay up and talk. But I'm beat. I feel like someone used the sledgehammer on *me*. I summon the energy to brush and floss, all the while inspecting the fleshy part of my neck for signs of inflation or sagging. Once, after lamenting the scourge of the Fink double chin, Peter asked me if I'd rather go blind or get "the chin." I actually had to think about it.

After a thorough spit-and-rinse, I lock the bathroom door and whip up a batch of my miracle antiaging cream — one part aloe, one part Palmolive dishwashing liquid, and two parts Preparation H. I discovered the recipe on the Internet after a depressingly ominous family reunion, where I saw firsthand what would become of my flabby, wattled neck if I don't take steps to prevent it. I spread generous amounts of the balm, working it in until I feel the loose factions of epidermis knitting themselves back together, like the tightening of a thousand tiny shoelaces.

That done, I plummet into bed and wait for sleep to overtake me. But it never does. My mind is too busy logging detailed entries into my long-term memory — the way Geri tucked her carpenter's pencil behind her ear, the beads of sweat gathered in that little ridge that connects her nose to the swell of her lips, the way goose bumps sprung to life when our arms touched, the faraway look in her eye when Dan wondered aloud why Geri and I never got together. When I caught her smiling, she blushed mightily and ordered me to fetch an extension cord.

I refluff my pillows and scrunch into a fetal position, but it's no use. There's a song running through my head. I don't know how I know this, but I'm pretty sure it's from the movie *The Color Purple* — "Maybe God Is Trying To Tell You Something." It's a big, raucous gospel number that seems to actually be trying to tell me something.

Geri spent an entire day giving Dan detailed advice on how to woo a woman. A lot of it was common sense. But there was some real insider information in there too, stuff that men are supposed to know but women are too stubborn to tell us. I understand that it's probably just a wicked combination of desperation, hormones, and last night's teriyaki. But why not take this information, tailor it to my needs, and use it on Geri?

Sunday

I always assumed that exploring Katie's keepsakes and reading her journals would tenderize my heart. Or at least dredge up all the old hurts and plunge me into an intense and prolonged depression. But it had the opposite effect. I haven't been able to quit thinking about Katie ever since I pawed my way through her hope chest. It kick-started something in me, like the compressor on an antique freezer that sputters and coughs its way back into action after years of disuse. And now it keeps clicking on intermittently, rumbling below the surface. As soon as I wake this morning, it clicks on again. And since it's Sunday, I decide to go back and spend some more time with the memory of my sister.

My parents are probably still at Dad's new church, and the house is deserted. For the first time since coming home from New York University, I notice the smell. As a kid I was fascinated by this phenomenon, the fact that every house had its own signature scent. I could never really put it into words. But I tried once, to Ricky Tuturo, my next-door neighbor in elementary school.

"See, Ricky. If you mix all the smells up — your dog, your dad's Old Spice and cigars, your mom's garlic recipes and fruity candles, the cedar chest in the hall, your smelly Converse high-tops ..." I paused, striving for just the right word or gesture to make my point. "You know, *your* smell. The Tuturo house smell."

"You want to know what I think?" Ricky said with a look that left no doubt he was going to tell me whether I wanted to know or not.

"What?"

"I think it's a combination of your upper lip and your own B.O."

I never tried to explain the phenomenon again after that. But I never stopped noticing it.

This morning my parents' house smells more like home than I'd care to admit. It's that comforting scent that you stop noticing, at least until you leave and come back. But you always know it's there, reminding you that, like it or not, this is where you belong.

Mom's perfume lingers in the hallway and mixes with the smell of fresh coffee. And sure enough, the Mr. Coffee is still on. I'm half-tempted to leave it on, knowing full well my father will get an earful later. Instead I pour myself the last cup, switch it off, and make my way to the attic.

The hinge on Katie's hope chest squeals as I raise the lid. Her journal is still on top. I drain the last of the coffee and pick it up. I'm pleasantly surprised to see how often my name appears. There are a few rhyming poems and drawings, but mostly the simple recounting of the mundane events in the lives of the Fink children — ball games, petty fights, favorite flavors of ice cream. The handwriting is meticulous, painstakingly so, but her spelling is atrocious.

I take my time, savoring the simple musings and artwork. Most striking to me are all the prayer requests. She was convinced that God was going to heal her friends from the Miracle Ward, especially Charlie Baringer. According to her journal, Katie would have gladly offered her life as a sacrifice if God would just save Charlie. Judging by the number of heart-framed *C.B.*s, she must have loved him. I have no recollection of any kid named Charlie. Nor do I remember her talking about him. But then she was too busy in those last months consoling her twin brother to mention her own love life. I sit and grin at the idea of Katie experiencing romantic love — sweet and wholesome, untainted by Hollywood or raging hormones — at least once in her short life. I should have been strong for Katie instead of the other way around. At least I made her laugh. But that seems awfully hollow now.

As I dig through the other layers of the hope chest, it's clear that Charlie loved her too. He must have written her a dozen notes a day. There are many other expressions of his undying devotion, including homemade cards, clay sculptures, Popsicle-stick creations. There's a canary-yellow piece of construction paper where someone colored in a frame around the edges. I scan the bottom and am not surprised to see the fine print: *Love always, C. B.* Inside the mockup frame is a poem about true love and space travel written in purple crayon.

Katie's written prayers include everyone but her. She prayed for friends and family and hungry children and lost puppies and that everyone would get to know Jesus. But mostly she prayed for me, that I wouldn't be too sad, that I wouldn't blame Daddy or God, that I would never forget her.

I snap out of my stupor and start cramming things back inside the hope chest, feeling like an intruder again.

* * *

If not for the torrent of emotion sluicing around in my brain, I'm sure I would have doubled over in laughter. Gary Fink is decked out in a gray warm-up suit from the seventies — his belly straining against the elastic — and a new pair of expensive Nikes. Dark patches spread across his chest and under his arms. And he reeks of knock-off designer cologne and sour sweat.

215

"Russell. I wanted to apologize about the way we left things. Your mom told me about Sonny."

"It's okay." I'm bouncing on the balls of my feet, conflicted. Part of me wants to lash out at my father. Another part senses the Fink version of an olive branch about to be extended. "How come you're not preaching this morning?"

"Guest speaker. I left after the announcements."

He walks into the kitchen and pulls his favorite mug down from the cupboard. He turns and says, "So, no hard feelings?"

"Some."

He lifts the empty coffee pot, then looks pointedly at me and the mug in my hand. "Well then, I guess we're even."

"What's with the Richard Simmons routine? I thought you hated exercise."

"Since I'm going to be on TV again soon …" He pats his belly as he says the words, hinting at obvious good news like a kid trying to prolong the suspense of a good report card. "Are you still up for helping me out on the TV spot?"

"You want me to talk about you on live national TV?"

Dad bends at the waist and begins a series of old man stretches. I expect a hamstring to snap any second. "Your mother will be there too. The producer said I could use a few of your paintings on the set."

"And … all the threats about you appearing on the air?"

"Threats?" As if he didn't know.

"Mom told me." This whole conversation reminds me that we typically communicate *through* my mother, casting her in the role of emissary, Pony Express courier, or maybe just a carrier pigeon. Maybe Mom was right. Maybe we are too much alike. I watch his double chin jiggle and my knees go weak with dread.

He switches from toe touches to side stretches. "Comes with the territory."

"So … fame and fortune, someone in your family dying …" I hold my hands up like scales, balancing the worth of the two options.

My father stops, looks at me.

"It's not like that, Russell."

"What's it like then?"

"When something bad happens, it's not always someone's fault."

* * *

The plan is to talk Geri into accompanying me to see Gramps. She used to grill me about him in college, more fascinated with his jailhouse conversion than the fact that he accidentally killed his wife. And since he left a message on my cell phone last night, saying not to worry, but that he'd been moved from his cell to the adjoining infirmary, I decided I'd better check on him and see what's up.

It would be an understatement to say Geri shared my religious cynicism in those days. If skepticism were a virtue, she would have been a caped superhero, able to malign smarmy preachers with a single snarky remark. When I first learned of her aversion to all things religious, I asked, "So I guess it's safe to say you deny the very existence of God?"

"Absolutely. I just hope He doesn't hold it against me later on."

But lately it seems that she's retreated into at least some form of belief. At some point I plan to investigate the change, but for now I don't want to jinx my master plan of using her own romantic advice against her. We stop at a Chick-fil-A and Geri insists on buying my lunch. When I protest, she reminds me again that she owes me twenty dollars.

"I still have no idea what you're talking about."

"In that case, forget it then."

"I'm not above freeloading, I just need a hint."

The grin on Geri's face is deliciously wicked. "Okay, how's this? One-rail, six-nine combo in the corner pocket."

The memory snaps into place with the *thunk* of a floppy disk. Midway through finals and in desperate need of blowing off steam, Geri and I ditched our highlighters and textbooks in favor of a couple of pool cues. As usual, the student center smelled like the inside of a pizza box. Other than Oprah crying on the TV in the corner, we had the place to ourselves.

Competition always brought out the flirt in Geri. Winning merely intensified it. So I suggested we play Nine-Ball. While she chalked her cue, I did my best to steer the conversation to our respective love lives. I asked leading and transparent questions about Tom, goading her into complaining about her fiancé's sales job that kept him on the road. When she finally conceded that he hadn't bothered to call and ask her how her finals were going, I seized my opportunity. I'm still not sure if my desperation stemmed from the fact that summer break began in three short days or if I was acknowledging at some subatomic level that I really was falling for Geri. Either way, I ventured down the low road, the one most traveled, criticizing Alyssa behind her back. Normally, Geri would never abide such talk. But that day was different. We took turns piling on, kidding ourselves into believing we were engaged in some sort of shared therapy.

After Geri made a bank shot look way too easy, and for no apparent reason, I just blurted it out. "Hey, why don't we blow off our finals and just fly to Vegas for an Elvis wedding?"

"Hah! You're all talk." She lined up a cut shot on the four. "Alyssa has you wrapped around her pinkie toe."

"Care to make it interesting?"

She paused mid-stroke, all squinty-eyed with her tongue poking out of the corner of her mouth. Without breaking stance, she cut her eyes at me and said, "Twenty bucks says you won't do it."

"Won't do what? Break up with her?"

Between sinking the four ball, then the five, Geri said, "Yep, that's exactly what I'm saying. I'm calling you chicken." Finally, she eyed an impossible, yet potentially game-winning combination on the nine ball.

"Is there a time limit? I mean, I don't have to break up with her today, do I?"

"If you'll shut up and let me line up this shot, you can take as long as you like."

"How about five years?" I regretted it at once, and Geri's stifled laugh confirmed my idiocy. My goal was to furtively explore the possibility of converting Geri from friend to lover; I mention running off to Vegas and she doesn't even shoot me down, but instead of seizing the moment with a bold declaration of undying love, I suggest she allow me a half-decade to bump her up in the romantic batting order.

"Whatever."

"Twenty bucks it is then." I don't even think she heard me, and I'm glad.

She struck the cue ball with side English. It caromed off the side rail, whispering past the eight ball, and striking the six with just enough force to send it careening the length of the table. I held my breath. Geri never moved as the six kissed the nine, and two slow revolutions later, it tumbled into the corner pocket.

"Nice shot," I said, still dumbfounded.

"Thanks. Which means you owe me a pepperoni slice and a giant root beer today." Geri giggles into the back of her hand. "And twenty bucks in exactly five years from today."

I dropped hints all through dinner, hoping that Geri would steer the conversation back toward Vegas or Tom or Alyssa or breakups. Instead we talked about finals and summer jobs and what we wanted to be when we grew up. Geri mentioned leaving for North Carolina to spend the summer break alternating between her fiancé's family estate in Charlotte and her grandparents' farm in the middle of nowhere.

Back on campus, we staved off our studies with several games of Yahtzee in the dorm lobby. I'm pretty sure Geri cheated. When she finally insisted we hit the books, I suggested we needed a change of scenery, using chocolate cake as bait. A half hour later, we found ourselves at the Opryland Hotel, eating rich dessert, leisurely strolling through the atrium, and not studying.

I should have kissed her when I had the chance.

* * *

We can see the prison a mile before we get there. More than a few heads turn as we pull into the visitor lot in the Mary Kay Mobile.

"You sure you're okay with this?"

"Are you kidding? I can hardly wait."

I don't know what I was expecting, but I'm disappointed by the ordinariness of the hospital. It's older but looks and feels like every other hospital in America. The intercom is a bit scratchy, but the nurse's shoes still squeak. The air is still rife with rubbing alcohol and disease. The staff bustles from station to station, room to room, with quiet urgency. We follow the ascending room numbers until we get to the one on my note. I half expect to see an armed guard, but the only thing holding Gramps in check appears to be a thin wooden door and a complicated web of tubes and wires.

He's reclining in his bed, staring up at the television, and completely oblivious to the fact that he's falling out of his thin gown. It takes him a second to snap out of his stupor.

"Russell! Sorry I didn't hear you come in." He notices Geri and pulls the covers up over his bony white body. "This TV is fascinating. We only get two channels in the community room—cartoons and preachers. Sometimes it's hard to tell the difference."

"So," I say, trying to mask the worry in my voice, "what are you in for?"

"Tests, mostly. But I don't want to talk about that. I want to have a look at this beautiful girl you brought to see me."

"I'm Geri," she says, stepping forward to shake his hand. "Pleased to meet you."

"It's all mine, dear." He kisses the back of her hand reverently, pausing to breathe in her scent — nothing lewd, rather unbridled admiration. "Pleasure is all mine."

I clear my throat and wonder if I'll have to forcibly extract Geri's hand from his. But she sits on the edge of his bed and cups his spotted hand in both of hers. He sighs with his whole body and grins like an absolute idiot.

"What kind of tests?" I say.

"The testy kind. Lots of needles and X-rays and whatnot."

"You have to have some idea what they're looking for. Are they taking X-rays of your feet, your brain, your heart?"

He jerks his thumb toward me and addresses Geri. "Is he always this uptight?"

"Afraid so. He can be a real ninny sometimes."

Gramps laughs like he's never heard anything so funny.

"But you know he's just worried about you because he loves you."

He looks past her and says, "Son, if you let this one go, so help me, I'll kick my way out of my grave and haunt you all the days of your life."

Geri and I speak at the same time, some convoluted version of, "No, we're just friends."

"He's not still going steady with that Looney Toon, is he? The actress? She's like an infernal prom queen. That girl's been rotting his brain and abusing his heart for years now, and he just tucks his tail and keeps coming back for more."

"Can't argue with you there," Geri says. "But I'm happy to report that our man Russell finally did the deed. He is now officially unengaged and back on the market. But I think he has his sights set on a nurse with a temper."

He looks at me pointedly and says, "Is that smart?"

I shrug and look away, the way I've always responded to that question.

"Nonsense," he says. "Now you listen up, son. Don't you dare let this beauty go. Either you figure out a way to woo this girlie, or I'll do it myself. I haven't had a proper date in nearly two decades."

"Sorry, Geri. He has this habit of talking about people like they're not in the room."

"In fact, Miss Geri, what are you doing this weekend?"

A brawny nurse buzzes into the room. "Cool it, lover boy. How are we supposed to keep an eye on that ticker of yours if you get all excited?"

"Is that what he's in here for?" I ask. "His heart?"

But the nurse is busy jamming a thermometer in Gramps's mouth and silently counting the palpitations in his wrist. I have to look away when she draws blood. She checks the monitors and flicks the IV bag, then jots a few notes on the clipboard attached to the end of his bed and disappears. When I hear Geri ask Gramps how he found Jesus behind bars, I decide to try and decipher the chart to see if I can figure out the nature of his condition. Besides, I know the story by heart.

Gramps spent his life dashing from one altar to another — money, power, women, the law books, golf, and more women. His appetite always managed to stay a step ahead of his ability to quench it, like a carrot on the stick. And once he got a nibble, his tastes changed. After months of binging on eighty-hour work weeks that inevitably led to a favorable verdict, his proclivities would shift to a new girlfriend or a new boat or sports car or custom-made golf clubs. But as much as he fancied the spoils of his burgeoning law practice, the one thing he adored above all else was his wife, though admittedly he did a reprehensible job showing it. Still, Deloris (aka Dot) Fink remained his rock and his salvation until death did indeed set them apart. He'd carelessly wounded her numerous times. Then one night, he got drunk and used a bullet. He still maintains that prison saved his life — twice. The wretched one he inflicted on his loved ones for nearly five decades, and his new life with Jesus.

One of Gramps's favorite pastimes was to get drunk and ridicule his son. Literally, he treated it like a pastime; once sufficiently liquored up, he would call his friends and colleagues and clients, inviting them to his son's house to get healed. As far as the elder Fink was concerned, his son, Gary, was wasting his life with all that religious mumbo jumbo. And the healings. But now Gramps is a true blue believer.

I scan the series of acronyms on the clipboard and am able to reasonably conclude by the handwritten "Post Myocard Infarc" that Gramps most likely had a heart attack.

"Tell me something, Miss Geri. Do you believe in miracles?"

I look up at my grandfather. Geri stares at the floor and twists her bottom lip for several moments.

"Yeah, I do. A little more every day."

Her response troubles me. I hide behind the clipboard, wondering what's happened to my sweet, self-avowed atheist friend.

"Good," he says. "Glad to hear it. Because gauging by the worried look on all the faces in this place, I think I could use one."

"It's your heart, isn't it?" I say.

He nods. "They tell me I need a new one. But I have no intention of letting them give me one."

"Why not?" Geri and I say in unison.

"I don't deserve it, that's why. I abused the one God gave me — physically, spiritually, and just about every other way imaginable.

223

Jesus cleaned it up once already. And that'll just have to be good enough. Besides, hearts in good working order are pretty rare. If I take one off the market, that's one less for some young father who can put it to good use."

I don't realize I'm angry until I hear the words pouring out of my mouth. "So you're just going to lie here until yours gives out?"

"As long as I'm lying here, I'm not lying in prison. 'Sides, I simply cannot wait to see Dot and tell her I'm sorry."

Gramps then changes the subject and keeps insisting that we would make a perfect couple. Geri keeps dodging and weaving, but at some point, he ignores her and tells me all the reasons he thinks Geri would make a great mother. When he finally turns to her and asks, "So how many do you want to have?" Geri blanches. Her face reddens and her eyes tear up. She excuses herself to the restroom, leaving Gramps and me to shrug at each other, mutually embarrassed. Maybe she's been told she can't have kids. I'm about to whisper this to Gramps when the intercom announces that visiting hours are officially over.

Three minutes later, Geri returns fully composed. Then she does the unthinkable. She suggests we pray together for Gramps, for a miracle no less. Arms extended, she stands on the opposite side of his bed and waits for us all to join hands.

Geri goes first. What she lacks in eloquence, she makes up for in sincerity. But as much as I'd love to stand and listen to her voice, my insides are roiling. Both hands turn cold and sweaty. My eyelids turn to spastic butterfly wings. My mouth dries up and my heart chugs furiously in its cage. I'm vaguely aware of my grandfather's words. What I can pick up is all about Geri and me. He's beseeching God to turn our hearts toward each other, for love to take root and soar, for us to marry and make babies and grow old together. Geri's grip tightens — and despite my mounting embarrassment at Gramps's audacious prayers — I can only hope it's for the right reasons.

Finally the room falls silent. It's my turn. But the words won't come. The monitors beep and footsteps fill the halls. Finally, the nurse comes in and shoos us out of the room.

Gramps thanks us for coming and makes us promise to do it again soon. Geri kisses him on the crown of his head, making him look thirty years younger. When we get to the door Gramps says, "Russell, my boy. Do you believe Jesus is who He said He was?"

I've heard the whole "ask Jesus into your heart" so many times that it doesn't register. It's become like elevator music or a refrigerator magnet that you learn to ignore, just another part of the overlooked landscape of my life. As a kid, I prayed it thousands of times — after sneaking peeks down a classmate's blouse or stealing bubble gum from the 7-Eleven or railing against God for letting me kill my sister. I've never been quite comfortable with the heart-as-house imagery, anyway. I always picture Hitchcock's *Psycho* house stuck out of a large patch of land like a tombstone.

"Come on, Gramps."

He nods once, and for the first time ever, I'd swear he doubts me.

* * *

Geri and I are sitting on opposite ends of Dan's sofa, with two decks of playing cards spread out before us. She's trying to teach me some elaborate game she invented as a kid. But either the rules keep changing or I'm more interested in flirting with her than focusing on strategy. In fact, I keep zoning out, scheming details for the surprise date I'm going to spring on her for this weekend. Gramps has inspired me to not "let this one get away."

"What's wrong, Russell? Are my freckles glowing?"

"Oh, sorry. Guess I was daydreaming again."

"Well knock it off. Makes me feel like I'm playing solitaire in a fishbowl."

I stare at my cards, clueless but trying to make an effort. Geri picks up my discard and begins a complicated series of moves. I go back to my scheming.

The plan is to recreate a montage of *Russell and Geri's Greatest Hits*, a walking retrospective of our most memorable moments together. According to Geri's sage advice to Dan, I need to leave no doubt of my intentions. Geri must feel pursued, beautiful, worthy of adoration and sacrifice. In short, she needs to know I care. That should be simple enough. As will the various locales — Geri's favorite hamburger joint, a stroll around the Parthenon, a felonious trip to the local zoo, and an exact reenactment of our last trip to the Opryland Hotel. However, it's the details that confound me. For instance, I have all these props, things that only have meaning for Geri and me. But when do I use them? And how much is too much? And where's that fine line between subtle romance and blatant, ham-fisted exaggeration? And will I recognize the line when I see it? I begin a mental inventory — roll of quarters for feeding lambs, sample strip of Brut cologne, a pack of Teaberry gum, pocketknife for carving, and two wrapped packages. That's when I realize I need a blindfold.

The memory makes me grin.

One night when we were supposed to be studying, Geri blurted out the fact that she could feel it when she crossed time zones.

"Feel it how?" I asked.

"I don't know, something just sort of moves inside me. And it works on airplanes too."

Of course I had to make her prove it. We piled into my VW Beetle and headed off to Chattanooga. About thirty minutes outside the city — and the Eastern time zone — I rummaged around the back seat until I came up with an old bandanna.

"Here, put this on. And no cheating or I'll drop you off at the bus station."

"What's the bet?"

"Whatever you want it to be," I said. "Because as soon as I figure out your scam, you're toast."

"Okay, you're on. But my reward must involve jewelry."

I kept one eye on her as we approached the sign, certain I could figure out whatever stunt she was about to pull. But she just sat there, her head bowed, humming under her breath. Just when I thought she was going to miss it, she said, "There it was. I felt it."

She nailed it.

I still doubted her. So I tightened the blindfold and started driving around in circles, making nonsense turns and crossing back and forth across the posted time zones. But she got it right every single time. She even informed me that we crossed it a few times on back roads as well. Although there were no signs, I believed her. When it came time to pay up, Geri made me pull into a gas station with the most garish display of fireworks and goofy souvenirs I've ever seen. After fifteen minutes of browsing the aisles, she decided on a candy necklace, a pair of wax lips, and a pack of candy cigarettes.

On the way home that night, our conversation turned philosophical. We were buzzing on too much caffeine, sleep deprivation, and a postadolescent combination of invincibility and insecurity. She talked about how Tom was the perfect man for her. She sounded like she was trying too hard to convince me — or maybe convince herself, as if repeating the words would somehow make them true. They'd invested so much time and emotional energy into their relationship that it seemed she felt obligated to let things play out.

Every time Geri mentioned my relationship with Alyssa, I found I was embarrassed, maybe even ashamed of it. I kept changing the subject.

To stave off drowsiness, Geri dug through her purse until she found a cassette tape and popped it into the deck. This ignited one of our pet arguments. Me being an album guy, I considered mix tapes an affront to my artistic sensibilities. She called me a dweeb and kept on singing at the top of her lungs.

We stopped at a red light near her apartment, and she said with a muffled voice, "Kiss me, dahling!" I turned to see her eyes closed dreamily, her giant wax lips puckered in my direction. I tilted my head, involuntarily matching her dreamy pucker, and moved in for the proverbial kill. A horn blared behind us. Our eyes popped open. She looked shocked, and maybe even a little disappointed. The light had turned green.

Only recently, after scouring my memory and a handful of used CD shops, did it dawn on me that Geri's mix tape may have been more than a random sampling of her favorite tunes. That maybe she was sending a message. One that I missed completely.

I make a mental note to recreate Geri's mix tape for my upcoming ambush.

That's when I notice her looking at me, her face a mixture of triumph and irritation. She's holding two cards in her hand with a huge stack facedown in front of her.

"You can only stall so long, Russell Fink. Draw a card, I'm sure it will be your last."

"Ha!" I say, drawing a three of clubs from one of several piles and using it to "capture the kitty," whatever the heck that means.

"Not so fast." She trumps my black three with a pair of red sevens. She then scoops the kitty pile into her left hand and plucks three cards from my hand with her right. "Aha. I haven't seen the Valentine Sweep since I was eleven. Do you know how rare this is? And how unfortunate for you?" She scribbles a few thousand points into her running tally. "You'll need a miracle to come back from this one."

"So you do believe in miracles." I pick a card from the pile nearest me and compare it to the ones in my hand. Utterly baffled now, I drop this new card onto the discard pile.

"I'm officially rethinking the matter."

"You're what? An agnostic now?"

"More of an explorer." She fans out a row of even-numbered cards, alternating between red and black, then yells "One-eyed Jack Attack" loud enough to startle Dan from his calculations. "And I do believe you now owe me ... let's see ... eighty-one thousand dollars and a chocolate shake."

"Hope your newfound faith is strong. Otherwise, you'll have to put that on my tab."

"So what about you, son of a preacher man? Don't you believe in miracles?"

"Begrudgingly. And only the ones I've seen with my own eyes."

"Well, that's no good." Geri looks genuinely disappointed as she gathers all the cards into one big pile.

"What's that supposed to mean?"

She ignores me and says, "Hey, Dan. I want you to settle something for your new roomie and me."

A pile of gadgetry litters the kitchen table. Dan claims he's working on a controller for a Russian satellite he bought on eBay. I'm learning never to doubt him. He looks up from his tinkering and cups one hand behind his ear, a signal for her to speak up. The logical thing would be for him to remove his ridiculous hat, a furry Klondike affair complete with wraparound earflaps. When I commented earlier that it looked like there was a muskrat hibernating on his head, Dan looked up and simply stated that muskrats don't hibernate.

Geri raises her voice and says, "Russell and I are having a friendly argument about miracles. Any thoughts?"

Dan flicks his eyes back and forth between us. I can't tell if he thinks he misheard or if we're pulling his leg. Or if he's trying to figure out a discreet way to nestle in between us on the sofa. He scratches his chin, lost in thought.

Geri winks at me and says, "See how fair I can be? I'm allowing a scientist to act as judge and jury."

"He's your cousin."

Speaking much too loud, Dan says, "Miracles, eh?"

"Yeah," she says. "Water into wine, healing the lame, raising the dead, Russell actually winning at cards?"

"Why not? If I were God, there's nothing I'd like better than to set up this elaborate network of atoms and DNA and brainwaves, then spend some time monkeying around with the system just to see the looks on the faces of the fascinated humans. Like a giant laboratory where nature is made up of constants and God keeps tossing in variables to keep things interesting."

Geri pumps her fist once. "Score one for the home team."

"I knew he'd take your side. But why would God need a laboratory? He supposedly already knows everything."

"I'm not taking sides, really." Dan pauses, eyes on the ceiling, pondering. "It's a simple question of whether you believe there's a God, a divine order to things."

"I don't know," I say. "And what difference does it make anyway? He's going to do whatever He wants, whether we ask Him or not. There's too many people starving and dying, too much sadness to think He's really paying attention to what we have to say. People pray for miracles all the time and nothing happens."

Geri fingers the hem of her Guatemalan flag blouse. I've never seen her look more in need of a hug. She doesn't seem comfortable with this conversation any more, in fact, she looks a little queasy.

Something starts buzzing on the kitchen table and it seems we've lost Dan again. He slides an earpiece under the fuzzy flap of his hat and starts punching buttons.

"Are you really asking," Geri says, "or are you just playing devil's advocate?"

"Both."

"I'm no expert, but I pray because it makes me feel close to God. It's more like pillow talk than a laundry list."

"You do ask Him for stuff though, right? But He only delivers when He wants to. Doesn't really matter what you want."

"I dare say if there's something you really want, you ask God for it. And although you may not like the answer you get — if you ask sincerely — you'll eventually be satisfied with the answer."

"Tried that. Lots of times. I'm still not satisfied. Here," I say, handing Geri the deck of cards. "Why don't you deal again?"

"What do you want, Russell? More than anything in the world? What is the one thing that would just rock your world and make it complete?"

She's staring right through me and down into my soul. She wants an answer, a real one. And I have the distinct impression that if I back-pedal or try to be funny, that I won't just make her mad. I'll hurt her. "I'm working on it."

We're still staring at each other when Dan yells, "Hey! Hey guys. We're getting a call. There's some crazy man yelling at your mom on the phone."

Geri and I rush to Dan's side, looking over his shoulder at a small screen that means nothing to either one of us.

"Can you tell where — ?"

"Ssshh!" Dan punches a few keys on his homemade computer gizmo and a voice fills the room: "Whoa unto thee, O spawn of the father of lies. You're fixin' to reap the wrath of a thousand leprous blind men."

He types again and the screen freezes on an address. "Let's go."

"Where to?" I say.

"The bowling alley off I-65."

* * *

Despite the adrenaline rush from our amateur sleuthing, our trip to the bowling alley is a blissfully bumpy one. Dan's not a great driver when he's obeying the speed limit; he's downright dangerous when he's not. So the tactical maneuver of resting my left arm on the back of the seat pays off in spades. Every time Dan hits a pothole or takes a sharp turn, Geri's body nestles further into the crook of my arm. Eventually we're pressed together like the singular silhouette of a redneck couple in a pickup truck. I know it's juvenile. But infatuation knows no shame.

Dan and I open the doors for Geri, and our senses are immediately assaulted. The place smells like popcorn, burnt hotdogs, the waxy smell of breathless children after recess, and a thousand pairs of dirty socks. The drone of conversation and balls humming down lanes is punctuated with sporadic intercom blasts, occasional cheers, or muffled curses.

We split up and go searching for pay phones and crazy-eyed prank callers we've never seen before. Dan made us memorize the number of the pay phone in question. His plan is to keep calling the number until we isolate the right one. Geri takes the restrooms, Dan the snack bar, and I head toward the arcade. I spot my quarry between a *Raiders of the Lost Ark* pinball machine and a *Ms. Pac-Man* machine with most of the graphics worn off from overuse. The receiver is covered with disgusting fingerprints and smudges. When I'm five feet from the phone, a grade-schooler with expensive sneakers and blue hair jumps in front of me and snatches the phone off the hook. He turns and smirks at me, as if we were racing and he won. At least now I won't have to touch the grimy thing. While the kid drops coins into the slot and begins dialing, I squint at the typed phone number above the keypad. The area code and prefix match, but the last four digits are not even close. The kid turns and gives me a dirty look as a parting gift.

I nearly run over Geri when I step out of noisy gloom. "How'd you make out?"

"No pay phone," she says. "But I'm pleased to report that at least the restroom was clean."

We make our way to the snack bar and find Dan in a Formica booth gnawing on a corn dog. His satisfied grin tells us everything we need to know.

"I take it you found the phone?" He points at a glassed-in phone booth by the bar, then wipes mustard from the corner of his mouth. "Which narrows our list of suspects down to pretty much everyone in the building."

He nods, still chewing enthusiastically.

Geri sits down across from him and says, "What do we do now?"

Dan swallows, then chases it with a swig of microwaved Yoo-hoo. "Not sure. I guess maybe we could take turns staking out the place."

I sit by Geri and prop my feet up on Dan's seat across from me. Every surface in the place is covered in a thin layer of filth, like hotel room carpet that turns your socks black. I'm thinking how tired I am and how useless this venture is turning out to be, when my peripheral vision latches onto something familiar — a man leaning forward, his left ear cocked in our direction, staring vacantly at a spot on the floor. And then he's up and approaching our table. It's Claude Beaman, Santa's cousin and Peter's private investigator, carrying a mug of weak yellow beer.

"May I?" he says. He doesn't wait for a reply, but works his bulky frame into the booth next to Dan. The starched fabric of his button-down swishes loudly when he moves. I have to jerk my feet back to keep him from sitting on them. He takes a long pull from his beer and casts his eyes casually around the room. "Don't suppose you see anyone in here that looks familiar?"

"Just you." I study his face, taking in his lazy eye for the first time.

And the way he constantly wets his lips. "And I'm starting to think you're following me."

"Nope. I'm following whoever is following you and your brother. You just keep popping up. In fact, if I didn't know better, I might suspect you were making those calls."

"And I could say the same about you."

His lips glisten when he smiles. It gives me the creeps. "Phone records indicate that at least a few of those menacing calls were made from that phone booth right over there." He points and squints through the secondhand smoke.

"I know," I say.

Beaman draws his head back in surprise. Geri and Dan watch in silence.

"And how would you know that? If you don't mind my asking."

I motion toward Dan who offers an overly friendly wave. "That's Dan. He traced a call here just twenty minutes ago."

"Claude Beaman," he says, offering his hand first to Geri, then to Dan. "That's pretty impressive work, tracing calls. Your technology is obviously better than mine. I do it the old-fashioned way, phone records and legwork. I got here ten minutes ago and was planning to kill an hour or two watching the pay phone. Then you guys showed up."

Dan looks proud. I can tell he's about to launch into an explanation of his computer thingy, so I cut him off before he begins. "Pardon me for saying so, but what are you really doing here?"

"Same as you, I suppose. Looking for your brother."

"He's never been much of a bowler."

He cocks his head at me, like Sonny used to do. "I find your sarcasm a little less than helpful. So I'll be blunt. I'm worried about Peter."

"Worried?"

"Sure. He's disappeared."

"Disappeared?" I can't decide if I think Beaman knows too much or too little. "If he's gone, then what's your interest in all this now?"

"Simple. Your brother is a client. If I can't find him, I don't get paid."

"So what's your plan? Other than to hang around the bowling alley and wait for the bad guys to show up and use the pay phone?"

His laugh is supposed to be good-natured. But it sounds forced. "You needn't worry. I've caught my fair share of bad guys in the past."

"Oh yeah," Dan says. "Me too. I once caught the FBI's third most-wanted criminal. Maybe you saw me on *America's Most Wanted*?"

He looks disappointed when Beaman shakes his head.

"I was in line behind him at the post office, saw his mug shot on the wall, then smeared peanut butter all over his face to subdue him till the cops came."

"Peanut butter?"

"Yeah, it was right there under his height, weight, and photo. Severe peanut allergy. Nearly killed the poor guy."

Geri says, "I've seen the tape a few times. Pretty impressive, really. Dan's a real hero."

Then Dan gives us the five-minute version. You can tell he's delivered this monologue before.

Beaman is grinning and nodding like crazy. "I think I do remember hearing about this."

"I think you're all nuts," I say. "And any minute, Alan Fundt is going to jump out and tell us to smile, that we're on *Candid Camera*."

Beaman chuckles while retrieving a small baggie from his breast pocket. He deftly slits the seal and dumps a dose of powder into his beer. The baggie disappears and he begins stirring his beer with a butter knife.

"What was that?" I ask.

Dan says. "Smells like orange juice."

235

"If you must know, it's fiber." His face reddens, giving him that Santa glow again. "Doc says I need to keep my colon happy."

Dan's PDA rings to life, treating us all to a back-masked version of "Stairway to Heaven." He gnaws on his bottom lip as he listens intently, peppering the caller with monosyllabic grunts of "yeah" and "uh huh" and "you sure?" After disconnecting, he stares at a spot on the ceiling until Geri says, "Spill it, Danno."

"My NASA guy calling. The toxicology screens are back on Sonny. Looks like they found traces of pentobarbital in his system."

"Pento-what?" Geri says.

"It's a euthanasia drug."

"What does that mean, exactly?" I say.

"Well, the mixture of alcohol, antifreeze, and barbiturates is more than a little peculiar. But if nothing else, the presence of pentobarbital probably means he didn't suffer much at the end."

"That's something, I guess. Anything else?"

"Yeah … Tang."

"Wait," Beaman says, his voice wet with incredulity. "Someone from NASA calls to tell you they found *Tang* in Sonny's system? What is going on here? Maybe I can help."

I fill Beaman in on what I know so far, how I found Sonny, about Peter and the Prestone, and even the traces of alcohol (conveniently omitting any mention of whiskey biscuits). We all stare at each other for a long beat, then start swapping crazy theories. As much as I hate to admit it, Beaman seems to make the most sense.

"Someone's been threatening your parents on the one hand and following Peter on the other. Up to now, I think we all assumed it was two different people. But now I'm not so sure. Maybe whoever's been harassing the family mixed the euthanasia drug in with the orange drink to get Sonny to drink it?"

We're silent for a while, mulling, looking for holes in his hypothesis. Finally, I say, "My next-door neighbor only saw one strange car that day. And whoever that was never got out. Guess Simmons could have missed the guy."

I look to Beaman for his reaction. He seems to be blushing when he clears his throat and says, "That was probably me."

"You?" Geri and I say in unison.

"Yeah, I was following the guy who was following Peter. Assumed it was the gambling goons coming to collect. But I lost him in your neighborhood. So if your neighbor is right, maybe whoever it is snuck in the back?"

"Maybe so," I say. And this seems to be the final word on the topic.

Beaman and Dan agree to exchange numbers with the intent of getting together soon to talk shop. While Beaman scribbles his information on a dry-cleaning ticket, Dan makes a phone call on his computer gizmo. It sounds like he's arranging for a car to pick him up at the airport. I don't move, because Geri has wilted into me. It started with her right thigh resting against my left. Then her head drooped, coming to rest on my shoulder. At some point, she locked her arm into mine and nodded off. Her warm breath on my neck makes me dizzy.

Beaman excuses himself, his knees popping as he gets up. Once he's out of earshot, I ask Dan, "So, are you really going to get together with that guy?"

"Nah, but it never hurts to be well-connected."

I grin back at Dan, distracted. Something about that Tang doesn't seem right. I resolve to check it out when Geri stirs beside me. Dan uses his version of a whisper. "Time to play Dick Tracy."

Monday

I haven't anticipated showing up for work this much since the weekend Bernie was arrested for bank robbery. Of course he didn't do it; it was a case of mistaken identity, but it brought me immeasurable gratification. It was short-lived once I saw the deflated look on Mr. Hengle's face and decided I should repent. It took three tries because I kept giggling.

The first thing I do at the office is check out The Leader Board, a giant construction-paper replica of a golf tournament scoreboard that tracks the progress of our company-wide sales contest. Mandy and Robin spent an entire Saturday afternoon creating the monstrosity, which possesses all the professionalism of an elementary school bulletin board. Prior to my latest conquest, the girls had calculated Bernie's sales to be sixteen under par. As of this morning, I should be atop the Leader Board with a ridiculous score of thirty-seven under par.

I'm not disappointed.

When I walk by the coffeemaker, Mandy and Robin halt their gossiping to applaud. Gladys from accounting joins in and I take a small bow. Bernie leers at me from the threshold of his father's office, then disappears inside.

I check my mail trilogy — voice, e-, and snail — then pour myself a cup of coffee and make my way to the conference room for our weekly sales meeting. For once I eschew hiding out in the back and opt for a seat in the second to last row instead. Ten minutes later, the rest of the crew files in and I receive a few more attaboys and literal pats on the back. I practice not looking smug as I imagine what a fuss Mr. Hengle will make over landing the TB&S order. But the look on his face when he grips the lectern dashes any thoughts of this meeting being about me. He looks like he's about to cry, like he's aged a decade in a single weekend. Like he did after Bernie's false arrest.

But his voice is strong and sure as he delivers another repackaged version of the history of Hengle's Supply, Inc. He falters a bit when he gets to the era of Max Junior. But after some throat-clearing and eye-wiping, he continues. Robin fishes a wad of tissues out of her purse and offers them around to the rest of us. Mandy grabs a handful. I take one to be polite. But Bernie stares ahead with an unreadable expression. Then it all makes sense when I hear the words "impending retirement" followed shortly thereafter with the phrase "ongoing health concerns."

He mentions Mrs. Hengle's failing health and something about quelling the rumors before they get started. He assures us that the company will continue to thrive, that there's nothing at all to worry about. Hengle's will be in good hands. Bernie nods imperceptibly, and my esophagus fills with hot sand.

"Now if you'll all join me in a round of applause," Hengle says and I notice he's smiling at me, "for Russell Fink who just snared the largest single order in the company of Hengle's Supply."

The applause is muted, no doubt a hangover from Mr. Hengle's news. It's dawning on us all that the heir apparent is the only man in the room *not* applauding my heroics. Bernie does eventually turn and smile at me. But it's not a happy smile.

The meeting adjourns and Nancy materializes out of thin air to invite me into her office. Once the door is shut, she sits and faces me. I prepare myself for the worst. She's going to fire me, and probably enjoy every second of it. And why not? She's earned it.

"Congratulations, Mr. Fink."

"Thanks, Nancy ... ?"

"It's Clancy. My name is Nancy Clancy." Her face is defiant, practically daring me to laugh. But I can't help myself. Then she does the unthinkable, and joins me — well, sort of — and I nearly miss it. But it was definitely there, an involuntarily reflex that included vertical parting of the lips to reveal teeth. Plus, a noise escaped her that definitely shared the DNA of laughter. I'm surprised at how pleasant it sounds.

"At least it's not Schmancy," I say.

That's when decorum gets the better of her. She coughs into the back of her hand and says, "I confess I had to check the employee handbook to see if there was a clause in there about moonlighting. Seems our star salesman has a part-time construction gig as a subcontractor."

"I like to think of it as overtime."

"I hope you don't expect additional compensation."

"No ma'am. Just a huge commission check."

"Believe it or not, I'm looking forward to signing it."

I check her expression for traces of irony. But either my radar is broken or she's genuinely pleased with my accomplishment.

"I had my doubts when I noticed you outsourced all the lumber and tools and additional labor. But you pulled it off."

"Mr. Hengle has always preached going the extra mile, giving the customer exactly what they want. And we now have one very big and very happy customer."

"That we do. I've already spoken with someone from Tyler, Billingham & Sneed this morning. They seem to have nothing but the highest praise for Hengle's Supply. And of course, for our current top salesman."

Nancy gives me another of her tight-lipped smiles, then folds her hands in front of her again and stares at me.

"And?" I say, waiting for the bad news.

"That's it. Congratulations. You've done us all proud. And …" She pauses to clear her throat. "And it seems that I may have been wrong about you, Mr. Fink."

"Don't beat yourself up too bad. I can be a real slacker when I set my mind to it."

"That's not funny, Russell."

"Sorry. And for a second there, I thought I was going to make you like me."

Her mouth forms a surprised *O*. When she speaks, her words sound brittle, as if she's trying to keep from crying. "Liking you has got nothing to do with it." She spins a photo frame around. "That's Reginald. He's a year or two younger than you."

"Handsome kid. What does he do?"

"He's doing time, Russell. For selling drugs to minors."

"I'm sorry. I had no idea."

"His father called him a slacker so many times that Reginald started to believe it." Nancy stares at me with moist eyes. For a scary second I think she's going to get up and hug me. Actually, I'm a little sad when she doesn't. "You ever call yourself that again in my presence and I'll fire you for sure."

We stare at each other a moment longer, then she says, "I was wrong about you, Russell Fink. And I'm sorry."

I decide to leave on a high note. But I have to ask, "Just curious. Who did you speak to at TB&S? Was it Sneed?"

"No." She looks at the ceiling for help. "It was a woman. And she had a funny name." The irony here is killing me, but I keep quiet.

"Fran Tarkenton or something. Anyway, she was very complimentary. Sounded to me like she might have a crush on you."

It takes real effort to keep the grin from sliding off my face. "I'll have to remember to look her up and thank her personally."

Back in my cubicle, I do just that. Geri answers on the first ring.

I pitch my voice low, like a nasal voice-over guy. "Yes, I'm calling from Hengle's Supply, and I need to speak with the employee with a funny name who's been saying nice things about one Russell Fink."

"May I ask what this call is concerning?"

"Mr. Fink would like to take said employee to dinner on Saturday. To show his gratitude."

"Funny name? Probably Billingham. Please hold."

Before I can hang up, Baxter Billingham says, "What can I do for you, Russell?"

"Oh, nothing sir. Sorry to bother you. I just wanted to check and make sure you were happy with the new copiers."

I hear a rustling sound, then he whispers, "Say, how's it coming on those photos of Barbie?"

"Still working on it."

"Excellent!"

My phone buzzes on my hip. A text message from Geri: "PICK ME UP AT SIX."

243

Wednesday

The name *Miracle Ward* came after the fact, coined by the reporter who ran the feature article in the *Tennessean*. He heard the story from his wife who learned the miraculous details from a nurse in her Bible study.

About six months before Katie's death, a support group grew out of the children's wing of Nashville Memorial's cancer wing. After months of grieving together in waiting rooms, fretting in hallways to and from therapy, weeping over cold coffee in the cafeteria, an organic bond had formed. Play dates were scheduled, meals ferried from house to house, desperate phone calls fielded at ungodly hours, prayers submitted with varying degrees of expectancy. When Katie suggested in front of the whole group that her daddy come and heal all the sick kids, it was met with surprising enthusiasm. She had a knack for unearthing glittery trinkets of faith and hope in the rocky fields of helplessness and despair. And what was her father to do? Say no? Gary Fink appeared one cold Wednesday morning, looking sheepish and uptight, then began reluctantly laying on hands and praying over frail, bald-headed children.

The dramatic accounts of remission and outright

recovery came trickling in weeks later. Katie was the only person who didn't seem the least bit surprised. The physicians remained stoic at first, exchanging dubious and suspicious glances. But eventually they joined several sets of parents in joyful, head-scratching celebration. Soon the entire ward was buzzing with renewed optimism. The news story made a local celebrity out of our father. Mom and Peter remained hopeful, but confused at Katie's lack of improvement. My sister beamed at the good fortune of her friends. I just held her hand and allowed the bitterness to eat away at my insides.

Of the eleven children present, four were eventually proclaimed cancer-free; five others went into remission. Two kids didn't make it. The local news anchors called it a miracle. The only medical expert willing to go on camera deemed it a very fortunate and welcomed co-incidence. Since Katie was not one of the fortunate few, I never really formed an opinion.

I asked Dan to take a look at Peter's Miracle Ward page and to get back to me. It didn't take long to whittle Dan's research down to just a handful of candidates. Of the eleven Miracle Ward patients, only four actually survived my father's healing into adulthood. Of those, only two still live in the area.

When I call and introduce myself to Fred Pryor, he sounds annoyed. That is, until I explain my connection to Gary Fink and the Miracle Ward. Then his grumbly tone graduates to one of sheer giddiness as he repeats, "Oh, you just *have* to talk to Sally about this," and "Go see Sally, she'll tell you *everything* you need to know ... and *more*." Each mention of his wife's name is followed by a short wheezy burst of laughter. It's hard to tell if he's infatuated, insane, or severely asthmatic. I attribute his eagerness and enthusiasm to an unyielding gratitude for my father's handiwork.

Sally Pryor changes all that.

The covered porch smells like well water and corn chips. It's lit-

tered with cigarette butts, a half-dozen coffee mugs, and a decompos-
ing mouse carcass. Sally, on the other hand, is done up like a realtor
on a billboard.

She begins screaming curses the moment she sees me through
the screen door. Apparently, Fred told her I was coming. Other than
the pulsing, distended veins on her neck and the globs of spittle careening from the corners of her mouth, the resemblance between
mother and daughter is astounding. Based on the group photo from
Katie's hope chest, my version of Misty Pryor's life would have included a stint as cheerleading captain, two years of dental hygiene
school, and a relatively quiet life with her accountant husband and
two-point-six kids.

"You got some nerve coming here." The screen door shrieks on
its hinges, then slams against the mildew-crusted vinyl siding as Sally
steps out to accost me.

"Your husband said — "

"Ahhh ... that flaming pile of — " Evidently, he failed to mention
that he's now her acrimoniously estranged ex-husband.

"I just have a couple of questions about Misty."

"Join the club, kid." She picks a fleck of something off the lapel of
her pantsuit and squints at it. "I got questions galore."

"Like what?"

"Like why God allows perfectly normal kids to get cancer?" I have
the same question but keep quiet. In part, because she looks like she'd
like to take a swing at me. "Then why He sees fit to heal that same kid,
then turn around and scramble her brains?"

"So she's still alive? I mean, she really was healed then?"

"Hah! Depends on your definition of healing." Sally Pryor reaches
inside her jacket. I wait for my life to pass before my eyes, certain that
she's going to shoot me. Instead she hands me Misty's business card.
"Here, see for yourself."

Spawn

Wiccan Goddess, Soothsayer, Bovine Deliverance

There's a tiny photo on the back of what looks to be the Gothic queen of some cartoon underworld. Her pale complexion is offset with black paint and so many piercings that her face appears to be attached with rivets.

"That's right. My daughter now credits some medieval wench named Aradia for her healing. And she makes her living casting spells out of unsuspecting farm animals and running a meth lab with her boyfriend."

"Oh," I say.

"Any other questions?"

"I don't know. Someone's been stalking my family. And I think that same person may have murdered my dog."

"And you think my daughter is involved, that it?"

"I don't think anything. I'm just poking around, trying to make connections."

"Yeah? Then try poking around the Middle Tennessee Women's Home for the Criminally Insane."

As she slams the door in my face I cross Misty Pryor off my mental checklist.

Thursday

When I finally get a hold of Mary Ann Leonard, she sounds sweet and relatively normal. "Sure! I'd love to visit with you. But we'll have to do it soon. Our flight leaves in a few hours."

It turns out she and her husband are headed to a South American rain forest to visit their daughter, Bonnie, a missionary. I'm not sure why this makes me feel so inadequate. She gives me directions, and ten minutes later I'm knocking on her bright green door with my nylon backpack slung over one shoulder. For some reason, it feels much heavier than its contents would suggest. Makes me wonder if I'm coming down with something or if I'm just nervous. Probably a little of both.

"Well, well. Look at you, Russell Fink. I always wondered if you'd ever top ninety pounds."

I'm guessing she's my mother's age, but she looks ten years younger. Her poofy blonde hair appears natural, her clothes bright and stylish. Even her wrinkles make her seem more impish than old. All in all, she does look vaguely familiar, but I can't quite place her. I'm sure my face gives me away. It usually does.

"You probably don't remember me at all, do you?"

I shake my head, relieved. She motions for me to sit down. "Not surprised. Whenever you came around, you either stared into your sister's eyes or directly at the floor. You two were something else, I tell you. Never seen anything like it since."

"How do you mean?"

"I've always heard that twins have a special bond. But you and Katie seemed to almost be an extension of each other. Kind of like those broken heart necklaces. You seemed to, I don't know, complete each other."

She excuses herself to the kitchen. I hear the sound of ice tumbling into glasses as I survey the living room. It's best described as a shrine, tastefully appointed, but a shrine nonetheless. Ceiling fans waft the foresty smells of potting soil and a variety of flora. The vaulted ceiling seems to go on forever. And the room is alive with greens and whites, from the shimmering curtains to the plaid sectional, from the marble-hearthed fireplace to the dozens of plants — hanging, potted, swinging, climbing. And then there are frames, nestled and tucked into every available space. Gauging by the photos, the Leonards are a happy bunch.

Mary Ann returns, carrying a tray of iced tea. She notices my gaping and frowns. "I know, I kind of go overboard with the plants and pictures and stuff."

"No, it's great. Kind of like a greenhouse without all the humidity."

"I guess we went a little crazy when Bonnie got sick. She developed a real fascination with plants. So I guess we just went all out trying to make her happy. My memory's kind of fuzzy now, but I think a lot of the parents did the same thing. You know, indulging every whim as some desperate attempt to make a suffering kid forget he's sick. Or offer a little hope. I'm convinced that's what helped our Bonnie."

I can't help but think that all this foliage has the same effect on

Bonnie's parents now, providing hope for their little girl who's not so little any more.

"So you don't buy the theory that my father healed your daughter?"

Her gaze drops to her lap. She starts to speak, then sips her tea instead. It's obvious she wants to get this right.

"I hope you won't take this wrong, but quite simply, no."

"Don't worry, me neither. I have a hard time with God singling out a few lucky ones just because of one man's prayer."

"Don't get me wrong, Russell. Bonnie's healing was an absolute medical miracle. We prayed a lot — for all of the kids. But we also watched Bonnie's diet and did everything in our power to keep filling her with hope. That's why she loved the greenery so much. When her father and I broke down under the stress, Bonnie always held up a palm full of seeds and pointed to one of her plants. Her logic was that if God could turn a crusty little tear-shaped rock into a beautiful flower, then scrubbing some cancer out of her system was no problem. And she was right. She had enough faith for all of us."

"Sounds like she was an amazing kid."

"She still is."

"Oh, right. Of course she is." As usual, I inflate a simple slip of the tongue into full-blown embarrassment.

"And as far as I'm concerned, God *did* single her out. I don't know why. And we've all had to deal with some guilt over that one. But He does what He does and we just try to keep up. Speaking of which ..." Mary Ann taps her watch playfully and says, "You came here looking for answers and I'm just blathering on."

"At the risk of sounding dramatic," I pause to unzip my backpack, "someone is stalking our family. And I think it has something to do with this."

I hold up the sand art for her inspection. She grins at the sight of it.

"Ah, Little Charlie Baringer's handiwork." She extends her hand and I give the jar to her. She rolls it around as if every granule contains a fresh memory. When she tears up, it makes me feel terrible. "Talk about indulging a kid's fascination. There was a rumor going around that Charlie's father managed to get Neil Armstrong's home number, determined to set up a meeting between his son and the famous astronaut. He ended up with a restraining order. And I suppose you heard he called the factory and ordered dozens of cases of Tang." She hands the sand art back to me. "That's where these came from."

"I guess I don't remember." But I'm not at all surprised.

"Little Charlie was obsessed with two things in this world — outer space and your sister."

"So I'm learning. But he died, right?"

A tear drops on the still spinning bottle. "A month or so after Katie. Like Bonnie and her plants, he wrapped his hope in the love of a little girl. When she didn't make it, well ..." She retrieves a tissue from behind a nearby plant and blows her nose. "Did you ever meet Charlie's father? Charlie Senior?"

I shake my head.

"He and his wife didn't exactly see eye to eye on how to deal with their son's illness. When your father performed his healing service, Charlie's mother became an instant convert. She was convinced that her son was healed and would not be dissuaded. She pulled him out of the hospital and refused any further treatment. They had a particularly nasty argument right there in the cancer ward one afternoon. She told her husband in no uncertain terms that his lack of faith was killing their son. She packed Charlie up in the middle of the night and took off. Charlie senior never saw his son alive again. And as far as I can tell, no one has seen Charlie Senior in over a decade."

"So you think he might be the one threatening my family?"

She makes a face like I just asked her for the recipe for ice cubes.

"Hang on a second," she says. "I may have something that'll help." Then she disappears into a back bedroom and returns several minutes later with a single slip of paper. It's a letter, handwritten in blocky pencil and signed by Charlie Baringer.

"You can keep it. We probably received two dozen or more of these. He was quite obsessed."

I do a quick scan to get the gist of it. It seems Charlie Baringer Senior had launched a campaign to not only keep my father from ever "stepping his defiled feet back into the ministry of our Lord," but it seems he wanted to send him to jail as well.

So that's it then. Charlie Baringer has been making the threats, stoking his vendetta against my father for years, even trying to enlist the help of other Miracle Ward parents. So it stands to reason that he's the one following Peter, not the gambling goons.

"All things considered, I guess I owe my brother an apology."

"Excuse me?" Mary Ann says. Apparently I was thinking out loud.

"Oh, I'm sorry. Thank you for your time. If you think of anything else, please call."

She walks me to the door and surprises me with a long hug. Not long enough, I realize.

Once behind the wheel, I dial Peter's number and wait for the beep, trying to remain calm. But worry seeps into my system anyway, slow and persistent, like an IV drip. He may have abused Sonny, but he didn't kill him. Charlie Baringer did. I skip the apology for now and warn him to be on the lookout for Charlie Baringer, if it's not already too late.

Saturday

I knock three times on the door, then twirl my old bandanna-cum-blindfold around my index finger to burn off some nervous energy. The sight of Geri when she answers is both delectable and disconcerting. A laser show crackles in my head while my insides flow with warm caramel. The changes are subtle, yet deliberate. Her cottony top is a complicated quilting of camouflage greens and eerily familiar red splotches with blue letters. It hangs on her like a hockey sweater, giving way to tan cargo pants and frayed Birkenstock clogs. She always had a knack for making comfy look cool. But she's outdone herself tonight, bohemian chic garnished with a beaded necklace and matching earrings. The effect is anything but casual, more like staggering. So much so, I don't realize I've dropped my blindfold until Geri picks it up and loops it around her wrist.

"Wow, your outfit is ..." I pause, still reeling from such intense adorability. "It's amazing, Geri."

Her happy eyes turn somber. She thinks I'm making fun of her. "Well, you did say to wear something comfortable."

"Let me rephrase that. You look lovely." She smiles in spite of herself. "And your hair is down."

She absently twirls a lock of what could pass for doll hair. "Yeah, well, ponytails give me a headache after awhile."

"I'm not complaining."

She squints when she smiles. And her nose scrunches up, making her freckles dance. But when I look closer, I notice her freckles are gone. How sad; I love Geri's freckles.

"Are you wearing makeup?"

Geri lapses into some unfamiliar posture, somewhere between blithe and demure. It looks good on her. Better than good. I'm trying to figure out a way to tell her this when she wraps the blindfold onto her index finger and spins it.

"Here," she says. "*You* put this on. You're giving me the creeps."

"Oh, sorry. I'll stop staring."

She looks more disappointed than relieved as she ushers me out and locks the door behind us.

"Wait a second." Geri pauses to buckle her seatbelt. "You're not going to make me do the time zone trick again, are you?"

"Oh man." I pretend to look deflated. "You ruined my surprise. Now I'll have to think of something else."

I put the Mary Kay Cadillac in gear, take a deep breath, then insert the CD version of our mix tape.

"I love this song. That's David Gray, right?"

I nod.

"Man, I haven't heard this in years."

I resist the urge to ask her to be quiet and listen to the words. But then I don't have to. When the chorus comes, Geri is singing "Sail away with me honey, I put my heart in your hands ..." in her squeaky, off-key alto. By the time it reaches my ears, it's as sweet and velvety as Billie Holiday. This same scenario is duplicated each time another song starts. When she realizes we're in the Vanderbilt area, Geri says, "No offense, Russell. But I'm not really in the mood for fried bologna."

"Not to worry."

Two turns later I parallel park and Geri squeals. "Rotier's? Perfect choice. I am so in the mood for a giant burger and a sinfully thick shake."

The restaurant hasn't changed a bit. It's dark and cramped, smoky and loud, and rife with fond memories. I signal the manager on duty, and he escorts us through the maze of tables to the exact spot Geri and I ate the last time we were here, nearly five years ago. We take our seats and I wait for recognition to bloom on her face. I have to settle for joy — not a bad consolation prize.

After we order, Geri wastes no time. "Okay, where's my present?"

"What present?"

"You said you had a surprise for me, right? So where is it?"

"Isn't sitting down for a meal with me surprise enough?"

"Sure, but I saw you sneak that package in your pocket when we got out of the car." Her grin is devilish and kissable and oh-so-hard to resist.

"Okay, smarty pants." I remove two small boxes and place them on the table — one a smallish square and the other an elongated version of the first. "Pick one."

She makes a big deal about trying to choose, lifting and shaking and smelling the boxes. Finally, she decides on the smaller one and reaches for it. "Okay, I want this one."

I'm suddenly blindsided with panic. I'm not ready, not yet. I snatch the chosen box out from under her fingers and cram it back into my hip pocket.

"Hey, what are you doing?"

"That was an executive decision. As the gift-giver, I can do that. If you play your cards right, maybe you'll get the other one later."

"We'll see about that. I might just decide to beat you up and take it from you. Lord knows, I outweigh you by about fifty pounds now."

257

She lifts the other box, peels the tissue paper off, and makes a big deal about the velvety box inside. "This better not be expensive, Russell Fink. Or you'll be taking it right back."

"Just open it."

She does. Her eyes go wide, and she makes small gasping noises. "It's perfect." She lifts it out and holds it up to the light, as if it were laden with diamonds. A few heads turn to see what all the commotion is about. But Geri ignores them, instead fondling the beads on her candy necklace.

"What do you think?" I say.

"I love it."

She slips it over her head, and I'm struck again by something about her homemade blouse. "That shirt looks familiar. Have I seen it before?"

"Nope, brand new. Just finished it today, in fact."

The meal comes and I catch myself steering the conversation back to the night I'm trying so hard to recreate. The burgers are so fat and juicy, I feel my arteries choking at once. When we've eaten all we can handle, I escort Geri to the door and say, "Shall we walk off dinner?"

Ten minutes later we're standing at the base of the steps of the Parthenon, a Nashville replica of the original temple of Athena, the poster child of ancient Greek architecture. We ascend the steps and circle the perimeter of the building, pausing occasionally to lean against the massive columns.

I've strategically picked our parking spot to coincide with a particular park bench. My hope is Geri will tucker out and ask to sit and rest, but if not, I suppose I can fake an ankle sprain. My brain is so consumed with the park bench that I interrupt Geri's lamenting about needing to pack for her trip to her mother's.

"Hey." I'm trying to sound casual but missing by a mile. "Isn't this the bench we graffitied last time we were here?"

"You may be right." At least she remembers.

"So," I say a little too quickly. "You think our names are still here?"

"I doubt it —"

"Hey! There we are!"

I kneel down to inspect it, leaning in close enough to smell Geri's skin.

"And look at that." I pause, trying to purge my voice of subterfuge. I stopped on my way home from work yesterday to carve out the necessary improvements. "Somebody took the time to draw a heart around our names. Ooh, and a plus sign between our initials."

She's quiet for a full minute, tracing the heart with her finger. I try to read her expression but the sun seems to be setting on her shoulders, making her look like a shadow. Her knees pop when she stands, and we head back toward the car. With every step our silence grows more tangible, a hushed indictment. It makes me wonder if I should just bag the whole idea.

Once behind the wheel again, I muster some enthusiasm and say, "Blindfold time."

As soon as I start the engine, Geri pops the CD back in, dons the blindfold, and nestles into her seat for more singing. The package in my pocket starts to feel like an anchor.

As I pull away from the curb, my own scattered thoughts assail me. Have I overplayed my hand? Been too obvious? Surely she can see through my transparent attempts at recreating our most memorable moments. I imagine she saw the freshly carved wood for what it was. What seemed like such a fabulous idea a few hours ago now strikes me as cheesy and obvious. I try to relax and just enjoy Geri's singing.

She fumbles some of the words, but at least she appears to be having fun again. When I refuse to sing along, she punches me in the arm. Eventually we end up harmonizing our way through songs by

Elvis Costello, Jonatha Brooke, more David Gray, Steely Dan, and even a Camper Van Beethoven song about bowling with skinheads.

* * *

After a series of complicated turns, I veer onto a secluded driveway canopied by tall oaks and evergreens.

"Wait a second." Geri tilts her head to one side. "We're going to the Nashville Zoo, aren't we!"

"Unbelievable! You peeked, didn't you?"

"No, silly. I can smell the manure."

"So, are you up for it?"

"I'll give it the old college try."

She removes the blindfold as I slow down to search for the secluded gravel road. I get out and unhook the thick chain, its purpose to keep people like us out. Back behind the wheel, I turn off the headlights and creep along the overgrown drive toward the familiar private entrance. Before getting out of the car, I turn what should be a three-point turn into five or six, aiming the pink behemoth in the opposite direction we came from. Just in case we need to make a getaway.

We make our way to a decrepit wooden door, the sound of gravel and crabgrass crunching under our feet. The last time we were here, I was able to hoist Geri up in the air by lacing my fingers together to make a stirrup, but I was in better shape then. So I play the hero and scale the rickety wall myself. Several abrasions and stifled curses later, I'm able to reach over the gate and trip the flimsy deadbolt lock. The door creaks open, and Geri and I begin our trespassing in earnest.

"You still have a thing for lambs?" I ask, keeping my voice at a near-whisper.

"Yeah, I do. More so than ever."

I realize now that we must have been much braver five years ago. We were never this jumpy before. But every squeal or bark or hiss gives me the willies. The upside is that Geri is hanging on to my arm and pressing herself closer to me with every step. At one point we whisper, "Lions, tigers, and bears … oh, my," as we make our way to the petting zoo and let ourselves in. I fish out some quarters and begin filling plastic cups with dried wafer thingies that the sheep seem to adore. I toss the food on the ground and watch the lambs jostle and squirm over it. Geri lets them eat out of her hand.

"Remember not to wipe your eyes," I say. The first time we broke into this very zoo, Geri ended up with a nasty E. coli-like illness that landed her in the hospital for three days. "I brought hand sanitizer, just in case."

When we run out of quarters, Geri and I lean against the railing. A pair of lambs keeps nuzzling her, and she can't seem to get enough of stroking their faces and letting them lick her hands. Their satisfied bleating sounds sweet. But the noise makes me more than a little nervous.

To combat that, I do what I always do and start talking again. "You really love those woolly beasts, don't you?"

She nods without looking up. I know something's bugging her. And I also know her well enough to know that she's incapable of letting things fester. In time, she'll tell me what's on her mind. She has to. It's how she's wired. I selfishly just hope it doesn't screw up the rest of my plan.

"You know, Russell, you never really answered your grandfather's question."

"Well, I would think the answer's obvious."

"Humor me."

"Of course I do. Me and Jesus go way back. I even did the 'invite Him into your heart' prayer when I was, like, seven." I pause for effect, then exploit the part of my voice reserved for punch lines. "So, yeah. I believe in Him, but I'm not so sure He believes in me anymore."

"Guess this is all a big joke to you then."

I have indeed screwed up. She's not the least bit amused. Quite the contrary, in fact. But instead of feeling guilty, I find myself resenting her pouty tone. I went to a lot of trouble to make this night special. This is not the conversation I was hoping to have by this juncture in the evening.

Geri wipes her hands on her homemade cargo pants. Then she just stands there, facing me, holding me hostage with her gaze. "Because I do believe it, Russell. I know it's not the Geri you knew in college, but now I've never believed anything so fiercely in my life."

I'm surprised by how much that stings. I've spent countless hours trying to make her believe in *me*. My pity party is cut short when we hear someone shout, "Hey!"

Geri looks at me. Then we're scrambling for the gate.

"Security! Stop right there and keep your hands where I can see them."

* * *

This is not the first time we've been chased by security in this zoo. But we were younger then, unassailable, teeming with brash ignorance. Still, we make a valiant effort at running away. But after fifty paces or so, Geri stops to catch her breath. And she grabs my shirttail to make sure I stop too.

"Sorry, Russell. I can't do it."

"Is it your back?"

She laughs. "Among other things."

Then the security guard is right on top of us. He's young, shockingly thin, and looks scared to death.

"Okay, you two. Hold still and don't pull any funny business." After he too catches his breath, he says, "Now what do you think you're doing in here after hours?"

"Actually," I say, "we were just leaving."

"The zoo closes at six."

"I know that now. Why do you think we're in such a hurry to get out?" He doesn't think I'm funny. But at least I get a worried smile out of Geri. "So if you'll excuse us." I grab Geri's arm, turn to leave, and for a second I almost believe I'm going to get away with it.

"Hold it right there. I'm calling the cops."

He unclips his walkie-talkie and is about to officially turn us in when Geri says, "Please don't do that."

The security guard and I swivel our heads toward her. Something in her tone brings us both up short.

"Why on earth not?" The security guard sounds incredulous.

Geri pauses, pondering her words, then says, "Look, my name is Geri Tarkanian and this is Russell Fink."

"Those names sound made up," he says.

"He's right," I say, nodding vigorously. "They do. Actually my name is Peter and this is Alyssa —"

Geri ignores us both. "We were just having some fun, for old times sake. We used to break in here regularly when we were in college. We never hurt anything, just strolled around and fed the lambs. Tonight we just thought we'd go back and try to relive our glory days. Russell here was trying to create a special moment. And well ..."

I swear I heard her voice crack.

"Well what?" the security guard says.

"It's too late for me."

"What's that supposed to mean?"

I expect Geri to tell him how sad she is that she's moving away — not a complete fabrication. She's mentioned going to visit her mother in North Carolina a few times tonight, but I've been too distracted to remember when or for how long.

"I'm sick," she says. "And I don't know how many fun days I have left."

We all quietly stare at the tops of our shoes for a while. I wish I could see Geri's face, to see if her smile is as big as the one I'm trying to hide.

Finally, the security guard tells us he's going to let us go with a warning. And that next time he catches us sneaking around the premises, he'll shoot us with a tranquilizer gun and feed us to the lions. We thank him profusely and immensely, then he tells us to go back out the way we came in.

Back in the car, I'm bouncing off the walls with excitement. "Wow, I didn't know you had it in you. I almost believed you back there."

But Geri's withdrawn again, probably feeling guilty about transitioning straight from Jesus talk to fudging her way out of trouble. I pop in the mix CD and try to work up my courage to finish the night strong while we drive to our final destination of the evening.

* * *

The Opryland Hotel used to be a cheap date, that is, before management started charging twelve bucks just to park there. Whenever college boys ran short on cash, they brought their dates here to stroll the lush grounds and "just talk." The result was a low-budget date with the fringe benefit of getting credit for having a more sensitive side.

Tonight I escort Geri to the revolving restaurant where we order dessert and coffee. I'm still buzzing from all the excitement at the zoo. Geri seems distracted, still humming remnants from the mix CD.

"You okay?" I ask. "You didn't hurt your back again or anything, did you?"

"No, I'm fine. I guess I'm just a little tired." She runs her finger around her water glass. "Sorry, guess I'm not as much fun as I used to be."

"Don't be ridiculous."

"No, I act and feel like someone two decades older. I'm fatter, more emotional, and just plain tired all the time."

"Knock it off." Without thinking, I reach across the maze of dishes and stemware, taking both of Geri's hands in mine. "You're absolutely perfect, just like you are."

She's about to say something. And it looks important. But the waiter shows up and deposits our matching slabs of chocolate cake, thus ruining whatever moment we were about to share. I can't help thinking Geri looks relieved. We attack our desserts and keep the conversation on safer terrain. Although it now seems defined by the things we're not saying.

"Okay, Geri. I'm dying to know what's up with your shirt."

She sits back and holds the fabric out. Something trips my memory.

I'm about to make some ridiculous joke when it dawns on me. I begin pointing out letters in the air. "Hey, that's my sweatshirt!"

Her grin is proud and more than a little embarrassed. It was summer break and I was taking her to the airport. She complained of being cold, and I made her borrow my red Belmont University Bruins sweatshirt. After that, we didn't see each other for years. And now here it is again. But what does it say?

Apparently, I spoke this last thought aloud.

"Oh, it's nothing. I just wanted to use all the letters."

"It's never nothing with you, Geri. It's always something." I affect a slightly mocking tone that I try to twist into more of a flirtatious one. She rolls her eyes and stares at an elderly couple holding hands and watching the colored fountains.

"What?" I say lamely.

She holds my gaze then, practically daring me to say something stupid. When I finally look away, she scrapes the last bit of icing from

265

her plate. When she looks up, her eyes are glistening. "This has been a wonderful evening, Russell. I know you worked hard to make it special. And I'm going to miss you when I'm gone."

I feel my face falling. Geri must see it too.

"I think I've decided—or it's been decided for me—to leave a little early for my mother's."

"How early?"

"A week from today. Saturday. I'm taking a leave of absence from work." She glances up to gauge my reaction. I doubt she likes what she sees. "I'm going to be there a while. Like maybe a couple of months. Maybe longer."

"Oh." I try to hide the shock and frustration and panic of this news by looking down at my plate. But I'm quite convinced that my scalp is glowing red.

"This has been the perfect evening. But you really shouldn't have spent the money ..."

"Your twenty bucks helped." This, of course, is a pathetic attempt to guide the conversation back toward our stalled love lives.

She wrinkles her nose at me and says, "I really should get some sleep."

"Not so fast," I say. "I do have one more little surprise."

Her smile is wary, but at least she smiled. And I wish I were half as confident as I sound. And frankly, I don't really sound all that confident. But I've set the wheels in motion. The last time I had this opportunity, I let it slip away. And I've regretted it ever since. So no matter what happens, I plan to finish what I came here for.

We wind our way through both levels of the atrium, pausing to toss coins in the rippling ponds and comment on the exotic fish. When I hear the waterfall, my heart starts to pound like a stallion trapped in a closet with its tail on fire. Geri yawns—big and loud—then threads her right arm through my left and rests her head on my shoulder. I take this as a sign of affection, a boon to my weak-kneed confidence. But she's probably just tired. Finally, we make our way to the back side of the waterfall where the memories come flooding back. I just hope she feels it too.

The weight of the moment strikes my lungs first, then my knees. I've reached the moment-of-truth part of the evening. It's time to decide to lay it all on the line or chicken out and go home. But my mind is suddenly a blur, ambushed with images of our shared history — walks around the Parthenon, shooting pool, staying up late and not studying, time zone tricks, Opryland waterfalls, and the time we got kicked out of a department store for starting a squirt gun battle with the cologne samples. That was a few short hours before our last trip to this very spot. At some point Geri accused me of cheating at Yahtzee. Our playful banter eventually led to a small wrestling match. I pinned her arms behind her back and was threatening to hold her face under the wall of water unless she admitted that she cheated. But instead of confessing, Geri executed a marvelous spin move that landed her in my arms. Somehow we'd ended up in a full-on embrace, noses almost touching. Tourists and raging waterfalls faded into background music. As did summer vacations, revolving restaurants, boyfriends named Tom, and girlfriends named Alyssa. We stared at each other, breathless, lips parted, inches away from consummating what we'd spent the last nine months nurturing on the one hand and denying on the other. My every molecule screamed at me to kiss her. But I hesitated, probably out of fear and some loyalty to Alyssa. My hesitation turned to an awkward pause, which was all the trio of German tourists needed to interrupt us and ask if we would take their picture behind the waterfall.

Now we're here again, under the same waterfall. Geri sneezes. Then she sneezes again. "Yikes. Sorry about that. Seems like I've developed an allergy to chlorine."

"Oops, I almost forgot." I fish around in my pockets and produce two small packages. First, I rip the corner off a cologne sample I pilfered from a drugstore and dab some under my chin.

"Is that Brut?" Geri says.

"By Faberge," we both say in unison.

Next, I tear into a pink wrapper and shove a long stick of gum into Geri's palm. "This still your favorite?"

"Cool. Teaberry. I haven't seen this stuff in years."

I read somewhere that our sense of smell is most closely related to memory. Now I can only pray that I've set the mood and let Lady Nostalgia do her thing. I have no clue what I'm about to say when I open my mouth, but that doesn't stop me. Not tonight. "You know why I brought you here tonight?"

"I have some ideas." She toes a loosed pebble on the aggregate walkway, her grin furtive and begrudging.

"You never admitted that you cheated," I say, relishing the temporary confusion in her eyes. "At Yahtzee."

She shoves my shoulder, hard enough to knock me off balance. "You're right. I didn't, did I?"

"Didn't what? Cheat? Or apologize?"

"I'm not telling."

I grab her shoulders, expecting resistance as I pretend to shove her head under the water. But she melts into me. And before I have time to think about it, our lips meet. Then again. When I pull back, Geri tightens her grip on my neck, relaxing only when I kiss her again.

The weight of the world has been lifted.

When it's over, we pull back and both mutter, "Wow."

Before I lose my nerve, I take the box out of my pocket and place it in her hand. I drop to one knee and say, "Geri, I should have found a way to do this years ago."

Her eyes widen and her jaw drops. Then she sneezes again. Her eyes alternate between the velvety box in her hands and the man genuflecting before her.

"Come on, open it up. My knee's getting all wet."

"Russell, I can't ..."

"Sure you can. Just flip the lid up and take a look."

Reluctantly, she does. Her expression is impossible to read, so I just blurt it out before I can talk myself out of it.

"I'm out of my mind, Geri. I love you like a crazy person. I was an idiot for ever letting you get away the first time. Heck, I'm probably still an idiot. But I'm nuts about you, and I don't want to spend another day without you in my life."

"Russell—"

"Don't you remember Gramps's prayer?" My tone is supposed to be suave, confident and creamy. It comes out all cracked and panicky. "You can't possibly deny an old man's dying wish. Just like you said, Geri. I'm ready to follow you to the moon. And I *know* you can see it in my eyes."

Her face is alive with emotion.

"Will you marry me?"

Tears prick her eyes and run down her cheeks. She's can't seem to find her words, probably a combination of shock and joy.

"Please say you will, Geri."

"No, Russell. I can't. I'm sorry. But I could never do that to you."

* * *

The night is colder than it should be. Or maybe my face is just hotter. We walk aimlessly around the parking lot, shoulders hunched like refugees, all too aware of the distance between us. I think it dawns on her the same time it does me—neither of us has a clue where the car is parked. But we don't talk about it. I suspect her voice is as unreliable as mine, although for different reasons. So we keep walking until the pink backside of Dan's Caddy appears in my peripheral vision.

I open the door for Geri, then walk around to the driver's side. If not for her phobia, I might just toss her the keys and keep on walking. She still hasn't moved when I open my own door.

"Russell ..."

Our eyes meet over the pink Caddy for the first time since she unstitched my heart.

"You know I'm sorry, right? And the kiss was wonderful ... the best ever."

I shrug, feeling guilty at once. It's obvious she's in pain. And I should be man enough to put her heart ahead of my hurt feelings. I swallow hard, but can only manage a limp nod.

"I know this won't make sense. Not now, anyway. But you have to believe me when I tell you this is for the best." When I don't respond, she adds, "You'll understand some day and thank me for it."

I look away, trying to find my voice. Finally, I turn back and say "I'll *never* understand."

But instead of looking at Geri, I'm staring across the roof of the car at a beefy guy in overalls sitting in his pickup truck. He grins like we just shared a secret. "Me neither, boss. Meeeee neeeither."

The silent drive to Geri's apartment is swarming with unspoken thoughts. The only real sound emanates from the car's speakers. The mix CD mocks us, countering the chatter in our respective heads with poetic pledges of undying love. What a ridiculous notion. But neither of us can muster the nerve to turn it off. Geri fingers the hem of her blouse while I strangle the steering wheel and ignore the apologies that seem to be coming off her in waves. But I'll have none of it. My heart is officially closed for business.

I park in front of her building and try to think of something to say. Nothing brilliant, mind you. I'd settle for something neutral or kind or even lightly sarcastic. Geri's gaze warms my cheek, and I know I should turn and thank her for a lovely evening and assure her that everything will be okay. Finally, she clears her throat and says, "Okay, then."

I watch Geri walk away again. She looks even more like the scared eight-year-old girl entering a new school. Only she's given up on the brave front. Before she disappears into her apartment, a few of the bright blue letters on her cottony top jump out at me and form actual words. I would swear I saw the words *love in ruins*.

I put the car in drive but can't seem to get my foot off the brake. Minutes later her bedroom light goes on. Some time after that I see her silhouette at the window. Our shadows stare at each other. The car's transmission rumbles under me. Once my foot slips off the brake, and I almost slam into the back of the car parked in front of me. I replant my foot on the brake and stare some more. It's nearly three in the morning when the car runs out of gas.

Monday

A quick search of the Caddy's trunk nets a box full of wires and electronic gear, along with a hibachi, a toaster, a microwave, some firewood, a sleeping bag, three blankets, and four cans of lighter fluid. But no gas can.

I start walking, head down and sulking my way into full-blown despair. The lump in my pocket rubs against my thigh, every step a fresh reminder that Geri turned me down. I'm wondering what I did with the jeweler's receipt when a siren wails a few blocks away, making me walk faster for some reason. Eventually, a rich, woody smell finds me. It's not unlike a campfire, and I can't help wondering if vandals haven't broken into Dan's car and are joyriding around, smoking sausages and roasting marshmallows on his Hibachi.

When I step out of Geri's neighborhood and into the commercial glare of 21st Avenue, I notice the bustle of emergency personnel and the awestruck voices of on-lookers, pointing and gasping at the fiery spectacle before them.

I stop and stare too. The flames are too big, too bright, too orange for my overwrought brain to process. I have the insane thought that Peter's coffee shop is right around here somewhere, followed by the even crazier realization that the Bean Bag is indeed burning to the ground before my eyes.

I watch the blaze.

Until my phone rings.

It's my mother. Her voice is thick with emotion when she says, "Russell ... Gramps is dead."

Part Three

Thursday

The funeral is generously attended, filling the church of my youth to capacity. When I see Dan walk in, I'm touched. His suit looks good, save for the bulges of who knows how many thermal layers underneath. But then I wonder if some absurd intersection of fate crossed Dan's path with Gramps'. A bizarre image flickers in my mind, one of Dan presiding over my grandfather's service, eulogizing in seven languages. Then I remember Mom mentioning the name of the minister on the ride over, Amos something. Of course Gramps would have thought a casket equipped with state-of-the-art stereo speakers was just the coolest.

Then I see Geri sidle up to Dan and take his arm. I feel a tinge of jealousy at the sight of her hand resting on his arm. Geri looks magnificent, the first time I've seen her in store-bought clothes since college. Dan offers a tight-lipped nod, then studies the tops of his shoes. Geri's gaze bores into mine — relentless, pursuing, consoling, delicate — a lifeline for my failing spirit. But it comes up short. I'm about to venture over and apologize for not returning her calls the last three days, maybe even steal a hug. But the funeral director corrals my family and escorts us to the front row of the aging chapel.

The wooden pew groans under the weight of family, sans Peter (I really should have told my parents about the fake kidnapping letter by now). But Peter's a grown man, and although it's no secret he never forgave Gramps for killing Grandma, he should be here anyway. I left him a dozen messages telling him when and where.

Muted sunlight refracts through stained glass windows, pale vignettes of Jesus healing, teaching, forgiving, dying, ascending. His eyes follow me around the room, offering comfort. But I ignore it. The familiar organ music subsides, and a gangly middle-ager in an off-the-rack blue suit takes the podium. Tight, oily curls taper into a widow's peak. He has a face like a shovel, broad and flat and severely scarred. But his voice is surprisingly smooth.

"Take a good look, brothers and sisters. Russell Allen Fink is gone. By my calculations ..." He pauses to glance at a pocket watch. " ... I'd say our friend has spent the last couple of days doting on that pretty wife of his. And now he's probably scaring up a game of checkers with whoever's in charge of guarding the pearly gates."

This elicits some raucous laughter from the motley gathering across the aisle, a patchwork of longish gray hair, leather, denim, braided ponytails, tattoos, and eyes like drying cement. Several of these former brutes catch my eye and nod their condolences.

The preacher is speaking again, and I can't help wondering who he is and how he knew my grandfather. As if reading my mind, he says, "Most of you folks don't know me. My name is Amos Ironside. I did some bad stuff in my life; there ain't a death penalty or a corner of hell severe enough for me." Someone mumbles an *Amen*. "By the time they put me in a cell with Russell, I'd already decided that the world would be a much better place without me in it. But he had other plans." This is met with a round of snorts and stifled laughter. "For those of you who don't know the story, every night after lights-out, Russell would start quoting Scripture at me. He could do the whole gospel of John from memory. He'd whisper so only I could hear it. Drove me batty. And when I couldn't handle it no more, I'd start screaming at him to shut the — um, to keep quiet. But all that got me was black eyes and cracked ribs from keeping my fellow inmates up all night. It didn't take long for me to learn to just shut up and endure it. But one night I'd had enough, and I told Russell I was gonna kill myself if he didn't pipe down. And that it was going to be on his head. Actually, I said all kinds of awful things, but he was unfazed. He just kept quoting his Scripture about how God couldn't remember a single bad thing I'd ever done. But that's all I *could* remember when I shut my eyes and tried to sleep. When it came to what I'd done, my memory was much better than God's. See, I used to … I was …"

He pauses, staring at something only he can see. Whatever it is, I hope I never see it. He coughs once, bringing himself back, then continues.

"So I finally told Russell that either he shuts his mouth or I'm gonna rip open my own throat. I was going to bleed out and Russell Fink would have another murder on his eternal rap sheet. And I was prepared to do it too. But the next thing I know, Russell is off his bunk and dragging me off of mine. He's all wild-eyed, grinning, and choking me. Squeezing the very life out of me, still quoting his Scripture.

"Every now and then he'd pause and scream at me, 'You want to die so bad? You just say the word and it's done. Won't be the first time I took a life.' Then he dug his thumb in harder, cutting all my wind off, still preaching at me with that crazy look in his eye.

"That's when I started fighting back, fighting for my life. He knew I would too; he knew me better than I knew myself. I wanted to die, but at the same time, I didn't. I just wanted someone to convince me that there was a shred of hope, something worth fighting for. So Russell strangled some sense into me, proved to me that even my pathetic life was worth living. He spent the rest of the night introducing me to Jesus. Then he spent the next three nights in solitary confinement." I'm surprised at the ripple of laughter behind me. "That's right, because the next morning he marched right up to the warden and confessed to choking me half to death."

"Because of Russell, I eventually made parole." This sets off a low rumble of approval and amens from the section of parolees. "He wrote me letters every day, encouraging me to get my GED and a job. Every time I came to visit him, he'd make me recite whatever part of John's gospel I was memorizing at the time. He never looked happier than hearing one of his disciples quoting the Word. Most of all he encouraged me to —"

His voice falters here, then crumbles. His tortured sobs fill every crevice in the room. He wraps his long fingers around his skull and squeezes.

While he squeaks out barely audible apologies and pounds his thighs with his fist, I sense movement to my left. One by one, the entire section of hippies, hooligans, gangsters, and thugs file out of their pews and make their way to the front. They lay rough hands on the heaving man and offer loud beseeching prayers on his wretched behalf. At first I think they're oblivious to their own spectacle. But after studying their faces, I can't detect an ounce of pretense. They just don't care who's watching or what they think about it.

The guy in the tattered red flannel shirt keeps cutting his eyes at me, like we've met before and he's trying to place me. I can't be sure, but I think it's the weeping man from prison, forced to meet his newborn daughter under the scrutiny of inmates, guards, Gramps, and me. Either that, or it's Peter in disguise.

Amos finds his legs, then his voice. With ragged words he tells us how he found the people he'd hurt and confessed his sin. Only one of his victims offered any semblance of forgiveness. And that was one more than he'd expected, one more than he deserved.

Amos wrapped up his story with a prayer, igniting a chain of impromptu testimonies from the crowd of rough men.

Apparently, when Gramps wasn't preparing wills or playing checkers, he spent the bulk of his time in prison loving the unlovely and reforming the unreformable, all in the name of Jesus. Several of these former inmates referred to my grandfather as the Repo Man—he saw no shame in using whatever dramatic means necessary to make his—or God's—point. More than one man quoted Gramps as saying, "We can do this hard or we can do it easy. But the good Lord tells me your number is up. Time to fess up and find your wings. Either that or die resisting it."

Story after story filled the room. Drug dealers, white supremacists, petty thieves, and even a murderer all stood to speak on behalf of my grandfather. But it didn't stop there. Three prison guards and a retired warden stood and bore witness to the miracles they saw with their own eyes, the hardest of men changed from the inside out. Not everyone, but enough to make believers out of them all. There were even a few documented cases of physical healing at the hands of my father's father. He became one of the most feared men in prison, not for his physical presence or his menacing spirit, but because he had the reputation of being God's pet monkey.

It seems his constant refrain was a single question: "Do you believe Jesus is who He said He was? Really *believe* it?"

At some point I have the sensation that Gramps is sitting beside me, grinning at my discomfort and relishing the words of his friends. But I can't indulge this image long. For some reason I feel like I might look down the aisle and see Sonny sitting there too.

But then it dawns on me that no one named Fink is speaking up for Gramps. I try to catch my father's eye. But he stares forward with his jaw set and his eyes moist. What a travesty it would be to let this service end without someone from his own family standing and paying some respect. My pulse quickens; I know I should stand and say something. But I'm too chicken. It's like my fear of praying out loud, only on steroids, magnified to some ridiculous power, paralyzing me. And besides, my father is the preacher, the professional orator, the man of the house, the spiritual leader. Another glance in his direction is all the proof I need that he's not going to do a single thing but sit there and grind his teeth.

Then all at once, my chest and head are filled with helium. I practically float up out of my seat. And since I'm in the front row, there's no way to miss me. I feel the weight of a thousand eyes on me as I make my way to the pulpit, driven by some unseen but undeniable force.

The retired warden wraps up his thoughts with a quick prayer, then welcomes me to the podium. My legs are like cold linguine and my entire body is wet with sweat. I find my spot behind the microphone and realize that I haven't planned a single thing to say. I scan the room, barely aware of the thick, awkward silence. Still I can't speak. I squint at the faces of distant relatives and complete strangers for inspiration. Nothing comes, just a swelling panic. I grip the podium tighter, but my hands are so slick I can't even do that right. I open my mouth, just to see if anything will come out, but it doesn't.

Now people are starting to squirm and fidget in their seats. I know I can't sit down without saying something. Still, nothing will come. Not even the tears.

My eyes find Geri, but hers are focused in her lap. Then she shifts her weight to one side and I'm temporarily convinced she's going to stand. That she'll make her way to the podium, squeeze my arm, maybe even feed me a few lines. But she shifts again and settles deeper into her seat. When her head tilts up toward mine, I look away. I clear my throat and say the first thing that comes to mind.

"My name is Russell Fink." My shaky voice rolls across the congregation like a wave. It laps gently against the far wall, then returns softly and crashes over me. "I loved my grandfather. And I couldn't be prouder to share my name with him."

I pause here, surprised I've made it this far and unsure what to say next. Then it dawns on me that maybe I've said enough already. I retake my seat, hide my face in my hands, and focus on trying to make my lips stop trembling. Someone makes a few closing remarks. Someone else offers directions to the cemetery and a final prayer. Sometime later I find myself staring out the window of a limousine, imagining Sonny perched stubbornly on a cloud and refusing to play fetch with Gramps and Katie.

* * *

The post-funeral festivities are just too depressing. So instead of standing in line, shaking hands and making stilted small talk with relatives I hardly know, I sneak out the back and call a cab. It smells like yesterday's lunch and the driver hums incessantly. I end up at Hengle's Supply. I figure I might as well check my messages and get my mind off things. It doesn't dawn on me that this may be a bad idea until I walk through the doors and see the back of Bernie's head. He's laboring under some heavy load that I can't see as he enters his father's office. I hear a loud, wooden thump followed by a lengthy sigh. Although I'm not feeling particularly snarky — I'm not feeling much of anything, actually — I decide to duck into my office before getting into anything with my boss's son. My plan is to clear out the voice mails and the emails, then allow my brain to idle while I play computer solitaire until quitting time.

When I round the corner to my cubicle, I'm confronted with a huge cardboard box perched in the middle of my otherwise empty desk. The carpeted walls are bare except for the dimples and discolorations where my photos used to hang. I don't have to dig through the box to see what's inside. But I do it anyway. Under my computer generated photo of Sonny wearing a cowboy hat is my Rembrandt desk calendar, a couple of dog-eared novels along with a Dale Carnegie book I never got around to reading, my three favorite coffee mugs, the fancy pen set my mother gave me when I got the job, and all of the dusty photos of Alyssa and me that I'd stowed in a filing cabinet.

The ramifications are obvious. But that's not what makes me mad. It's the fact that someone, probably Bernie, has been pawing through my personal stuff. All at once I'm transported back to my college dorm room, realizing that my acoustic guitar, about sixty CD's, and the contents of my savings account have gone missing. But then I notice the lights go out in the elder Hengle's office. He emerges, looking older and more haggard than I've ever seen him before. He sees me staring and seems to wilt. We stare at each other from across the room and he shakes his head. After a long moment he makes his way to my cubicle, smiling sadly.

"I was very sorry to hear about your grandfather, Russell. I know it's only a small token, but I do hope the flowers arrived in time."

I shrug and point toward the box. "Does this mean I'm getting a promotion and a bigger office?" My voice is laced with more anger than I would have thought possible after today.

"No, son. But I think you already knew that."

"Would you care to explain it to me then? I've had the best month in company history and I'm rewarded with a pink slip?"

"I'm afraid it's out of my hands." He motions with his chin toward the trio of Bernie, Mandy, and Robin as they lug computer equipment out of the conference room and into Mr. Hengle's office. "You weren't here this morning, Russell. Mrs. Hengle took another turn for the worse, had another stroke. And the doctors tell me she'll be in need of constant care." At this, his voice breaks. "And I refuse to send her away.

So it appears that this is my last day too. Bernie's in charge. As of today, it's his company now; I just hope all those history lessons stick."

I know I should quell the voices in my head; that I should make some sort of overture or gesture to the grieving man in front of me. But I'm simply too stunned to process all this new information. When the fog lifts, I'm sure I'll feel terrible.

"For what it's worth, I argued on your behalf." He puts his hand on my shoulder and waits for our eyes to meet. "I'm very proud of the way you've come around, Russell. You'll be an asset wherever you land. And please don't hesitate to use me as a reference."

"Thanks," I say. "And I hope Mrs. Hengle gets better soon."

"The doctors say she'll never be the same. But I'm still holding out hope, praying for another miracle." His hopeful look breaks my heart. He squeezes my arm and it's not hard to imagine another desperate walk up my father's front steps, only with his wife hanging on his arm instead of Ray.

I stare at the corner office for a long time, listening to the laughter and the bustle of activity inside. Scenarios play out in my mind, some angry, some sarcastic, and all very ugly. In the end I decide to take my toys and go home.

But then Bernie pokes his head out of his new office and wants to have a word with me. Mandy and Robin scurry out like two frightened birds. Against my better judgment, I make my way to Bernie's new office. He punches a button on his speakerphone and says, "Nancy, could I see you for a moment? And please bring the Fink file."

"You're really enjoying this, aren't you?"

He doesn't answer. Instead he pretends to study some single-spaced document on his virgin desk blotter. I know he's not really reading it because his lips aren't moving.

If I were smart, I'd grab my box and go home. Instead, I keep talking. "Guess I shouldn't be surprised. While most kids were playing cops and robbers or cowboys and Indians, you were acting out corporate mergers and mass layoffs."

"Nothing pretty about this, Fink. Just doing my job."

"That is total crap and you know it. You've been dreaming of this day ever since you met me."

"Don't flatter yourself." He makes a strained noise that could loosely be interpreted as laughter. "I spend a lot less time thinking about you than you'd imagine."

But I can tell by the way his lip twitches that I'm right. His hands are shaking and his eyeballs are Riverdancing. It's suddenly clear to me that he's rehearsing his speech. He's the boy in the backyard, after scoring thousands of imaginary winning touchdowns, who's finally getting his shot. That, and he's waiting for Nancy to show up so she can hear his little speech. I decide to take a play out of Alyssa's handbook and not give him the satisfaction.

"Look, Bernie. If you have something to say, say it." His eyes flick to a spot over my shoulder. Then Nancy is standing there, squinting through the dense cloud of testosterone in the room. I ignore them both and say, "On second thought, save it. Just cut me that commission check and I'll get out of your hair."

"What commission check would that be, Fink?"

I stand up and try to look imposing. But the tremors breaking out all over my body give me away.

Bernie looks to Nancy for help. It's obvious she's about to deliver more bad news, but neither Bernie nor I know who it's for. She opens the manila folder in her hand and begins flipping and scanning pages. Bernie rounds his desk and looks over Nancy's shoulder, probably sensing he's losing control of the situation. Nancy taps a spot on the paper with a long fingernail. Bernie's eyes find the spot and a grin breaks out on his face.

"Sorry, Russell," he says. "But your contract clearly spells out the condition of outstanding commissions at the time of termination."

I snatch the folder out of Nancy's hands, startling them both. Several documents spill out and flutter around our ankles. I try to read the lines, but they're tinged red and wriggling across the page.

Finally, when I can't think of anything sensible to say, I hear myself shouting, "I want that commission, Bernie. I earned it. It's mine."

He's shaking his head while Nancy is trying to pick the scattered papers up off the carpet.

"You tell him, Nancy." She can't, or won't, meet my gaze. "I need that money."

"I'm sure you do, Russell." The condescending smirk on Bernie's face makes my fist curl and tighten. "But you're holding the contract in your hands. That is your signature at the bottom, is it not? Go ahead and read it. I'll even help you with the big words if you—"

Nancy clears her throat and says, "Bernie, I'm sure that's enough."

"I'm not leaving here without that check."

"I'm afraid Daddy doesn't sign the checks anymore. I do. And I have no intention of signing anything but your pink slip. Something he should have done a long time ago."

Nancy is still on one knee, trying to dislodge a few papers from under the sole of Bernie's tasseled loafer.

"You know, Fink. I never could see what my father saw in you. It certainly wasn't potential. But I'm pretty sure now he just felt sorry for you."

Nancy says, "Bernie, knock it off. *Now.*" She gives up tugging on the sheaf of papers under his foot. She's standing up now, probably to go call the cops.

"No, somebody needs to explain the facts of life to this guy. You walk around here, feeling sorry for yourself when you should be out

287

learning how to become an impact player." He takes another step toward me, jabbing the air with his forefinger. "You think you're funny, but you're not. You're pathetic. You're ..."

My balled fist makes a wide arc from my hip to a spot above my right shoulder.

Bernie's eyes widen. He raises both hands for protection, fingers fanned and trembling.

My poised fist then rockets toward Bernie's lower lip. And no amount of mental gymnastics can undo the launch sequence.

Bernie tries to backpedal, losing his footing on the part of my personnel file. I think it's the actual pink slip he was so proud of.

Nancy reaches her full height just as Bernie disappears from view. All but his feet, which flash where his belly used to be. He lands with a winded thud as my fist smashes into Nancy Clancy's nose.

Even as I'm kneeling beside her, my first thought is how much my knuckles hurt. Blood seeps through Nancy's fingers as lame apologies come tumbling out of me. I turn to grab a box of tissues, but never make it. Bernie barrels into me, leading with his shoulder. I bounce once on the carpet before the top of my head smashes into the doorjamb. When I look up, Bernie has already found a first aid kit. He's using his teeth to tear a long strip of gauze, while cradling his phone between his ear and shoulder. He's already dialed 911.

"That's right," he says calmly into the mouthpiece. "His name is Russell Fink. He's armed and dangerous and out of his mind."

Nancy's voice is thick and garbled. But I'm certain I hear the words *hospital first* and *you idiot.* Apparently Bernie values my apprehension and arrest over the health and welfare of poor Nancy Clancy. When I realize I can't do anything to help, I do the only thing I can think of.

I run.

A mocking voice inside my head says, *Liar, I thought you said you don't hit girls.*

* * *

When I ask the cabbie to wait outside my parents' house, he points at the meter and shrugs.

It takes three tries before the tumblers align and the door clicks free. My gaze darts to the familiar spot — bottom shelf, right-hand side. But it's not there. No glimmering glass bottle, no black label. I step back, blinking, attempting deep breaths and scanning every shelf again. When I still don't see it, I begin tearing into boxes of legal documents and a few of Mom's spare purses that litter the floor.

Nothing. No vodka to drown my misery. So I do the intelligent thing and kick one of the shelves, upsetting a stack of papers and an old Dutch Masters cigar box. Pain ripples upward and outward from my big toe.

I shove the loose papers back onto the shelf and scoop up the cigar box. But the flimsy lid gives way and the contents spill out all over the floor. It's letters, mostly. They are all in pencil, block lettering that tilts to the right as if bracing against a sharp wind.

The letters all contain threats, some subtle, some over the top. I sit with my back to the safe and drop the cigar box into my lap. They are all signed the same — *CB*, capitalized and devoid of personality. Many of them are scrawled on newspaper clippings. There are a few that recount my father's fall from grace, his fraudulent healing practices and tax evasion. But worse than that are the grainy photos of Peter and me in our high school uniforms. Peter was a baseball standout and I played soccer and basketball. Each one is captioned in the same blocky red lettering: *Eye for an Eye. Son for a Son.*

When I slip the last letter back to its envelope, I sense more than see something fall out. It takes a few seconds to find it, a tiny sand dune of orange crystals on the carpet. The scent of artificial flavoring is unmistakable.

Tang.

As I start to close the box, I notice one final letter pasted to the top inside of the lid, likely with dried dog slobber. The edges are tattered and tinged in orange ...

It's the letter I found next to Sonny the day he died.

That would mean the Tang came from the letter itself. But if so, what does that do to our theory that his killer mixed the orange drink to entice Sonny to drink the euthanasia drug? And if that's the case, I still have no idea who really killed him.

I take my time putting things back where they belong, all but the orange-stained letter. Instead I fold it once and slip it into my hip pocket. It was, after all, the last thing Sonny ever did.

* * *

I make two more stops on the way home, one at the liquor store where I buy a bottle of my mother's preferred brand of vodka. The humming cabbie thinks I'm nuts when I then duck into a pet store for a box of Sonny's favorite doggie treats. He keeps looking at me in the rearview and shaking his head. Ten minutes later he drops me at the curb in front of Dan's house and I give him a twenty-dollar tip.

The first thing I do is crank the air-conditioning up. Next, to fully milk my despair, I retrieve the crinkled envelope from Dr. K's office and the unaccepted engagement ring. I plop onto the sofa, fiddle with a few remote controls until I'm simultaneously listening to John Coltrane, watching *The Price Is Right*, and sitting in a living room cold enough to chill Jell-O. I marinate a doggie biscuit, raise it as a toast to Sonny, then try to eat it. I gag a third of it down and have to fight not to retch on Dan's carpet. Since the vodka is mostly tasteless, I load up on a mouthful of chocolate chips to get the grainy taste out of my mouth. I take two more quick pulls on the bottle and shout answers at the contestants about the price of Brillo pads and low-fat peanuts—wrong answers. This makes me miss Sonny terribly.

I decide that I deserve the dog biscuits, but not the alcohol. So I dump it down the drain and return to watching *The Price Is Right*, hugging an empty vodka bottle and a box of biscuits in place of Sonny. Eventually I feel my body taking on the same shape as the sofa as I melt into the cushions and give in to my drowsiness. I have a vague notion of Geri and Dan walking in on me, concern darkening their features. Dan complains about the temperature while Geri plays with my eyelids.

"If you insist on turning the heat up even more, I'm taking this ridiculous dress off."

"Aren't you afraid lover boy will see?"

"Hah. He won't see anything straight for at least a day or two." She holds up the empty vodka bottle and shakes the box of dog biscuits like a broken maraca. "Poor thing. And please don't call him that. He's not my lover boy."

"Would be if you gave him half a chance."

"That's ridiculous. He has the hots for that nurse." Geri hikes up her dress and lifts her arms. I know if I don't close my eyes, they'll bulge open and blow my cover.

Too late. The dress is off, revealing a pair of jogging shorts and one very large, very round belly.

How could I have missed *that*?

Dan laughs. "You guys crack me up. I've never seen a more perfect couple. You're both crazy about each other."

"What's that supposed to mean? Has Russell said something about me?"

"Your poker face stinks, Geri."

"Oh," she says, resituating herself in the recliner and resting her

291

hands on her considerable middle. It looks like she swallowed a basket-ball. "So, what did he say about me?"

"Not much. Just that he's madly, head-over-heels, out of his stinking mind, in love with you."

"Liar." But she's grinning. "Really? He said that?"

"And you feel the same way about him. You just won't admit it."

"So what if I did? The last thing in the world Russell Fink needs is to be saddled with someone else's kid."

"Somehow I don't think he'd see it that way."

I keep waiting for Sonny to jump out, so I'll know for sure I'm dreaming. But this is making too much sense. I'm trapped in some limbo-like state of semi-consciousness, staring at the woman I love through slitted eyes, as carefully guarded secrets spill out all over the floor. Should I be offended? Relieved? Overjoyed?

Geri is pregnant.

I have no idea who the father is.

And remarkably, I don't care.

Dan tries to talk her into staying over. But she says she needs to finish packing. I lay still until they leave.

Friday

I have no idea how long I've been here. Or, for that matter, what I'm looking at. The canvas before me is a brilliant disaster with shades both temporal and divine. At some point my muse must have snuck up on me. Now she's nowhere in sight, but her seat is still warm. I shake my head in wonder, trying to remember the strokes that led me here.

Abstract art has never really been my forte. But this thing, this delightful regurgitation of body and soul and spirit, stirs something in me. Some part of me that was tourniquetted off and left for dead. At first glance all I see is the kaleidoscope of unexamined pain—bruises, infection, scar tissue, old wounds with cruddy scabs. But below the surface, at its core, there's light. Its rays pierce the ugliness. Like the sun, hope is rising and will not be deterred.

"That's hard to look at."

I nearly topple with shock at the sound of Alyssa's voice. Where did she come from? How long has she been watching me? And how did she get inside Dan's house?

"Whatever happened to knocking?" I say. "You scared the bejeebers out of me."

293

"I did knock. About thirty times. But it looks like you were in one of your zones."

All at once I'm compelled to shield the painting. There's an unexplored intimacy there that I'm not ready to share with anyone. Especially not Alyssa. Without thinking I grab the easel and start to turn it away from her view.

"Don't, Russell."

"It's not finished. I'm not even sure if it's any good."

"Who cares if it's good? It's real. And you've always been brilliant when you're real."

I don't know what to say to that. So I stand there and fidget.

"You don't have to say anything, Russell. Just get over yourself a little, get out of the way, and let the work speak for itself." We stare at my creation in silence. "You know what it reminds me of?"

I'm just too drained for smart aleck banter.

"It's the way you used to paint when we first started dating. You used to call me 'Muse,' remember?"

"I do."

"Guess we kind of screwed things up, huh? But you know, despite the fact that we've accumulated enough baggage to open a thrift store, I do still love you. Not the crazy kind. But I think the real kind."

I open my mouth before I know what to say. "Alyssa, I don't know what to — "

"Don't try to explain anything. You're too far gone already. That's obvious. But if this painting is any indication of things to come, something big and bright and beautiful is about to explode all over your life. And I don't mind saying I wish it were me."

"Alyssa, I'm sorry. I don't know what to say."

She bites her lip. Her eyes well up, and I can't tell if she's restraining a smile or a sob. She stares at the ceiling in frustration as the tears spill down either side of her face. I track their progress, like the world's saddest downhill slalom competition. I know I should hug her. But I simply cannot risk that kind of intimacy again. I know I should be overjoyed. I'm getting exactly what I wanted — a clean break. But I can't help feeling sad. And more than a little scared. If I had any clue where my spleen was located, I'm sure it would be tingling.

"I'm sorry, I — "

"No, Russell. I'm the one that's sorry. About your car. About the ring. About Sonny and your sister, and well, everything. In fact ..." She digs her hand deep into her jeans pocket and retrieves a Ziploc sandwich bag. I have to squint to see the diamond inside. "Here, this is yours."

I waste no time shoving it into my pocket. "Thanks. And speaking of Sonny, I wanted to apologize for him."

"Apologize?"

"Yeah, he pretty much hated you. And he wants you to know he's sorry ... or, you know, he would if he could ... want you to know, that is."

"Okay." She draws this out, implying my insanity with two stretched syllables.

"And I hope you won't take this the wrong way, but, um, I suppose you have an alibi for the morning he was killed?"

I'm prepared for some kind of tirade, either verbal or with her fists. But she smiles as if my amateur investigation is the sweetest thing she's ever seen. "I was sitting in a room, waiting my turn to audition for a Kenny Chesney video." She raises her right hand solemnly. "With thirty-seven bottle-blondes as my witness, I swear I didn't hurt Sonny."

We swap sad grins, realizing together that it really is over and we have very little else to say. Finally, she says, "Guess I need to get going. I was hoping I was wrong, but I needed to stop and see for myself. But it's obvious your mother was right. You're still in love." She looks up, finding confirmation in my eyes. "Just not with me."

"Come on, Alyssa. Don't."

"Actually, this makes things easy for me. For both of us. I am, as they say, heading for Hollywood."

"You're serious. You're finally going to do it?"

"I leave tomorrow morning to start shooting the Kenny Chesney video. After all, there's nothing here for me … is there?"

It takes real effort to keep my resolve intact. She thumbs a tear from the corner of her eye. "So I guess this is good-bye."

We hug. And it feels good, right, blessedly final.

* * *

It takes Simmons forever to answer his door. He looks much sicker than before, old and unkempt. Worse, he smells sick and stale and probably knows it.

"Come on in," he says, then steps away as quickly as his stick legs will take him. He falls into his recliner and eyes the parcel in my hand. "I'd love to offer you some tea, but I'm afraid you'd have to make it yourself. And the kitchen is a mess."

"That's okay. Just wanted to bring you something."

I place the framed canvas on his footstool, then peel the brown paper back to reveal my portrait of Sherry Simmons.

"I hope you like it," I say. "I did it from memory."

He puts a trembling hand to his mouth. I watch as moisture gathers in his right eye, then spills over into a single tear. If I could only learn to paint that — loneliness and joy captured in a single, salty drop.

"You did that?" His voice is ragged but sturdy. And tinged with wonder.

I nod, then watch him stare at the painting a while longer. Finally, I clear my throat and say, "I guess I better get going then."

Still firmly under the spell of his wife, he doesn't even glance in my direction.

* * *

It's dark, and the plan is to drive to Geri's apartment, park outside her building, and stare at her window for a while. Granted, it lacks the intimacy of actually watching her sleep. But I can't help myself. I just want to be near her. Tomorrow she leaves, and when she wakes up, I can drive her to the bus station and make one final pitch.

I stop at a convenience store around the corner from her place for some Yoo-hoo, Fig Newtons, and a strong cup of coffee. "Love Hurts" blares through a boom box held together with duct tape. The raspy, overcast vocals make my throat hurt. The clerk is ageless, willowy, and covered in colorful tattoos. Her smile reveals smoker's teeth and some serious gum disease. And when she talks, the black metal stud through her tongue bobs like some medieval weapon. It looks like a pitchfork, and the thought of it makes the roof of my mouth hurt. I can tell she wants to talk so I feign drowsiness and keep my eyes on the counter. She's not dissuaded.

"What's a cute boy like you doing out at this hour all by his lonesome?"

The words sound like a cheap pickup line. But her delivery is alarmingly innocent, bordering on angelic.

"Believe it or not, I'm about to park outside a girl's window and just sit there, thinking about her."

"Must be love."

"Yeah, I love her." There's something magical about telling a total stranger. Or maybe it's the giant smile breaking out on her otherwise scary face.

297

She rings up my groceries, and we swap paper money for coins. That's when I notice her plastic nametag. The name *Page* is etched in red letters. But someone has added a tail to the letter *P*, making it *Rage*.

She says, "You're not going to sing, are you?"

"Huh?"

"Like in the movies. No serenading or cheesy love songs on a boom box?"

"Nope. Probably just sit there."

"Well pardon me for saying so, but that plan kinda sucks." She grins at my gaping expression. "What good is loving someone if you're not going to do anything about it? Sounds kind of selfish if you ask me—which you didn't, of course."

"You're right, I didn't ask."

"And cowardly too."

"Thanks for the advice," I say. "But I really need to get going. So if you could put this stuff in a bag for me?"

She has to think about this. In fact, she stands motionless for so long, I'm wondering if she's not high on something. Then she grabs a plastic bag, snaps it into a mini parachute, and starts cramming my things inside. I reach for the bag, but she hangs on to it, her bloodshot eyes fixed on mine.

"Tell me something, lover boy. You believe in Jesus?" Great, here we go again. I'm a little offended that, in the eternal scheme of things, I'm in line behind my homicidal grandfather, his band of reformed hooligans, my dysfunctional parents, and now this Goth girl riddled with piercings. When I don't answer, she says, "Well?"

"Yeah, most of the time. Why?"

"What if He decided to just show up on His donkey and sit around drinking chocolate milk?"

"Actually, there's no milk in Yoo-hoo."

"Better check that label, funny boy." While I'm scanning the fine print for dairy content, she continues. "Jesus took one look at the people He loved and decided to do something about it. He actually got His hands dirty."

"Didn't those same people kill Him for His trouble?"

She smiles. "Love hurts."

* * *

It's after midnight when I get to Geri's. I try humming the corresponding Eric Clapton tune, but my head is still swimming with the words of Rage, the Goth-girl/amateur-theologian. As much as I hate to admit it, she has a point—but not the point that Gramps and Geri have been trying to make. My father, the writers of the four gospels, the apostle Paul, and dozens of preachers have convinced me that Jesus is exactly who He said He was. I'm not always comfortable with it, but it's part of me. I get that. It's like a subscription that won't run out, no matter how many renewal notices I ignore.

I'm struggling with the love hurts part and what, if anything, to do about it. The examples are plentiful—my nutty family, Sonny, Katie, Geri, and yes, even Alyssa. I was brainwashed into believing that love was patient and kind and never envies and all that. But experience tells me otherwise. On good days, love is merely a hassle. But mostly it's just plain excruciating, an imbalanced yoke, an anchor with a short chain. So maybe the scratchy-voiced singer was right. Love is doomed to hurt. Or I'm just not doing it right.

I park Dan's Caddy by the curb, as close to Geri's window as possible without violating any more civic codes. There's a light on in her apartment, but no movement.

The Fig Newtons and Yoo-hoo don't sound so good to me now. I sip the coffee, but it burns the tip of my tongue. A layer of fog emerges on the windshield so I power down the windows and pocket the keys so I won't accidentally lock them in the car. That's when I feel the envelope from Dr. K's in my pocket. The plastic address window makes crinkling sounds when I pull it out. I turn it over in my hands, fingering the flap, waiting for the fear to stop swirling and to settle into my gut.

Maybe this is the impetus I need to get me off the fence. The contents of this letter offer either a short reprieve from worry or a death notice.

I decide to strike a deal with myself. If it's cancer, I'll just sit here and feel sorry for myself. When morning comes, I'll drive Geri to the bus station — heck, I might volunteer to drive her all the way to her mother's house in North Carolina — then I'll kiss her on the forehead, tell her again that I love her, and go home to finish a few paintings while I wait to die. If the results are negative, I'll allow myself to celebrate by storming her apartment and making another sloppy plea for her affections.

I slide my finger under the flap until I can feel the gummy residue. Tingles shoot through various body parts as I hear the first rip. Then a pair of headlights converges on my face like twin spotlights. My eyes go wide, like I've been caught doing something naughty. I hunker down in my seat until the car passes like a shadow.

I hold the envelope up to a street light and squint at it, trying to read what's inside without having to open it. For one frightful second, I'm convinced it's ticking, a clear sign that my time on earth is drawing nigh. But it's just the engine cooling.

Sensing movement, my eyes are drawn back to Geri's window. I feel guilty watching, but can't seem to tear my gaze away. Her ghostly form passes behind the curtains, like the mythic Siren, only with a potbelly.

What I should do is toss the envelope in the backseat and go convince Geri to stay. What I do instead is peel the flap all the way back.

I pause, taking two deep breaths. As I remove the documents from their paper prison, I realize I'm praying, totally against my will. The funny thing is, I'm not praying for a certain outcome. In my mind, I only have a few months to live. No, I've already skipped ahead and am praying for a miraculous healing, which fills me with disgust. If God couldn't—or wouldn't—heal Katie, then He has no business wasting His time on me.

The papers are out in the open, unfolded in my lap, and waiting to be read. I have to will my eyes open. Then I have to wait for them to adjust to the dimness.

I'm staring at two sheets of paper on Dr. Kozinski's official letterhead. It's a customer service survey, asking me to rank specific aspects of their performance on a scale from one to ten. There's not a single word about my cancer—real or imagined.

A familiar turbulence works its way through my system. I recognize the sound first, then the emotion. Laughter. My body and my brain are wracked with it. And when I realize how long it's been since the last time, I laugh even harder. I can't stop. Then I hear a familiar voice.

"Russell?" Geri is peering through her screen window. "What on earth are you doing out there? And what's so funny?"

The answer is just too pathetic to say out loud.

* * *

The sound of mulch crunching underfoot sounds harsh and indicting as I approach Geri's window. In all the years I've known her, I've never seen Geri's bedroom before. I imagined a tasteful blending of homemade curtains, antique black-and-white movie posters, and a few choice remnants of girlhood. But instead of purple unicorns or teddy bears clad with miniature flags, the walls are scuffed and mostly bare. It feels transient, and unbelievably sad.

301

I need to say something, so I just blurt out the first thing that comes to mind. "I'm sorry I was rude the other night when I dropped you off."

"That's okay, Russell. I know you feel weird, like you've delivered some fatal blow to our relationship and it'll never be the same. But you're wrong. I haven't been exactly honest about things either. When I get back from my mom's, maybe we can just pick up where we left off."

Geri winces as she repositions herself behind the window. For the first time ever, her fruity perfume depresses me. It's yet another reminder that she turned me down.

"If I'm not in jail."

"What's that supposed to mean?"

I tell her all about my confrontation with Bernie. And how I punched Nancy Clancy in the schnoz.

"You did what?" Geri is not amused.

"It wasn't on purpose. Bernie got lucky and fell down at the last second. Nancy just happened to be in the right place at the wrong time."

"Give me your cell phone." She doesn't wait for me to comply. She takes two steps back and begins stabbing digits on her cordless handset.

"I hope you're not calling Nancy—"

"Dan? It's Geri. I need you to find me an address. Her name is Nancy —hang on a sec." Geri hisses at me through the window, "Nancy what?"

"Clancy. Her name is Nancy Clancy."

A smile plays around the corners of Geri's mouth. But she recovers at once and arches forward as if she's going to slap me. "Come on now, I'm serious."

"Nancy Clancy."

She balances the phone on her shoulder and scribbles on the back of a receipt. Before telling Dan good-bye, she blows a powerful gust from the corner of her mouth, causing her bangs to fly back into place. I stand there and gape under the stark realization that I could spend the rest of my life brushing Geri's bangs back into place.

"Here. Good thing for you, she only lives a few miles from here." She thrusts Nancy's address through the window. "I'm not speaking to you again until you make this right."

"What if I say no?"

"I'll shut the window and go to bed."

"What if I just hang around your window and serenade you until your resolve cracks?"

"You're not that good a singer."

"If I do this, you have to let me come back. I have some really big news I need to talk to you about."

She tilts her head and stares at me. "Deal. Now get out of here before I call the cops on you."

When we're both convinced she's serious, she stands up and closes the window.

* * *

Fifteen minutes later, I pull to the curb of a quaint English Tudor. A huge trash can lies on its side, and the brown grass stands in stark contrast to Nancy's pristine Volvo gleaming under a floodlight. I stare at the brick facade and listen to my own ragged breathing.

I wade through an invisible bog of trepidation and attempt to script an impromptu apology. But the lines get all tangled and garbled in my mind. The knuckles on my right hand start to tingle where I splintered the cartilage of Nancy's most distinguished feature. I trace a few lines on her front door where the paint is peeling, still trying to muster the courage to knock, when I sense movement. Something white flashes in my peripheral vision. It's a sheer curtain fluttering back into place, a signal that someone's home. I take a deep breath and pound on the door. A minute passes, still no answer. Of course it's nearing midnight. I cock my arm to knock again when I hear a swooshing sound behind my left ear.

I'm actually contemplating air displacement and trajectory and velocity as a hockey stick slams into my shoulder blade, then ricochets up and smashes my right ear against my head. I turn to see the rabid eyes of Nancy Clancy shrouded in bruises and white gauze. She says something terrible about my mother, then relaunches the hockey stick. Animal instinct ignites somewhere inside me and I perform a sophisticated duck-and-lunge move that sweeps Nancy Clancy and myself off the rickety porch and into her front yard. One of us makes a wounded, gasping sound and I realize that my left ankle is on fire. Dried grass fills my mouth. And when I try to dislodge it, Nancy's eyes grow wider. She must think I'm trying to spit on her.

After another sixty seconds of clumsy squirming and jockeying, I'm able to hoist myself into a sitting position on her stomach. We stare at each other, both heaving from exertion.

"I came to apologize."

"I don't accept it."

"I'm trying to make amends here."

"I don't care what you're trying to"

"I don't have much time so I'll cut right to it. You have to know I didn't mean to hit you. So I want to apologize."

"I'm still pressing charges."

I feel her arm tense beneath me and see her grip tighten on the hockey stick. I press my knee onto her forearm until she winces and finally lets it go. When I feel her relaxing a little, I let her up. It takes several minutes to convince her that I'm not on crack.

"You want to know something funny?" she says. "I quit today too."

We swap begrudging grins. "Feels pretty good, doesn't it?"

"Bernie will run that company into the ground before the end of the year. I don't need that on my résumé."

I stand up, offer her my hand, and pull her to her full height.

"I really am sorry, you know."

"I know."

"If you want to, you can belt me with the hockey stick again."

She laughs in a way that makes me think that in another life, I could grow to like Nancy Clancy. "I'd best take a rain check."

"Well the least you can do is send me the doctor bill." She begins to say something, but I cut her off. "Seriously, at least let me pay the deductible."

"You should have quit while you were ahead."

"What's that supposed to mean?"

"I resigned, remember? There is no deductible."

I hobble back to the Caddy, not knowing whether to laugh or cry.

* * *

Geri's changed into an oversized peasant blouse made from a Canadian flag. I never knew a giant red maple leaf could look so good. Since she still hasn't invited me in, I lean on a nearby dogwood.

"I should warn you, Russell. Mrs. Tatlock in 4B called to inform me that we won't have to worry about that Peeping Tom anymore. She called the cops."

It takes a few paranoid glances over my shoulder to realize she's talking about me.

Geri hands me a steaming mug of decaf, then rests her chin atop her folded arms on the windowsill. My inner artist takes a snapshot. The red brick porthole and bare walls are no match for the beauty streaming through the window.

"Don't get me wrong, Russell. I love hanging out with you and all.

But it's a little after my bedtime." She pauses to take a loud slurp of her coffee. "So what's this really big news you were talking about?"

Confronting her about her pregnancy seems too scary, sharing my non-news from Dr. Kozinski's office too pathetic. So I opt for the path of least resistance. "I guess I kind of lied about that."

"That's not very nice."

"I panicked."

"Make something up, you know, so my opinion of you doesn't suffer."

After a moment of surprisingly painless deliberation, I clear my throat and begin. "Okay. Once upon a time, there was this boy and this girl who—"

I hear a siren in the distance and Geri laughs at the stricken look on my face. I use this to my advantage, stoking my own sense of urgency to say what needs to be said before I lose my nerve. I've always worked better with a firm deadline. And something tells me if I don't get this right, I may not get another chance.

"Russell? You were saying? About the boy and girl?"

"Right, right. Once upon a time there was this boy. A boy who loved a girl. He was pretty sure she loved him back, but for some bizarre and unfathomable reason she wouldn't admit it."

Geri fingers a button on her Canadian flag shirt.

"The boy learned that the girl was keeping sec—"

"Wait," Geri says, still looking straight ahead. "What did the girl look like?"

"She's the most beautiful girl in the whole wide world."

Geri grins with one side of her face. "You've confused your tenses."

"What's that?"

"You started in past tense, then switched to present."

"Doesn't matter. It's a love story. They're supposed to be eternal."

"Keep going."

"So the boy—"

"Wait. What does the boy look like?"

"Um, well, like me."

Geri nods her approval and wipes both of her eyes with her sleeve.

"Anyway, the boy tried like mad to win the girl's heart. He bought her expensive jewelry." Geri bats her eyes and fingers the beads of her candy necklace. "He took her to exotic places and freshened his breath with Teaberry before he kissed her. But the girl had secrets."

Geri's breath catches, a soft rattle that makes my heart wobble.

"I know about the baby, Geri."

Her bottom lip quivers and her head drops to her chest. I take her hand and squeeze it, all at once frustrated and comforted by our windowsill barrier. She still won't look at me. I lean in close and wrap both her hands in mine.

"I know you're pregnant. And I don't care."

This elicits a ragged laugh. "Well, that's not very nice."

"I mean, obviously I care. But you know, it doesn't matter, like as far as our relationship goes." She stares at her fidgeting hands. When I can't stand the silence any longer, I say, "Why didn't you tell me?"

"I don't know, take your pick—fear, shame, you name it. But you're absolutely right. I should have told you and I'm sorry. You're my friend. And that's what I need right now, Russell. A very best friend."

"What if I need more?"

"That's the whole point, Russell. You deserve more. You deserve better."

"You're wrong, Geri."

"Look, Russell. I don't mean to be so cryptic. I just—I don't know—Why do we have to complicate things?"

"Because ..." I wait until she looks up. "Because you turned my

307

heart to Silly Putty. Because I can't take my mind off of you. Or my eyes. And if I ever get my hands on you, there's a good chance I'll die from sheer delight. When I'm with you I feel like I'm breathing helium, or laughing gas, as if I'm floating through the atmosphere like Dan's girlfriend. And when I'm not, I can barely breathe at all. My insides turn to sludge. The world turns gray and heavy. Even my taste buds go on strike."

Her face scrunches into a question mark.

"Seriously. Just yesterday I got all depressed thinking about us and tried a little experiment. I ate some chocolate cake, a fingerful of peppercorn dressing, and an orange. And you know what? They all tasted like dog biscuits."

"I'm flattered, Russell. I really am."

"No offense, but I'm way past flattery." I'm surprised by the heat of my words.

"I'm sorry, Russell. You have to know that. But I don't know what you want me to do."

"I want you to love me back."

I'd swear she mouthed the words *I do* before turning her head toward the ringing telephone. "Uh-oh. It's Mrs. Tatlock." The machine clicks on and I hear a tenuous alto warning Geri to lock her windows.

"So what's the problem?"

"It's complicated."

I shake my head. "That's my line. There's something you're not telling me. Something else." Her quiet tears confirm what I've just said. "That's what hurts the most. You don't trust me."

Geri is quiet, shaking her head.

An eternal pause later, she says, "I'm sorry, Russell. I can't do this to you."

"Geri? Do *what* to me?"

"Look, Russell. Even if you manage to crack my resolve — and trust me, you're much closer than you think — we're missing a pretty key ingredient."

"Yeah, what's that?"

"You don't believe in miracles. That kind of dooms us from the start."

I want to scream at her, to ask her what on earth that means. But she's staring off to where a police cruiser is turning onto the block, shining its spotlight in the bushes across the street.

"I do love you, Russell." She takes my face in both her hands and holds it there. "You know I do."

"Just not in that way, right." I shake my head in pathetic, futile, and utter defeat. Her grip tightens, stilling my body, but not the accusing voices in my head.

The spotlight creeps closer and I have to duck behind some prickly azaleas. The cops train the cruiser's headlights on the Caddy's license plate. I crawl along the side of Geri's building, bricks scraping one shoulder and prickly leaves poking the other. I'm trying to ignore the jagged pieces of mulch digging into my palms when I think I hear Geri say, "But I do, Russell Fink. In *every* way."

* * *

Once out of sight of the cops, I jog back around the corner to the convenience store. I'm greeted by the ding of an overhead cowbell and the familiar voice of Rage.

"Lover boy! How'd it go?"

"Not great. The cops are after me."

"You didn't do it right then."

"Actually, I did. I didn't just show up. I got down off my donkey and did something about it. Even got my hands dirty."

I hold my mulch-laden palms for her inspection. She smiles, then flicks her eyes at the door. "Good for you. Let's celebrate." I follow her

309

gaze and see two middle-aged guys in shirtsleeves climbing out of an unmarked squad car. "Uh-oh. Why don't you grab yourself another Yoo-hoo — it's on the house — and hang out in the ladies' restroom for a few minutes?"

I do as instructed, leaving the door cracked enough to see through.

The cops make small talk with Rage, then ask if she's seen any suspicious characters loitering about.

"Just you guys," she says.

The taller one says, "This about that coffee shop that burned?"

"Yep. Owner's name is Peter Fink. Kid brother named Russell, who by the way, has an outstanding arrest warrant for assault. Punched a woman, his boss I think."

"Not a nice boy," the short investigator says. "Do you know where the Brothers Fink are keeping themselves?"

I shrink further into the restroom, allowing the door to close even more. I have to strain to hear the next part of the conversation.

"Got a tip from a local PI, claims the brothers have been scheming their insurance scam for a while."

"Idiots."

"Yeah, probably find 'em with a trunkful of gas cans and matches."

They laugh a little too hard, then adjourn to the coffee station. I strain to hear the conversation but I can't make it out. All I can think about is the cache of explosives in Dan's trunk and how long it will take the cops to link it to me.

The lawmen amble up to the register, but Rage waves them through. "On the house, boys."

I wait another two minutes or so, then poke my head out. Rage beckons me forward. "Your name Peter?"

"Nope, Russell."

"Good. My ex's name is Peter."

I down my Yoo-hoo and walk in the opposite direction of Geri's place with my head down. I have no plan other than walking. The blister on my left heel is competing with the slight burn in my thighs when I see a familiar sign.

* * *

After surviving a terrifying climb, I'm now sitting in what I've come to refer to as Alyssa's tree house, staring through the leaves at the unlit neon sign of *As a Jaybird*. I didn't come here on purpose. In fact, when I left the gas station, I had no plan at all. Instead I was trying to wrap my waterlogged brain around Geri's last few sentences under the window. *Yes, Russell. In every way.*

I stretch my legs to keep them from falling asleep, then find myself taking stock of just what my life has become over the last few months. I have no money, no job, and no prospects. My family is as screwed up as ever, and somehow it's still my fault. I'm in love with a pregnant woman who supposedly loves me back, but for some reason, refuses to act on it. Not only that, she's boarding a Greyhound in the morning and I won't see her again for months. Maybe never. I haven't seen my brother since I broke into his apartment. My grandfather and my sweet clairvoyant dog are both dead. Although I still have no idea who killed Sonny, I know that someone's been sending my family threats that might not be idle.

I'm wondering whether I'd rather spend the rest of my days hiding in Mexico or Canada when my phone rings. Dan sounds like he just woke up.

"Geri just called. She's worried about you."

"That makes two of us."

I consider asking Dan what he thinks my chances are of getting Geri to move to Vancouver with me. Instead, a piercing beep fills my head. My phone's dead. I resist the urge to chuck it in the street. Instead

311

I lace my fingers behind my head and lie on my back. A few stars are visible through the leaves. Next thing I know I'm pondering Gramps's pesky question. Do I really believe Jesus is who He said He was?

Clouds scoot across the sky, clearing a path for the moon. It's a mere sliver, a cuticle against a velvety blue backdrop. I can't help thinking of the Great Oz hiding behind his curtain, pulling his levers, and generally making a mess of things. It's been drilled into my psyche that God loves me and that His mercies endure forever and His grace is sufficient and all that tripe. That He's great and He's good—let us thank Him for this food. I get all that. Makes for a quaint caption on a cheesy painting, but I'm not buying it. Not tonight.

Then my bravado is taken out at the knees, double-teamed by the thuggish tag team of guilt and doubt. Maybe it's just me. Maybe I'm to blame for insisting that God punch my Get-Out-of-Hell-Free card, then relegating Him to the dank crawl space in my mind. The easy thing would be to curl up into a fetal position and take the beating I probably deserve. But instead, I decide to go down swinging.

I realize that now I'm praying—out loud, even. And just like when Alyssa was up here alone, it's quite by accident. Must be something about this tree. I tell myself to cut it out, but I can't. This is an inevitable conversation that I've been avoiding for far too long. So I decide to go for it, unleashing my full arsenal of pent-up frustration.

My brain is blaming God for everything that comes to mind. My mouth is just trying to keep up.

I stop and stare at the sky. I've never bought into the lightning bolt theory of God's retribution. But I scan the horizon just in case. A speeding dark cloud crosses over the half-moon, and I'm convinced God is winking at me. Just like Geri does.

And speaking of Geri, she's leaving and I'm stuck up this tree talking to my imaginary friend.

I uncross my legs and stretch my back. The floor of the tree fort creaks, moaning in sympathy. As I try to think of something else to yell at God about, a new sensation spreads inside me.

It's warm and buttery and rather annoying.

I look to the heavens again and say, "I don't want Your comfort, I want answers. And if I can't get the right answers, I want to fight."

I'm struck with an image of Sonny, regarding me with a tilted head and an amused doggy grin. I would never stoop to comparing Sonny to God or vice versa, but I can't help thinking that not unlike my canine companion, that God is just happy to hear from me. Despite my ranting and my whiny insistence that my life has been doused in dog pee, He refuses to get defensive or angry.

Before I know it, I'm apologizing for some things and confessing some others. When I go overboard and start calling myself names — things like a selfish and neurotic loser, a finger-pointing imposter who carries grudges, a faithless swine — the Sonny version of God places a paw to His lips and reminds me that I'm His.

It's more than a little disconcerting. But in a good way.

It never dawns on me to ask what I should do next. But I'm sure it's implied.

I think I'm supposed to paint.

Saturday

I hear Dan's version of a whisper over the sound of an idling engine. "Russell? Are you up there?"

I sit up, too quickly. It's still dark. My body aches all over, as if Santa's pointy-eared helpers spent the twilight hours hammering away at my entire backside. My head seems to have endured the brunt of the punishment.

Dan calls my name again. My croaky response gets lodged in my windpipe. When I open my mouth to try again, a marble-sized piece of gravel cracks me in the forehead.

"Ouch! What are you doing?"

"Oops, sorry about that. You okay?"

"I'll live. If I don't get freaked out and fall out of the tree."

"What's the matter? You afraid of heights?"

"You could say that."

"Just don't look down."

"Do you have any idea how lame that advice is?" I sneak another look, hoping the darkness will help. But from this vantage, it looks like I could just go on falling forever.

"What can I do to help?"

"Tell Geri to marry me?"

"Okay, hang on."

Despite the fear roiling around in my belly, I venture another peek downward, hoping to see the pregnant form of Geri. But all I see is the bluish glow of Dan's face. After a few whispered exchanges, he clicks his computer thingy off and says, "You're in luck."

"Oh yeah, how's that?"

"I called Geri and told her you were up a tree and out of your mind. And that you refused to come down until she agreed to marry you."

"What did she say?"

"She said maybe."

* * *

"Nice ride," I say, squirming in the passenger seat. "Looks familiar, but not all that comfortable."

Dan's driving my Taurus. "It just needed a new alternator."

"How'd you find me anyway? And please don't tell me you implanted some weird microchip in my neck and used your satellite."

"That's closer than you think." Dan lifts his computer thingy and wiggles it at me. "My satellite pinpointed your cell call within a half-mile radius. When I got to the naked bar, I just followed a hunch."

"Well, thanks for rescuing me."

I arch my back and retrieve whatever it is I'm sitting on — the small bundle of mail from my birthday lunch with Mom. I flip through junk mail and bills for no other reason than to stay awake.

It works.

The unsealed flap of one credit card offer has inadvertently pasted itself to another letter. When I peel them apart, I find a handwritten envelope with no return address, no stamp, and no postmark. The block letters seem familiar, slanting forward, the same as Sonny's letter, except for the reference to Peter's kidnapping.

316

Reverend Fink,

If you want to see your firstborn alive again, heed my warnings. Stay off the air, or else. An eye for an eye; a son for a son.

The IV drip is now an open faucet. I'm genuinely worried about Peter now. I pull Sonny's note out of my pocket and realize it's not postmarked either. So ... that can only mean they were hand-delivered. Both of them. Which means Charlie Baringer is *in* Nashville and really has kidnapped Peter.

I follow Dan through the back door of Heavenly Pastures, and I notice that it's nearly five-thirty in the morning. Fatigue catches up with me and I fall over backward on the familiar leather couch while Dan makes coffee.

"Orange?" Dan holds a pair of giant fruity orbs up for my inspection.

I shake my head, lost in thought.

"You sure? I'll warm it up for you." He begins peeling his orange, noisily sucking the nectar off his fingertips.

I don't answer. The tangy citrus smell has awakened something inside me. Dan gets up and pours coffee. Citrus — beer — orange crystals — coffee. Blocky handwriting.

I got it.

"Do you still have that note from Claude Beaman? From the bowling alley?"

Frustrated, Dan says, "Okay, hang on a sec. I'm sure I entered his contact information in here." His computer thingy materializes from one of his many layers of clothing and he immediately starts punching buttons.

"No, I don't need his number. I need the actual scrap of paper he wrote his name and number on. And please don't tell me you pitched it."

"Oh." He looks deflated, but after a few seconds of pocket patting, he digs his wallet out. I sip coffee and watch him flip through the dozens of papers in his wallet. "Here we go."

I get up and look over his shoulder. It feels like my grin will wrap itself around my head. I take the slip of paper from Dan's hand and say, "I knew it."

We're staring at the back of a dry-cleaning claim ticket. The meticulously crafted block letters are all lined up and heavily slanted to the right.

"What?" Dan says. "You knew what?"

"*That's* how he knew about the threatening phone calls at the bowling alley. He *made* them."

"Who did? What are you talking about?"

"Claude Beaman and Charlie Baringer are the same man."

Dan reaches for the dry cleaning ticket, no doubt anxious to see how I gleaned this information from a name and phone number. But I'm not ready to give it up yet. The awkward handoff results in the note slipping from both our grasps and fluttering to the ground. It lands face up and my eyes are drawn to the line at the bottom.

The ticket shows that six shirts were laundered — extra heavy starch, two sport coats and three pairs of slacks dry-cleaned. The first initial — a capital letter *C* — is followed by a patch of scribbles, then the name Beaman. I hold it up to the light and squint at the scratched-through section. I'd swear I can make out *Baringer*.

So if I'm right, then the man Simmons saw by my parents' mailbox was Baringer, hand-delivering his threats. He wasn't following the person following Peter — *he* was following Peter. *An eye for an eye, a son for a son ...*

* * *

I realize as I punch the last number into Dan's super-geek computer that I have never called my father's cell phone before. In fact, Dan had to find the number for me. After four rings, I expect it to click into voice mail, but he answers sounding professional, yet breathless.

"What do you need, Russell? I'm preparing to go on live TV here."

"I need to talk to you."

"Well, start talking. I've got a couple of minutes before I go to makeup."

"In person."

"Oh, okay. Can't it wait a few hours?"

"No, I'm afraid it can't."

"Well, you're supposed to be here at nine anyway. Get here a little early and maybe we can talk then."

When I don't answer at first, he says, "Let me guess. You forgot all about the fact that you're scheduled to go on live television this morning. Am I right?"

My first impulse is to lie. But I check myself. "Yeah Dad, I'm sorry. I completely forgot. But I'll be there."

* * *

My father is studying some kind of script when I let myself into his dressing room. He looks up and smiles as if he's genuinely pleased to see me. It's a little disarming, given my mission.

"You said you had something to talk to me about?"

I nod, not quite sure where to begin.

I want to blurt it all out, to tell him everything I know about Charlie Baringer and Claude Beaman, and all the suspicions I have about Peter's disappearance. I want to ask him how much he knows about Baringer and how he could possibly dare to put his family in harm's way by ignoring all those threats. And I want to tell him about the ransom note. I want it all out of my brain and into his, so he can do his fatherly duty and tell me not to worry, that everything is going to be okay.

Instead I realize that, based on what I know about Baringer, he's just like me. Or I'm just like him. Either way, we both blame ourselves for not saving someone we love. All our leftover blame is directed at Gary Fink. I've been nurturing this grudge too long — at myself, at my father, and ultimately at God.

"Russell?" My dad snaps his fingers. "You were saying?"

"I forgive you, Dad."

"You what?"

"That's right, I forgive you. I want to — "

"Is this another message from Sonny?"

"No, Dad. This one's from me. And you don't have to accept or anything. Mostly I blame myself for Katie's death. But I've spent way too much time blaming you as well. Katie thought you could heal her. And when you didn't, I blamed you. I was wrong to do that and I'm sorry."

"Sure you don't want to save some for the camera, Russell? You're not making much sense here."

"And I forgive you for kicking me out of the house, for not speaking up at Gramps's funeral, and for rarely ever being around when we needed you."

He shrugs and says, "I don't know what to say."

"You don't have to say anything. But I did."

"Okay, well, thanks." The combination of pride and embarrassment make him look ten years younger, like I might look in ten years. And other than the double chin, I find I don't mind it so much. "Now why don't you get yourself cleaned up. You're on after the first commercial break. We can talk more later."

I follow my father's gaze up and over my right shoulder. An intimidating female with thick forearms and a complicated headset squeezes my elbow. "Right this way, Mr. Fink. You need to be out of makeup and on the stage in about three minutes."

She ushers me into the hallway, applying more force than I deem necessary to steer me into a small room full of lights and mirrors. On the way in, something eerily familiar distracts me. I stop and whip my head down the hallway. It's the guy from Gramps's funeral, wearing the same red flannel shirt. But instead of cutting his eyes at me, he tugs on what I now see is a fake beard. He grins at me and winks, then disappears into the studio. I was right, it was Peter in disguise. And I guess it still is. But what does it mean?

I don't have time to answer, the burly producer woman is wrestling me into the makeup chair.

* * *

I'm onstage now, seated just off camera on a secondary set. My father is onstage as well, huddled with Geoffrey Sinclair and the show's producer. I overhear him explaining that some of his family members may not be able to make it. There's a disturbance in the crowd. I whip around in time to see a man righting himself after tripping over the knees of an elderly Asian woman. The producer stops and chats with a cameraman that looks familiar in some odd way. I stare for a moment and decide that my sleep-deprived imagination is working overtime. The camera guy's face is a dead ringer for a Buddha statue wearing a Member's Only jacket.

I scan the small studio again, looking for Peter. Dan is sitting in the front row of the crowd. Mom has been through makeup and is seated across from me on the secondary stage. She looks sober, but not at all happy. I still can't find anything suspicious, but the eerie sensation has gotten worse. Then the house lights dim and the cheesy synthesizer music starts up. A man in headphones does a silent countdown and points to the camera nearest me. I see the red light go on. In the monitor I see my father and Sinclair grinning back at me.

From the front row, Dan catches my eye and says, "I've tried to call him a dozen times, but I keep getting his voice mail."

"Who?"

"Beaman," Dan says. His failed attempt at whispering coincides tragically with the director's signal to cut the music and cue the men on stage. Heads turn from every direction. The bald cameraman turns toward the sound of Dan's voice and our eyes meet. We blink our mutual recognition, and he turns back to the camera. I have the sensation of someone lighting a fuse at the base of my spine, the sparks snaking their way through my insides.

A beefy security guard gives Dan a dirty look and tells him to keep quiet.

Suddenly Dan's PDA is ringing — Elvis Costello crooning "God Give Me Strength." The security guard snatches Dan's invention and hurls it at the ground, silencing it. Dan doesn't wait to check the damage. He's incensed. He bull rushes the security guard and they land in a heap on the studio floor. If Sinclair's microphones are as sensitive as I suspect they are, the live studio audience is now receiving a PG–13 viewing experience — for adult language and a scene of violence.

But it's about to get worse. The bald, clean-shaven version of Claude Beaman/Charlie Baringer has left his camera and is heading straight for the stage. When his hand disappears into his jacket, I leap over the punching mass of bodies in front of me and rush the stage.

* * *

Someone is howling.

At first I assume it's Baringer — if indeed one can actually assume anything while making a mad dash into the throes of danger. But time seems to have slowed down, again making me wonder if this is the end for me. And amid all this assuming and wondering, I find that I still have enough brain cells to pray as well.

But the howling is making it hard to focus on the words.

Baringer's mouth is definitely moving. But despite the crazed look in his eyes, I can tell he's forming actual syllables.

No, the prolonged yowl is coming from somewhere inside me. Even though I've now added embarrassment to my litany of ponderings, I can't seem to make myself stop. I decide this really is the end of the line for me.

As confirmation, Baringer raises his arm and something glints in the stage lights. I wait to see the muzzle of a gun, followed by a small explosion. Although the flash never comes, I am pretty sure I hear sirens.

Whatever Baringer's holding, it's too big to be a gun. It's more like a tube. A nightstick? A small bazooka perhaps?

He's on the stage now, less than five feet from the cowering preachers on the couch.

Baringer stops and turns back toward the camera. That's when he unfurls the shiny cylinder he's been wielding.

It's a laminated poster. And since I'm still hurtling forward, merely a yard or two from Baringer, I see it clearly. The poster is an oversized version of the Miracle Ward photograph from Katie's hope chest. All I can really see is Katie, but my mind fills in the blanks — twelve grinning kids in various stages of deterioration surrounded by a few nurses and teenage volunteers.

I try to put the brakes on, now that it's clear he's not shooting anyone. But it's no use. As I close the distance on Baringer and finally smash into his mid-section, I hear his tearful plea to keep Gary Fink off television. Words like *false teacher, fraud, heretic*, wash over me as we tumble to the floor.

I can't breathe, and for one brief moment, I look up expecting to see the dreamy form of Sonny perched on my chest. Somehow Baringer ends up practically sitting on me—he's still pointing at my father, weeping, slinging accusations, and repeating the name of his dead son. My writhing and struggling has little to do with the pitiful man straddling me like a barstool. I just want to breathe again, more than ever. And I want this man off me so I can dash off to the bus station and see if I can do a better job with *that* dramatic ending than I did with this one.

Just when I think I'm about to pass out, I catch glimpse of red flannel. Peter wraps Beaman in a bear hug and begins wrenching him off me. I scoot out from underneath him, gasp a quick thank you to Peter, and sprint toward the exit. The security guard spots me and runs my way, cutting off my angle to the exit. Dan is between us, punching buttons on his PDA, oblivious to the pandemonium around him. I'm about to scream at him for help when I see one of his big feet shoot out, catching the security guard in the ankles, a brilliantly executed playground maneuver.

I leap over the skidding uniformed body and through the doorway, only to be met by a platoon of cops on my way out. I point to Baringer and shout, "Stop that man." That seems to merely pique their curiosity. So I scream, "Officer down!" and they sprint into the studio, guns drawn and shouting.

* * *

I make the twenty-minute drive to the bus station in ten (would have been less if not for that lunatic ambulance driver that kept cutting me off in traffic). I notice it's slightly filthier than the bowling alley as I stop and stare at the TV monitor, trying to distinguish between arrivals and departures. But my mind is so scrambled, I can't remember the initials for North Carolina. The line is only three deep at the one ticket counter that's open. So when I elbow my way to the front and demand to know about the Charlotte departure, I only have to endure a half dozen lasers boring into the back of my head.

The prunish lady in blue polyester ignores me and points to the billowing back end of a giant Greyhound. I turn and run, bursting through the double glass doors. The plan is ... well, I don't know.

The bus lurches forward, dousing me in exhaust fumes. I watch through bleary eyes, coughing, as it picks up speed and heads toward the exit. I chase after it, waving my arms and shouting, just like in the movies. If only Alyssa could see me now.

My only chance is to cut off the angle to the exit and hope the driver has to wait for a break in traffic. I leap over an upturned garbage can. The bus makes a wide arc, its left blinker mocking me. I scan the windows, searching for Geri. But all I can see is the yellow glow of the setting sun.

I scream Geri's name and wave my arms. My legs and lungs are burning, and I realize it's no use. I can't catch up. My legs find another gear, pumping faster, and in sheer desperation, I hear myself bellowing a single word ... "Geri!"

I have a vague notion of illuminated brake lights as I run head-long into the side of the bus.

Thankfully the massive rear tire absorbs most of the impact. But my flailing elbow thumps off the side of the bus, followed closely by the side of my head. The driver's bulging eyes meet mine in the large sideview mirror. My chest is heaving and everything hurts. Yet some-how I swallow enough oxygen to shout Geri's name again.

The bus driver's hand slides through a small opening and he waves me forward. I ignore his window and make my way around the front of the bus to the passenger door. It opens with a hiss, like the top popping on the world's largest can of soda. My hands are resting on my sore thighs and I'm still trying to catch my breath.

The driver's voice is gruff, bordering on panicky. "What's got into you, boy?"

"Geri ..."

"What?" the man says, clearly annoyed.

"I'm looking for Geri."

I hear a voice, floating from some impossible distance, calling my name. It sounds like Geri, but I know it's the voice of dementia.

"Well?" The bus driver says again. "What is it?"

"Let me on the bus. I have to talk to Geri."

"I don't think so. If you got something to say, I'm sitting right here."

"Russell?" It's the floaty Geri voice again.

"Geri? Is that you?"

"Look, mister. I ain't got all day to ..."

"I love you, Geri!"

The driver blanches, looking truly horrified. "Pervert!"

That's when I notice the blue and white stitching on the driver's breast pocket. *Jerry.* All in one motion, he shuts the door and swings the enormous vehicle onto the street. Tires screech and horns honk, but it doesn't matter. Jerry cannot get away from me fast enough.

I manage to stand to my full height, then blink twice at the swirling red lights of an ambulance right in front of me. A pair of EMT's are attending to a woman on a stretcher. Only the top of her head is visible, but it's the most lovely scalp in all of human history.

"Russell? How did you find me here?"

"Geri?" I hover over a pair of EMT's tending to her. "Are you okay? What's going on?"

"Her water just broke." The EMT in charge is great-looking, obviously intelligent, poised, and worst of all — so utterly good at something. Something useful. Just the kind of guy Geri *should* fall for.

They load her into the idling ambulance and slap an oxygen mask into place. When I try to climb in after her, the more burly of the two medical technicians places a restraining forearm on my already tender chest.

I point to Geri and say, "I'm with her."

He looks to her for confirmation. She nods and motions me forward with both hands. She looks frightened to death.

Finally, the burly EMT announces to the rest of his crew, "Make room for Daddy."

A few cops arrive, looking curious and making me wonder how much time I have left with Geri. As far as I know, I'm still a wanted man. Maybe more so now than ever before.

Once inside the ambulance, the non-beefcake EMT drives while the hunky one coaches Geri along, soothing and cajoling her, telling her that she's doing great. My jealousy dissipates in an instant. In fact, I fear I'm developing a man-crush on the EMT. Then Geri grabs my hand, pulls me close, and the world starts spinning again.

* * *

Medical staff fly into and out of the room. Introductions sail over my head. The sleepy-looking guy is the anesthesiologist. I'm pretty sure Geri's gynecologist is a woman. But I can't remember which one.

Geri's job is to *not* push yet. Mine is to feed her ice chips, remind her to breathe, and to *stop* saying encouraging things. I fend off notions of complete inadequacy while keeping one paranoid eye on the door. I just know Officer Peebles is going to show up and arrest me for multiple assault charges before Junior gets here.

Gauging by the look on Geri's face, I can only assume a contraction is the uterine equivalent of an industrial mop ringer and a blowtorch. When the cataclysmic cramping subsides, Geri informs me that the plan all along was to carry the baby to term and put him or her up for adoption.

"What's the plan now?"

Geri's face cracks into quiet sobs. The attending nurse shoots me a warning look, as if this is all my fault. While she prattles on about effacement percentages and dilation, I fill Geri's mouth with ice chips and wait for my next instruction, or the next tidal wave of pain. But Geri reaches for my hand and squeezes it. "I don't know what to do, Russell. I don't ... I don't ..."

She's wincing and writhing again, fighting back more sobs. The nurse gives me another dirty look and whispers encouragement to Geri. When I do that, Geri yells at me. I try not to be offended and try to figure out something I can do to make her feel better. She seems to sense this. And when she catches her breath, she says, "Pray, Russell. Pray for a miracle."

"Okay, sweetheart. I will. But could you be a little more specific? Are we talking about the miracle of childbirth or some special something that I'm missing?"

Just then Geri's gynecologist bustles into the room. Somehow she's able to juggle compassion and medical prowess with seemingly no effort. It's just another reminder of how bad I was at my job. After a few more encouraging words, she announces that Dr. Frederickson is stuck in traffic and will be here shortly.

I glance up, apparently looking worried or confused or both. The good doctor decides to answer my puzzled expression with real words.

"Frederickson is the oncologist."

Geri's face drops and her eyes look dead. I know what I'm supposed to be praying for now. Her hand goes limp in mine. She looks sad, defeated, horrified, somewhat resigned, and scared to death.

"Oh," the gynecologist says, clearly mortified at having spilled Geri's secret. "I'm sorry." She looks at Geri who still has her eyes closed, tears spilling over her splotchy cheeks. "He didn't know?"

Geri shakes her head.

* * *

Other than beeping monitors, the space between contractions is now laden with silence. The stress seems to have slowed her labor down. The nurse has replaced her dirty looks with pitiable ones.

Finally, Geri says. "It's ovarian."

"What's that?" I say, surprised to hear her voice.

"The cancer. They call it the silent killer."

The nurse looks like she wants to say something, to contradict Geri. But she just busies herself with more charts and dials and wrappers.

"I don't know what to say, Geri. 'Sorry' sounds cheap. You know I love you but even that sounds hollow."

"There's nothing to say, really. It sucks and that's that."

She goes limp again. Then she turns her head away, trying to bury it in the pillowcase. The nurse tries to steady Geri to keep her from upsetting the tangle of wires and tubes. A low moan escapes her, building steam into an all-out wail. Geri is balling bed sheets in one fist and pounding the bed rail with the other.

I hurry around to the other side of the bed. But Geri is writhing again. The nurse stabs an emergency button and exchanges anxious words with the scratchy voice in the speaker. Words spill out my mouth, but even I can hear how vacuous they sound. Every attempt at trying to comfort her is met with more writhing, more sobbing, more yelling at me.

The room is filling with worried medical specialists. It seems there's a very real possibility that Geri could lose the baby if they cannot get her under control.

Then it occurs to me what needs to be done. I use both of my hands to corral one of Geri's. Then I squeeze it between mine, clear my throat, and do the unthinkable.

"God, you need to stop this. Now!"

I hear someone ask if they should alert security. But I ignore them and keep on praying.

"I don't know if you're listening or not, but we need a miracle, and I happen to think You're long overdue in sending one. And if this is somehow my fault, then strike me dead. But don't let my puny faith stand in the way of doing what needs to be done."

Geri moans. It sounds to me like she's dying.

"I know it's possible. I've seen You do it before, but I wouldn't believe. But I'm willing to believe it all now, every word of it — creation, fall, redemption, pillars of salt, virgin births, talking donkeys, that whole water to wine chardonization thing. Just do — "

Then I hear the most blessed sound in the universe. Geri's laugh. It lasts only a short time, but it's enough. I open my eyes and see that she's calmed a bit. She tightens her grip on my hand and nods a silent thank you. She lapses into small bursts of moaning and crying out, but at least the doctors and nurses seem to be making some progress.

The pressure in my hands increases until I feel like Geri's grip will disintegrate the bones. When I start praying again, she relents to a tolerable level. Eventually, my prayers find a less obnoxious rhythm. I even hear myself mixing in a few praises and some long-ago memorized Scripture.

* * *

When I get to Geri's room, she's sleeping. I hold her hand and whisper subliminal "marry me" messages until the nurse runs me off. I decide to go have a look at baby Katie, and I only get lost twice on the way to the nursery. When I find a guy about my age who looks like he's taken an unauthorized furlough from a criminal asylum (or maybe he's just the world's preppiest heroin addict) — feet dragging, eyes red and swollen, under heavy lids yet beaming like a lottery winner and speaking in giddy, rapid-fire fragments to a gaggle of cousins and in-laws — I follow him. He taps on the smudged window and makes baby noises while two uncle-types jockey for position with their movie cameras.

From my side of the giant Plexiglas window, I scan the pink and blue placards until I find her. Despite the scary resemblance to Winston Churchill, this Katie is every bit as beautiful as my twin sister. She's splotchy and bruised, all belly and spindly limbs and wearing a doll-sized toboggan hat. I watch her tiny chest rise and fall under the glow of her own heat lamp. I want nothing more than to barge in and smother her little pink face with kisses.

I don't realize my head is pressed against the glass until someone touches my shoulder. A nice voice says, "She's beautiful."

"Yeah, so's her mom."

"You should go in and hold her."

"I'd love to. But I don't think I'm, um, authorized."

"Let me see," the lady with the nice voice says. I'm sure if I could tear my gaze away from baby Katie, I'd realize she's a nurse. She pulls my left arm down to examine the wristband they accosted me with in triage. Her hand feels nice, warm. I have this vague notion of her squinting through the glass, then tapping on it and pointing me out to one of the nurses. She shakes my wrist and says, "According to this wristband, it says you're the father. So if you'll follow me ..."

She punches a few numbers into a security keypad, then ushers me through the giant, mechanized saloon doors. The nurse holding Katie offers me the sweetest snaggletoothed grin, then places all eight pounds-three ounces and eighteen-and-a-half inches into my shaking arms. I stare at Katie's tiny fist, then work my finger under her miniature replicas. Everything is to scale, from the wrinkled knuckles to the fingernails that already need clipping. When she tugs on my finger, my knees nearly give out. Now I understand that crazed, heroin-addict expression.

For one fleeting second I wonder who the father is, not so much

331

because I care about his identity or the story behind Katie's conception. What I want to know is whether I'll have to compete for baby Katie's affection.

I'm still not completely sure how I feel about miracles. But the strongest evidence so far is my expanded heart that is filled with love for a baby girl I've just met.

* * *

Geri's awake now, hearing the story of the TV station melee piecemeal while holding Katie in her arms. I'm handling most of the narration, with Dan and both of my parents interrupting with their own colorful observations of Baringer's ambush. Geri's eyelids are still fluttering when she asks, "So, who is this guy anyway?"

"His name is Claude Beaman."

Geri says, "You mean the private investigator guy from the bowling alley?"

"Yeah, sort of. He was posing as a PI to get close to the family. When he heard about *Second Chances*, he returned to Nashville and delivered his threats directly to our mailbox. I think his plan was to kidnap Peter and make good on his warnings. At some point his plans changed from murder to public humiliation."

"But why?" my mother asks.

"His real name is Charlie Baringer."

She makes a small gasping noise, blinking recognition and exchanging wary looks with her husband.

"Charlie's son was also named Charlie Baringer."

Geri looks confused so I fill her in. "Charlie Junior was one of the Miracle Ward kids. But not just any kid. He was Katie's best friend and confidante, a Tang-loving wannabe astronaut who was in love with my little sister." Mom dabs at her eyes, no doubt remembering. "When Dad performed his healing service at the hospital, little Charlie's mother declared her son healed. She refused any further medical treatment, as an act of faith I guess. When Charlie senior protested, she took their son away. The boy died two months later. His father blamed my father."

Dad offers an imperceptible nod, then busies himself cleaning his thumbnail with Nancy Clancy-like proficiency.

Finally Geri says, "So how'd you make the connection?"

"A combination of handwriting, Dan's detective work, and Tang. I thought it was peculiar how Beaman was always sprinkling orange crystals in his coffee, his beer, and who knows what else. He claimed it was medicinal but always seemed a bit cagey about it. What confirmed it though was his handwriting. When he wrote his number on a napkin at the Bean Bag, I noticed how everything tilted forward as if bracing for a sharp gust. Other stuff too, like the way his sevens had little flags on them or how his fours looked more like tents than goalposts. Once I compared that to the dry cleaning ticket and all those threatening letters in dad's cigar box, things sort of fell into place."

"Yeah," Geri says. "What was up with him sprinkling Tang everywhere?"

"Not sure, but I think seasoning his drinks with it is like paying homage to his kid. And maybe like his calling card too, a way to remain 'anonymous' while making sure Dad knew he was keeping tabs."

"They say smell is closely related to memory." Geri hugs baby Katie a little tighter to her chest and kisses her forehead. "But it's kinda sad, if you think about it too long."

Dan punctures the awkward silence by breathing warm air into his cupped hands.

Then baby Katie is make suckling noises, what I have now decided is the sweetest sound on earth. Geri still looks tired, but not sleepy. "So did Baringer kidnap Peter or not?"

On cue, Peter walks into the hospital room.

"I guess not."

Peter nods greetings all around, managing to look smug and sheepish at the same time.

"The first ransom note demanded cash, lots of it. It was also stamped and officially postmarked. So I didn't worry too much about that, figured Peter was up to something." My brother shrugs, noncommittal. "He knew I knew the gambling debts were real, how scared he was, and how deep Sinclair's pockets are. When the second note came — the one from Baringer with no postmark — I did start to worry a little. That is, until I saw Peter again at the TV station."

"Hey, like I told you, I needed the money."

"So, you went into hiding because of the gambling goons. Then you realized someone else was following you, but ... that's where it gets fuzzy."

"I started following him instead. Figured he was up to something, might as well see if I could use it to my advantage. Then when I got your message warning me about this Charlie Baringer guy, I knew I was onto something. Just wasn't sure what. Guess you never took my demands to Dad or Sinclair, eh?"

"I might have ... if I hadn't seen you staring at your apartment through a pair of binoculars."

"Oh," Peter says, his cheeks turning pink.

"But your trashed apartment *was* pretty convincing ... well, almost. I'm guessing once your extortion plan was in place, you came out of hiding long enough to ransack your own place. It was impressive work, but it took a while for me to figure out why your big-screen TV, framed baseball cards, and coffee maker survived unscathed. While your sectional sofa, portable TV, cheesy hotel art, and ancient stereo were all in smithereens. Why destroy a ratty sofa with a brand new plasma TV hanging on the wall?"

I pause for dramatic effect. But no one clutches their heart at my startling revelations. Or even whistles admiringly.

"Still can't figure out why you left your little black book behind. Unless you just wanted me to see your trashed apartment."

"Of course I did—you, the gambling thugs, the police, and anybody else who happened by. More the merrier; just made the kidnapping look more legit."

"But you needed that address book. It had the running tally of your gambling debts, a list of bookies and loan sharks, complete with phone numbers and exact dollar amounts. I guess you figured if the extortion worked, you could satisfy the gambling thugs with the promise of Sinclair's money."

"Yeah, and it would have worked too if you would have just asked for the money."

I ignore Peter and focus on the synapses firing in my brain. "Wait a second ... that entry in your book, the *$78K Slip* sounded suspiciously familiar, the same amount that was stolen from me my freshman year—the Gramps fund. I kept my PIN number hidden in my Gumby bedroom slippers."

I say this with a little too much authority, and Geri calls me on it. "You're really enjoying this, aren't you?"

"Yep, I'm a regular Agatha Lansbury." The fact that everyone laughs but me should be a clue, one that I apparently miss. Whatever it is, I'm sure Geri will tease me about it later. I look hard at Peter and say, "So I'm right? *You* stole my money?"

"Gramps's money," Peter corrects me. "And yeah, I used it to finance the Bean Bag. *That* was my college. Gramps had plenty more money where that came from. Besides, I was going to pay you back—with interest—from the money I made on the coffee shop."

"Guess we'll never find out," I say. "So what happened to the thousand bucks I loaned you? And will I ever see it again?"

"Oh, that. I paid the insurance premiums on the Bean Bag, including fire insurance. So yeah, you'll get it back. All of it." He pauses to grin at my shocked expression, then winks and adds, "With interest."

"I thought we were arson suspects."

"Nope. As of thirty minutes ago, the official cause is faulty wiring inside the espresso machine."

Geri's nurse bounds into the room wielding a tiny paper shot glass full of pills. "From the hallway it sounds like the end of a *Charlie's Angels* episode." With stealth and precision she deposits a freshly swabbed thermometer under Geri's tongue, cuffs her arm, and clothespins her index finger. The equipment dings and whirs and flashes numbers. While scribbling notes on a clipboard, she says, "Which one of y'all is the detective?"

Several fingers single me out. I try not to blush.

"Okay, Kojak. Let's finish it up soon. Mama needs to get some rest."

Before the door clicks shut behind her, Geri says, "So tell us, did Beaman kill Sonny or not?"

"That's seems like the obvious choice. But when it happened, I just knew it was Simmons. I even called the cops on him, then later went over to his house and accused him."

"That poor man," my mother says. "You should be ashamed."

I hit the highlights of my interrogation of Simmons about the morning Sonny died—who arrived when, and in what car. I let the fact that my mother was there the whole time slide for now. "He may have had the motive, but he didn't do it. And neither did Baringer."

Peter shakes his head. "I agree. He's basically harmless, more sad than homicidal."

"What about *you* then?"

"Me?" Peter tries to sound indignant. "That's just nuts."

"Is it? No one hated Sonny more. You obviously had the motive and the opportunity. Sonny had just finished destroying your latest memoir notebook. Simmons saw you at the house that day. And when Dan told me about the antifreeze in Sonny's system, I immediately remembered your weird apology in Mom and Dad's garage. And the funnel."

"Oh?"

"I found it the next day, still slick with antifreeze."

"It's not what you think. I just wanted to make him sick."

"Peter!" My mother looks horrified.

"I swear," Peter says. "After Sonny lapped up a few drops, I felt guilty and made him stop. I poured it back into the Prestone container with the funnel. I did not kill Sonny. He didn't get enough to kill him."

"How would you know that?" I ask, pausing between each word.

"I looked it up on the Internet," Peter says.

"I believe you ... but only because Dan discovered the pentobarbital in his system."

"The what?" Peter says.

"It's a euthanasia drug."

"Wouldn't you have to be a vet or something to get your hands on something like that?"

The only sound in the room is an occasional beep from Geri's IV tree, and of course the pounding in my ears.

"Mom?" It was a legitimate question when it left my brain. But by the time it floats out of my mouth and into the sterile hospital air, it sounds like an accusation.

She sighs with her whole body. Then makes a clumsy stab at intercepting a single tear streaking down her cheek. She misses, which makes her cry harder.

"He was sick," she says. "Terminal, actually."

"Here ..." Dan fumbles a wrinkled handkerchief out of his pocket and hands it to my mother. "It's warm."

She nods her thanks and continues. "I kept meaning to tell you. But I just couldn't. Not with your constant moping around, thinking you'd killed your sister and fretting about cancerous moles. I just knew you'd find a way to blame yourself." We share a knowing glance. I just hope Peter keeps quiet about the whiskey biscuits. "Sonny was in the final stages of renal failure. His kidneys were shutting down, and affecting several other vital organs as well. I took him to three different vets, but he was inoperable. So I kept a loaded syringe hidden in the fridge just in case I needed it. I guess I hoped you would just assume it was old age. Anyway, when I found Sonny staggering around the kitchen, traipsing through pools of his own sickness, I just knew his time was up." She looks up sharply at Peter. "But I didn't know about the antifreeze.

"My plan was to clean him up and get him to a vet before you got home. But I decided I needed one quick drink before I got started. The first one led to three or four more. When I finally woke up, you and Sonny were gone. Your father informed me I'd screwed up his dinner party. But all I could think about was how sad you must be. And what I'd become. I'm sorry, Russell ..."

She breaks down. It dawns on me then, she's not apologizing for putting Sonny down. "I should have been there with you, but I got drunk instead."

I can just see her sitting in the kitchen, Sonny's head in her lap, stroking the fur under his chin while his breathing slowed, then stopped.

I'm about to cross the room and hug her. But my father beats me to it. And that's a good thing.

Then it's over. We all stare at each other, collectively embarrassed. I wait for someone to applaud, but Dan starts punching buttons on his PDA gizmo while my family files out the door and Geri snores softly. I move to her bedside and kiss her forehead. That's when I notice baby

Katie peering up at me, a quick flash of bright eyes followed by a tooth-less, crooked grin. And that's all the applause I need.

* * *

It doesn't take a lot of convincing for Geri and Dan to insist I go back to Dan's for a much-needed nap and shower. I can't remember the last time I slept ten hours straight, much less in the middle of the day. But I do. And it's warm and sweet.

* * *

Dan and I stop off for flowers on our way back to the hospital.

When we enter Geri's room, she's cradling baby Katie close to her chest. It takes a few seconds for me to notice the other people in the room. My parents are there, grinning like crazy people. Peter is perched in the window, looking more than a little humbled. He hops down, wraps me in an enthusiastic hug, and whispers, "I'm proud of you, little brother. Always have been."

"What did I do?'

"Plenty," he says, winking. I can't help but think he's about to ask to borrow money again. But he just grins and punches me in the arm.

"Somebody want to tell me what's going on?" I say.

Geri pats the bed next to her and says, "Have a seat."

I do and she places baby Katie in my arms. To my great surprise, I burst into tears. And everyone in the room bursts into laughter.

When I look up, Dan is standing at the head of the bed with a Bible open in his hands.

"Dearly beloved," he says. "We are gathered here today — " He pauses to check his watch. "Okay, well, tonight, to be exact."

"Don't I get a say in this?" I ask.

The group of onlookers (and some nurses) exchange scandalous murmurs. But Geri knows better. She just grins up at me.

"Go ahead," she says. "Have your say."

My eyes meet my father's, and I ask, "Would you do the honors?"

He points at himself, questioning either my intentions or my sanity. Dan places the Bible at the foot of the bed and makes way for my father. Geri rests her warm hand on my arm, then baby Katie wraps her tiny fist around my finger and gives it a squeeze. Without a doubt, I know Sonny would approve.

Z+

Insights,
Interviews,
& More

Contents

Q & A with Author Michael Snyder

Q: Russell Fink, Mike Snyder. One and the same?

MS: I did have a basset hound growing up, but to the best of my knowledge, she was not clairvoyant. During a routine mole removal surgery, my doctor did indeed say, "Oops!" That, and I did share Russell's irrational belief that one tiny miscue with the scalpel would fill my body with cancer. I'm not overly fond of praying out loud. My appendix burst during the editing stages of *Russell* — but no helicopter ride for me. (*Ed. note: That line got cut. Mike's memory is a little thin.*) Also, I work in sales. But I've never sold copiers, and I am not a slacker.

I've never tasted whiskey biscuits or broken into a zoo or tackled anyone in a TV studio. I've never applied hemorrhoid cream to my neck or shoulders. (I do have a deceased relative who did, although I don't think it was the ointment that caused her ultimate demise.)

I've never met anyone named Nancy Clancy. I did, however, punch a girl in the nose once. But I had a good excuse. You see, there was this Snoopy trash can on my head ...

343

Q: We don't have time for your stories. Tell me about your writing process for *Russell Fink*.

MS: Much to the chagrin of my very patient editor, the process did not involve much plotting. Russell (the character) kept showing up in short stories. He first appeared to me, nameless, alongside Dan at their breakfast table. The scene where Dan steals Russell's cereal bowl and spoon is pretty much verbatim from a story called *The Inheritance*. That first iteration of Russell was a bit too smart-alecky though. The next story was entitled *My Name Is Russell Fink* (odd coincidence, eh?) and included an outlandish love interest, a roommate named Peter, and the inklings of Russell's vocational tug toward painting. The third story was the best of the lot, although the only real resemblance to Russell was the death of his twin sister, Katie. So out of the three disparate stories, a hybrid version of *Russell Fink* was born. I shelved the other two novel ideas I was tinkering with and plunged headlong into Russell's mixed bag of neuroses and tried to cobble together something that resembled a cohesive story. For the most part I allowed the characters to dictate the story. Maybe next time I should employ more reliable characters.

Q: Speaking of hybrids, there's no mention of alien intelligence or life on other planets in *Russell Fink*. Why?

MS: Life on other planets seems just plain weird to me. Everyone traipsing around in fancy pajamas, fiddling with giant *Lite Brites*, and firing pink and green lasers (Lasers? Really? That's where technology stopped?) at any mangled piece of cutlery that dares to cross into their orbit. Very melodramatic times, I fear.

I will say this: if you think the mere mention of those things will sell more books, we could have Dan marry Trish on Mars, maybe have Russell and the gang doing "La Macarena" at the wedding reception?

The more accurate reason, however, is that my tiny brain is most comfortable in modern times. What interests me most is what's happening around us right now, the wealth of humanity and unique predicaments in the house across the street. Almost anyone you meet is all at once funny, interesting, unique, and filled with love and fear and hate and peculiar notions about how life is supposed to work. I merely spy on those people and write down what they say. I've only been arrested twice.

Q: Who are your literary heroes?

MS: My literary heroes are too many to mention, and for good reason I'm pretty much enamored with anyone who can conjure up a good sentence. Fondness turns to infatuation if said author can massage those sentences into paragraphs. And if he or she can then stack those paragraphs into a great novel, well ... I'm smitten. So here's a partial list, in no particular order: Anne Tyler, Nick Hornby, Douglas Coupland, Flannery O'Connor, Richard Russo, Ernest J. Gaines, Steve Martin (yes, *that* Steve Martin), John Irving, the Coen Brothers, Neil Simon ...

And if I may be so bold to bend the rules a bit ... Woody Allen, Jerry Seinfeld, Steven Wright, Rick Reynolds (comedians are writers too!) ... Jonatha Brooke, John Hiatt, Over the Rhine, Elvis Costello, Sarah Masen, Patty Griffin, Radiohead, Walter Becker & Donald Fagen, Miles Davis, Thelonious Monk, those four guys from Liverpool ...

Q: Please just stick to the questions asked. So, what can we expect from your next novel?

MS: My next novel, tentatively entitled *Return Policy*, will be similar in style and scope — the intersection of likable yet neurotic characters, hopefully funny, and with big hearts. My guess is that a few familiar themes from *Russell* will emerge, as well as a fresh take or two on the role of one's heart when dealing with friends and lovers and jobs and badgers named Rufus. (Okay, just one badger named Rufus. More than one would be peculiar.)

The germ of the idea was a character angry with God and trying to return his salvation. I refer to him as my prodigal Samaritan. Unfortunately, Father Joe is slowly taking a backseat to the three main characters, all answering similar questions in their own unique ways ... What if the arc of our lives is just one big meaningless circle? Or what if it's not? Does the arc have a definitive target? Or is it destined to languish into some random nothingness? Who took Willy's toothbrush and why?

The point-of-view alternates between Willy Finneran (a narcoleptic transplant survivor bent on destroying an espresso machine and finding his toothbrush), Ozena Webb (a customer service operator with a fake family and too many notions of romantic love), and the inimitable Shaq (a quasi-homeless man with blank spots on his memory, a few strong convictions, a big heart, and nary a clue).

Q: What, no *Russell Fink 2: Russell the Muscle?* He's back, and ready to kick some —

MS: Okay, *Russell the Muscle* is just funny enough to make me waste a few nights imagining our hero in tights and knee-high vinyl boots. But then I'd have to decide ... color schemes? Mask or no mask? Cape or no cape? Whether to make Dan his sidekick or resurrect Sonny? And what of his super power? The ability to infuse enormous doses of worry and regret on unsuspecting villains, thus rendering them incurably sidetracked? And what if Wonder Woman made a pass at him? What then? Huh?

Deleted Scenes

MS: First up, this was my original idea for the opening of the novel:

In the dream, my entire life has been reduced to a single hardback book. Sonny is there too, adding to the prophetic quality. He looks younger and a bit sadder than normal, even for a basset hound. The book lies between us and I'm pleased by its thickness, as it seems to bode well for my longevity. Sonny blinks, swiveling his gaze between the hardback and me. When I fail to take the hint, he uses his wet nose to nudge it toward me, his paws clicking on the kitchen tiles. The wordless cover reveals a grainy black-and-white photo of Katie and me in matching sailor suits — holding hands, wide-eyed, and trying to stop giggling long enough to extinguish our birthday candles. Sonny barks, an obvious signal — or so it seems in dream vernacular — for me to proceed. I rifle through the pages, but they're blank, all of them, save for the dust jacket. So I lift the cover and begin reading the inside flap:

My name is Russell Fink.

I still live with my parents and I hate my job. I do not hate my parents, although I tend to blame them for every bad thing that's ever happened in my life. So I guess it's safe to say that I love them; I just don't like them all that much. And I'm sure the feeling is mutual. My best friend in the world is my paternal grandfather, currently serving consecutive life sentences for first-degree murder. My doctor vehemently disagrees with my diagnosis, that I suffer from eventual cancer. In other words, I'm certain the afflicted cells are splashing around in my DNA pool, waiting to manifest themselves in one of my major organs. And speaking of terminal malignancies, I gave my sister cancer when she was nine. She died eighteen months later, leaving just me and my older brother, Peter.

I miss her terribly.

(Continued on back flap ...)

I pause and look to Sonny for clues, unable to fathom these random tidbits from a memoir that exists only in my imagination. He stares back with mottled eyes, brimming with liquid sadness, as if he's just realized the implications of calculating dog years.

My headshot, stern and writerly, takes up the bottom one-third. The photo was taken from above and left, no doubt to mask my drooping right eye and burgeoning Fink double chin.
On the back cover, a few obligatory quotes:

"Sure, Russell's got his issues. But he's good people, a phenomenal painter. And there's something about the way his blood moves in his veins that wreaks havoc on watch batteries. He's able to maintain that 'just shaved' smell all day. Oh yeah, he's the best Nerf basketball player ever." Peter Fink, author of Fink & Stein's Monster

"He's not a particularly good kisser, but he's just so darn reliable. And protective. And nice." Alyssa "Muse" DeMartini, future multiple Emmy winner and author's former fiancée

"Russell is the only man I've ever loved. Really loved. I just wish that were a good thing." Geri Tarkanian, administrative assistant, Tyler, Billingham & Sneed

"He's downright toasty." Dan, inventor and friend

I set the book aside and try to meet Sonny's gaze. But he's fading now, like heat shimmering off hot pavement, as the dream takes on a telepathic quality. Random thoughts stagger and collide as I wake exactly one minute before my scheduled alarm. First, see if Dr. Kozinski can squeeze me in this morning. Next, check on Sonny. Then let Mr. Hengle know I'll be burning another sick day. And if Alyssa does call with one of her harebrained schemes, ignore her.

Finally, who the heck is Dan?

MS: Here's the "long form" of Dan's encounter with one of America's most wanted bad guys ...

"Oh yeah," Dan says. "Me too. I once caught the FBI's third most-wanted criminal. Maybe you saw me on *America's Most Wanted*?"

He looks disappointed when Beaman shakes his head. Geri says, "I've seen the tape a few times. Pretty impressive, really. Dan's a real hero."

Then Dan gives us the five-minute version. You can tell he's delivered this monologue before. As usual, his hands are in constant motion, his voice fluid and calm, save for an occasional sibilant whistle. While Dan speaks, I doodle on one side of the envelope from Dr. K's office.

"I was mailing a care package to my girlfriend—she's an astronaut—from the tiny post office in Spring Hill. That's back when it was a one-stoplight town. Anyhow, while I was studying the FBI's Most Wanted posters on the wall, I kept accidentally bumping the guy in front of me. I tend to crowd people sometimes because I get really cold. I'm staring at the black-and-white pictures, trying to memorize the names and features—just in case—when the man in front of me turns and tells me all the disgusting things he plans to do to me if I bump him again. So I take a step back and busy myself with the next photo. That's when I saw him ... the guy in the photo was the guy in front of me. At first I didn't believe it. But I kept reading the statistics. He was obviously a white male.

He appeared to be taller than five-foot-eight — until I noticed the heels on his motorcycle boots. The brown eyes checked out. But his hair was too long from behind to see if he really was missing his left earlobe. I read his name again, followed by a long list of aliases. The idea popped into my head and out of my mouth before I had the chance to think about trying to trip up a mass murderer with no way to defend myself. I decided to go with the name his mother gave him. I cleared my throat and said, 'Milton?' He turned on me, mildly surprised, then really angry. When I saw the missing earlobe, my mouth dropped open and he knew he'd been made."

"Let me guess." I don't even try to hide my incredulity. "You wrestled him to the ground, hog-tied him, and sat on him until the cops came."

"Shh," Geri says. She sounds groggy. "Let him finish, Russell."

"No," Dan says. "I wish. What happened next was he started choking me. The problem was that nobody was in line behind me. I could see the customers in front of us, but they were all facing forward. And I couldn't make any noise since my windpipe was getting crushed. All I could think of was to snap my fingers. But I was still holding the care package with both hands and I could not force myself to drop it."

"What about the postal clerk?" Beaman asks. "He must have been facing forward."

"Yeah, but he never looked up. Not once. So when Milton lifted me off the ground, I knew I had to act fast or I'd become another notch in his belt. So I dug my hand into the care package — it wasn't taped up yet, which was one of the reasons I was in line at the post office; I was out of tape — and removed the jar of peanut butter. It was difficult to manage, but I eventually removed the lid, scooped two fingers into the creamy spread, and raised my hand where he could see it. His grip slackened ever so slightly and his eyes widened, broadening my target. I thrust both peanut-buttered fingers into his eyes and began to rub."

Beaman is grinning and nodding like crazy. "I think I do remember hearing about this."

"I think you're all nuts," I say. "And any minute Alan Fundt is going to jump out and tell us to smile, that we're on *Candid Camera.*"

"No, no, this is for real." Beaman has turned in the booth to face Dan. "He was allergic, right?"

"Bingo," Dan says, pointing dramatically at his newest fan. "His poster stated clearly: *Severe peanut allergy.* So while he was writhing around on the floor, I dialed 9–1–1 on my PDA. Then I sat on the man's chest and had some peanut butter until the cops came."

MS: Here we have Dan asking his beloved to Trish to marry him on national television ...

"What is all this?" I ask. Geri shushes me and drags me toward the newly expanded conference room of Tyler, Billingham & Sneed. I can't help feeling a little proud as I breathe in the opulence and inspect my handiwork. She called my office this morning — all business — and insisted I come to her office immediately to check on the copiers. Now we're standing in the darkened conference room while Geri remotely controls the television into action.

"Ssshhh. Just be quiet and listen."

The perky theme song of the *Today Show* comes on and Geri cranks the remote up to ear-splitting levels. The camera pans to the crowd outside with their homemade posters, shouting unintelligible greetings and flashing hand signals to their loved ones at home.

Finally the producer cuts to the studio where Matt, Meredith, and Al are all grouped around a gangly, yet familiar form. "No way," I hear myself say.

"Welcome back," Matt Lauer says with a smile that looks like it could slide off his face any second. "As we promised at the top of the show, we're going to make a little history on the program this morning." The camera swivels toward Dan, then zooms in tight. His spastic grin fills the entire screen. He licks his lips incessantly and his eyes seem to scurry about like a nervous bunny rabbit. "We're here with Dan Holtzendorf of Nashville, Tennessee, who has an important question for a real American hero." The screen splits, revealing the grainy image of a Spartan blonde woman in a space suit.

"You're kidding," I say to no one in particular.

"Shush," Geri says.

While the cohosts trade serious questions about the mission, Commander Trish Davis squints vacantly into the camera and fiddles with her earpiece. The complicated nature of the connection makes for awkward delays between responses. All the technical details sail over my head, something about space dust and repairing a broken satellite. Finally, Matt chimes in again and says, "Well, Commander, we have a little surprise for you."

Pause ... blank stare ... blink ...

"Oh," she says, venturing a look to her left. "Okay."

"We have a friend of yours here in the studio. Say hello to Dan."

They exchange self-conscious greetings, then Matt interrupts again. "Okay, we're a little short on time — and I know you can't see us here in the studio, so I'll give you the play-by-play. Is that alright?"

"Sure." Embarrassed grins threaten to break out on Trish's face. But mostly she looks confused.

"Okay," Matt says. "Dan is down on one knee and wants to ask you a question."

The camera pulls back. Dan is kneeling, his left arm extended in a hackneyed thespian pose. I'm thoroughly embarrassed for him. And kinda proud too.

"Trish —" He pauses to gulp for air. "Will you marry me?"

At first it appears that the connection has been lost. Trish just stares. She blinks. Then she stares some more.

Dan is getting wobbly and looking more than a little panicky.

"Um, could you hurry it up a bit, sweetheart? The guy in my earpiece says we're up against a commercial break."

Nervous laughter titters in the background.

After another long pause, Trish brightens and says, "Yes, Daniel. I think I will. And thanks for asking."

The space camera jiggles a little, causing Trish's image to flicker. When it settles into place again, we see an arm extend from off-camera, holding a black jewelry box. Trish opens it and tries in vain to fit the biggest diamond I've ever seen on her ring finger.

After three attempts, she slides it onto her pinkie.

The studio audience cheers. Geri is wiping her eyes. And I'm looking everywhere for Sonny.

"Okay kids," Matt says, his voice brimming with giddiness. "Congratulations. And we'll be right b — "

"Wait," Dan says. "Do you think we could go ahead and get married now? I don't think I can wait."

The studio audience erupts with laughter. Matt, Al, and Meredith all shrug at each other with giant grins plastered on their made-up faces. Then Al Roker yells, "Is there a preacher in the house?"

"Stay tuned, folks," Meredith says. "After a word from our sponsors, we may come back and make a little more history."

Three minutes later, Dan and Trish are pronounced man and wife on national television.

1. What kind of name is Russell Fink, anyway? Do you think there is significance behind the name?

2. If someone told you to quit your current job to do something you really love (like Dr. K advises Russell), would you do it? What if the thing you really love to do is to scam people in the name of God?

3. Answer Russell's question: "How do you exact revenge on an ailing, crotchety neighbor without risking either jail time or a rather severe dent in your self-esteem?"

4. Russell, Peter, and their parents all struggle at random jobs to make ends meet. Is financial trouble simply bad luck, or is there a source and underlying problem?

5. Do you pile your eights like a snowman or swoop them like a racetrack?

6. How many times have you responded to "I'm not talking to you" with "Ah, but you just did." Where does the satisfaction from that retort come from?

7. Do you ever search through your purse/briefcase/pockets in order to avoid speaking to someone? Why? Why does Russell?

8. When is the last time you stopped to look at a fly? Really look?

9. Russell compares his relationship with his father to sharing a prison cell. What was their crime? Who imprisoned them? Who is their lawyer? Will the court hear their appeal? Are they falsely accused? What color are their prison clothes? Are there legal loopholes that they can exploit?

10. Sonny becomes Russell's drinking buddy. What else do they have in common?

11. Sonny's death becomes the catalyst for many things in Russell's life. Has the death of a pet ever caused such change in your life?

12. On Russell's birthday, he presents to his potential clients, has lunch with his mother, and has dinner with Geri and Dan. What event has the most significance?

13. What does Russell want, more than anything in the world?

14. In tracking down Sonny's killer, Russell stumbles upon his past. Who do you think *really* killed Sonny? Why?

15. Geri says, "You don't believe in miracles. That kind of dooms us from the start." Considering everything Geri and Russell have been through together, is this true?

16. Russell says, "I don't want Your comfort, I want answers. And if I can't get the right answers, I want to fight." How does this philosophy play out in Russell's life? Do you ever feel this way?

Read an excerpt from *Return Policy*,
Michael Snyder's next book. Coming December 2008!

Willy:

Once a year, my senile aunt tries to kill me.

Her name is Mavis and she's really my great-aunt, my mother's mother's sister. And although she may not be *trying* to murder me, it darn near works every September. These days Mavis only remembers names and birthdays. And in my case she actually puts the name and the date together correctly.

For the past six years, she's sent the exact same *Happy 30th Birthday* card — a pastel bouquet of balloons, streamers, and tumbling confetti on the outside, and the words *Embrace the Zero ... Happy 30th!* on the inside. (The accidental double meaning of her palsied scrawl, "hugs and kisses," shouldn't offend me, but it does.) I cannot begin to explain the terror this simple act of kindness evokes in me. Mavis only deviated from her torturous routine once, the year before Lucy left me. That year she sent a chintzy alarm clock with the card. As a result I spent three days in the hospital under constant observation for hypertension, post-traumatic stress disorder, and suicide watch. Lucy was probably right. I may have overreacted.

I came home and buried the clock in a shoebox, then tucked it under Lucy's side of the bed. That same night I got up, unearthed it, and severed its power cord for good measure. Unexpected shrill noises are bad enough for my health; this one could be fatal. It's why I leave my cell phone on mute and keep my windows up in traffic.

For years I've imagined the ticking in my chest as a pawnshop alarm clock, wrapped in pink pumping flesh. It's set for half-past some unknown hour in the not too distant future, sometime around my thirtieth birthday. I turned twenty-nine yesterday. That leaves three hundred and sixty-three days to ignore my To-Do List and play solitaire. And pray I'm sleeping when the alarm goes off.

I spent the better part of a decade figuring out who to blame. Was it God for knitting together such a weak heart in my mother's womb? My mother because she smoked through two out of three trimesters? My father for driving my mother to the nasty habit in the first place? The surgeon for not waiting on a sturdier, more durable organ? The donor himself for not eating more vegetables and shunning elevators? At some point I decided to blame them all equally, then abandoned my accusations altogether and turned my attention to my list, officially titled "Things to Do before I Die." It's not a bad list. It just needs one more item, namely, stop wallowing and actually do something about the list.

Even at fourteen, the harsh truth of my situation was evident. Someone had to die for me to live. I felt guilty before my surgery and every day since. Several days after opening my chest, removing my diseased heart, and installing its donated replacement, I overheard a conversation between the surgeon and my mom. Despite her prayers and constant reassurance, she was terrified the new heart wouldn't take. "Not to worry, Ms. Finneran. William's procedure went swimmingly well. If we're lucky, we just added another decade and a half to his life."

I was never very good at math, but I believe that puts my expiration date at about thirty ... if I'm lucky. And I don't believe in anything but bad luck.

When I can't bear to look at the card any longer, I push back from the kitchen table. Espresso lips over the edge of my "World's Worst Teacher" mug, which now appears to be shedding dirty tears in mourning.

My grandfather's lockbox is tucked into the corner of my underwear drawer. I flip the top and toss the birthday card inside. But before closing the lid I catch a glimpse of my first novel. It's a shiny library copy of *The Handyman*, the first in a series of detective novels about Ralph Handy (my unlucky one-eyed, one-handed repairman-cum-sleuth, first name synonymous with vomit, last name a cruel reminder of his handicap—and yeah, his middle initial is *I*). The cover shows the sleeve of a tan overcoat emerging from the shadows, a revolver protruding like a vacuum cleaner attachment where the hand was supposed to be. I open the back flap and stare at the smirking, black and white version of me. The version that knew he wouldn't live forever but didn't seem to care.

I flip to the dedication page. I scrawled my list under the words, *For Walter, my brother, mentor, and friend.* I was just young enough and dumb enough to think a list like this would matter. That the act of jotting down a few goals would magically produce the internal fortitude to accomplish a few worthy things. I study the list, mentally crossing off the few things I've managed to do already — buy my grandparents' house, finish my "serious" novel, go for a ride in a helicopter — and scoff at the rest. Fall in love ... for real this time? What a joke.

Then it dawns on me. I should have done this years ago.

I snap the book shut, grab my stack of birthday cards, then carry them to the kitchen and toss them into the sink. I root around in the junk drawer, finding every candle that Lucy left behind but not a single match. I check all the usual places — the spice rack, the bill drawer, the bathroom — all to no avail. Then I remember my grandfather's pipe rack. I pause to inhale the rich aroma of wet tobacco, then snatch his favorite flip-top lighter and hurry back to the kitchen wondering if this is a purging or a sacrifice. A refiner's fire or flaming lunacy?

I decide to toss the cursed espresso maker into the fire as well, but only after I get my kindling ablaze first. I hold the copy of my novel aloft, then flick the lighter open. I spin the flint wheel once, then again before it ignites. I touch the flame to the edge of the dangling book cover and wait.

Nothing. The yellow tendrils flirt with the edge but don't catch. I let the pages dangle and waft, hoping the resulting breeze will fan the flame. Then my thumb starts to burn and I have to let go of the lighter.

I stare at the book, wondering if it's been treated with some secret flame retardant to prevent the library from burning. I pick up the stack of birthday cards instead. When my thumb has sufficiently cooled, I flick the lighter into action again and hold the edge of Mavis's death notice to the flame.

The flame catches and I see my distorted grin reflecting in the belly of my teakettle.

That's when the alarm goes off, a shrill pulsing chirp that literally stops my heart. I drop the lighter and the flaming card into the sink and hold the edge of the counter with both hands.

When my breathing returns to normal, I urge my wobbly legs across the living room, under the familiar archway, and into the bedroom. There on the floor by the nightstand is Mavis's alarm clock, its cord repaired and snaking into the outlet. Angry red numbers flash 12:29. I flip the alarm button to Off.

I'm not typically one for omens, but I decide now to do something else about my list. Or maybe it's been decided for me.

Willy:

The sight of Lucy always made my scar tingle. These days it happens whenever the phone rings. It's ringing now, in fact, but I ignore it. Instead I thumb through the deck of cards in my hand (searching for a much needed black nine) while I wait for the machine to pick up. Call me a coward if you like, but a man can only absorb so much bad news.

I place the nine of spades on the ten of diamonds, then resume turning cards over. After a long beep, I hear the habitual throat clearing of my literary agent. His voice sounds like a drowsy Muppet.

"William ..." Sigh. "We need to talk ..." Elongated nasal breathing. "Soon ..." Bigger sigh. "And in person ... so please call me." Medium sigh, but with feeling. "I have news."

The word *news* is bloated with meaning, conjuring the image of a grim-faced soap opera doctor — *I'm sorry, Mr. Finneran. We did everything we could ...*

Despite Stan's perpetual grogginess, he's a real animal when it comes to business dealings. This proved invaluable when my books were actually selling. But I haven't heard from Stan in months, not since the last puny royalty check arrived. He didn't even bother with a Christmas card this year. This morning his bored monotone sounds more despairing than normal, if that's even possible.

I take another sip of espresso — a vile beverage — and place a red jack on a black queen. I've been playing solitaire for what seems like days now. At some point I took the aces out of the deck and replaced them with the following:

-An index card with Doug's cell number on it — clubs, because we used to play nightclubs

-A photograph of Lucy celebrating our first anniversary (the fleck of red sauce on her chin makes me cry if I stare at it too long) — hearts, for obvious reasons

-A greeting card I found tucked between the pages of Song of Solomon in Lucy's Bible — spades, for digging graves

-The receipt for Lucy's espresso machine — diamonds, still not sure why

She's been gone for nearly three years now. And what I hate more than the loneliness is the fact that I've lost Lucy's scent. I used to stand in our closet and sniff the sleeves of her shirts and the necklines of her best dresses. A smarter man than me would have taken her pillowcase and favorite pajamas and had them hermetically sealed. That way I could open the package for a quick whiff on special occasions. Specifically it's her skin I miss most — the sight of it, the warm touch, but mostly the smell.

One night I got the bright idea to stuff Lucy's favorite pj's with sweaters and balled up sheets. I just knew I couldn't suffer another night of waking up at two in the morning and weeping at the sight of the empty spot beside me. She didn't own any wigs so I used a volleyball and a new mop I found in the garage. It didn't have to be perfect, just passable, since Lucy always slept with her head under a pillow. I washed the mop with Lucy's shampoo, then doused it with perfume and lotion and tucked it between the covers. With the lights on, my handiwork resembled a Lucy scarecrow. Of course I still woke up at two a.m. The only difference was screaming in fright before the sobbing started up. Of course the really pathetic part of all this is that Lucy and I never really loved each other. Ours was a marriage of convenience.

I've gone thirty seconds without a play when my homemade ace of spades appears. I place it in the first foundations position and pause to study it. The card was from a guy named Rex. On the outside it said, "Thinking of you." Folded inside was a printed version of a long back-and-forth email with conflicting versions of what transpired between Rex and my wife. From the evidence I've managed to cobble together, he used words like *bliss* and *affair* and *love*. She called it an "emotional hiccup" that could have led to a "physical disaster" that should be "filed under *Things Best Forgotten.*" This last bit should make me feel better, but it doesn't. Every time I read it I feel my borrowed heart nudge sideways a fraction of an inch, like when a stranger squeezes into the seat next to you on the subway.

The phone rings. Caller ID flashes the name DOUG TURKO, making me regret the pitiful message I left on his machine last night. I ignore the phone and search for a black three. When the ringing ceases I allow my head to drop into my hands. This is what my life has become — avoiding my best friend, drinking bitter coffee from my wife's lover's immortal espresso machine, and cheating at solitaire.

Some time later the phone rings again. Without looking at the number, I fling the cordless handset at the espresso machine. A direct hit. The phone explodes into a hundred plastic shards. The malevolent coffee machine hisses at me. I would swear under oath that the amber power light winked at me.

I pour another cup of espresso and use the soles of my bedroom slippers to sweep all the phone pieces into a pile. A few moments later the answering machine clicks on in the bedroom. I crane one ear toward the familiar voice. It's Alistair "the Dean" Langstrom, my boss, and he doesn't sound pleased.

Three grimacing swallows later I rinse my cup and change my shoes. A trip to Wal-Mart is in order because I'm out of espresso mix and I need to replace my phone.

That's when Doug shows up, letting himself in with the key I keep hidden in plain view on my front porch. Once inside, he tosses a giant stack of mail in the middle of my cards and croons, "Avon calling!"

"I thought you reserved the prissy burlesque shtick for the Dean. By the way, I think I may have just been fired."

"Not on my watch." Doug plants his fists on his thick hips like an effeminate superhero; a move his wife finds adorable. "They don't call me the Filibuster Queen for nothing."

When Dean Langstrom inherited the current Edwards University English Department he was more than a little dismayed to find a hack, genre writer on his otherwise esteemed staff. Blatantly ousting me however could be a political nightmare. My students may admire me, but my colleagues simply adore having such a convenient target for their literary disdain. So Langstrom has settled on alternating strategies of either shaming me or annoying me into resignation. He scrutinizes my work, talks down to me, and peppers me with trivial questions about obscure literary figures at faculty meetings. But Doug proves too staunch an advocate, his cries of discrimination only a breath away. His moderate politics and conservative religion notwithstanding, Doug can play the flaming liberal to the hilt, boycotting everything from local zoos to Planned Parenthood facilities. He once staged a sit-in to protest the Girl Scouts preying on the obese and elderly when hawking their chocolate devil wafers. The Dean knows better than to fire Willy Finneran with Doug standing guard.

"Is all that gay humor a sword?" I ask. "Or a shield?"

"Maybe a little bit of both. As you know, I didn't ask for this affliction."

"Which one?"

"Touché."

Doug claims to have undergone a period of sexual *dis*orientation in college. It ended on a blind date with Maggie, another sojourner of nebulous sexuality. They made a pact, more spiritual than carnal. The result was a modern-day arranged marriage, complete with two-point-six kids.

"How is Maggie?"

"We're fat and grumpy and more beautiful than ever. At least the morning sickness is behind us." Doug always refers to his wife's pregnancies in plural possessive, owning inasmuch as possible all the pain and suffering as any man can. I have to admit, he does an admirable job. In fact, their love is so complete and endearing and, let's face it, sickeningly idyllic, it depresses everyone in its soupy green wake.

"Won't the arrival of your bouncing baby boy tip Langstrom off to your rampant straightness?"

"Nah, it'll confound him more. But enough chitchat. Why didn't you answer your phone?"

"I don't know. I'm busy."

"Should I check the tub?"